KING HARVEST

THE KANSAS MURDER TRILOGY
BOOK 1

BY MELVIN LITTON

PROLOGUE

They stand on a high bluff beneath the starlit sky, two errant figures made more ragged by their shirttails blown in a warm south wind. Fires etch the distant landscape, burning wheat stubble off fields where phantom shapes stir alive before the flames. The men gesture through the broad expanse, friends in the flesh who will one day be ghosts like the buffalo they envision covering the horizon for thirty crow-miles south.

The larger man arches a whiskey bottle that glitters briefly before falling away, then war whoops as if his throw spans the entire valley. The other howls to the sky. In their stoned haze they perceive the hoof-beats of a million beasts, audible as their voices in the muffled wind, racing their hearts like they've reached back over a hundred years and are standing at the very scene once witnessed by early settlers:

"I've seen a herd of seven thousand cattle," an old-timer vouched in a turn-of-the-century gazette, "all in one roundup. Yet compared to that sea of buffalo they weren't but one drop in a bucket of water, and that bucket but one drop in the ocean..."

A host that defies numbering, like stars in the prairie night.

Held in the cusp of the moment, mindless to all else but their shared vision, the conjurors drift for a time. Now and then a restive cloud passes over, obscuring the stars like a smoke signal gone awry; yet the greater number shine on as the fires recede and slowly fold into the land. Silent, at last sobered by fatigue and wary of the approaching dawn, the two men stagger downslope and edge along a low gully, their forms all but lost in the greater darkness.

Doors latch shut. An engine growls low. Their truck soon emerges onto the road to follow a tenuous beam towards the distant town. A short while later the lingering shades disperse in the cool clear dawn.

"Sundown and yellow moon and pretty soon a carnival at the edge of town,
King Harvest will surely come..."—Robbie Robertson (The Band)

I. INTO THE WIND

"We're like buffalo hunters," Lee hollered above the roar of the wind and engine as the pickup raced down a back road, dust rolling up through the rusted floorboard. He hung his arm out the window, slapped the side panel and repeated, "Yep, just like buffalo hunters." Riding shotgun, his eyes fixed to the land.

But the buffalo were long gone and the prairie had been farmed for well over a century, the surrounding fields, recently disked or plowed, overflowed the ditches. Dust skimmed the horizon like remnant smoke from wheat stubble as if the fires that had blazed and died over a month before still clung to the edge of things. Little to brighten the view in dry August except for clusters of sunflowers in the ravines and ditches, while the land seemingly stretched on forever beneath the arching sky where an occasional white cloud appeared like a snow-capped mountain, which would have proved a welcome sight though there was no chance of such on the Kansas plains. What they hunted was hemp, wild hemp, what the authorities referred to as *marijuana.*

"Damn straight," Will shot back, gripping the wheel, "and the hunt is on."

Their practiced eyes scanned the terrain in search of the telltale green, somewhat vague and pale at a distance, but closer up it sheened, swaying in the wind like a grove of Christmas trees—hemp, there for the taking, uncontested, lowly, unlike the highly prized varieties from Columbia and Mexico, a mere weed to many eyes, but contraband nonetheless, for while it lacked the narcotic effect of its more potent cousins, it shared the very look, taste, and smell, so it was readily marketable as a blending agent. Always someone waiting to buy and given the requisite gumption and guile and a certain leap of faith, it was possible, just possible, to spin said straw into gold. An attractive prospect, trading wild hemp for greenbacks. The pair now hunting had done so many times and aimed to do so again, with even greater faith.

Buff Hunters... Will smiled at the thought. Less of a romantic than Lee, still he liked the notion. His full name was Will Wolnofsky, Wolfer for short, but none dared call him "Wolf," because an older brother had thus shortened their name for sake of business: Wolf's Fine Clothing for Men. *"The Fuck!"* Will cursed at the time and often since, him pissing on their father's name to make a buck. But laughing now, "This season we're gonna make a killing, with or without Frankie," nearly had to shout to be heard, "though Frankie may have an angle, we'll see. Either way, make a killing or go to jail trying. This time we do it right, Lee, 'cause I ain't goin' back to construction. Not after trying to breathe life into that poor bastard last winter..."

The victim had been standing next to a moving crane, resting his hand on an outrigger when the boom snagged a power line and the discharge hit him like a bolt of lightning. Will rushed over and gave mouth to mouth while another man pumped the chest. But the fool was already dead as dirt, eyes burst and bloody, smoke oozing from the soles of his boots. His face, ashen as split wood, soon darkened, blending like his tattered clothes with the rutted landscape by the time the ambulance arrived. Will was still trying to raise the dead when they pulled him off.

"Guess that was my payback for not going to Nam," he later told friends. There were moments he could still taste the burnt lips and tongue, and the hard breath like a cigarette doused in an empty beer left to sour. The fool had definitely been drinking the night before, and hungover, not paying attention, next instant dead as dirt.

"That's all we are, dead men," Will declared. "Dead men if we don't put enough cash in our pockets to break free of this shit. If a man can't go his own way, he might as well be dead or in jail. 'Cause it's all a damn prison anyway. And damned if I'll do like most, spend my whole life swimming upstream to lay one damn egg 'n die. Belly up like a damned salmon..." Remembered his dad lying in that room, flat on his back, staring up at the ceiling, hardly said a word the entire year before he died, struck down at age 50 by a stroke for all his frantic efforts. "I'm done dragging my boots through the muck, Lee. Let's fill our pockets with cash or go to jail trying. You bet, prison or cash, buddy. Prison or cash."

Lee simply gave a nod. Liked the idea of cash in his pocket, stuffed tight as the stems in a bale of hay, but had no desire to see the inside of a jail. Had a pretty wife to keep an eye on and a young son to raise. But he let Will sing his song.

Will was more like a big brother and wasn't half as reckless as he might sound, actually quite cautious in a desperate way, the kind of man who'd turn blue in the face trying to breathe life back into a dead one. Big, strong, hell of a full back in high school, he would have played college ball but for a slipped disc suffered while heaving a 12-pound shot sixty-odd feet. Rotten luck, like shooting seven and snake eyes in a single roll. They cut him open, fused his lower spine, left him bedridden for six months, staring up at the ceiling like his old man and addicted to pain killers, mostly pot, ever since. At least the pot relaxed him, took his mind off the pain. That's why he'd missed Vietnam, rated 4-F due to his back. Though he felt no pain at the moment, enthused, laughing as he took a deep hit and passed the joint to Lee.

Lee pinched the nub, took a whiff and tossed the ash to the wind. He held the smoke briefly then slowly exhaled and glanced to his friend. Despite the amiable smile, Will definitely had the look of one you wouldn't want to mess with: a broad forehead fit like a helmet above dark deep-set eyes, though his most prominent feature was his jaw, a classic boxer's jaw that would make a Marine wince if not graced by that smile. Lee had no doubt that Wolfer was tough enough to weather prison, and likely he was too, though not as big, only a welterweight, but prison was one fate he'd sooner not tempt.

Lee set his battered cowboy hat to the back of his head, straw unraveling at the crown and brim, and gazed out at the passing fence line. Will seldom wore a cap or hat, hard to find one big enough, wore a red bandana to keep the hair out of his eyes. Dark hair just starting to gray—this his 30th year and he felt time grabbing him by the neck, hurling him on. He'd cut his eye-teeth watching Brando in the *Wild Ones* and James Dean in *Rebel Without a Cause* and still retained much of the manner and style of that era, wore white t-shirts and blue jeans, classic Levi 501's, never touched bell bottoms unless fit tight to a woman's thighs.

They rode in silence for another mile or so then pulled to a stop in a cloud of dust. Both men jumped out to take a leak, piss puddling at the base of each back tire. Neither said a word. Late afternoon, beer almost gone. A tumbleweed cut loose by disc or plow bounded across the road and caught in the fence alongside a dozen others bristling like trapped coyotes in tawny transparency below a "No Trespassing" sign blasted by buckshot, the wind humming through the barbed wire and thistles.

Will for one hated the wind, sensed it was no live thing, in fact was indifferent to live things and would be there long after life had gone. And he said as much as they shook their dicks and re-holstered.

"Goddamn wind. Don't matter if it's summer or winter, it chills me to the bone."

To Lee the wind sang a song, an oddly reassuring song. Maybe it was no live thing, but it had been there from the beginning.

"Hell, it stirs things to life, Wolfer. Combs the land, scatters seeds...like them tumbleweeds yonder. Wind caught 'em in the fence, it'll cut 'em loose. Weaves and unweaves all kinds of things. Like an old voice in an old tale."

"Okay, I might can buy that," Will said climbing back into the old green Chevy, named Ol' Green for its faded color and faithful service. "But like Frankie said last night, and the one thing I agree with him on, 'If the answer my friend is blowin' in the wind, so does horseshit once it's stomped to dust.' And that's why it's so damned unsettling, it mocks us. Trails like a shadow. Like some howling beast. If it tells a story or gives an answer, in the end it's simply this, *We're gonna die.*"

"Aw now, Wolfer, not so fast," Lee countered as he popped each a last can of cold beer. "We've got miles to go before we sleep, ol' bud, miles to go..."

They let the suds bubble to their lips and cut the dust as they philosophized on the wind racing in through the windows, coloring their minds, their speech, while their eyes scanned the horizons, creek banks, and fencerows for the least sign of hemp.

The land, formed by centuries of storm and drought, eroded, transformed, wounded and scarred by the plow, lay like a rumpled patchwork quilt. Various fields, some freshly planted, others green with milo, set neatly squared to a patch of clover or purple alfalfa. And here and there a rent in the pattern revealed a creek pasture grazed by cattle, horses, or sheep—this wild uncultivated zone, hemmed in and stitched by fences as foreign to the natural flow of the land as a corset to a woman's flesh, stood in marked contrast, left unplowed, meandering, fly-infested and dense with weedy foliage, held in reverence or suspicion depending on your want and need.

"She's a bitch, this prairie," Will laughed. "She'll break your heart and tempt you. Done so all my life. All her gentle swells and far spaces set there to taunt us. And the wind is a good part of her wiles. Each time I leave for some wooded place so calm and quiet you can hear your own breath, she calls me back."

"Why is that?"

"Guess I belong to her. Like she's got first claim. On you and me both."

"Could be her mild winters you miss?"

"Yeah, icy wind biting down like nails hammered in cold flesh."

"How 'bout her fruitful summers?"

"You bet, like now, so hot 'n dry, nothing but baked dirt and brittle grass. So fucking merciless you can taste the ash 'n dust of the dead."

"But you can't fault spring. She's fine and fair."

"Got that right. Sweet as a puppy's breath."

"And autumn, Wolfer. You gotta admit, autumn is golden."

"Damn straight. Like good memories and old whiskey. That's our time, Lee. Autumn. Days to die for. Except for the wind, the *cur-sed fuc-king* wind."

Lee caught the wind in his mouth and made a hollow whistle.

"Don't fight it, Will," he laughed. "Just breathe it in. Breathe it in..."

On this much they agreed as they drank their beer and rambled on: The wind is a trickster and a tease that keeps much hidden and never tells the whole truth, the entire story, as it covers and uncovers traces—a fragment of speech, a scent, a trail of dust or smoke. Clues that appear by chance or whim as they do on any given day in any given life. Yet the wind moans on, echoing each, as if it were the author—there at the coming of the horse and man's extended range, and the iron horse of steel and steam as it ate up the land and spewed forth men to farm the plains before Fords, Chevys, and GTO's raced in thundering duel down dirt roads and blacktop highways, and even then, witnessing young flesh encased in steel, daring death and one another, laughing as young questers always laugh exceeding limits and giving chase. Like Will and Lee heading into the wind, primed, defiant, undiminished, young. This is their time and telling, Range County Kansas, late summer 1975.

II. THE BOYS

The wind had all but died the previous evening when the sun set low in the west, coloring the dust trail blood-pink as Frankie Sage blew into Will's place with Jack Kelly and Gabe Swenson in tow. The old stone house stood out in the middle of a section of plowed ground surrounded by nothing but a few cedars, the wind, earth, and sky, owned by Ned Furburgh, a true cowboy fated to farm, and hated tractors, plows, combines, the whole works, but farming paid for horses and gave Ned time to hunt deer in Texas and Wyoming, so he'd horse-traded with life so to speak and made the best deal he could. He rented the place to Will for a pittance and pretty much turned a blind eye to the boys and their doings. Along with most folks in those parts, Ned liked the boys, had known them all their lives, had watched them play ball and go to war. Besides, the boys were always respectful and considerate of their own.

As Frankie was wont to advise, "Remember what Jesse said, 'Keep 'em smiling, fellas, they might be on your jury someday.'"

Of all the boys Frankie was the most jocular, convivial, and cunning. Swarthy, handsome, with piercing brown eyes and thick dark hair that whipped like a stallion's mane with each jerk of his head—always ready with a quip or laugh, except when in a foul mood or weary of weak-minded chatter, then he could turn vicious and biting, turn his considerable bombast and rancor on whoever or whatever. Drive his point with a slashing hand or stabbing finger, deriding and declaiming like an arch fascist. That's when they called him "Franco" and he didn't care one bit if they did.

"You point that finger at me once more," Will warned, "I'll bust it off!"

"You try it, big boy. Just try it…"

Frankie and Will had nearly come to blows. Harsh words and gestures filled the room like a dark wind hurled to the far walls and ceiling. Jack, Lee, and Gabe watched from the doorway as the rivals rose from their chairs and cast their shadows above the flickering lamp. Good thing the table stood between them. In the next instant an angry hand clipped the ashtray like a hockey puck. Jack reached out and caught it just before it spilled to the floor. His greater concern was that a coming thrust would send the lamp crashing in a pool of flames. He set the ashtray safely beyond reach and turned a wary eye on the pair, like a horse will its head to size you up.

Jack, who often went by Jacko, had only one good eye. The other was a glass orb embedded in place of the one pierced by a pitchfork when he was a small boy. And right then, witnessing their hot words and quick hands jabbing through light and shadow, he sensed the sharp prong from his father's errant thrust flash to his eye and feared he might see blood again. Even the glass orb, which usually stared off to another time and place, seemed fixed to the moment.

The argument was this: Frankie wanted to organize the boys in a greater scheme, a more rational scheme that would put more money in everyone's pocket. It made sense, what he proposed, and Frankie had the grit and daring to captain such a scheme.

Problem was Will had always seen himself as the leader; after all it was Will who helped Frankie kick smack when Frankie first got back from Vietnam in '69, weighing less than 140 pounds, badly in need of 40 or 50 more to flesh out his six-foot one inch frame. Will took Frankie's dope and flushed it down the stool, locked him in a room, practically sat on him and made him eat and sleep. Breathed life back into that corpse. In a couple of weeks Frankie roared back, bags under his eyes went from half dollars to dimes, up and striding, full of dash and swagger, ready to whip the world, run guns, seize the prize, talking evolution, revolution, and absolution all in one breath. A full-blown iconoclast. And *Hell yes!* still liked nose candy, good pot, and could get drunk on two beers any day or night, but steered clear of smack ever since. Owed that much to Will and ever grateful. Actually giving Doc Will a fair listen.

"*Jesus H Christ, Frankie!* Don't you make a fine picture of a horse's ass standing there talking that shit! Acting like the big chief out to wear the big feathers. Ain't it you who always said we didn't need a leader? Just two years ago you told me to *Fuck off!* when I tried to get things rolling."

"Yes, Will, that's true. I remember. But that was then, and this is now. Things are different. We're all different." Frankie trying to lower the tension, achieve his end, the great heat and argument nearly over. They'd traded a dozen *Fuck you's!* and kicked their chairs to opposite walls, stood nose to nose like two bulls in a pasture deciding whether to charge or whether the cows were worth the fucking headache. Will's wife JoAnn, a delicate Bible-raised blonde, was hiding in the kitchen, her hands thrust in dishwater, wondering what she'd married into, wishing they'd lower their voices, raised to be a good wife and fearing she'd be a widow most any minute. But Frankie's quieter tone chipped away at Will's hard anger, ever persuasive, soothing old wounds.

"Look Will, we've got a sweet deal going. And I want you in on it. I want everyone in on it. All I ask is that you hear me out."

"I'm all ears, Frankie. *Ah-l-ll* ears." Edgy, blunt, keeping his distance.

"Good. Then like I was saying, we…Jack, Gabe, and I have a chance to buy a little place, a hundred 'n forty acres, about fifty miles east, halfway to Manhattan. On over into Clay County. It's off the main road, secluded, hidden by hedgerows, with a high bluff in back. Sixty acres tillable, the rest creek and pasture. It has a ramshackle house and outbuildings. We made an offer and should know in a couple days. Take possession late next week. It's perfect. Perfect for drying and keying. We can move stuff through there by the ton and no one to ask by your leave. Gabe has new contacts, says he can sell every leaf cut in Kansas. Jack will stay at the place and keep an eye on things. Get the stuff dried and bagged. I'll work with the crews back here and on west. Not to be boss or big chief, but simply to keep things moving. We can keep ten to twelve guys busy. Everyone makes money and all you have to do is cut."

Which sounded sweet, because sitting on the stuff was a pain and made everyone antsy. And selling it was always a risk. Not so much due to the law, though selling was a felony while cutting was a mere misdemeanor—but because selling led to the murkier side of things, to people from other places, people you didn't know or trust. As Frankie always cautioned, "It's not the law, it's our own kind we've gotta watch out for."

None of them carried guns, not in a patch or at any time while working hemp. That only asked for trouble. But when dealing, making a sell, yes, they carried guns. Had to because that's when you dealt with the other guys and they sure as hell did. Everyone showed their guns as they showed the goods and the money to keep each honest as the trade was made. All part of the game.

"Okay," said Will, "I'll think on it. You get that place bought, we'll see. But I'll have a few more questions don't think I won't." Still wary, still suspicious, still held a grudge from last year. No sweet deal then. He thought Frankie had tried to rip him off and had said so. Frankie told him where to stick it. Another night they'd shook the rafters. Will still hadn't put it to rest.

But Lee saw it otherwise. Thought Frankie had done the best he could. A bad year for selling hemp, like any crop, the market always up and down, subject to supply and demand. Frankie attempted to market for several groups of pickers, pooled all the hemp to make one deal. And succeeded, in part. For it was a two-part deal and the second part fell through, cash undelivered. The middleman claimed he'd been robbed, middle of the night: two masked gunmen took cash, stereo, coke and left him hanging like a limp dick caught in a zipper. A likely jive, but he had the look of an easy mark, too slack-jawed and frightened to work a scam. Frankie took him at his word and did what he could, what he thought was best. Split the cash in hand even to all concerned. Will didn't see it that way, said his dope was part of the first exchange and didn't get ripped off, so he wanted full payment. Frankie didn't budge, said the dope was all part of one deal, all shared in the profit, all shared in the loss. No one liked it, not really, getting only half of what was expected. Like seeing wages taxed at 50%. Lee wanted to know who the fool was that got ripped off and lost their money. Frankie told him.

"I know that jerk, seen 'im around. He thinks he's a painter. Does tie-dye for chrissake. What a frigging goofball. Did it ever cross your mind he might be lying? Might've stashed the cash and faked the whole thing?"

"Yes. It crossed my mind. He might have. Who's to say? But three or four thousand dollars, what's a life worth, Lee? Would you kill a man for that?"

"Maybe, if I knew he'd ripped me off."

"Well let's find out. Let's go shake him up. Bust a finger or two. Hell, take his car and sell it." Frankie calling the bluff, plenty willing to do his part, driving the devil's bargain. Is it worth it? Are you willing? That was his question as he gazed, eyes held steady, unblinking, dark yet lucent, hinting at once of the serpent or a father confessor. You could never tell which. Which made you think.

For a moment Lee thought *You damn right!*—wanted to hurt the guy bad, for it was dead winter and he was broke, had a wife and son to care for, and self to feed. But no, he had to admit, it didn't make sense, unseemly even to lay a hand on the fool. Not a road he wished to take. Best take the loss and better luck next time.

There it would have rested, except for Renee, Frankie's ex-wife. Bitter over the divorce and other women, and failing to wheedle her way back into favor, she went for the jugular. Let it out that Frankie had stiffed them all and kept the money for himself. Dishing up a real witch's brew and looked the witch as she said it. Lee wasn't buying it for a minute. Few did. But it caught in Will's craw and stuck, eating away, the thought, the possibility, because he'd long warned Lee that Frankie was a user.

"I mean it, he'll use you. I love him like a brother, but he'll use you, me, anybody."

Lee listened quietly and kept his own view. Up to a point

they all used one another. Sure, Frankie was calculating, but fair-minded and keen to everyone's interest. His own foremost, as he freely admitted any number of times.

"Look, I ain't out to fuck myself. I want every penny I can lay my filthy hands on, so help me God!" Raising his hands, laughing, extravagant in word and gesture, perhaps that was his guile, perhaps not. In any case, if he used people, he used them as they let themselves be used. He never pushed, unless pushed. Then he pushed hard.

Will, too, was keen to his own interest. When he felt his interest threatened, he set his stout jaw and turned badger. So they made quite a pair. A caution to watch.

But the storm had passed, both laughing now, off to the kitchen for more coffee. Frankie bantering with JoAnn drying the dishes, got her laughing too. Said, "Why don't you dump this hardhead and take those long legs dancing with me sometime?"

"In your dreams buster!" She backed him off with a snap of her towel, blushing as she shook her head—*Frankie such a tease, unconscionable!*—raised to be a good wife, wanted nothing to do with hanky-panky.

Watching them stand down, Gabe gave a low sigh. Hated to see them square off.

"Someday, I swear, they're gonna kill each other."

"Just a difference of opinion," Lee allowed.

While Jack cast that lone eye in doubt.

"Boy, I dunno. More a *big* difference, I'd say."

Gabe was still sighing, shaking his head. Overweight, smoked too much, always sighing and wheezing, asthmatic, suffered from hay fever. For Gabe cutting hemp was pure torture. He hated it. The pollen, the rough terrain, stumbling blind in the dark night, swinging a machete near hand and leg, stripping leaves till your fingers bled, and lugging fifty-pound bags of wet hemp a half mile or more to a roadside ditch in wait. Not to mention mosquitoes. He much preferred selling the stuff and was good at it, confident, at ease in his element. Bagging money, that was his gig. He didn't even mind the guns, at least they didn't make him sneeze and he hadn't needed to use one. Yet. He knew they were mostly for show, and that most exchanges, no matter the parties involved, were straightforward and businesslike. As long as everyone got what they wanted, all parted happy. Just avoid the narcs and don't party till you're home safe. Clear and clean. A rational approach.

And Gabe liked it that way, a man of reason: a former Hegelian radical turned running-dog capitalist, a hint of Lenin in his wisp of beard, but not in his eyes, no grim ideologue there, for they laughed like old Saint Nick if he was ever young and full of mischief. Gabe was crazy-fun like all the boys— not crazy-mad like certain fellow-travelers in the sixties, dour radicals who had no sense of proportion, no sense of humor, like their nemesis, Nixon. No, Gabe liked his fun writ large, but he was also curious and oddly mystical, ever gnawing at the root of things. Though the true beginning could never be known, that which came before Adam and Eve, all the Precambrian muddle locked in the mud. This was Gabe's suspicion. But the mystery could be explored and sifted like tobacco rolled and lit by a match, the smoke let to drift forth with thoughts warmed by the flavor, the scent, the dark aroma.

The boys all loved long nights of raw rambling discourse— talk of past and future deeds, of life and why, ideas and arguments spun one to the other as in a thousand-page genesis. All read too many books, stayed up too late, smoked too much dope, and drank too much beer. And when they were flush, had money, they snorted cocaine, which was seldom, but in which there was no moderation, snorted till it was gone, wide-eyed and focused, minds in full glory, conjuring every conflict and wonder known, answering every riddle, cutting to the quick, stirring the air and flames till the dust had settled and their minds were left ragged and tattered like buckshot road signs. Then they passed out, crashed for a day, a night, to wake feeling damned sorry and lowdown. And broke. Pockets emptied out by their own improvident glee.

Frankie was there to put cash in their pockets and spark that glee. Rouse them to the task. A sweet deal for all. And he'd been there from the beginning. Will had been there too, in witness, but Frankie was the instigator, the one who started it all. Hemp-picking. Summer of '65, following his first year at the university in Lawrence where he'd learned about marijuana, shared the curiosity, the craving, and saw money being made and knew just where he could get his hands on the stuff—the *pot*, or "hemp" as it was commonly called out where it grew wild, which was practically everywhere, it being a cash crop in Kansas since the 1850's, grown extensively throughout the state up and through WWI, till the market at last withered and died with the passage of the Marijuana Tax Act of 1937, effectively making possession of the plant illegal.

So back home in Cibola City for the summer, one warm night in August, he and Will drove out to a patch they'd scouted. Both hushed with excitement, listening to the murmur of the wind through the shouldering trees and the close chorus of cicadas and frogs, cautious and quiet as they crossed the fence. They carried along a pair of good scissors belonging to Frankie's mom and two white pillow cases that fluttered like ghosts in the moonlight as they reached to snip the leaves one by one, Will using his old scout knife, each of them careful and surgical in their work. They soon had two bags full. A pirate's booty. They rushed back to town, tied off the ends of the pillowcases and tossed them in the clothes dryer.

There they stood in the process of drying the hemp when Frankie's mother, Reba, came in late from a VFW dance, and drawn by the sweet-rank odor she walked down to the basement and caught them red-handed. Wise to the world and her son, at a glance she guessed what they were up to, rolled her eyes and said, "Sweet Jesus...just what do you two young fools expect to do with that?" Cynical and cutting at times, knew men were fools, had buried the father and now saw the son casting his talents to the wind; she didn't wait for an answer, gave a weary shrug and wandered off to bed.

But Frankie was none deterred, knew exactly what he would do. Giddy at the prospect. That night he and Will rolled over 200 marijuana cigarettes, *joints* as hipsters termed them, and that autumn back in Lawrence, Frankie sold them one or two at a time for $5 each—sold to frat rats, sorority chicks, academics, libertines, artists, musicians, rambling souls, all the grand pretenders and hangers-on that gather to sup from the mother institution, the University. And if a single one ever got stoned, they were the greatest pretender of all, for you could smoke a bushel full and not cop a buzz.

Ditchweed. It definitely had the same look, taste, and smell, but was nothing like the primo Sensimilla that Frankie presently lit up and passed around. California grown, select and seedless, like he planned to grow in the future. And *smooth*, filled the lungs with sweet delight. Filled the mind as well. Made you see the colors and shapes of songs. Close your eyes and think you were floating, free and weightless through a tapestry of your own weave, and if not floating, for certain set your mind adrift. All drifting now, listening to "The Band" singing: *"Across the Great Dee-vi-i-IDE, grab your hat and take that Ri-i-IDE...!"* And Frankie riding it for all it was worth, drawing them in with fond remembrance and camaraderie.

"Remember that first night, Will? With Mom's scissors, cutting it leaf by leaf?"

"Yeah, yeah..." chuckling, "damn fools, like your mom said."

Young and green, but things had evolved considerably since then. Each year the harvest grew more efficient, the technique more refined, till by now they were using hydraulics to press keys they had once stomped by boot. In essence hemp-picking was a prime example of bootstrap capitalism, all the processes needed to take a raw product from field to market—all except for advertisement and that came the old-fashioned way, by word of mouth and caveat emptor: *Buyer beware!* Harvest was an enterprise requiring considerable pluck and daring. Not for the timid and meek. It was hard, hard work. At peak season, in mid-to-late September when the seeds matured and stems were full, on any given night a crew of four good men could take out 1000 pounds of wet hemp that would yield a dry weight of 200 pounds. Once keyed and sold at roughly $25 a pound, or $50 a kilo, that came to over $1000 per man. Not bad for a night's work, especially when construction only paid $4 to $5 an hour, less than $40 a day after taxes for a ten-hour day in the hot sun. No doubt about it, Frankie promised a sweet deal.

"We can move everything you cut. Ain't that right, Gabe?"
Gabe and Jack both gave a nod, but Frankie wasn't waiting for
an answer. "We've got contacts in California, Detroit, Florida.
They want all they can get to mix with the good stuff coming
in. Or maybe sell it straight out. Hell, sell it to niggers, college
kids—"

"That's blacks, Franco," Lee prompted.

"Oh Lordy me, did I say—*Niggers?* Blacks, blacks, oh my yes,
by all means, sell it to the blacks..." Frankie not missing a beat,
"to liberal schmucks and Jane Fonda too for all I care. If they're
dumb enough to buy it, *who gives a shit!*"

Incorrigible, effusive, laughing and declaiming, striding
forth, framing the action, forging his gang. And to mark the
moment and sweeten the pie, Frankie laid out a quarter gram
of cocaine, powdered it with a razor and sliced a line for each,
no great indulgence, just a good whiff and taste, enough for
a brief delight and leave you wanting more. Each leaned
forth and sniffed while Frankie stood center of the table like
Christ breaking bread with the disciples, arms spread wide in
summons.

"It's all there for the taking, boys. A fortune, all set and
waiting. Just open the door and walk on through."

Just walk on through...

The phrase struck Lee in echo of something Frankie had
said six years before. Autumn of '69. Frankie had returned
from Vietnam about the same time Lee had left the Air Force
Academy disillusioned by the spit-shine regimen and the
distant war. He'd went there as Arran Clayton straight out of
high school and left using his middle name, Lee. It seemed to
suit him. He wanted to change a lot of things but didn't know
quite how or where to begin. He'd lost his dream of blasting
off into space and touching the red planet, having dreamt one
night of landing there to witness nothing but empty plains of
red dust hemmed in by mountains all shoved up like graves,
not a single river, tree, or winged thing—only a lifeless wind,
barren and cold, like the one Will hated.

His dream upended, Lee turned from math and physics,
forgot all about vectors and ellipses, the pitch and yaw of

motion. He preferred the pitch and yaw of riding a horse, of sitting a saddle and setting his spurs—of tasting the sun, the living wind, and the pure freedom of a rhythmic stride, as if he could reach through the distance and grasp the blue sky extending west to the real mountains. The Rockies! All that blue infinitude that the Cheyenne had called "The Blue Vision." He no longer looked to the red planet but to the good earth, the blue-emerald jewel around which all else revolves. Still the center of the Universe if the heart and womb are given their due. The sacred center.

That was the trouble with the University in Lawrence where he enrolled following the Academy. He found no center. All his efforts grew lame and unfocused. He tried philosophy, literature, but nothing took root or offered a path to "The Blue Vision." He thought about painting, but they were all "moderns" caught up in the splash and daub of color theory and design. He loved painting from Cezanne on back, even Picasso in his "Blue period," but anything thereafter just sucked—*"Alotta dada blada"*—and no one and nothing could change his mind. His force and impetus flattered their intellect and disdain, but he stuck to his guns.

"Dada blada... Fuck it!"

He set his boots bounding down the stairs and out the door. Sick of it all. The premise, the pose, the refutation. His part and presence in the whole charade. Knew there was a war on, albeit a stupid war, but boys his age were fighting and dying every day. And he should be there with them. His thoughts, his feelings that day as he headed down the hill, crossing the park towards Mass Street, when he met Frankie coming up from the other way. Frankie wore a thick wool stocking cap of variegated color, Navy pee coat, blue jeans tucked in knee-high boots, marching up like a land-locked buccaneer clasping his pilfered treasure, a bright new silvery coffee pot in one hand and a book, *The Stranger* by Camus, in the other. Though they were as yet only marginal friends, Frankie greeted his young compatriot from the old hometown with a hearty smile.

"Good to see ya, Lee. Where ya headed?"

"Down to the recruiting office to sign up."

"Sign up? Who with?"

"The Army, I reckon."

"Why?"

"Vietnam."

Frankie's face paled. "No, no," he said, "you don't wanna do that."

"Why not? You went."

"Yes, I went. And that's why you should listen. And why I say don't go. You going there won't help a thing."

"Others are there. Doing their part."

"Yeah, and their part is shit. Look Lee, war is bigger than any man. Dropping down a slit trench with mortars and rockets crashing all around, poppin' like corn in a hot kettle and you thinking you're next as you stare into the chaos, hoping for a way out. No, don't go. Listen, on the best day Vietnam is the most fucked up mess you can imagine. Any average day can get you killed. And that's the worst part. The waste. I zipped too many young guys just like you into body bags. Poor bastards with no choice. At least stop and think. Come on up to my place, we'll brew some coffee, smoke some hash, give it a rest. Hell, what's the rush? What's the problem?"

Lee might've said that he had the urge to die. Simply fall to the fire and have done with it. Life, the world, and self. Because that's always part of a young man's rush to war. But no one ever says that.

"I'm tired of school. Sick of the game."

"So? There's better choices than Vietnam. What do you want to do? I mean, what do you really want to do?"

Lee paused, didn't know quite how to say it, because he'd never said it before.

"I want to paint. You know, really paint. Real paintings, like the masters."

"Well then—*Do it!*" Frankie said, gripping the coffee pot and book in the spread of his arms, looking for all the world like Moses herding a straggler to the Promised Land. "Hell, it's right here, Lee," he pointed to the very air before them, "the hole is right here. All you have to do is *crawl on through...*"

Next day Lee bought a book on anatomy and started drawing every night. He was soon studying the anatomy of Diana, his future wife. Studied each contour and sinuous line, for Diana had an anatomy well worth study. And a heart and a womb. And later on, when she gave him a son to love, he discovered that life provided many battles. Some well worth the fight.

A great part of Frankie's charm was that no matter the situation he always made it sound so easy: *walking through that door, climbing through that hole...* Among those presently gathered, each had a similar echo in mind. Typical of many a good shepherd he often promised more than he could deliver, pointing to the moon as if he touched the very surface. But that was a trait, not a fault. The fault was always too little faith. And Frankie's faith was deep, and not at all Christian. His faith was in himself, in his own spirit and experience, and in his friends.

Frankie's mother had the same raw faith, the same tough center. She'd died the year before. Gathered her kids around her death bed, gave them a pep talk on who was to look after who. Frankie being the oldest, Reba expected him to step up to the plate. Grim, quietly assured, tough to the end, she brooked no sympathy. Dead of cancer at age 48. They buried her a week before Christmas. Frankie didn't say much about it. He looked up Lee on Christmas Eve and they went to a tavern, played some pool, drank some beer, then drove out to Will's place, stayed up all night, tending the stove, talking quiet.

"Helluva thing not having a mother or a home to go to," Frankie said along towards dawn. "Helluva thing..."

Frankie had the faith and the boys knew it. That's what galvanized them. The problem was how to keep the faith. How to tap the spirit that had claimed them since birth. For they had set themselves apart, the boys, and returned to their origins, each in his own way honed to the ripening moment.

Call them "boys," though all were grown, as most men in their 20's or 30's are yet boys, full of vim and vigor, the spirit of youth, in need of something extra, some greater thrill or challenge, unless so scarred by fate or war as to prematurely take solace in a job and routine. While several had been to war, they were not so jaded that they could not laugh at their lot or still take joy in risk. And they knew the risk, having seen death and dealt in death—particularly Ry. He'd fired on the enemy any number of times never certain of who or what he'd hit.

"That's the jungle for you," he'd say with a smile. A killer smile.

Ryan Harling: handsome as young Adonis with marble smooth flesh and thick ringlets of dark hair framing finely honed features, sky-blue eyes, and a smile of quiet irony that rarely left his lips, that expressed the same ironic delight whether sipping wine or coffee or watching Frankie dish up yet another line of coke.

"Here Ry, sit you down," Frankie urged. "Have a snort 'n clear the dust."

Ry had worked late in the field and missed the big argument but arrived in time to partake. He merely smiled and took a chair. Tall, well-mannered, invariably polite, he took pleasure in nearly everything he saw. Especially women, made each one feel special treated to that smile, that manner, and few could resist. Even a woman raised to be a good wife might give it a thought.

Frankie set the plate before him and said, "Finish 'er up. It'll prick your ears and make ya feel better."

Ry took a blast up each nostril then leaned back and grinned.

"Since Nam, I always feel better..."

His first day in-country, jumping from a helicopter into a hot LZ, the first casualty he came to had his nuts blown away. From that moment on Ry forgot all about *The Red Badge of Courage*. He'd spent six months in the bush, served with a company of 200 men that suffered over 70% killed and wounded in a score of firefights, ambushes, land mines—mostly claymores the enemy disarmed and reset—and booby traps of every shape and kind right down to shit on sharpened punji sticks. Yet for all that and what fed irony to his smile was that he was only certain of one day's kill. Five black-pajamaed VC nailed by a 50 caliber at 1000 yards as they tried to cross an irrigation canal. Three floated off like garbage bags in the blood-stained current while two reached the bamboo foliage where they likely died of their wounds, though they were never looked for nor found.

You didn't go rummaging through the underbrush for dead or dying VC. So they added those 5 to the 1 water buffalo and 7 squealing pigs killed earlier that day to make for a grand total of 13 enemy KIA's.

"Flat out amazing, thirteen KIA's," Ry declared with a tight smile, relating an absurdity beyond resolve. "Biggest score in the whole sweep. HQ choppered out a case of cold beer. Piss-warm once we got it. Good though."

Meanwhile their own dead piled up all too vivid and near. Before they cycled out his platoon was down to 50%, counting FNG's, and they'd lost 3 lieutenants.

"The third one didn't last a day," he said. "Out on patrol as usual, playing us as bait, we came under fire around noon. Took cover against an embankment. The LT told us to keep our heads down, like we needed telling. Then the damn fool stuck his up for a look-see. Caught a piece of shrapnel, just a neat little hole. Right about here," Ry tapped a finger to his brow.

"He say anything?" Gabe asked in quiet wonder.

"No, just fell back and sort of whimpered like a rabbit. That was it."

"Man, what a thing, one moment young and vital, the next moment dead. You'd think there'd be something...something more when a person dies."

"Well, what do you want, Gabe? Trumpets and a grand choir?"

"No, Frankie, that's not—"

"Oh, I suppose it's the mystical connection we're lacking here. All them answers blowin' in the wind. Well, so does horseshit once it's stomped to dust."

"No, it's the notion of death and war, that's all. It's tragic."

"Well I was in the war and I saw death," Frankie said, fully roused, for they'd tangled earlier that day over the nature of death and whether the soul transcends or simply ends. Frankie had heard enough. "Damn right, it's tragic. So...? Think that boy's karma got mangled, now we all join hands and sing Kumbaya?"

"No, that's not it. Say what you like, but death happens everywhere, every day. You forget I saw Cory die not two months ago. And sure, he took a fool chance and got swept under that semi, him and his Harley chewed up in a blink of an eye. I remember how he laughed at me when he gunned past, like he was a thing eternal, brother to the wind. Man, there were parts of him scattered all over that pavement..."

This sobered the boys. Even backed Frankie off. But he soon grimaced and jerked his head, couldn't abide their stone-faces, the pained silence.

"Okay, okay, I grieve for ol' Cory too. He was wild and gutsy, fired all his guns at once and died hard. And those second louies had it rough as well," he allowed. But he wouldn't leave it be, slapped the table and added, "Poor devils fell faster'n cheerleaders after a big game."

Which sparked further protest but moved the evening on.

Strangely, Ry's greatest fear and panic didn't occur in combat.

"Don't think I ever told you this," he said, catching Frankie's eye, trying to coax him to friendlier ground. "My worst moment over there..."

"No, don't recall you saying," Frankie eased back.

"We'd been humping the bush a week or more. You know how it was in the rainy season," Ry said, his smile all but vanished, "constant downpour, mud everywhere, you could never get dry. A pitch-black night, we each crouched under a poncho, rain dripping down our necks, filling our boots, soaking in through every rip and seam. No one slept, we all palmed a cigarette and huddled up for warmth. No thought of Charlie. Suddenly I felt a clawed weight latch to my arm. At first I thought someone had grabbed me. Then I cupped my cigarette and looked down..."

All eyes followed as he mimed the very move, straining for a glimpse.

"So? What was it?"

"A foot-long cicada. I kid you not, that sucker was as big as my forearm. I freaked, it flew. My heart clicked on full auto. I swear I couldn't stop shaking till sunup."

The jungle harbored fears worse than man, primal fears dispelled only by daylight and a hearty laugh. "Just a big fucking bug and I've never been so scared..."

But his favorite war story, the one he didn't mind telling and told again that night as time lulled and the boys sobered and listened, was the mystery of the VC tank, though the VC lacked armor so it must have been Chinese, manned by NVA regulars. "No way it was one of ours," Ry noted. "The tracks were too small, like the difference between a narrow-gauge railroad and the modern UP. Obvious at a glance to anyone standing there..." He gazed to the table and saw a war map in the oak grain, the trails, ravines, and elevations. "We were in the Central Highlands. It was clear and dry, a real pleasant day. We came across the tracks in late afternoon and followed them to the edge of a cliff. Then the tracks simply vanished. No crumbling embankment, no sign of wreckage in the trees below. Everyone knew the enemy lacked airlift. Hell, they weren't even supposed to have tanks. But even then, why pick a tank off the edge of a cliff?"

And Frankie—who had no patience for hocus-pocus and went off like a clap of thunder at any mention of Castaneda's Yaqui sorcerer or Von Daniken's ancient astronauts, declaring one "A hopped-up Mexican" and the other "A flying Dutchman" as he scoffed, "What a crock!"—could not doubt Ry's account of the missing tank, could not doubt the context. Each time he sat riveted, utterly perplexed by the notion of all that tonnage made to vanish in the mist. Because he knew that whatever Ry related from the war was in earnest. And whenever Frankie would curl back his lip and snarl "Naw!" at hearing another *could be* or *what if*, preparing to unleash his arsenal of doubt, squelch said thought on the hard anvil of reason, Ry would simply smile and say, "So? Explain to me those tank tracks." Frankie would pause and grow quiet, admittedly stumped by the fact, the reminder that certain phenomena trumped reason, ran parallel to and beyond its grasp. And to see Frankie stumped was a wonder in itself.

Ry accepted the inexplicable, saw it all around him. Neither a skeptic nor a blind believer, he embraced the real and the possible, and whatever luck came his way.

"There's one mystery I have solved, though," he said.

"What? That VA quack finally cure your gut worms?"

"No, Frankie, still got 'em. Eat all I want and not gain an ounce," showing his smile like a hidden ace. "It's the Jeep. Think I got it running."

"Thought you overhauled it a month ago?"

"I did. But it was still not running right, if anything a little worse."

"I told you not to buy that piece of junk."

"That you did. But it wasn't the Jeep. Last week I tore it down again."

"Again...?"

"Yep. Only took me half the time. Laid out all the parts like Mom's good china at Christmas. Checked ratios and tolerances. Couldn't find a blessed thing wrong. Then putting it all back together, it hit me. First thing I should've checked," he slowly shook his head. "So simple I missed it. Too blamed obvious. You know that little screw on the regulator valve?"—nodding to Frankie, for both were good mechanics, having grown up repairing farm equipment, proficient by age 14 and near masters by 18.

"Oh Ry, don't tell me, surely not. Not the air-intake?"

"You got it. Hiding in plain sight. Took a screwdriver and gave it a couple turns. Presto, the motor purred like a kitten. I'd been up all night, nearly sunup. Too tired to even cuss myself or throw a wrench. Just leaned over the hood and laughed till I damned near cried..."

He had them all laughing while he held that smile. He'd seen it a hundred times in Nam, how little things could trip you up. And back home—well, it always paid to keep an eye out.

III. NIGHT JITTERS

The day lengthened in a whirl of hot wind and dust and occasional tumbleweed. Will and Lee had been roving the countryside for several hours with no real luck. They'd found a few patches of hemp, but each grew too close to a house or road to risk cutting. They needed something more secluded. Will slowed Ol' Green and pulled to a stop by a pasture gate. A lightning-struck oak stood beyond the fence, its jagged trunk sheared and blackened like a dark stave set to mark a boundary best not crossed.

"There's an old pond down over that rise," Will said. "I fished there a couple years back. On the far bank are three of the finest cottonwoods you'll ever lay eyes on. Now the wind through a cottonwood makes a song I like, bright and silvery, like the leaves. I camped there one night."

"That the night you heard the panther?"

"Yeah, heard the panther." Will again looked to the rise. "And that's the place, right over yonder…" He'd fallen asleep on past midnight, campfire crackling low, and woke to a scream that bristled his hair and hushed the night. At the second scream he knew he wasn't dreaming. He jumped up and dragged a chunk of deadfall over the fire, stoked it till the cinders flared like a backyard fireworks display. While all around he felt those yellow eyes watching. Time passed, the flames settled low. Finally the bullfrogs started croaking and the wind sang through the leaves.

"That was some night out there alone. The fire, the panther, and me with nothing but a damned fishing pole. You can bet I was glad of that fire. Damn glad," Will grinned and turned to

Lee. "Felt like Cro-Magnon without an ax. Anyhow, if memory serves me well, there's a fair stand of hemp up along a feeder draw that angles north. You might check it out whilst I drive on around the section."

"Sure thing, need to limber my legs."

Lee tossed his hat to the seat so as not to draw an eye, jumped out and side-hopped the fence, lithe as a shadow. He cut past the thistles and soon merged into the knee-high brome. Meanwhile Will cruised on north and rounded a curve.

They used Ol' Green to hunt patches by day because it looked like any other old beat-up farm truck—the bumper sticker read: *One Kansas Farmer feeds you and 79 other people.* For night hauls they used Lee's F-150 Ford, a dark maroon with good tires and a V-8 tuned to run. Ry had rigged a switch on the steering column to cut dash and brake lights, so at a flick of a finger it could blend with the night.

About fifteen minutes later Ol' Green rolled up from the south and stopped by the gate. Lee jumped out from a stand of sunflowers and popped the door.

"Damn!" Will said. "Didn't see ya."

"That's the point, ain't it?" Lee hopped in and they drove on.

"Well…?"

"You were right. There's some great old cottonwoods back in there. Though the pond's all but dry. But a fair stand of hemp. A little weedy in places, but there's enough for three to cut. Should make a decent showing."

"There's a full moon tonight. You ready?"

"You bet, time to make hay."

Ry would be their third man.

Early evening, about an hour past sundown, the crickets and locusts ratcheted like air wrenches on lug nuts in a frenzied *click, click, clatter,* sounding out a brisk cacophony in the fluid night air. A warm wind blew gently from the south and several clouds skiffed low beneath the moon as Will, Ry, and Lee crossed the fence and headed into the pasture. Ry's younger brother Rowdy had dropped them off and was not the least tempted when Ry ribbed him about joining in.

"I mean it, Rowdy. You really oughta try hemp-picking sometime. We'll start you off right. Make you water boy."

"Bullshit!" he said. "Got better things to do—"

Tires spun out gravel and dust as he roared off. Eighteen years old, had worked hard plowing in the hot sun all day. Maybe there wasn't a war on, but there were plenty of wild times and hot women to be had. They didn't call him "Rowdy" for nothing. Off to town, ready to splash his name on the water tower if so dared.

They stood at the rise and watched him go, headlights bearing south towards the lights of Cibola City. They waited briefly to let their eyes adjust then moved on. Each wore dark clothing and a web belt with machete, canteen, and running pack. Ry carried the stripping tarp and gunny sacks rolled over his shoulder like a Civil War ruck. Will brought up the rear and kept an eye to the road while Lee took the lead, having covered the ground earlier that day.

The moon lit the way with fair clarity, but there were always badger holes and barbed wire to watch for. Badger holes, edged by telltale mounds, were easily spotted; wire, on the other hand, left to tangle in the grass, gave little warning and had lamed many a horse and man. So they each scanned the ground, noting any obstacle, the least rise and fall in terrain.

While their vision was more broadly focused than during the day, once their eyes fully adjusted it was amazing what they could sense and see. Each blade of grass cast its shadow to another and all wore the tawny color of late August, except for the scattered bluestem spiked with red, or the blossomed milkweed so freshly white it glistened, and in clusters it earned its more poetic designation, Snow on the Mountain. Bull thistles, which the boys gave a wide berth, stood lone and tall as a man, aggressive and lean, showing a bluish tint on their spiny leaves.

On ahead loomed a darker presence, like a blacked-out cityscape of towering spires with all the crenelated variances of a gothic skyline—closer up it resembled a regiment of black knights, some afoot, others mounted, grouped in wait, lances held ready, their helmet crests and pennants aflutter in the wind. Closer still the boys discerned the deep green hemp shooting up like a miniature forest from the surrounding grass. Female plants stood dominant, full-leafed and hearty, next to which the males leaned frail and withered, having shared their pollen—in another week they'd be nothing but stalk and stem. But it was the females and their lusty limbs laced with five-fingered foliage that beckoned. The boys spread out the tarp, dropped their web belts and waded in, gripping their machetes with gloved hands.

To select a plant they gauged it against the sky, careful to avoid any males still showing a latent vigor. Choice made, they bent it over and made a crisp down-stroke near the base, then cradling the plant in their free arm, they moved on to select another and continued in like fashion till they'd gathered a good bundle to shoulder back to the tarp. There they began stripping the leaves from the stem, tedious work requiring a strong grip and constant arm motion. It was usually best to strip against the direction of growth, from stem to stalk, what they called "back-stripping," though later in the season, after the first frost, when the leaves loosened and the seeds budded full, dropping to the tarp with a dull *thump*, it worked easily either way. But it was still early, the seeds barely on. Once stripped, stalks and stems were tossed to an outer pile to be later hidden in a gully or in the middle of the patch to make the harvest less evident. Likewise each man worked here and there through the patch, never clear-cutting like a sickle, but moving constantly about, culling the best, leaving a number of plants standing visible to the eye. In truth many plants were too scraggly to bother with, and morning glories grew so thick through the entire northwest corner that it wasn't worth hacking your way in.

On they worked, alone or in tandem, either cutting or stripping, depending on their mood, hardly saying a word, each lost in the fever and prospect of the task, breathing hard, finding the rhythm, listening to the night sounds, the wind, the hum of the traffic along the distant highway, and near at hand the swish and rip of stripped leaves and the intermittent *thwing* and *thwack* of a machete slicing through a bent stalk. Every few minutes one or the other would stop and blow a green wad from their nose, wipe it on their jeans and press on. For each rustled stem dropped a mist of green pollen in the moonlight, a pungent dust that made you sneeze, but magical as well. Part of the allure of hemp-picking aside from the money was its more fanciful and elemental aspects: the night, the moon, a machete, working simply with your hands alongside your friends to turn a mere weed into hard cash. The irony, of course, made it all the more fun.

The stars blinked in mute witness. The moon drifted west. From time to time the boys glanced towards town, noting the lights of the carnival camped at the northeast edge. The Ferris wheel spun like a crowned jewel surrounded by the lesser lights of lesser rides—the octopus, tilt-o-whirl, rocket plane, and such. And no one could miss the searchlight that beamed on its axis, sweeping the sky throughout the horizon, calling all to the fair. On past midnight the great color and swirl ceased as the carnival shut down and the town dimmed in the distance like a lamp turned low. The boys kept on working, soaked in sweat, didn't take a break till 1:30.

"Let's bag this stuff," Will said, wiping his brow. "Then let's have a smoke."

Lee snatched up a gunny sack which he and Ry held open while Will stuffed in the leaves, bearing down with the press of his knee after every few handfuls till it was packed full, leaving only enough slack at the top to twist shut and duct tape a handle to grip it by. They bagged four more to add to the three bagged earlier then squatted Indian style in the belly of the old buffalo wallow where the tarp lay, all in all making for a nice nest down out of the wind.

Will tossed Ry a ready-made and they lit up, careful to cup the flare of the match and the glow of their cigarettes—tricks Ry had learned in the war which came in handy in the patch. Lee had quit smoking and no one smoked while cutting, they chewed, mostly "Red Man," adding its *splat!* and slaver to the leaves as they stripped, laughing about what a fine kick it would give the hemp.

"Make some hippie see green," Lee said, pretending to take a toke. "Wow! What's in this shit, man? Tincture of swamp lizard?"

All laughing at the thought, the antic, when Will suddenly hushed, "*Quiet—!*"

They listened for a minute and heard nothing but their own breathing and the tall sheaves of hemp rustling in the wind.

"Guess it's nothing," Will said, squinting hard, still alert. "Thought I heard a limb snap. A little edgy, I guess, first night and all. Gotta work out the kinks."

Will was prone to caution, at times overly cautious. But it was always wise to attend the senses because the boys had been surprised on several occasions in the past by sheriff and deputies and had to scatter like coyotes to make their escape. That's why they each carried a running pack with a change of clothes and some spare ration. Will's idea. And only a fool parked a vehicle in a patch, like waving a red flag at a bull, a sure way to draw heat. Whereas a determined man afoot at night was hard to catch no matter what hounds they sent.

Ry sat across the way, bouncing on his haunches, at ease but ready.

"Doubt if there's anyone out here besides us, Will. Probably just a tree limb."

"Yeah, you're probably right."

When they finished smoking their cigarettes, Will poured a cup of honey-laced coffee into the lid of his thermos and passed it around to give each a boast before going back to work.

"You sure it's okay to keep the stuff at your place?" he asked as Lee took a sip and handed back the cup. Lee had agreed to dry the hemp and sit on it at least until Frankie's plan came into play. Will couldn't keep it, his place too open, though Ned was tolerant, he didn't care to push his luck. Nor did Ry, not with his father poking his nose into every corner of the farm every waking minute, constantly in need of something to do. Cole had been a hard drinker in his day, running buddy with Frankie's old man, the notorious Justin Sage. And while he hadn't touched a drop in over ten years, not since the day they buried Justin, he still had the fevered urge and knew it. So did Ry. Being the oldest, he'd taken the brunt of his father's rages in those darker times. Which partly explained Ry's calm concern.

"That's right, Lee, no need to risk it," he said. "We can dry it up some creek or pasture. Take turns checking."

"No, someone's more likely to see us. And I don't see any problem. Dry it under those cedars out back. No one can see in there. And ol' John doesn't snoop none. Heck, he's hoping I'll buy the place."

"You gonna buy it?" Ry asked. Will curious too.

"Might. He only wants twelve thousand for the house, barn, and that forty-acre pasture. A good pond back there. Helluva buy, really."

For the house was truly a mansion, three stories high with wrap-around porch, a winding staircase, oak floors and bird's eye maple woodwork throughout, built in 1911 and still solid. All it needed was paint—*About a 1000 gallons worth!* was the standing joke. But given paint and set in any sizable town it would have easily fetched a hundred thousand or more. Lee liked it right where it was. It set back from the road with a huge front lawn and spacious corrals out by the barn, all in good repair and all empty, like the house before Lee moved in. Empty for three years. The old Tannis place, something of a legend. So big and so far out of the way that nobody wanted to live there. Yet only 13 miles from town.

"Not to worry you," Will said. "But some say it's haunted. Ned thinks so."

Lee laughed. "If it's haunted, so's my hat. Nothing in there except the damn mice. And those kittens you gave us made short work of them." The mice had enjoyed the run of the place, raiding at will, and the carnage had lasted a week or more with the skitter and chase through empty halls, the crunch of bones late in the night, now mostly quiet, the remaining few cowed and meek. Lee and his wife and son had been living there since wheat harvest, well over a month, and already felt at home. Tempted to buy the place once he had cash in hand. Put a horse in the corral, cattle in the pasture. Tempted to put down roots. Though he had to admit, the house contained some odd spaces, strangely cold and distant, but he supposed any big house did.

"Oh, that's just people and their talk," Will shrugged as he cast out the dregs, "wouldn't lose any sleep over it." Then he

stood and stretched, attempting to pop his back and relieve the
ache. Suddenly he shot back to one knee.

"*Look—!*" he said in an urgent whisper, pointing towards
the road. "There…in that low draw. See? Someone coming our
way. See the cigarette? There again. *See…?*"

Ry and Lee crouched directly behind Will, eyes intent,
nodding anxiously.

"Yeah…think so," Lee answered, noting the flicker of light
and apparent movement. He flexed his knees like a halfback set
to bolt at the signal. All three ready to scram like a wishbone on
a sweep. Then another flicker appeared, and yet another, here,
there, and all around. Scores, then hundreds of tiny lanterns
flicking on and off.

"Fireflies, Will," Ry announced with a low chuckle. "Fireflies
damn near ran us out of the patch."

The wind had died down and fireflies were out by the
thousands, appearing through the pasture, the patch, down by
the pond, like a galaxy of stars gently settling to earth in quiet
play and motion. The boys gazed on, drawn by the rife magic
and wonder.

"Jesus, have I got the jitters," Will confessed, breaking
the spell, his senses a little punchy after being up all day and
working half the night. "Bad as a damned rookie." But relieved
and ready to get back to work. Though the relief didn't last, for
they'd no more than reached for their machetes when a horde of
mosquitoes struck, following the fireflies by mere minutes, as if
the fireflies were scouts leading them to prey. No question they'd
flown up from the pond—the shallow mossy water overgrown
with rushes and cattails provided an ideal breeding ground.

Damn! Fuck the devils! Christ Almighty!!!

The boys cursed and slapped their arms and faces as
the mosquitoes swarmed, buzzing in their eyes and ears in
relentless hunt and hunger, determined to feed.

"Lord, wouldn't you know," Ry groaned, all irony and no
smile. "Left my *DEET* at the house. The one thing I should of
packed." DEET was the insect repellent used in Vietnam, highly
effective, and Ry swore by it, but didn't think he'd need any that
night out in the open with a steady wind.

"I didn't pack anything either," Will said, thinking maybe they should call it a night, then quickly vetoed the thought. "Hate to quit now. Hell, we can cut another two hours. Got any ideas?"

"Might try smearing on mud," Lee suggested.

*Yeah, yeah...*they gave it a thought. Damn near ready to run down and roll in the stinking pond mud when Ry had another idea.

"Let's try tobacco juice. Stuff's pretty potent. They give it to horses and dogs for tapeworms. Kills about any stomach worms except the ones I've got. Maybe it'll scare these dang skeeters."

Worth a try, desperate by now, each took a big chaw and started chewing, soon smearing dark tobacco juice over their face, neck, and arms, and felt their skin tighten as the astringent took effect. Lo and Behold! the mosquitoes withdrew, still humming close, but loathe to land. Cheered by success the boys smeared on more, coated their stomachs, backs and chests, looked a savage sight and smelled worse, but felt great. Refreshed, even. They grabbed their machetes and went back to work. By 3:30 they had two more bags packed and ready.

"That makes ten in all," Will declared. "Time to saddle up 'n head out."

"Suppose we better," Ry said. "I need a good half hour to make it to the house 'n fetch the truck." Because Rowdy for damned sure wasn't going to pick them up, he'd made that clear when he dropped them off. Told his big brother in so many words that he planned to be waylaid by a woman or drunk on his ass by that hour, not running up and down country roads, checking his rear-view mirror for sign of Sheriff Guy.

The Harling place lay less than two miles directly south. Ry would help make one tote to the road before heading on. That would give Will and Lee time to have all ready to load on his return. They clipped on their web belts and were preparing to shoulder a bag when they heard a loud snap. All three froze and listened, moving only their eyes. Definitely something out there this time. Something big and hunched, moving up the draw. And something else, further back, in the direction of the pond, lumbering through the hemp. Steady, unhurried. Then nothing.

"What the devil's that...?"
Each spoke in a bare whisper.
"I dunno..."
"Do you hear anything?"
"No, not now..."
Waiting, watching, listening.

Then an old cow mooed in lowing query as if to ask, *What are you boys doing out here this time of night wrecking our pasture? And why isn't the salt block back where I last licked it? When I's up here last it was down by the dam, now where's it got off to?* Cattle strung out towards the pond, all joining in, bellowing questions and complaints. *That's right, you tell 'em Bossy, where's it got off to? We want that salt block and how about a mineral block to go with it? Huh? How about some sweet hay? And whatever come of that handsome bull you dropped off last spring? My, he had good heft and thrust. My oh my, just the thought makes me MO-OAN!!!*

By now the cows were raising a righteous chorus of throaty moo's. A dog started barking in the near distance, threatening to wake the whole countryside.

"Shut the fuck up you old hussies!" Will threw a stick to silence the nearest one. She merely swished her tail and mooed again as if to say, *Why'd you do that for?*

"Christ, what a night," he said. "First off I jump at my own shadow. Then the fireflies, mosquitoes, and now these damned cows. If Sheriff Guy's waiting out by the road, I'm gonna bum a smoke and catch a ride to town."

The boys each shouldered two bags and marched off, putting tracks between themselves and the cattle left milling about the hemp, lowing back and forth like old women at a rummage sale, poking here and there, somewhat curious, somewhat critical, *Now where's that salt block? Where'd they put it? Is it over your way Martha? NO-O-O! Well then, MO-O-OVE on over, 'cause this ol' heifer wants to see for herself!*

The stars shone in greater multitude and clarity as the moon vanished in the west. The boys had no problem following the cow path up through the pasture. Nor were they worried about meeting the sheriff out by the road, what with the carnival and fair and young bucks like Rowdy on the loose, he'd have his hands full. Nor was he a deep concern on any other night. Sheriff Guy Craig, who most people referred to simply as Sheriff Guy, was an older man in his mid-fifties, respected and well-liked. The boys liked him too. For one thing he didn't get too riled about hemp-picking, unlike some, didn't consider it a grave social menace. As long as you were discrete and took care not to harm person or property, he pretty much let things ride. You practically had to land in his lap before he'd take you in. But anything too obvious he'd step on.

He'd caught two bona fide hippies the year before. Rastafarians with wild braided hair and lit-up eyes that hit town in a psychedelic van with California plates and every *peace-love anti-this-that'n-the-other* sticker pasted to the back door and bumper. They got stuck in a plowed field trying to reach a creek bottom full of hemp. *What a bummer!* Then they had the bright idea to walk to the nearest farmhouse and ask the farmer to pull them out. They were polite enough, standing in the porch light, faces pressed up against the screen like two giant June bugs.

"Hey man… Can you help us?"

They offered twenty dollars.

The farmer said, "Sure, fellas. Be out directly. Just need to fetch a lantern and tell the wife." He told the wife to call the sheriff then went out and loaded self and the two lost causes on his old "Johnny Pop," a three-cylinder John Deere used for row-cropping. They chugged off down the road, shooting black smoke with a loud *pop! pop! pop!* every third stroke as the Rastas tried to plug their ears and hold onto the fender wells to keep from falling, big tires spinning like paddle wheels on a river boat, threatening to suck them under and pave them to the road. The dark of night, no lights, clouds breaking up below a bright silver moon, and those ungainly silhouettes speeding past looked highly suspect to any coyote or raccoon that happened to gaze up and notice.

The tractor arrived at the field to find Sheriff Guy and the wrecker in wait. Sheriff cuffed the hippies; wrecker towed the van. Next day the judge sentenced each culprit to a haircut and a bath, levied a $50 fine for trespassing and sent them on their way, with a faintly sober cast to their eyes. Whole county had a good laugh over that one.

But it was an entirely different story in the neighboring county east. The Sky County Sheriff, Hoss Wayne, was an ex-marine and acted like Wyatt Earp taming a cowtown when it came to nailing hemp-pickers. The previous year he'd nailed 50 plus, practically stuffed the jail. Again, mostly out-of-staters coming in to feast on the wild hemp. But the easy pickings were all Sheriff Wayne's. And over there, if caught, you faced a $500 fine or 30 days and loss of vehicle. So after a few close scrapes the boys steered clear of Sky County, no matter how tempting. Besides, there was even better cutting to the north and west in Hill and Smith Counties. Tonight was more of practice run than anything; they simply wanted something close at hand, something to get their feet wet and their blood pumping.

They'd covered a quarter of a mile, still following the cow path, breathing hard, leaning forward with the weight of the bags, straining to maintain their grip, when they reached the rise and stopped dead in their tracks. They let the bags slip to the ground. And it wasn't the weight of the bags that stopped them. It was a light. Not a spotlight or searchlight of any kind. But a bright light in the eastern sky that shone brighter than the most brilliant star, three times as bright as Venus.

And it moved! Zig-zagged up and down then zipped to the north horizon and stopped, stationary a moment before moving again by fits and starts like a luminous water spider—or the tip of an otherwise invisible sword wielded by a black-capped master feinting here and there as if toying with them as he slashed a brilliant "Z" through the northeast sector of the sky. Then it vanished to reappear, dimmed and vanished once more. Then as suddenly it reappeared, gaining in brilliance, drawing close, before returning east where it slowed to hover in a relatively fixed position.

It was certainly no lightning bug, unless of cosmic variety. And though fatigued, the boys were clear-eyed and lucid. And no hallucination could produce the same effect on three separate minds. What they observed was a visible fact, a phenomenon that lay outside the perceived order, utterly beyond their understanding. Yet what is perceived must somehow be reasoned with and commented on.

"Holy shit..."

"You see that..."

"I'll be damned..."

Each felt like a kid conned by some trick and speaking merely confirmed they weren't the only fool watching. Yet certain before asking that there lay no answer, no explanation to ease their puzzlement. For there was no swamp gas in Kansas. Nor was this a reflected light—not a cloud in the sky. Whatever its origin or intent, it clearly contained its own force and energy. And there was no jet, no rocket, no meteorite that could move like that. Not even a weather balloon hurled by a twister.

Ry turned to Will, raised his brows and grinned.

"Well Wolfer...? Is that what you'd call a U...F...O?"

"I'll be damned. I'll be goddamned," Will repeated like a skeptic who'd doubted Santa Claus made to witness the flying sleigh and the red-nosed reindeer. "Serves me right. Never thought I'd see such a thing."

Because they'd had an argument not a month before over the very thing—the notion of aliens, the mere possibility, most particularly Von Danikin's theory of ancient astronauts having visited the earth. Will scoffed absolutely, wouldn't buy it for a minute, sided with Frankie in pooh-poohing the whole idea of little green men. But given what they now saw, Will had to admit that the notion of aliens and ancient astronauts no longer seemed so farfetched. And his "I'll be damned" was offered by way of apology for being such a bonehead.

Too bad Frankie wasn't there to eat crow as well.

Not that Ry was gloating as he chuckled and grinned like a kid having told you so, simply expressing his usual delight, perhaps a bit more than usual. Wholly amazed in fact. Most definitely the craziest thing he'd ever seen. Crazier than a foot-long cicada or those tank tracks left on the ridge above the jungle. He decided to check with Lee and see what he thought, knowing Lee had once aspired to be an astronaut.

"How about you, Lee? Got any ideas?"

"Not a one," he said as he slowly uncapped his canteen and wet his lips, trying to call reason into play. "Can't even guess, not really. A pocket of energy, I suppose. A ball of light that must have some form or mass. Every light has a source. A flashlight, a skyrocket, a lightning bug. The sun, the moon. And they say every star glows in its own ball of fusion. Now if that thing is a small ball of fusion...of pure energy and somehow self-contained, that might explain why it doesn't burn up at those speeds. Because at that rate anything we know of would flare into ash in the time it takes to blink—"

In the next instant they watched it flash from east to north and back again.

"What would you guess it...ten, twenty, thirty miles out?" Lee observed. "Or it might be above the atmosphere at ninety miles or more. Which would better explain why it doesn't burn up or leave a trail like a falling star..." He fell silent a moment as each thought begat another and all fell short like rocks thrown at the moon. "But Christ, if not weightless, the stress from those kind of G's, that kind of acceleration...anyone in there would have their flesh ripped from their bones like jerking a coat off a hanger."

"Think they've come to pay a visit?" Ry asked, convinced that anyone or thing that could fly that fast was smart enough to avoid turning to mush in the process and surely had something in mind.

"I don't know. And sooner not find out. "

"Me neither," Will said. "Whatever they have in mind I bet we don't want."

"Maybe not," Ry mused. "Kind of like the prey seeing a hunter, isn't it?"

"Yeah, something like that."

All felt a slight unease, somehow threatened, even as they gazed like star struck lovers who swear that all the stars in heaven blink just for them. Without question they felt singled out, in a sense honored by what they saw. But light travels in all directions and stars blink whether anyone is watching. And what they saw flying through the sky, whatever its motive, it lay completely beyond their scope. Perhaps inimical to their will and desire. For certain indifferent. That was the suspicion and fear. Yet their greater fear and the more likely outcome was their being called fools.

"One thing I know," Will said, voicing the collective concern, "if we tell anyone, they won't believe us. They'll just think we're nuts." Having experienced a dubious conversion, he wasn't about to go tell it on the mountain.

No, a thing so extraordinary could only be shared with those who witnessed it. And what they now witnessed was so extraordinary it could not even be named. Yet instinct told them that there had to be an intelligence involved, because it was so lively, erratic, and playful—whereas dead mute matter did not change course or accelerate unless made to do so. But what kind of intelligence, what possible reason or purpose had it for being there, hovering like a star in the east, like something being born?

The boys scratched their heads in wonder. Wise men they were not.

Leave them to their wonder and mischief as Ry walks to his house to fetch the truck and Will and Lee finish toting the rest of the bags. Turn east to that light and focus to the earth below. To the adjacent region 30 miles east. To Sky County.

IV. BAD THINGS

Some things happen. Bad things. Beyond anyone's wish or will. At least anyone wishing otherwise. Such can only be witnessed, or told, no matter how much it turns the stomach or grieves the mind. The fact remains. Bad things happen.

Joseph Conners was 18 years old, blonde haired, blue eyed, an all-league halfback just out of high school, working that summer at the Farmer's Co-op tire shop in Arcadia, the queen city of Sky County. He planned to attend K-State in Manhattan that fall on an Air Force scholarship, dreamed of flying. But lately he couldn't focus on his plans or his dreams. He had seen something bad. And what he'd seen could not be shared, dared not share it. He was so scared that the previous morning he'd stepped out behind the tire shop and vomited. The fellow he worked with, Chris Boswick, heard him retching and joked, "What's the matter, Joey? Too much beer last night?"

"No. I saw something," he said, still spitting, catching his breath. "Something I shouldn't have. It's got me so I can't keep my food down."

Chris sobered, sensing the boy's fear like the smell of vomit. "Then go to the police—"

"NO! I can't!" His answer so sudden and final that it silenced them both.

Joey didn't say another word, already said too much. And he could judge the depth of his own fear by the other's reaction, because Chris Boswick's face paled as they went back to work and he didn't share any of his usual banter that day. They worked mostly in silence, either pointing to or reaching for a wrench or pry bar as if each sensed that words were now taboo and would only hasten bad luck. Chris was a veteran of Viet Nam and he'd seen many bad things, some of which he'd shared with Joey that summer, priming him like a kid brother to the dangers of war and life in general. "Afraid I've seen some bad shit," he'd say. Yet deep down Joey knew that what he'd seen was every bit as bad, all the more so because it was something he'd never imagined and involved someone he respected. But you can't compare bad things; they are all equally unimaginable till you see them, then you can imagine nothing else. He felt a wall form around him, looming like a shadowed cliff, closing him off as he dropped down a deep dark shaft, irrevocably drawn by the fear and consequence of what he'd seen. He no longer perceived a future, could not think of college or flying. He sensed his life coming to an abrupt end, a cold certainty gripping the pit of his stomach.

But he felt wholly alive that evening in the arms of his girlfriend Cathy as they danced to the music in the open air in front of the band stand. She was so pretty, warm, and vibrant. Beautiful to hold. They'd met at a Catholic youth camp the previous summer and had dated ever since. Even though she lived 40 miles south in Salina, they still managed to see one another two or three times a week. By now they were deeply in love, had eyes for no other. And her eyes were brown.

Her parents came from Mexico and her father worked on a hog farm at the old air base near Smolan, southwest of Salina. Her full name was Catalina Rosa Maria Torres. Though she insisted everyone call her Cathy, even chastised her mother till she relented. Only her father called her Catalina, and him she did not chastise, for he doted on her, his "Catalina bonita," saying it with such fondness that she could not refuse to answer. Still, she wished their last name was Terrel, Terrance, or Tillman. Anything but *Torres*. She'd grown up hating her brown skin, her black hair, and dark eyes. Longed to be blonde and fair. But lately she had blossomed and began to accept her color. Since meeting Joey and having his blue eyes gaze to her, she knew she was pretty, because he was so handsome and would not think her so if she were not.

Tonight, dancing before him like a butterfly fluttering in the moonlight, she was beyond pretty. Dazzling, seductive in

her white dress which revealed the brief swell of her breasts
and flared at mid-thigh with the shift and sway of her hips,
her tapered legs prancing in perfect rhythm to the rapid rock
beat which she loved and danced to with such abandon and
grace that it made him want to catch her up and hold her. And
he caught her now, took her in his arms and spun her around
and around in dizzy swirl and laughter then set her free again.
Admiring her flesh and form and movement, biding his time
till the music slowed. And she loved the slow songs too. Loved
leaning to him, raising her face to his, brushing lips, sharing
their breath and scent, letting her breasts heave freely against
him, melting to his embrace with the press of her hips, feeling
his flesh swell in want of her. And she wanted him so.

A half hour later parked in seclusion off a hillside road at the
south edge of town, they nearly went all the way. She let him
unzip her dress, remove her bra and panties. Her hair hung to
her waist; her crucifix to her breasts. He nibbled at her ear, her
neck, her nipples. She unbuckled his pants, freed his hardened
flesh and gripped him in her hands. He felt so large that she
could not imagine him in her, yet wanted him there. They
groped and grasped, fingers exploring hidden recesses where
juices flowed in want of further touch and friction, stroking
one another till they grew faint, the urge so strong. She leaned
back and spread her thighs as he shifted over and prepared to
enter. Then she touched the crucifix at her breast. They stared,
waiting, their eyes wild with want. With fear and doubt. She
bit her lip; he drew back. They wanted her a virgin on their
wedding night. And they planned to wed the following spring
after her graduation. Attend college as man and wife.

"Is it so long to wait?" she asked, soothing his ache and
need. Yet searching his eyes, she saw something else, something
troubling him. Something wrong.

"What is it, Joey? Tell me." Then she panicked. "Is it another
girl?"

"No, Cathy...no." He looked to her and shook his head.
"There'll never be another girl, Cathy. Never. It's just..."

"Then tell me. Please?" She perched up beside him with her
legs tucked under, brushing the hair from his eyes.

"Nothing really. It's just...sometimes life seems so short. Like it's about to end."

"Ah Joey, it's just beginning. We've got forever, you and me." Then she fluffed his hair, teasing him. "And soon enough, big boy, you'll have this chica all to yourself. Huh?" Which made him laugh. She could always cheer him up with some little antic or another. They teased and laughed as they readjusted their clothing, dreaming of the day when their love would be sanctioned and they could savor it free of guilt and constraint. And he tried to forget his fear of what he'd seen, the bloodied leg under the canvas and the voice on the phone that warned:

"*Say one word, your little brown bitch is dead...*"

He drove his parent's 1972 Ford LTD, royal blue with gray interior. A four-door with automatic transmission. A family car. Certainly no hot rod. But with a 396 V-8 and a four-barrel carburetor it could move, and he could drive. He often topped 120 down the long stretches of Highway 81 to and from Salina, and hadn't yet been caught. A month earlier he'd skidded off the highway onto a country road to lose a trooper in hot pursuit. He threw up a cloud of gravel as he fishtailed to the ditch, then straightened out and sped over a hill, turned into a field and cut the lights. Half a minute later the trooper roared past with full siren and red light flashing. At the next mile he slowed and cruised on around the section, finally reaching the highway and heading south.

Joey watched him go, waited a few minutes, then eased out and followed country roads back to Arcadia. Thrilled at his escape. And confident he could drive. He loved speed. Didn't smoke or drink, something of a straight arrow. And when his friends called him that, he'd say, "That's right, I'm a straight arrow. And I'll be flying jets some day while you're still poking along on a tractor."

Heading down the hill towards the main drag that ran north and south through town, he noticed headlights coming up fast in his rearview mirror and thought it might be a carload of friends out to razz the young lovers, honk their horn, stick their heads out the window and ogle. Like usual he'd play it cool, smile and wave them on.

But the black pickup that pulled abreast didn't belong to any friend. It crowded him to the curb as both vehicles came to a screeching halt. A spotlight glared, flooding the windshield. Joey shifted in reverse and burned rubber back up the hill, whipped around and took the only escape he saw—a gravel road heading south. He told Cathy to buckle up and hold on. She didn't need telling, having already bruised her lip against the dash in their abrupt stop. She glanced back and saw the pickup in pursuit.

"Are they some of your crazy friends?" she asked, hoping it was all in fun.

"No, Cathy. I'm not sure who they are. But they're not friends."

The speedometer hit 60, then 70. He had no fear of speed and knew the road, could anticipate each dip and turn. In fact he knew all the roads through the region and could map them in his mind, mark each blind curve and intersection, having hunted along them since he was a boy. Only now he felt like a rabbit trying to lose a hound. He checked in the mirror and saw the haze of headlights in the dust behind. He pushed harder, faster, trying to distance himself and her, racing beyond his headlights over the quick-shifting terrain as trees and fencerows flashed past like grainy film.

Cathy tensed with each rise in speed, growing ever more anxious.

"We're going awfully fast, Joey?" She looked to him in wonder of his haste.

"I know. You've got to trust me."

"What is it? Are you in trouble?"

"We're both in trouble. I'm sorry, Cathy. But I saw something. Something terrible. And I think they were part of it."

"What? What did you see?"

"I can't tell you. I can't tell anyone. I *can't*. *Can't—!*" He slammed the steering wheel with his fist, then caught himself and calmed. "Please, Cathy, trust me. Trust me and pray...pray for us both."

She said no more, gripped the crucifix pendant at her breasts and prayed. Prayed to the Virgin Mary, to baby Jesus, to Saint Christopher and to all the other saints for their timely intercession. For deliverance and mercy. Prayed in English, in Spanish. And she prayed that her mother and father would forgive her many tantrums.

Nearly five miles south of town they cleared a hill doing 80 and went airborne briefly before landing with successive bounce and jolt. Both gave a shout of laughter, giddy at the weightless moment and the wild thrill of holding the road. Then silent again as Joey quickly slowed, cut the lights, and turned onto a dirt road that dead-ended from the west—the intersection all but hidden by a hedgerow that overgrew the ditch. They sat, panting in fear and wait. Within seconds the trailing headlights rose over the hill and descended their way, their pursuers traveling somewhat slower, steady and controlled. The pickup passed on down the hill then stopped. The spotlight speared through the darkness, sweeping up through the pasture and trees like a broadsword stabbing at the undergrowth, poking for prey. Then the spotlight dimmed and vanished while the red glow of back-up lights filled the view. In the next instant the pickup appeared in full profile like a dark menace as the spotlight shot through the window, lighting the interior with Cathy's frightened scream.

Joey gunned the engine and raced on, cleared two more hills before taking the first turn south. Heading south in frantic flight as if instinct and duty drove him there. Heard Cathy crying. Had to get her home or her father would worry. Had to save her. There had to be a route of escape. *Had to be!*

But nothing and no one in this world has to be. The wind settled the dust of their chase within minutes of their passing as it would one day scatter the dust of all involved. Only love is immortal, and only in song.

Joey gripped the wheel, making ready for the curve up ahead, an "S" curve that rounded a hill and made a sharp descent down the far side. He skidded fine through the initial bend, but on the second he edged too close to the shoulder and the soft gravel left piled by a season of farm traffic caught his tires and pulled him to the ditch. He ramped a culvert at 50 miles an hour, took out a fence post, and swerved back onto the road, grinding to a halt on a broken drive shaft.

He only had time to grasp Cathy's hand before the pickup sped down...

A great horned owl lands on the upper limb of a hillside oak. Blinks its yellow eyes and scans the scene. Interrupts its flight to observe the rude approach of man, the rush of light and mass, like hounds in chase on the road below. Sees the first hound leap through the fence then kick and spin till it lies wounded, its lone eye shining off into the darkness. Soon the larger hound bears down, eyes beamed straight ahead, tracking with intent and vigor as it approaches the first and stops.

Doors kick open and three jagged shadows appear, ghastly in form and aspect like scarecrows blown in the wind, clothed in dread and hollow of heart and mind. They circle their prey. From the near side comes a brief cry silenced by a sudden flash and shot. The owl draws alert, knows the sound of gunfire as well as the scent of the hunter and of blood. From the opposite side emerges yet another shadow with a cry of rage and grief answered by a series of angry shouts as the scarecrows converge and drag him forth into the harsh glare of the beaming eyes that cast the struggle far into the night. Man shadows loom over the creek bed to the hill beyond, stretched like huge tree limbs clashing in a hard storm. The very act staged in a wedge of light.

"Cathy? Why? Why did you...kill her, you—"

A pistol slams his head as he staggers to his knees. Rough hands gripe him by the hair and smash his face against a headlight, pinning him there. Faces starkly etched in black and white hover at the periphery, screaming harsh taunts.

"Why you running, lover boy? Who'd you tell!? Cat got your tongue?"

"I didn't tell, I didn't...I swear!"

"Oh, listen to this, he swears. Got us a real boy scout here."

"You killed her, you bastard, you fucking—"

His words cut short by a bullet fired into his gut. He clutches and falls in fetal agony. A frightful pause as he grimaces at his murderer in the glare of lights, gasping through his bloody teeth: "Fuck you, fuck you, fuck you...!" While the killer knells like a mock confessor, a harbinger of death, lingering a moment as if to savor his work.

"No, fuck you, boy..." Shoves the pistol between his legs and fires.

Headlights suddenly appear to the north. The scarecrows glance in alarm.

They drag their victim aside and vanish as they came.

The owl again scans the scene. Blinks indifferent to the death and agony it has witnessed, but ever keen to the scent of man and his acts, wise to and wary of the road. The wind ruffles its feathers; it turns its head to the skitter and rush of prey through the thickets below. Presently the owl spreads its wings and sweeps down over the creek in hunt, merging with shadows through the trees.

V: THE SHERIFFS

A dust devil the size of a man twisted down the road and broke up passing the vehicles parked on either side, then formed anew in a swirl of dust and continued on towards the narrow creek bridge at the bottom of the hill.

"County needs to widen that bridge. Two cars collided there in '71 and put a kid in the hospital."

The taller man standing somewhat distant did not answer.

The shorter man sat squatted on one knee, scratching at the road dust with a stick, trying to focus anywhere but on the bodies. "Need to fix that bridge," he repeated in idle drift, his thoughts left spinning from the brutal murder of two kids right there on County Line Road dividing Range and Sky Counties. Both sheriffs called.

Homer Evans, the old farmer who'd notified them, knew right-of-way and jurisdiction like he knew crops and weather. Knew by whose right you crossed which ditch into what field. Knew where his taxes went and whose salary they paid and he expected to see a job done right.

"So, by Golly, I called ya both out," he said. Homer, a wiry little man of 70, stood with his arms folded on the bib of his blue overalls, wore a clean white shirt and a red Co-op cap tipped back on his head, showing the sharp divide of his sun-weathered face and the bleach white above his brow. Bald as an egg and never took his cap off except at the table, in church, or when honoring the flag. "Me 'n the Missus jest heading over to the Disciples of Christ when we found 'em like that. The Missus didn't feel much up for church no more. I drove her home and give you fellers a call. Never thought I'd see the day, and hate to say it, but I'd rather live through the thirties agin than see such a thing as this. Seems the whole country's got more of the devil these days than of God. You don't think so, jest look for yourself."

Sheriff Craig had seen all he wanted at a glance. Knelt to calm his stomach.

Sheriff Wayne stood at the gravel edge of the road and stared down at the boy. Black blood and flies, twisted features and crusted vomit—shot in the groin and made to suffer. Sheriff Wayne blinked away and walked to the car. He'd seen death aplenty, but not in this context. And the young girl, her head slumped sideways, eyes staring down like she was thinking of a song being played, like she was ready to step out and dance, still radiant in her bloodied white dress and death pale skin. He leaned in at the window to examine the entry wound to the head, drawing back her hair with his pencil, careful not to touch anything or in any way mar the evidence, thinking, *sure was a pretty thing.* But already starting to stink. He noted his watch, 8:45. And hot as it was, already past 90 degrees, she couldn't have been dead more than five or six hours or she'd have smelled worse. Only now drawing flies. He shooed them away with his notepad and leaned in for a closer look—found her seat belt still fastened and saw no sign of rape. He stepped back and tapped his pencil to his notepad.

Yeah, she sure was pretty.

Meanwhile Sheriff Craig stood, hiked his pants and tucked his shirt. His clothes were of khaki and worn for comfort, wrinkled and durable like his face. The cuff of one pant leg caught on the boot of his brown Wellington's, leather so scuffed and worn like he'd walked 100 miles of rock desert to get there, though it was only 15 miles from Cibola. An old sweat-stained fedora purchased in the fifties sat slightly cocked to the side of his head. Sheriff Wayne on the other hand wore a brand-new white straw Stetson. He stood shoulders squared and dressed sharp, shirt and trousers neatly pressed, gig-line straight, seams perfectly creased from shoulder to cuff—left, right, left—like the drill sergeant he had been. He wore the hat of a good guy but his face was pure bad-ass ex-Marine, pock-mocked and fight scarred, the meanest face on any man this side of death was the common view, voiced only at a distance. He stood 6'6" in his boots—black boots that boasted their shine even through the skim of dust—and weighed in at 240. His name was Rob, or Robby, but most had called him Hoss since high school.

A real contrast in size, manner, and age—Sheriff Wayne right about 30 with dark cropped hair, and Sheriff Craig in his 50's, his hair gray and thinning, enough on top to furrow with a comb. But they got along. Not chummy. Kept their distance. Like now as Sheriff Craig walked slowly along the roadside, head down, examining the ditch for any sign or clue. Even took out his reading glasses to examine a bit of mica he'd picked up, then tossed it aside and folded his glasses to his shirt pocket.

"Can't spot a single shell casing. How about you?"

"No, and you won't," Sheriff Wayne answered, still jotting observations in his notepad. Then he looked up. "They used a revolver, Guy. Probably a thirty-eight, judging by the wound. Because it's too big for a twenty-two, and a forty-five up close would have blown half her head away." He packed a 45 himself, holstered on his hip, and he knew about wounds from two tours in Vietnam.

Sheriff Craig didn't carry a gun, kept one wrapped in a towel under the front seat. A 22 revolver. The only thing he wore on his belt was his badge. He nodded in answer and went back to examining the roadbed, the dust so powdery he couldn't detect a single footprint, not even his own as the wind blew steady, erasing all but his jagged shadow tugging at his heels. He detected nothing but shadows, dust, and wind.

The old farmer still stood by watching.

"Say Homer, you live about a mile east. You hear anything in the wee hours?"

"Ohhh, I dunno, Guy…" he paused, rubbing his chin. "Naw, nothing 'cept the dog barking along about two-thirty to three or so. The Missus has a winder fan blowing in my ear so's I can't make out road noises like I usta could. But ol' Jeff sure nuff took up a yip 'n howl. Figured he caught whiff of a coon. They terrible bad down in the corn this year. Them buzzards know it's ripe a'fore you do."

Then he wrinkled up his nose and stepped back, catching scent of the boy's corpse ripening in the sun. Flies swarmed about the vomit at his mouth and the foul mess of his lower body wounds. They were all appalled at the sight of the boy, his evident torture and suffering. They knew it was Joey Conners. They knew him from football. And they knew he was a good kid. The kind of kid that everyone liked to claim and no one liked to see anything bad happen to.

Homer backed off another two steps and addressed Sheriff Wayne.

"Any idea who done this?" Being a Sky County taxpayer, he knew who had best hear his concern and from who he'd like an answer.

"Nope, no idea as yet."

Homer frowned in disgust and looked to Sheriff Craig.

"Now you mayn't know this, Guy, but Hoss sure a'nuff does, 'cause he's looked into it. My neighbor to the south, Marion Campbell, lost some good stock awhile back. A dozen Hereford cattle and a registered bull. Rustlers, by gum. They left the bull dead, mut'lated like that boy. Cut out his wanker and drank his blood."

"Now Homer, I doubt anyone drank his blood," Sheriff Wayne countered wearily, he knew of the rumor and its likely source.

"By Howdy, I say they sucked 'im dry," the old man bristled. "'Cause there weren't a drop a blood on the ground anywheres. Cut out his wanker and his balls to boot. And that's the devil's work, I say. Kinda scary, too. And Dale Green is anuthern. In late May, his wheat 'bout ripe and ready to cut, he found three big patches all stomped down. Stomped in a big circle they was. Big a'nuff to turn a combine around in. Way out in the middle of a section a'ground and not a footprint or tire track leading in or out. And lots a folks this summer say they seen strange things in the sky." Nodding his head steady as he spoke. "Now I ain't seen none, but good folks as jest don't say it to hear themselves blow say they seen flying saucers and I believe 'em, by gum. Ain't none but spacemen could do Dale Green's wheat like that. No sir, and I wager good money it's spacemen or these dang kids on devil weed with their devil music and voodoo that's behind this right here. That's what I say," standing braced and ready like a little dog barking at a big one. "Yessir, that's what I say," repeating his concern for benefit of proper authority.

Sheriff Wayne remained unruffled. He didn't argue, he didn't scoff or laugh, he simply walked over, looked down at the old man and smiled. A smile that was all but imperceptible in that mask of mean, though he felt kindly towards the old man and only meant to calm him.

"Homer, I know you're concerned and upset. We all are. And I admit, I don't know who rustled Marion's cattle or what crushed Dale Green's wheat. But right now I want to focus right here on the murder of these two kids. Find out who did it and why. Now I want to thank you for calling us out and standing by. But I say you go on home now, look after your Missus. We'll handle things from here on."

The old man had stuffed his hands in his pockets and lowered his eyes like a kid being lectured by a principal. Hearing the last, he pursed his lips and nodded, turned and shuffled back to his rusty red Studebaker pickup, tailgate missing, the bumper bent and caked with manure. He climbed in, started with a lurch and drove off.

The wind blew the dust trail away as he disappeared over the hill.

"Any thoughts on this?" Guy asked as they watched him go.

"None I can act on. But my guess is whoever did it has killed before, because they worked fast. Chased them down... see where the car crashed through the fence there. They shot the girl right off. Didn't mess with her a bit. And I bet there were three or more, because Joey was a strong boy and would've been a handful. He'd been dating that little gal for a while. I'd see 'em around town, up and down the highway. She was from Salina, I think. He was a real decent kid, Joey. Didn't know him all that well, but I know his dad. It's the pissants you get to know. Little pricks so full of it they gotta stop and piss on everything they come to. Steal it or break it."

"Think they were kids? A jealous boyfriend, maybe?"

"Could be, but I doubt it. Whoever did this was a full-grown bastard out to kill. Didn't even touch his wallet or her purse. Did their bloody work and just left it. Like they were proud." Hoss gazed beyond the creek to the road south. "The KBI and their lab boys should be here within the hour. Maybe the bastards left us a print somewhere. But I wouldn't count on it."

He glanced back to the body in the ditch. And right then, if looks could kill, anyone caught in his stare would have dropped like a sprayed weed. Because he hated what he saw and hated whoever was behind it. If a bit rough, he had a good heart. Which didn't mean he wouldn't hurt a fly. He had and he would. He'd even drowned puppies when told to do so as a boy; obeyed his father and didn't flinch, though deep down he wanted every one of those pups for his own. And he would hurt a man if need be. He'd killed a fair number in Vietnam. The first one jumped him with a knife late one night while he was on garbage detail. A little black-pajamaed VC who couldn't have weighed much over 100 pounds, jumped to his back like a monkey. Hoss tossed him off and gutted him with his own knife. Suitably proud and savage in the act. For about a minute. Then the horror and revulsion set in. He wrote to a buddy back home, needed to touch base with someone beyond the war, told him what had happened and that he never wanted his mother to know. No, never wanted to kill again. But he did. Had to to survive and grew more accustomed to the act. Just didn't want his mother to know.

A good Marine. After two tours they sent him home to recruit and train. Things went fine for a while then something snapped. Seeing raw recruits made soldiers and sent off to die after all he'd seen, after years of war and no end in sight—well, the thought of those young boys filling body bags was a hurt he wanted no further part in. Simper Fi be damned. Passed over for promotion he resigned. Went home to police the streets, catch truants, corral drunks, and trap speeders. Soon made sheriff and as sheriff he hauled in a jail-full of hemp-pickers each season. Like he said, "I just catch 'em, I don't clean 'em." And sometimes he even tossed one back. No one looking over his shoulder telling him what move to make, when or why. He liked the freedom and the responsibility. But he hadn't counted on this: two kids murdered.

"Any leads on the cattle?" Guy asked.

"No, no leads. But I've got a hunch who. Just can't share that with Homer. But you and I both know who." Because there were cattle missing in Range County too.

"Well, I don't know. He could be up to his old tricks. Except this doesn't smell quite like him. He doesn't leave a calling card less he aims to. CC's pretty slick."

Colonel CC Holtz. They both knew him well. He was a real presence—a shrewd auctioneer and son of a bootlegger, among other things. He'd made his first money in the black market during WWII as he would boast to any and all when sipping good bourbon whiskey, which was almost daily.

"While our boys was off fighting Tojo 'n Hitler, I's fucking women and making a buck," he'd declare, slapping the very backs of those who'd fought, then growl, "Cleared a hunnerd grand in '43 alone, a'truckin' corn. Trucked southern corn up to cattlemen in Nebraska and Wyom so's they could fatten their stock and ship good beef to our soldier boys. All joining in the war effort. You betcha! *Pay-tree-odic* duty! Lemme tell ya, ain't no war wound, no war ribbon, no bronze, purple, or silver star worth a hunnerd grand. You wanna piece of this world, you wrap your fist around a wad of money, let the fools wrap themselves in the flag. And lemme tell ya, given the chance, most will shuck that flag fast as a woman'll slip her dress to taste that money *by God!*"

And he had a reputation with the women, that's where "CC" came from, short for Charles "Cannon" Holtz. Over the years a fair number of women had fallen to the Holtz cannon. Some said it measured 12 inches. Some claimed to have seen him lay it out on a bar top and place 10 half dollars end to end and still have room for a dime. He was a big bullnecked man and bulled his way to whatever he wanted. He owned the sale barn in both Sky and Range Counties, an auto shop, filling station, and grain elevator, as well as the Tri-County Ready Mix. So if you needed gas, grain, or concrete, or wished to buy or sell livestock, you dealt with CC. As they said, he had his finger in nearly everything and if he didn't have his finger in it then it wasn't worth a fuck. Sooner or later nearly everyone dealt with CC.

Many of his interests lay across the tracks. Seedy dealings. Aside from rustling, there were rumors of gambling and prostitution, and even a shooting some years before at Diamond Jack's Club, a converted barn outside Cibola City. But by day CC kept it reputable; he had an instinct for what played on mainstreet and before the school board. And he was generous. He helped fund little league, K-18, and Legion ball. Made certain the boys had good equipment and new uniforms. He even gave at Christmas. Sent hot meals to all the "Old Folks' homes" and the county jails. No bird meat either, but good beef and pork, prime rib and honey-cured hams. Old folks and jail birds sang his praise and swore by him. "Ol' CC playing Santee Claus," they'd say. "Ah don't care how he come by it, by Jinks or by Jesus. He shares! Yessiree!"

Colonel CC Holtz, native son and ranking citizen, full of bluster and good humor, ready to shake the hand of every man he met and call every woman "mother" or "honey," depending. The only thing he disliked was an honest man, because if you couldn't give them something you couldn't trust them. The Sheriff of Hill County, Patch Hyland, he liked, bought him a steak once a week and patted him on the back, like a good dog, Patch knew when to sit and when to stay. But Sheriff Craig and Sheriff Wayne were another story, both honest men, and whenever they sniffed too close CC would warn, "Every county has its king, boy. You best remember that."

"Yeah, he's slick alright," Hoss noted. "But one of these days he's gonna slip up and I'm gonna nail 'im."

Guy knitted his brow, doubted that day would be anytime soon. But one thing he did know and he shared it now.

"That wheat of Dale Green's? Them circles are caused by a fungus."

"*Fungus?*"

"Yeah, I forget the name. Some Latin word, no doubt. Anyhow, the fungus causes the stem to break down. Can do it to grass in a pasture too. Fairly uncommon, but it happens. The farm agent out of Manhattan explained it to me a while back. He said he didn't know exactly why, but it always works in a circle. Leaves a pattern like a tire left laid in the grass a spell."

"That's pretty much how it looked. Only a tire about fifty foot across."

"Yeah, it's an odd thing. And hard to figure if you don't know the cause. What folks way back when used to call 'fairy rings.' Because they thought 'the little people' came out at night and danced in a circle."

"Well, that's one puzzle solved. One I can tell Homer." Hoss made a check in his notepad, wished the rest would come that easy, simply fall into place and answer up like well-drilled recruits.

"See anything strange last night?" Guy asked.

"How do you mean?"

Guy again knitted his brow, doubted whether he should share it.

"Oh, you know, I had a long night what with the fair 'n all. It was on past two before I got in. Just about to pull my boots off when I got a call from Tom Baken up north of town. Said his dog woke him and he went out to check. Seen something in the sky off east and said it was the darndest thing and I'd better shake a leg and get on out and see for myself because it wouldn't do no good to explain. Well, Tom's no crackpot, so I drove on up to the north edge of town to get a clear look at the sky. Saw a bright light over east here, just lapping up there like a bobber on a current. Then it whipped north like a cast lure and stopped dead in its tracks...like it hit the end of a line. Then it took to jerking up 'n down like you were jigging for a fish. Like Tom said, it was the darndest sight." Guy drew a slow breath in wait, wondering whether Hoss would even give answer to such a thing.

"Yeah, I saw it. Got a call about the same time as you. I stepped out back and it was directly overhead. Bright as a flare. Watched it flicker a bit. Then it shot back north and just hung there. I went back to bed. Peculiar alright."

"Make anything of it?"

"Nope. And don't care to as long as it don't land and start killing people."

Which sounded reasonable to Guy. But it bothered Hoss more than he let on, and he admitted as much in the next breath.

"Christ, I don't know. Got this mess here. UFO's. Dead bulls minus their dicks. There's another three besides that one of Marion's that Homer doesn't know of yet. And that's probably the work of some damn woman. They're all going crazy lately, what with their rights and our wrongs." He thought of his own wife, with her diet pills and Pepsi, nagging him over an occasional beer. So what if he emptied a six-pack most evenings, a man had to relax. "We've got hemp-pickers showing up. Seems like a new batch every day. Half of 'em from out of state and some shady characters in the mix. A good few are packing guns. Got that to consider. And for all I know there may be a devil cult around here somewhere."

Not to mention the Vets—still dressing in camouflage, still caring weapons and staying stoned, like in Nam. There were at least a half-dozen hard-core Vets in his county alone caught in an aimless drift, often violent, who'd made it back in-country but not back in the world. He knew from his own experience that they carried a grudge and why. Pissed off at going. Pissed off at coming home to no welcome, no thank you, *no nuthin'*. Except for the GI Bill, and for the shit some of them had gone through and witnessed that was worse than nothing. Even pissed off deep down that they made it back and others didn't, the poor saps that got wasted.

"Somehow out of all this," Hoss continued, "we gotta find a thread or clue to catch these bastards. I swear I ever get my hands on 'em…that's some I'd like to clean myself. Hang 'em up in a big river oak and leave 'em for the crows."

Which again sounded reasonable to Guy.

They didn't say much more. The KBI and their forensics crew soon arrived and began taking photos and dusting for prints. A short while later the ambulance came to deliver the bodies to Sacred Heart Hospital in Arcadia—usually a destination of succor and hope, for it was a first-rate institution, pride of the county, an impressive five-story structure that stood on a high hill at the west edge of town, in fact its most prominent feature from a distance. But for all its status there would be no miracles performed at Sacred Heart that day, only the brutal facts of the autopsy as later reported by the coroner, confirming Sheriff

Wayne's assessment of the wounds and the caliber of weapon used. Seeing the bodies loaded and shrouded in white brought home the terrible finality and waste to the sheriffs paired at the scene. Whether it was the fact of the murders or simply that they were thrown together and made to deal with officials more remote and clinical, whatever the cause, by the time all had shaken hands, said their *Good days*, and headed off, the two sheriffs had formed a friendship of sorts and began addressing each other in a less guarded manner while settling final points of jurisdiction and concern.

"Since the girl was found on your side of the road, Guy, how about you do background on her."

"Sure. Need to make a trip to Salina anyway. I'll head down tomorrow."

"Okay. Well, like I said, I knew the boy. I'll see his parents later today. Then start checking around. Anything I find, I'll pass along."

"Same here, Sheriff. You can count on that."

"Good. We better stick together if we're gonna solve this. Because these boys from Topeka may know their lab work, but when it comes to things out here, I doubt the whole bunch could scare up a quail."

"Afraid you're right."

With that both nodded and went their way. Hoss Wayne headed north in his new white Ford Bronco which he would run through a car wash first thing upon reaching town. Guy Craig drove a light tan '72 Chevy Impala. Dust blended well with the color and he rarely washed the car—only following winter to flush the mud and salt from under the fenders, again at 4th of July when it was waxed and shined to lead the parade, and once more in the fall for homecoming and Veteran's Day. Of course he emptied the ashtray of gum wrappers when full and kicked the mud off his boots before getting in, otherwise he let the interior go. Dust layered on the dash so thick you could write in it, which he did on occasion, using his finger to jot a phone number or address.

One recent morning his deputy, Roy Kern, stuck his head in through the driver's window and asked how the hell he read the speedometer. Guy pressed his finger to the glass and traced a large arch revealing the whole range of numbers from 0 to 120. Likewise he drew a slash at the temperature and fuel gauges, then answered with a grin, "No problem, Roy, all clear as a bell."

Guy paid minimum heed to appearance. Changed the oil and filter at 2,000 miles, the plugs at 10,000, kept the tires aired and balanced and got where he was going in timely fashion. When needed, in an emergency, he was usually there first, directing the traffic, the fire truck, wrecker, or what-have-you. First on the scene that day as well. And glad to be leaving, only wished it was over and done with. He'd handled his share of fatal car wrecks, which were bad enough, but the last truly gruesome thing he'd dealt with was in the summer of '69, when Buddy Reeves was killed.

A happy-go-lucky kid just out of high school, working construction, hurrying to finish up his job at quitting time Friday, go to the big dance and see the girls—he was standing on the upper platform, hosing down the cement mixer when he slipped and fell headfirst into the iron bowels set churning in wait. A co-worker heard a sharp scream before the mixer ground the boy to sausage. Guy had to help dig him out, piece by piece. And had to be the one to tell his father who insisted on seeing what was left.

"That's my boy in there! Let me see my boy!" he cried as he shoved past the men grouped outside the funeral home. Guy wished he'd done something, anything to restrain him. But the father had his look. And that look, the shock and horror, hit him like a rock shatters glass. He staggered off and hadn't breathed a sober breath since.

That scene haunted Guy for the better part of a year. He couldn't sleep, not really. Mostly ate chicken noodle soup and unbuttered toast, or a little something on a cracker. That's about all. Anything else gave him heartburn. He quit drinking coffee. Took to drinking buttermilk to calm his stomach—bought a quart now and then and drank it till it soured. And he took to studying words, looking up each one he came across and didn't know, as if knowing the definition would somehow give meaning to his sense of things. His interest in words first sparked by a murder trial in the summer of 1960.

Guy's best friend Jack Marshal had stood charged for the murder of the man who'd impregnated Jack's fifteen-year-old daughter. Whether guilty or not was never known, no verdict ever reached—another situation that ended with more regrets than answers. Guy's regret was letting him out to swim that river. But Jack was the only one strong enough and desperately wanted to help, hated being caged and taunted with words. Guy knew how he felt, having sat in the witness stand while the prosecutor paced back and forth trying to rattle him, tossing out words that he didn't know, high-toned words that had no common use or meaning. By now Guy knew those words and while he didn't use them himself, they helped in part to size up certain men and situations. But the deeper meaning and mystery of things remained a hard nut to crack, indifferent, unmoved, unchanged by any form or use of words.

Guy had lost his wife two years earlier to diabetes. May, a large ruddy-faced woman, had looked so tiny and pale all alone in her coffin. He missed her with a deep abiding ache, like his heart pumped on empty, longing for her bulk and warmth. Most nights he sat up late, smoked a pipe, and worked crossword puzzles, thumbing through a dictionary or thesaurus, seeking some clue, definition, or meaning. He really couldn't say what he was looking for, only that the ritual and play of words helped him contend. Like tobacco, it created a drift for his thoughts to follow, vague, amorphous, nearly forming an image, a certainty, and in the next moment dissipating, leaving nothing but utter doubt and question. Like this life, this world, this murder. Who in hell would do such a thing? And why? Some fiend that ranks himself right up there with God.

Not that Guy lacked faith. He figured God was around. He just didn't trust Him. He'd seen Him take too many too young. And witnessing the torture May endured at the end, he saw no evidence of a loving God.

No, Guy didn't pray, but he hoped to hell none of the boys were involved in this thing. He knew Lee Clayton as Arran and knew him well. Liked that boy, practically helped raise him. Lee had grown up with Guy's own son, Ross, and slept over at least 100 nights in the old jail when Guy was under-sheriff in the late 50's. The old jail long since demolished and no one slept over in the new jail unless they were incarcerated. Times sure had changed, more strict in some ways, more lax in others. Lee, like the boy they found murdered, was another one the whole town liked to claim, full of promise, went to the Air Force Academy out of high school but left after a year or so. Some said he couldn't hack it. Guy doubted that was the case. Lee was tough enough; his whole family was tough. But he'd certainly drifted ever since. Like so many young people adrift, in search, like rootless seeds. Lee had recently moved into the old Tannis place with his wife and baby boy. Guy couldn't see that he was doing himself a whole lot of good living out there with no job other than occasional farm labor. And likely cutting hemp. But maybe no great harm either.

Guy knew all the boys—Will, Frankie, Ry, and others. He knew what they were up to and that Frankie was the ringleader. Frankie was always up to something, always had been. Reminded Guy of his old friend Jack. And claim him or not, if you didn't like Frankie you didn't like seeing the sun come up. He might get too hot at times but he definitely carried his own light. Guy always liked to see him coming, except when he was in high school and Guy had to pull him off another kid during a street fight outside a dance. In a score of scraps till his senior year when he grew big and strong and no one messed with him anymore. And smart, he had brains and wit coming out of his ears, could use every word in the dictionary and ones they dare not print. Full of talent and all off track. Before she died his mother would shake her head and declare, "That boy could be anything. Governor of this state. But he's determined to piss it away just like his father." Which was the root of the problem as Guy saw it, too many hard scrapes with his father. Justin Sage had been a good man too, somehow derailed. Nothing like a drunk for a father to leave a kid wary of authority in any guise.

Knowing each of them and their stories as he did, Guy didn't want to see any of the boys end up in prison. Not a one deserved it and it wouldn't do them any good. In Guy's view prison did one of two things: either weakened a man or made him mean. Like Valentine LaReese sent up two years prior and recently paroled. Always had a mean streak that boy. Or maybe it was the name his mama gave him—*Valentine*.

By now he was meaner and even more cunning. He had a job driving a bread truck. The Rainbow Man. Delivered all over the county. A real go-getter, you had to hand it to him, Valentine had energy, now delivering into Hill and Smith Counties beyond. Which somehow didn't figure, delivering bread that far. Maybe fooling most, but not Guy. That bread truck showing up too many places too late at night. Rumor had Valentine dealing everything from marijuana, cocaine, and LSD to the usual crowd, steroids to coaches and muscle boys, and speed to heavy equipment operators working around the clock on the new railroad right-of-way under construction north of Highway 36. Busy as a bee and a real hot head. Plus he had him a queen bee, a leggy blonde, and rumor had it that she liked to play. Valentine being so busy, it left her time to diddle.

He caught her one recent dawn and ran in waving his pistol like a rattler shaking his tail, threatening to murder whoever leapt out the back window. Dangerous and prone to strike, always coiling up and hissing at someone or thing. Yet even at that Guy suspected Valentine had more rattle than bite, or he'd do more than threaten a man caught with his wife. Still, Valentine was a mean little sidewinder and definitely bore watching.

Especially in light of the murders.

Lots of things beginning to happen out in Sky, Range, and Hill Counties. And through the prism of the morning's events, nearly everything Guy saw and thought took on a different shade and meaning.

VI. TANNIS PLACE

The large white house stood a stone's throw back from the road, framed by a sloping lawn and the starlit sky, quiet and dark except for the porch light left on. Lee turned up the drive and smiled again at the thought of it being haunted. It sat there like a big friendly dog in longing and wait; all it needed was someone to fill its emptiness and make it a home. As the pickup rolled to a stop a small white mongrel and a yellow Lab came out from under the porch, yawning and wagging their tails in greeting.

Lee quickly unloaded the hemp and hid it under the cedars behind the house, covered all with a tarp then ran inside and up the stairs. Took the back stairs off the kitchen, hitting the treads two at a time, anxious to wake her so she could see the strange light before it disappeared in the sunrise. She heard him bounding up the stairs, striding down the hall, always listened for his return and worried. But his bootsteps skipped light and happy and she knew he was excited, coming to share some adventure or experience. Sometimes he approached reluctant, troubled; he wouldn't say much and she usually had to wait to hear it from someone else. Like the time they were held at gunpoint by another crew of hemp pickers, trigger-happy fools out of Kansas City. And if Frankie hadn't blurted the details a week later—slapping his knee in hot riot, thinking it a great story for one and all—she would've never known. Worse yet was when Lee didn't return, like the year before when he was ran out of a patch in Sky County and he didn't show up till late the following day, his flesh and clothes cut and torn, feet blistered and bleeding. She had to smile even though it made her sick with worry as he leaned back and laughed, telling about the sudden arrival of cop cars and pickups, sirens and horns blazing while he and his buddies fled like coyotes, crossing miles of countryside to make their escape. So she was happy and relieved he was home, but she didn't turn, pretended to be asleep as he stood in the doorway catching his breath.

The sight of her lying naked always took his breath. A hot night, she'd kicked off the sheets while her t-shirt lay twisted above her waist, exposing her lower back, the full curve of her hips and thighs. Her body lush and toned like a dancer, though she claimed her breasts were too big for true ballet to which she had aspired. Lee didn't mind. They were perfect for a huntress, a sleeping Diana. And that was her name, though he often called her "Dita," which she didn't mind coming from him, but would hear it from no one else. In public or when he thought to be persuasive, he always referred to her as Diana, as in, "Diana, listen, I've got to cut hemp. How else can I make enough money for me to paint and for you to stay home with Jesse…?" Naturally, it was the latter point that convinced her, and though she'd vowed that last year would be the last time, she had consented yet again.

As he leaned down to kiss her neck the reek of him hit her nose. A sharp foul odor that she could not place.

"*Wahhh!*" She bolted up and shoved him away. "What *is* that?"

He stood laughing, his face stained like a heathen, his hair matted with the same.

"Ah, Dita…just one little kiss—"

"No! What's that gunk on you?"

"Chewing tobacca. Smeared it on to keep the mosquitoes off. It worked too."

"Yuk! I'd hope. It'll keep me off."

"Come on now, come with me…" He took her hands and pulled her to her feet, leading her on like he wanted to dance. "Quick, you gotta see this," he smiled, leading her from the room and down the hall.

"See what? What have you got?"

"Nothing I've got, Dita. But take look. Just look at that…"

He stood her before the hall window facing east and didn't say another word. She gazed at the light and smiled in wonder as it made a slight pirouette before spinning off to the left, then back to the right, then floated up like a soap bubble with effortless ballon to vanish and reappear in a blink. What it was, she didn't ask. They stood for a time, watching it slowly fade in the sunrise. She leaned to him now, not minding his rank scent so much as he caressed her lower back and further down. At last he slapped her flank and gave a wink.

"I'm gonna take a quick bath and see you in a minute."

She winked back and said, "Better hurry before Jesse wakes up."

The sun soon lit the window and filled the hallway while they made love in their room. Her green eyes were like gems unearthed and opened to the sun, like her person and clarity, so elemental, seemingly of another time, washed clean in offering to him, flesh perfumed by earth, wind, and water, so soft, warm, and inviting, she took and soothed his hard edge and tension, pleased his want and hers. Later, as the morning breeze blew in through the screen, drying the sweat of their passion, they listened to the mulberry limb sway against the porch roof outside their window. They lay face to face, touching, kissing. Her auburn hair curled in folds past her shoulders to the pillow; her flesh quivered as he traced a blue vein of her breast to the sweat at her nipple. Her breath and scent made him hunger in want to hold her and again feel her sweet warmth. But he felt the fatigue of the night coming on like every drop of blood being drained away.

"Do you know what's funny?" he said before dozing off.

"No. What's funny?"

"You are...and pretty too."

"No, besides that."

"Will says ol' Ned thinks this place is haunted. Others think so too. But if anything's haunted it's that old house across the road. They could film *Night of the Living Dead* over there..." He smiled and drifted off, soon breathing slow and easy.

The first evening upon moving in they'd walked up the road to explore the place. Still daylight, the dark outline of the rooftop and chimney appeared etched against the sky as the sun set in the harvest glow of early June. Hedge trees formed a tangled arch at the entrance. Further on, past bushes and weeds and a long curving drive, stood a stately old Victorian with peaked roof and tower, portico and filigrees, and weathered clapboard siding that hadn't seen a speck of paint in 50 years. The gate sagged off its hinge and the yard lay overgrown with bunchgrass and clover, shrubs and saplings. A cedar had taken root at the rocky base of the north foundation, spiraling up past the rusted eaves in tapered silhouette next to a tall Dutch elm, long dead, whose trunk and limbs stood bare and skeletal. From an upper limb an owl flew, veering south towards the barn and creek. They watched it disappear then they approached the house.

Nearly every window was busted out, plaster and wallpaper fallen, crumbling to dust, leaving nothing but a dark empty shell, a stark negative of what had once held life and color. Many shingles had rotted, slipped their nails or blown away, leaving scores of holes in the roof. The main floor had collapsed into the basement—the remnant joists and planking angled towards a jagged indeterminate darkness where you might toss a match and see its flame consumed before it hit bottom. Or so it seemed from their perspective. And from that dark center came a chill like the stale breath emitted from a deep well, or a grave. They went no further and turned away.

In leaving, Diana glanced and saw the flutter of a white curtain, ragged with age, marking a lonely presence in an upper window. Each time they passed along the road that image and the lingering chill made her shudder.

And now, listening to Lee drift off, she merely smiled in answer. She didn't have the heart to tell him—as if saying it would only make things worse and silence would perhaps make it go away—that Jesse had awakened crying the last two nights. Not like Jesse to cry in the night. And entering his room, she felt that same chill. And when she lifted him from his crib, Jesse, not quite two, pointed to the doorway and said, "Make her go away, Mommy!"

"Who, honey?" she asked, gently soothing him.

"The old woman. She cries."

"Oh, honey...there's no one. And why would she cry?"

"Cuz the old man hurt his leg. Make her go away, Mommy. Make her go..."

Each night she assured him that there was nothing, no one to be afraid of, but he would insist until finally calmed by her warm voice and enveloping arms, then his head would slowly nid-nod, fighting off sleep as she rocked and sang to him in a chair by the window. Since the end of breast-feeding he rarely woke in the night and had never been subject to nightmares, so she wondered at what he had dreamed and why, hoping it was just a passing faze.

Lee shot out of bed. He'd heard Diana scream. She screamed again as he pulled on his pants and ran down the stairs and out onto the porch. She stood at the base of the steps clutching Jesse in her arms while a calico kitten crawled, gasping for breath, dying at her feet. The next instant a tall lean greyhound dashed around the truck and snatched up yet another kitten in its sharp jaws.

"He's killing them all!" she cried.

Lee grabbed a fist-sized rock and hurled it, striking the hound in mid-flank. It dropped the kitten with a yelp and made a limping run across the yard. "Git outa here you hell hound! You sonuvabitch!" Lee fetched the rock and threw it again, hitting the hound on the bounce to speed it along. Then he ran back to check on Diana and Jesse. The first kitten was already dead; the second lay twisted, coughing blood.

"I was afraid he'd get Jesse," she said, trembling, wiping back her tears. "Now he's killed them all. I hate that dog."

The greyhound belonged to a neighbor a mile west. It strayed down from time to time to lord it over their own dogs, Rue and Keeps, who were only half grown. Lee had run it off at least a dozen times that summer. And the week before it had killed one of their kittens. Lee drove over and talked to the people, a pleasant old couple, Mr. and Mrs. Shafer. They were keeping the dog for their son who was away with the National Guard for summer drill. And they were real sorry to hear about the kitten,

but neither of them thought their son's dog would do such a
thing. As Mrs. Shafer said, "I just can't believe T-Bone would
hurt a little kitten." Lee remained polite and calm, but assured
her that the dog had indeed killed the kitten and asked that they
keep him home from then on. They said they would.

Today Lee headed back up the road with two dead kittens on
the truck seat beside him and he was not a bit calm. Mr. Shafer
was fueling up his tractor when Lee pulled in the yard. The old
man shut down the pump and walked over to say, "Good day."
The greyhound stood back by the house, and seeing Lee get out
it turned and slunk like a guilty shadow towards the barn.

Lee pointed and said, "Did you see that dog come up the
road a minute ago?"

"No, can't say as I did."

"Well he was just down to my place and killed two more
kittens."

"Oh, I can't believe T-Bone would do that," the old man said,
echoing his wife from a week before. And that tone and denial
lent an even sharper edge to Lee's words.

"Mr. Shafer, don't tell me your dog didn't do what I just saw
him do. He killed these two kittens"—Lee reached back in the
pickup and tossed them to his feet. "There, see for yourself.
They're still warm. Not only that, but my wife thought he was
gonna take Jesse. Scared her real bad. Now I like you folks, but I
don't trust that dog as far as he throws his shadow. I asked you
last week, now I'm telling you. Keep that dog home. If he comes
near my place again, I'll get my gun and I *will* shoot him. Do
you understand?"

The old man cast his eyes to the ground and gave a faint
nod.

Lee left the dead kittens lay and drove off. Hated being
hard on the old man and knew it wasn't wise to antagonize
a neighbor at the same time he was drying hemp in back of
his house, but he wouldn't have Diana and Jesse terrorized by
anyone or thing. Hated that slinking bastard of a dog, skin and
bones showing through its scant gray fur, its pale-yellow eyes.
Hated the whole greyhound breed as well as the coyote hunters
that kept them. Maybe because he felt like a coyote himself.

Though if he felt marginal and hunted it was his own fault, due to his own choice. What ate at him was knowing that the risk followed to his wife and son.

Back home Lee spread out the tarps and scattered the hemp in a thick even carpet beneath the cedars to catch the warm wind and sunlight filtering through. Finished, he went inside and told Diana what had happened while she fixed his lunch.

"I doubt he'll be back," he said of the dog. "But we'll keep the rifle by the door. If he shows up, I'll shoot 'im. If he shows up and I'm gone, you shoot 'im." He gave a wink and Diana felt mildly reassured. She could use a rifle and while she'd never killed a living thing, she would gladly shoot anything that threatened her child.

After eating a cold beef sandwich and hot soup, Lee laid down on the couch in front of the fan to catch up on his sleep. He soon found the deep slumber that follows long labor and a full belly—one from which you awaken not certain of where you are.

He heard a voice through the hum of the fan as Diana shook him awake.

"He's gone," she said, her face lined in worry. "I can't find him anywhere."

"Huh? Who's gone?" Lee sat up, blinking his eyes, clearing his head.

"Jesse. I went down to put a load of clothes in the washer. He was playing on the porch. I wasn't gone more than a few minutes. I came back up and there was no sign of him or the dogs..." She followed Lee out the door. "I looked all around the house and hollared for him. He always answers me. Where could he have gone to?"

That was Lee's question as well. The front yard was as big as a football field. He scanned the road. Nothing. He looked to the barn and other outbuildings and saw no movement.

"*JE-SEE! JE-SEEE!*" he called through his cupped hands. Again, no answer.

"Do you think the dog came back?" Diana's voice quavered in fear of what those jaws could do to Jesse.

"No, he...*Christ!* I don't know!"

Lee ran turning in circles, looking in all directions. Then he looked to the pasture and thought of the pond. He didn't say another word, broke into a dead sprint and hurtled the gate. Diana was close behind. Both had the same thought and fear, for they swam in the pond from time to time to escape the heat, strapping Jesse in a life jacket while they kicked about and lazed on inner tubes. Jesse loved going to the pond, loved to splash and play and squish fistfuls of mud. The pond lay about a hundred yards north of the house. As it came into view Lee slowed, fearing he'd see a little body floating face down in the water. But he saw nothing and no sign of the dogs. He ran on down to check along the edge for footprints. Frogs plopped in frenzied succession as he circled the pond. All he found were the paw prints of a raccoon, the slight trident etches of a Killdeer that flew at his approach, and deer tracks on below the dam. He met Diana coming around the other side, both breathing hard, relieved Jesse wasn't there, but plenty worried.

Lee cast his eyes to the distance. Fields and fences stretched to the horizon. Nothing but shimmering heat waves and the dust trail of a vehicle heading for the Scottsville grain elevator three miles northeast where Lee had worked during wheat harvest. The twin silos shouldered over a hundred feet into the sky like a giant alien structure risen on the prairie. Somehow incongruent, forbidding. Lee turned southeast towards the cluster of trees that marked the long-abandoned house.

"Know how he likes to kick up dust along the road? Maybe he headed over there."

Diana nodded hopefully.

"Yes, and there's lots of junk. He loves junk…"

They cut across the pasture and down through the gully, again at a run, thinking of Jesse fallen in the dark jagged hole or the old well in back. By the time they reached the road they could hear the faint yip of the dogs. Lee raced on ahead, up the drive and past the house, down towards the barn where the dogs were barking. A short distance beyond the corral he spied Jesse stopped up against the lower strand of a barbed wire fence like a little buffalo trying to bust through that which cut off his free range and will. He shoved and struck it with his fists in a crying rage while the dogs circled and yipped, cheering him on towards the canyon of the creek and wild vistas beyond—a whole wilderness waiting to be tasted, sniffed, and explored.

Lee had to admire his pluck and spirit, even his urge to wander off and see what lay around the next bend. An urge he shared. But he was also angry and frightened for his son. He grabbed him by the arm and gave him three or four hard swats on the rump and said, "Don't you ever run off again without telling me or your Momma!"

Jesse was already fit to be tied, and his father's harsh words and rough hand didn't make him any less so. He ran straight for his Momma.

"Diana! Don't you pick him up," Lee warned. "He ran down here on his own, he can make it back on his own."

"But Lee, he's just a little boy," she pleaded. "He doesn't know." And of course she wanted to sweep him up in her arms, thinking him lost, seeing him run to her.

"Then it's time he learned. After this he'll think twice before he runs off."

She did as Lee asked, gently touched Jesse's head and told him to run along, she would see him at the house. He glanced to his father and ran on, tears streaming down his face, trailed by the dogs. Diana gave Lee that silent look that said she'd gone deep inside and would not come out for a good week or more. That was his punishment and no amount of coaxing or sweet talk would help. How well he knew. Things already heading in a downward spiral after only one night of cutting hemp. Maybe he had been too hard on Jesse, but he didn't think so. Men and women were different. Their care and concern expressed in different ways.

He thought of his own father, sensed his ghost at times draw near like the wind in the leaves, perhaps made angry at his son's doings, longing to put a boot up his backside. And he wondered of that ghost and his own acts, and how he was judged. It seemed to Lee that a man had two choices, the only two worth considering: he could either make his own way in the world, like Will said, or failing that, take his own life. Lee didn't judge his father, but he was determined to make his own way no matter what.

"I'm gonna cut the whole season," he said as they walked along, not expecting her to answer, but knew she was listening. "Cut enough for us to buy this place or move on if we so choose. I'm tired of picking around the edges, making a few thousand, barely getting by. You hang tough, Diana. In two months, it'll be over."

"This'll be the last time?" Voiced in question and in warning.

"It will be if we do it right and don't back off."

They had each heard the other's arguments a hundred times and left it at that.

On ahead Jesse ran chasing his shadow and making motor noises. Every few steps he'd drag the toe of his shoe, kicking up a trail of dust. Grasshoppers crisscrossed his path or jumped aside in a thrash of legs and wings. A bumblebee flew from a drooping sunflower and whizzed past his ear. Jesse stopped briefly, watched it go, then ran on. Rue and Keeps trotted along on either side, their tongues lapping up the wind, laughing in the sunshine. Rue was a little white mongrel with one brown ear and a curly tail. Keeps was a playful Lab that would fetch anything thrown and keep it for himself.

When Diana and Lee arrived back at the house, Keeps stood licking Jesse's face. Jesse was laughing, pushing him away, saying, "No Keeps. Stop it!" Diana lifted him up and carried him to the steps and sat with him on her lap. Pleased to have him home safe in her arms, she wiped away the dirty streaks where his tears had dried. Jesse basked in her favor, full of himself and his adventure. But mother and child were both cool to the father as he strode past.

Lee walked on behind the house to turn the hemp so it could dry on the flip side. Always best to keep it turned. Come evening he would roll it in the tarps to keep the dew off. It would need at least another day to dry.

The action slows as it usually does in wait of another dawn and day. Troubles submerge in fitful sleep and mix with the past to form dreams at times as vivid and disconcerting as anything witnessed in the flesh. Hoss Wayne awoke with the grim realization that it was no dream playing through his mind, but the very scene. The murders. Up bright and early Monday morning, he showered and shaved and was soon out the door. At about the same time Sheriff Craig headed south for Salina where he had to deliver a prisoner to District Court by 8 o'clock and planned to spend the rest of the day gathering information on the murdered girl.

Hoss Wayne's concerns were more immediate and close at hand. Neither sheriff was a homicide detective nor even thought of themselves as such, each had a dozen other duties to perform daily. Plus numerous calls. But the murders weighed on them, overshadowing all else like the approach of a violent storm weighs on a farmer as he pens the cattle and stables the horses, wondering if the hard winds will spare his crops or leave the house and barn standing. And it was not like in the movies or on TV where jaded cops trade quips over a strange corpse—though the dead were always strange, belonging utterly to themselves. For Hoss had known the boy. He knew practically everyone in the county. Made it his business to know.

And he wasn't sentimental, hadn't cried at his father's funeral, only thought of what a sad lonely life the old man had led, always cold and distant, like it somehow seemed more fitting to lower him in the ground. Nor had he cried when he drowned the puppies as a boy. And the only tear he shed in Vietnam was when he got the clap, and that was from the pain of trying to piss. But it was gut-wrenching meeting with the father and mother the previous afternoon, watching them react. Like having your own knife twisted inside you. Everything in reverse of what it should be.

The father sat beside the mother on the sofa, shaking his head, saying how they'd planned to see Joey off to college the following week. Drive him down to Manhattan and meet his roommate. And no, he had no idea or inkling of any trouble. He and his wife didn't exactly approve of the girl, though she was Catholic and seemed nice enough. And Joey had insisted on dating her; he kept his grades up and did everything expected of him, so they couldn't very well refuse.

"But it was against our wishes," the mother added firmly. In truth they didn't approve at all, feared it would never work out, a different race and background. In fact she felt it was somehow the girl's fault that her son was dead.

"A mother's instinct," she said, breaking into tears. Her husband clasped her shoulder and drew her close. Always one's instinct to blame another. Hoss stood in the middle of the room, his hat in hand, feeling wholly out of place, happy to take his leave once the priest arrived. Consoling the aggrieved was not his bent or province.

Talk in the cafe centered on drugs, the general buzz and suspicion.

"Joey Connors was a good boy..."

"No doubt"—"I agree"—"None finer."

"But that gal of his was Mexican..."

"Uh-huh"—"Yep, a real hot tamale"—"That's what I hear."

"And she's outa Salina. You can bet they's drugs behind it. Mark my word."

Heads nodded and word spread like cream stirred in coffee, flavoring every tongue. Even details that Hoss would sooner not hear were divulged. Like the nature of the wounds and the boy's torture. But what with the ambulance crew and hospital staff, and a rural community of less than 10,000 souls where everyone knew everyone's business, you couldn't keep a lid on it. Walking into the Downtowner Cafe that morning, Hoss didn't even try. Murder was the hottest item on the menu.

"Any leads, Hoss?"

"Nope."

"How 'bout fingerprints?"

"Negative."

He shut out most of the talk with blunt answers, straddled the lone stool at the far end of the counter and ordered "The usual." Blackened his biscuits and gravy with pepper, ate about half, left a dollar tip, and took his coffee "To go." Heard enough talk most mornings to last the day.

Hoss turned left at the mid-town intersection and drove across the bridge to Co-op Tire. The manager, Carl Glover, a stout man with a broad friendly face stood behind the counter with his arms folded across his chest in a mass of hair and muscle. The hair grew thicker on his forearms than on his head.

Listening to Hoss ask about Joey, he rubbed a hand through that wan patch and gave a deep sigh. He'd already heard the news and like everyone was *Sorry as hell to hear it.*

"Joey showed up on time every day," he said. "Just the best kid. But hell, you know that. A big bright smile, he did his job and then some. Didn't shirk. That boy was headed places. A terrible thing. And I'm sorry, Sheriff...I ain't got a thing to tell you. I work up front here, meet customers and place orders. But Chris worked with him most days. Chris Boswick. He's in back opening up the shop. You might talk with him."

Chris was pushing up the overhead door as Hoss walked in. Sunlight flooded through casting both men's shadows across the shop floor. The air smelled of rubber, diesel, and solvent—a sharp mix of odors, crisp in the morning air, that hung heavy and nauseous as the day warmed. Chris wore a pair of greasy fatigues, torn t-shirt and tennis shoes. Ready for a long day of wrestling truck and tractor tires. He was only a couple of inches shorter than Hoss, husky through the neck and shoulders, wide in the girth. He had a shock of reddish blonde hair and pale blue eyes that squinted from the sunlight. His eyes slightly red most mornings from the joint he smoked on the way to work. Even redder this morning after hearing about Joey. Usually quick to laugh and happy to talk, but stood quiet and sober.

"Morning, Hoss," he nodded, attempting a grin.

"How ya doing, Chris?"

They knew each other fairly well. Both graduated from the same high school, though Chris was a mere freshman when Hoss was a senior. And they shared a deeper affinity, both veterans of Vietnam. They traded war stories from time to time over drinks at the VFW.

"Truth is I feel pretty bad about Joey. Feel like I should've done something."

"What do you mean? There's nothing you could do."

"I gotta tell ya, Joey was scared. So scared he ran out back Friday morning and threw up. I joshed him about drinking, ya know. But that wasn't it. He said he'd seen something. Something he shouldn't have. Wouldn't say what. I told him to go to the police. He said 'No!' like it was life or death. Guess it was." He glanced to the floor then to Hoss.

"Remember in Nam? You'd know some guy for months, hump the same trails, bunk side by side, share some close calls and good times. Then one day he gets this look, like he knows he's not gonna make it. And you know it too. That's the look Joey had, he was that scared. And I just...just backed off. I mean... like with these split rims..." He pointed to a large tractor tire that lay to the left of the door. "I don't touch 'em. I let Carl. Because no matter how careful you are, they can blow and cut a man clean in half. Leave part here and the rest strung out in the alley." Breathing fast as he spoke, growing anxious, recalling his own fears in attempt to explain.

"You know, like with booby traps in Nam..."

He'd once watched a Demo man try to disarm an abandoned jeep. The man was confident, joking one moment, and then he got that look just before he reached down to snip the last wire. Knew before he reached. The explosion ripped off his arms and legs and left his blackened torso smoldering 30 feet away. Chris had seen that look too many times not to know what it meant. He could read it like the written word.

Same with the hapless gook he crossed paths with one day along the Cambodian border. He and remnants of his platoon, lacking E-vac and Commo following a firefight, had wandered lost for the better part of two weeks, plagued by heat and rain and every rotten thing the jungle could spew out. His boots all but shot. Then fortune smiled and he got a new pair. Size 13. Yanked them off a dead NVA, a big sucker he happened on while rounding a jungle trail. They stood face to face, momentarily surprised, though the other knew even before Chris slipped the safety and stitched a burst across his chest that he was a dead man. Dead before he hit the ground.

So no, Chris had used up his luck long ago and knew there was some shit you never walked clear of no matter what boots your wore.

"I hate this, man...I really hate it." His eyes welled with tears. "Joey was a good boy. He wanted to be a fighter pilot, you know that? He'd made a good one...*Damn!*" He turned to hide his tears, cursing as he wept for Joey and all the good boys now dead who'd wanted to be something.

Hoss left quietly, walked out to his Bronco and drove off. Grateful for what little he'd learned. At least he had a thread, vague as it was: He knew the boy had seen something and was scared. But a thread to what? What had he seen? And why fear going to the police?

These thoughts and questions would dog him till he found the answer. But he would follow that thread and see what he could scare up. While he had no patience for deduction, common sense told him what any kid on the playground knows: The bully will hurt you if you tell. So there'd been a threat. That explained the fear of the police. But from who and why? More questions like hounds in chase—and Hoss didn't like being hounded even by his own questions. Trained for assault, he preferred to lead the chase. Everything was in reverse of what should be.

Guy delivered the prisoner on time then drove on to the high school the girl had attended. Classes at Salina West were already in session in late August, not like in the old days when they waited until after Labor Day to ring the bell. The principal, a Mr. Havel, who introduced himself as *"Doctor"* Havel, was a boyish looking man of about forty dressed in a light grey suit. He reminded Guy of a lawyer, somewhat haughty and preoccupied, like he had little time for questions, having already arranged to meet with the KBI on the matter. But all smiles nonetheless as he escorted Guy down the hall and into a room where he introduced him to a young woman seated at a desk.

"This was Cathy's English teacher, Sheriff," he said, extending his hand as she stood to greet them. "My erstwhile colleague, Miss Bayton."

"Oh? Has she resigned?" Guy asked. "Or did you just decide to fire her?"

"I, uh…don't. I have no idea what—?"

"Then you prob'ly meant to say my *worthwhile* or *worthy* colleague. Because *erstwhile* means in former times, in the past. Isn't that so, Miss Bayton?"

"Quite so," she answered, lightly gripping Guy's hand.

The principal forced a smile and ducked out the door, anxious to put tracks between himself and his blunder, had better things to do than bandy words with Miss Prim and a rural sheriff. In contrast Miss Bayton was pleased to speak with Guy.

"That was fun," she said. "He sticks his foot in it quite often. Though none of us dare correct him." But her smile was brief as she recalled the reason for their meeting, for Cathy had been one of her favorites.

"A very bright student," she said. "And a wonderful girl, Cathy. She wrote such marvelous stories. She was going to edit the school paper this year and planned to study journalism."

"She…have any problems?"

"No, none that were apparent."

"How about boys?"

"Well, the boys liked her of course. She was quite pretty. But as far as I know she only dated the boy from Arcadia. Perhaps you'd like to speak with Juanita Inez, she and Cathy were best friends. She might know something. She's my student aide this quarter, and just across the hall. I can bring her over if you like?"

Guy said he'd appreciate that and awaited their return. His main question at this point was the possibility of another boy—in fact it was his only question and the sole motive he could see. But Juantia quickly shook her head.

"No, definitely not," she answered when he asked of other boys. "Her parents wouldn't even let her date until she was sixteen. That was last summer. And when she met Joey, she had eyes for no one else. When other boys came on to her, she gave them the cold shoulder. She wouldn't even dance with them. And she loved to dance. Some people don't understand, but Cathy and Joey were truly in love."

So declared as if she were one of the true faith addressing a nonbeliever. But Guy needed no convincing; he knew about first love firsthand. He and his wife May had dated from age 13 and married right out of high school. They hit some rough spots later on but eventually smoothed things out. He still expected to find her when he woke in the night. Missed her in a mighty way.

Guy thanked Juanita and Miss Bayton for their help then
drove on to the Torres place. Juanita had given him the address.
It was a modest frame house on a quiet street, an airplane
bungalow common to the 1920s. He walked through the yard,
dreading the thought of meeting the mother and father, of
facing their grief. He nearly turned back as he stepped to the
porch, but the image of the boy and girl dead along the road
gave him purpose. He raised his hand and lightly knocked. A
few seconds later the door opened. A sweetly plump little lady
with pretty face and dark eyes stuck her head out and smiled
faintly as he gave a brief explanation of his presence there. Then
she opened the door wide in welcome.

"Please, please, Sheriff Craig, do come in," she said,
expansive in word and gesture. "You find our Catalina, our
Joey. You come in and sit down. No, I insist. *Mi casa es su casa.*
And you call me Teresa, and here, here is a nice chair for you.
Would you like tea or coffee?" she asked, folding her hands
expectantly. She wore a fine black dress with matching heels,
like she'd just been to church or planned to go.

"Well…I'll have tea. Thank you."

Guy sat down, placed his hat in his lap and looked around.
He'd never seen such bright colors in a house. Light green walls,
yellow ceiling, and red door and window trim. There were blue
cabinets in the kitchen. Several lush velvet paintings hung from
the walls depicting various scenes from Mexico: a mythical
creature, half bird and half snake; an Aztec dancer; a sun-god. A
large crucifix stared down from the wall, and on the table below
stood a figure of the Virgin, a darker Virgin than Guy had ever
seen, surrounded by a score of lit candles. On the far wall hung
assorted masks, carved and painted, garish, rude, and comical.
He glimpsed a dancing skeleton and a dozen other curios and
artifacts strange to his eye. On the bureau to his immediate left
sat the family portrait. He recognized the girl standing next
to her mother, her father and an older brother on either side,
and two younger brothers posed in front. Beside this stood a
photo of the older brother in uniform—with sergeant stripes,
numerous ribbons, and a Bronze Star pendant from his neck.

Mrs. Torres returned and handed Guy a glass of iced tea.

"That's our oldest son, James," she explained. "We are so proud. He is eight years in the army. And *twice!*" she said, holding up two fingers of her right hand, "He went to that terrible war. And *twice* God answered our prayers and sent him back to us." She turned to the Virgin and the crucifix and crossed herself. "Now God takes our Catalina. Our dear little angel, and God takes our angel home."

Her eyes lingered on the picture of the girl as a man appeared in the doorway of the back room and smoothed his coat and brushed back his hair.

"Ah, here's my husband, Carlo. He was just resting. Carlo, this is Sheriff Craig. He found our Catalina and our Joey."

"Gracias, señor," he said, stepping forth to clasp Guy's hand. "Tank you, for to visit our home...in our sorrows." Then he sat quietly on the sofa and listened as Mrs. Torres explained that her husband spoke very little English.

"Always so busy, so many days working, you see..."

He worked on a large hog farm about ten miles west near the little town of Smolan. While the farm was merely another slice of Colonel Holtz's empire, it operated under the name *Smolan Pork, Inc.* Guy knew of the place and knew that CC employed up to forty Mexicans out there. Worked them seven days on and two off in rotating shifts and paid no overtime. He liked to boast about how they'd work where a dog wouldn't shit. But good workers, he'd claim. Yessir, *damn* good workers!

Mrs. Torres told Guy that their son James was to fly in that evening from South Carolina where he served in a Ranger battalion stationed near Charlestown. She'd sent their two younger sons to school that day; she thought it was for the best. Again, Guy's only question was whether there had been another boy in Cathy's life.

"Oh no, Sheriff Craig. Catalina and Joey were so much in love, you see. Joey, he was like another son. They planned to marry in the spring. June the third. On Carlo's birthday."

Guy learned nothing more. Only that they were a close and caring family—and strangely expressed no bitterness at their daughter's death. He had to admit, he envied their faith, their lack of bitterness, but he could not share it. As he rose to leave, they thanked him again for coming and said they would pray for him. Mr. Torres followed to the door with his wife and said, "Pleez, Señor Craig. Find theez killer. Pleez?"

No promises, Guy answered only that he would do his best. And driving home to Cibalo City that afternoon he felt wholly inadequate to the task. He still faced a wall of mystery. Maybe it wasn't as blank as it had been that morning, but every bit as thick and *impenetrable*—and knowing the word didn't make it any less so.

The hemp was nearly dry when Lee last turned it. He scattered some of the deeper pockets and let it lay another two hours. Now Tuesday evening. He knelt and gripped a clump, watched it spring back. It looked about right, ready to bag. He liked the smell of hemp once it had dried, not as sweet as alfalfa, but a similar body and aroma. The ten bags they'd carried out had shrunk to five, which was normal; after drying, hemp usually lost half its volume and two-thirds its weight. He shook out the tarps and folded them, then carried the bags into the basement and weighed them on an old bathroom scale. Nothing too accurate, only wanted an estimate. The five bags weighed a bit over ninety pounds. Once keyed up and sold that would give each man six to seven hundred dollars. Only half of what they could expect at peak season, but enough to get things rolling.

He sat on the lower basement steps, running the figures through his mind. He enjoyed the cool basement—the walls and steps laid up in limestone blocks six to eight foot long, a bare earth floor except for a small slab of concrete where the washer stood. All good and dry with no hint of dampness, and definitely cool. Lee liked it down there during the day. But not at night. He hated to go down there when the breaker threw the switch on the pump. A lone bare bulb dangled from a twist of wire, dimly lighting the walls and shadowed corners, lending the aura of a cave or a crypt. He could imagine a hand reaching up through the dry earth floor, and everywhere a cold breath. And the stone steps leading down measured a full ten foot across. Spaced for what? Though he supposed they were built wide to help in delivering the large stones for the foundation, it was unusual.

Many odd features in the place, like the small diamond-shaped window set in the west wall above the winding staircase. The red pane caught the glow of the setting sun and cast a warm blush through the great room below. Diana said people once believed that such windows served to keep out evil spirits.

His thoughts were interrupted as a vehicle turned up the drive. By the rattle and groan he knew it was likely Will in Ol' Green. Probably wanted to check on the hemp, curious of the weight. Lee got up and walked outside, still a bit of daylight. Rue and Keeps circled the pickup, wagging their tails.

"Just got it bagged," he said.

"Good. Because you're gonna need to move it." Will looked grim, his eyes a darker, deeper set. He didn't ask about the weight. Didn't even get out of the pickup. Kept the motor running.

"The KBI's in town asking lots of questions. Tyke told me when I stopped by to gas up at Gerral's about a half hour ago. I drove straight out. Guess there were two kids murdered south of Arcadia over the weekend...out along Sky County Road. It's stirred up a real hornets' nest. Got 'em looking into everything. Anyhow, Tyke said they spoke with Mr. Gerral around noon and he heard our names mentioned. No telling what they're up to, could be planning a bust. So I'd get that stuff as far from the house as you can. I'd help but I gotta go warn Ry"—already turning the wheel, backing up to drive out—"then git home and hide my own stash. Good luck."

The panic was contagious. Lee ran down to the basement to grab the bags, his heart pounding as adrenalin kicked in. He could've cared less if a hand shot up through the dirt right then, simply given it a kick and ran on. By nightfall he had the bags stacked beyond the pasture fence. From there he began lugging them to the milo field east of the barn. The milo stood about knee high, full leafed and heading out. He counted off twenty rows then turned a hundred paces north. In two more trips he had all secure and covered with a tarp. The milo had only recently been cultivated and there'd be no one in the field till it was ready for harvest in late October. Everything well-hidden and beyond sight of the road. Nothing in the house but

guns, guitar, wife and son—all legal the last time he knew. Lee
breathed easier walking back.

Good ol' Tyke…

He'd have to thank him next time he stopped by Gerral's
66 to fill up. Tyke had worked there ever since Lee was a kid. If
you needed air in your football or bicycle tire, he always lent a
hand, gave a wink and a grin and asked you how it was going.
And that quick wink made you forget his cross-eyes and thick
glasses. A stubby little man, he could barely reach halfway
across a windshield with his squeegee, but still managed to wipe
it clean. Back and side windows too, always gave full service.
And he knew all the boys, had cheered them in their sports and
various doings through the years, and it didn't matter whether
they were playing ball or cutting hemp, he was on their side.
When their friend Sammy was committed by his parents—in
effect declared insane and locked up for nine months more or
less in punishment for skipping classes and drinking beer his
first year in college—of all the people from Cibola City, only
Tyke, a cross-eyed filling station attendant, bothered to make
the long trip to Topeka to pay a visit, drop in and say, "Hi ya,
Sammy, how's it goin'?" and share news from the hometown
with a boy who felt all but abandoned.

*Yeah, need to thank him…*Lee thought as he slowed to gaze on
the fresh array of stars, puzzling on the luck of some and the
fate of many. Then he lowered his gaze to the road west, hoping
there'd be no flashing lights headed his way.

All that night and the next morning Lee waited for the ax to fall.
Told Diana what little he knew about the murders and the KBI
being in town. Then asked if she'd still hang tough. She stood
barefoot in her white blouse and Daisy Mae cutoffs, sure looked
like a daisy to Lee. But still giving him the silent treatment.
After a long look she said, "I will…as long as nothing threatens
Jesse." It was an answer at least.

Lee didn't know himself what to think and slept hardly at
all that night. He tossed about, envisioning a flood of headlights
and sirens racing up the drive, kicks at the door, and shouts
of men entering with guns drawn. All imaginings, of course,

or maybe not. And that morning, walking outside, looking to the sky, he wondered if they might swoop down and land in the front yard, because it was plenty big and they had done the very thing at other places, the Attorney General and his boys, stirring up a mighty dust and creating headlines while landing helicopters to seize a little hemp.

By noon Lee was wholly fed up and wore out by his own fret and worry. He went back inside, grabbed his guitar and sat down to play. Where painting required monastic peace, he could summon a song from the wretched depths—even stumble in hung over at dawn favored by a grace note or lyric of wry promise. More of late he realized that his vital art lay in song and he began to explore with greater vision and focus, searching for a form that reflected his life and experience, a sound with roots to tradition yet reached to something else. To things he sensed and felt. In his gut he knew he no more belonged in Paris than on Mars, but to his own time and place. Thinking more of Nashville or Austin if he moved on.

He sat by the screen door in the kitchen so he could keep an eye on the road. But his attention gradually drew more to the song he was working on as he jotted lyrics in his journal or noted an occasional chord change, sipping iced tea and playing steadily, till by mid-afternoon he'd all but forgotten about the road. Pleased with his effort, he kicked back in his chair and began singing "Waiting for a Train," an old Jimmie Rodger's tune with a simple yodel that fit his voice and range. He took pleasure and instruction in learning such songs and played it through several times, giving accent and polish. Lost in the moment, the music, he didn't hear anyone drive in or even step to the porch, only a soft insistent knock at the door. He knew without looking that it wasn't Will, because Will would have simply walked on in.

So he was surprised, and a bit alarmed, when he turned to see Sheriff Craig.

"Why...hello Guy," he said, standing to let him in. "Or, should I say Sheriff?"

"No, no. Guy is fine, Lee. I was just out this way and—" he noticed the guitar slung at Lee's side and smiled. "Say now, that was you playing. I had no idea."

"Yeah, I've been at it a few years. Got a lot to learn."

"Sounded good to me. That song was one of my Dad's favorite."

"Yeah, me too. A great ol' song..."

While Lee managed a grin, he felt his anxiety deepen as he glanced to the road, wondering if Guy was merely the lead car for the whole posse. Diana had walked in from the other room, leading Jesse by the hand. Both stood quiet, somewhat hesitant, curious of their visitor. Jesse looked out from behind his momma's legs.

"Diana, this is Sheriff Craig," Lee said, pleased his voice held steady as he took the opportunity to introduce them. "Or Guy, as I always called him. You know, Ross's dad. I've told you about them. He ran the old jail when I was a kid."

Diana nodded, keeping her distance.

Guy doffed his hat and said, "Pleased to meet you."

"And this is our son, Jesse," Lee added as the boy walked forth, gazing up at the silver badge clipped to Guy's belt like it was the finest thing he'd ever seen. Giving Guy full scrutiny and a big smile. Jesse could sense people like a dog—if they were alright, he met them straight on, if not, he shied away. Seeing this helped Diana relax.

"Is there some problem?" Lee asked, anxious of Guy's reason for being there.

"Oh no. No problem, Lee. Just something I'd like to talk about. Won't take a minute. No need to disturb your family, we can talk outside."

"Sure." Lee laid his guitar on the table and followed Guy out.

They stood in the shade of the house beside Guy's car.

"Look...if this is about the Shafer's greyhound—"

"Matter of fact it is, Lee. Earl said you threatened to shoot it."

"Yes I did. Did he say why?"

"No, he was kind of vague on that."

"Right, well that greyhound's been straying down here all summer. Which wouldn't be so bad, but a week ago he killed one of our kittens. I went over and kindly told them about it. They didn't seem to believe me, but said they'd keep the dog home. Then Sunday morning the dog came back and killed our last two kittens. Right here by the porch. Diana said he made a dash at Jesse. Scared her real bad. So I took the dead kittens and drove over, dropped them at Mr. Shafer's feet and said if their dog ever came back, I'd shoot 'im. Now, I probably shouldn't have done that with those kittens."

"No, probably not, but can't say as I blame you. As I see it, you'd be in your rights to shoot the dog if he comes back. But I'll have a talk with Earl and Betty and see if we can't put a stop to it. They're good folks, the Shafers."

"Sure, Guy. I haven't a thing against them, except that greyhound."

"Well," Guy allowed with a faint smile, "I imagine you leaving those two dead kittens spooked them alright. That and the two murders..." He waited a moment then said, "I take it you've heard about that."

"Yeah, Will stopped by and told me. Hard to believe that happening around here."

"Well, it's a sorry mess. Two kids killed for no good reason. No reason at all as far as we can tell. Me and Sheriff Wayne over in Sky County, we're looking into it. And the KBI, of course, they're up checking on things..." They'd hit town the day before like fools kicking at anthills—*stirring up everything but a clue* is what Guy wanted to say. But he simply rubbed his palm and considered his question.

"Anyhow, another thing I'd like to ask. Well, you get around, Lee...what with this and that. You're a young man and all. And I've known you a long time, that's why I'm asking. I'm just fishing here. But have you heard any rumors, or know of anyone that might do such a thing?"

Lee shook his head.

"No one I can think of, Guy. The only gunplay I've heard of was that LaReese fellow who chased off some fool caught with his wife." A hot topic in barrooms and barnyards that summer— till by now most of the county had heard. But what Guy and few others knew was that the one ran off was Ry. When Will warned him of chasing after married women, particularly that one, Ry simply grinned and said, *"That don't plug no holes."*

"Okay, Lee. Like I said, just fishing. But you catch wind of anything, or see anything, anything at all, you let me know. Alright?"

"Sure, Guy. I'll do that."

"And take care out here. There's no telling what's behind this"—expressing his concern as he opened the car door, preparing to leave. "Just take care and watch out for your wife and that little boy."

As Guy got in to start the engine Lee laid a hand to the door to delay him.

"What is it?" Guy asked.

Lee smiled, hesitant, then said, "Aw, just this thing I saw. And it's way off track. But did you hear of any light in the sky late Saturday night? Or Sunday morning, I guess it was. A strange light that hovered over east then zipped north. Then back again. We were over at Will's, me 'n Ry, up late and saw it. Just wondered if you heard."

Guy gave a slow nod, almost as reluctant to answer as Lee was to ask.

"Yeah. Tom Baker called, told me to git out and see for myself. Said I wouldn't believe it if he told me. Strangest thing. What did you make of it?"

"No idea," Lee laughed. "I'm just glad someone else saw it besides us."

Guy was relieved too as he drove out. While he knew hardly a thing about the laws of physics, he had a practical sense of things. And he knew that if you dangled a fishing line in a deep pool of a creek or river, the line and your image would reflect directly over any catfish lying on the bottom, whereas if you cast to the distance, the line would cant at a severe angle to the water. Guy knew fishing and his line of sight, and recalling how Hoss described the light as being directly overhead, he knew that Lee and his friends, no matter what they were up to, had been nowhere near the scene of the murders.

Lee slept much better that night. He even felt Diana press warmly against him. Later on the wind blew in from the south, humming through the window, inducing a deep restful sleep.

In the adjacent room Jesse curled in his blanket, clutching it in his fist. He stirred fitfully as the curtain fluttered across his face like fingers softly brushing his skin. He wakened to see the curtain billow overhead, and beneath it appeared an old woman's vibrant image, vaguely transparent, shifting like the shadow of a flame.

Hel-lp, hel-l-lp us—her voice mournful as the wind, receding and emerging with each flutter of the curtain.

Jesse stood, gripped the crib railing and cried, "MOMMY! MOMMY!"

VII. THE PARLEZ

A heat storm blew up from the south. It came and went in the time it took Diana to rock Jesse to sleep, sending fissures of lightning through the horizon before rumbling on north like iron wheels over an old plank bridge. It merely rained enough to dimple the dust and sweeten the air. When the sun rose a few hours later evidence of the storm had vanished like a ghost in the night. The wind shifted, blowing from the desert southwest, boding another dry hot day through the length and breadth of the prairie.

Word spread from Will's place like waves from a rock dropped in a pond: A big powwow that evening. Frankie phoned and had the deed to the land, and the KBI had cleared out the day before. All the boys were to gather at sundown. Rus Berret drove in from Hays. And of course Frankie, Gabe, and Jacko were there along with Ry, Will, and Lee. Dave Autenburg, another friend, had ridden down with Frankie and his new flame, Dave's sister Alice—a little blonde fraulein with milk-maid hips, arched brow, and a knowing smile that promised she knew enough to keep Frankie distracted even in the grip of ill-gotten gain. Other women were there as well: Rus's steady live-in Lori, Will's wife JoAnn, and Ry's young lady Kara Hesten.

Kara loved to dote on Jesse—she sat on the lower porch step sharing a slice of watermelon with him, breaking off big red bites while daubing his mouth with a napkin. Diana sat on the upper step and smiled, proud of her charming boy. Everyone was eating off paper plates, enjoying a late-evening picnic beneath a glorious sunset. They had fried chicken, potato salad, fresh tomatoes, and corn on the cob all washed down with

either cold beer or iced tea. Finished, they tossed the cobs and
rinds to the chickens and fed the bones to the dogs. The women
washed what few dishes remained and came back out on the
porch to sit and chat while the dogs and goats milled about the
yard trailed by Jesse dragging a long stick in the dirt.

Then, as in a ritual, the men filed inside the old stone house
and gathered around the large oak table. There were eight in
all, and each nearly as eccentric and bullheaded as the hunters,
scouts, and warriors who rendezvoused in those regions a
century and a half before to discuss terms and territory and by
whose say they traveled and camped.

Frankie acted the war chief, ready to raid far and wide on
a broad campaign, nothing as drastic as scalps or captives, but
certain to make them flush with plenty of wampum and horses
to trade. Will was acting the contrary, and not exactly as peace
chief, more a die-hard traditionalist set in the old ways and not
yet willing to trust or follow Frankie.

"Don't know if I'm into this," he declared right off.

"What do you mean, Will? What's the problem?" Frankie
thought they'd made peace and smoked on it.

"We've already cut. Lee, Ry, and me. Got it dry. We don't
need all this."

"You gonna sell it?"

"Damn right!"

"Like last year?" Frankie challenged as Will set his jaw.

"Listen, Will"—Lee stepped in, hoping to keep things civil,
tired of the on-going argument. "I like Frankie's plan. And I'm
the one sitting on the stuff. You can't keep it and neither can Ry.
You didn't know this, but Sheriff Craig stopped by yesterday.
Yeah, stepped right up to the door and knocked. Came to ask
about the Shafer dog. He was nice enough and all, but he more
or less hinted that he knew what I was up to."

"That's right, Will. Guy's no fool. He knows our game."

"Then that's another damn thing." Will was scowling now,
feeling betrayed all around. "You get too many involved it's
bound to call down the heat. Already had the KBI hit town."

"Aw fuck the KBI!" Frankie scoffed. "They couldn't find
pork in sausage. Hell, them city boys won't drive a dirt road let

alone walk in cow shit. Only a sheriff'll do that, and the only one we need to worry about is over in Sky County. And that's the beauty of our game. We cut here, there, and yon...and by sun-up the stuff's back at our farm, sixty to eighty miles away."

"Yeah, and you've gotta go through Sky County to git there. And the heat is for shit-sure on in Sky County."

"No, Will. Look," Frankie held up his palms, appealing to his old friend, "we all know the best hemp grows up in Hill and Smith Counties, north of Highway 36. And that's where we'll cut. Then truck it east on 36, skirt Sky County to the north and take back roads south to our farm in Clay County. We've already scouted three different routes. All good gravel roads, passable rain or shine. No need to sweat Hoss Wayne. Hell, I don't want to tangle with the big bastard either. Because that sonuvabitch *does* know how the hog ate the cabbage and sure-as-shit where to find pork."

This comment even got Will to smile, though he still had a question.

"So you can sell all that we cut?" Cagey as ever, sniffing out the deal.

"We can sell it, Will. What do you have now?"

"A little over ninety pounds," Lee answered.

"We can sell that and have the money in your pockets by next week."

"I've got a deal going in Detroit," Gabe said, standing back of Frankie and smiling like he'd made the sale of the century. "We call it Mexican Leaf and sell it for thirty-five a pound. They think it's something real exotic. Bright green Mexican Leaf. Sold them a load last week and they called back wanting all I can get."

"How about that!" Frankie laughed. "Gabe's got them motor heads puffing on K-pot. We take your ninety and add to our one-fifty, key it up and have it there by Sunday. You'll see your money by Tuesday...Wednesday at the latest. Green leaf for greenbacks, boys. What do ya say?"

"Okay, that's all well and good for ninety pounds," Will continued. "But we've got eight guys here and you're looking to cut twenty nights minimum. Say you can even find enough good patches—"

"We'll find 'em, Will."

"Okay, say you do. That's several tons of pot. Four to five thousand pounds."

"That's right. That's where we're aiming. And we can sell it."

"Yeah, well that's what Earl Butz told the farmers. Said, 'Plant 'er fencerow to fencerow, boys, and we'll sell all ya grow.' He sold 'em a crock of shit. Now they're sitting on surpluses and taking it up the ass while prices hit rock bottom."

"Definitely got 'em between a rock and a hard spot," Ry nodded. "All those young tigers that jumped in and borrowed big are feeling pretty sick right now."

Lee agreed, his brother was one of them.

"Look, I ain't Earl Butz," Frankie said. "It's my ass too. And I ain't looking to fuck myself."

"Yeah, but you ain't above fucking someone else."

"Dammit Will!" Frankie slapped the table and stood. "You got a fair deal. Same as everyone. No one could sell it last year and I sold it. You didn't sell one lousy ounce. So I don't want any more crap. And that fucking hippie you deal with down in Lawrence couldn't sell it either. Ricky 'Rich' Easton couldn't move his fat ass if it was on fire. All he does is stand out front of the Rock Chalk telling lies and dealing coke…what little he don't snort. This year the shit will sell and I'll sell it. Guaranteed! You wanna go your own way. Go! Go deal with Slo Mo Ricky. The only fast move he's got is his right hand pumping his dick, if he can find the sorry thing."

"Okay, Frankie," Will grinned, easing off. "I'm not too hot on Ricky 'Rich' myself, not after last year. And I admit, thirty-five a pound sounds real good."

"That's another thing we need to clear up," Frankie announced in a more sober tone, tapping his fingers to the table.

Silence followed like a sudden chill. The clock ticked. Eyes focused.

"Just what is it we need to clear up?" Will asked, sensing a raw deal.

Frankie hardened his gaze and said, "We sell for thirty-five, you get twenty. If we sell for forty, you'll get twenty-five."

"*Whoa there!*"—"*Bullshit!*"—"*Fuck that!*" All this from Lee, Ry, and Will while Rus added "*You dern right!*" from his listening post in the far corner.

"Look," Frankie quickly countered, "Gabe, Jack, and I each put down four thousand dollars and signed our names on a thirty thousand dollar note to buy that farm. That's a serious investment. None of you had the money or made the commitment. Plus we'll truck the stuff, sit on it, and get it sold. All you have to do is cut."

"Now you've shown your true colors. I was waiting for this," Will said, pointing a hard finger at Frankie. "You know we've always split even. You know that."

"Yeah, no way this is gonna fly," Lee sided with Will.

"Look, you can bitch all you like. But we carry the burden of investment."

"Yeah, and you reap the fruit of investment," Lee struck right back. "You wanted a farm, you've got it. And you need to remember something. You, Gabe, and Jack, all the times I dried and sat on the stuff for you. Sat on it for several months, several times, and didn't charge one red cent. And Will got it sold back then."

Frankie, Gabe, and Jacko exchanged glances, all looking a little shamefaced.

"Yes, that's true," Gabe softly allowed. "But if you recall, we offered you a bigger share even then."

"That you did. And I said no thanks. Said we'd split even. And that's all I ask now. An even split."

"*Damn straight!*"—"*Fuckin' A!*" Will and Ry hammered in chorus.

"Look, things change. This is business," Frankie said. "It's *business.*"

"Oh great, like that's some grand reason or excuse—*business!*" Lee mocked. "People use that word as a smokescreen to break faith and take advantage. Forget obligation and understanding. Like the sun no longer shines and the rivers no longer flow. Suddenly you're all big landowners out to treat us like tenants and take a third of the crop. My dad busted his butt farming on shares and I don't aim to."

"Lee, everyone still wins. You're gonna make a lot of money."

"But you're gonna make a whole lot more. And get our labor to boot, just to sit on it and sell it, which is your preference anyway. It's too cushy. Because any of us can out-cut you on any given night. I can out-cut Jack 'n Gabe double. And Rus and Dixie here can each out-cut me." Lee turned to Dave Autenburg and asked, "Dixie, surely you don't buy into this?"

Frankie had tagged Dave with the nickname "Dixie" years before to bait him for his radical views. Now Dave wore it like a badge of honor, usually eager to argue his point. But tonight he merely shrugged, reluctant to be drawn into the fray.

"You know I'm not in for the long haul," he said. "Makes me too paranoid. I'm just out to cut a few good nights and get back to work."

He was definitely a good worker, if not the best worker among them. Quick, spry, full of nervous energy. Like a boxer pacing the ring. When he received his draft notice his final semester of college, he barged into the chancellor's office and denounced the startled exec as a stuffed-shirt Fascist, declaring himself a true proletariat, son of a hard-working carpenter who fought the Fascists in the Big War and raised nine kids, drank beer, rolled his own, and fished on Sundays—carrying on in like manner till the campus police hauled him away. This earned him a mental deferment, deemed too crazy to serve in a mad war. Yet another badge of honor. And now he was a hard-working carpenter himself, looking to make a fast buck so he could attend guitar-making school. Honest and good-natured, smiling as he ran a hand through his curly brown hair, giving his head a shake as if only now awakening to the argument.

"Come on, Dixie," Lee urged, pushing for a commitment. "You're a good union man. You gonna let these guys act like management and stick it to us."

All eyes turned to Dixie as if he were an arbitrator.

"Well..." he said, showing a combative grin. "A fifteen-dollar spread does seem a mite too big, Frankie. Borders on exploitation in my view."

With that pronouncement the argument renewed with a vengeance. Each party puffed up their chests, arguing three ways at once. Gabe, Jacko, and Frankie against the rest—everyone repeating prior points in their favor, shouting down their opponent, stabbing fingers, shaking heads, pounding the table, trading heated words. Negotiations had clearly entered a troubled stage.

Rus Berret stood with one boot propped against the wall, listening, stroking his foot-long beard, reddish-blonde in color same as his thick unruly hair. He arched an eyebrow and had a wary glint in his pale blue eyes that said he was keen to certain things being said and not so keen to others. Always a hint of fight in his gaze. Cocky. They used to call him "The Rustler"—and at times still did—because he was quite a cockhound in his teens. Outscored Ry and Frankie put together. Brash, handsome, the lead singer for a rock group in the mid-sixties, The Wild Reatas, a show band with slick matching suits, back-up brass, bright lights, dance steps and all. He could sing "Donna" to make the young girls scream. And he rustled his fair share of sweet-little-sixteens and a few no doubt younger. Not entirely proud in hindsight of his manner and approach. He'd sucker them with love, or its vague promise. And at times, to gain their favor, he used a fake diamond delicately placed on a willing finger. In a day or two he'd be gone, on to the next town, the next conquest. No, not entirely proud, but he gave each a moment to remember, like a song, even if the song saddened in time. As they say, all's fair in love and war. And war is what changed him. Vietnam, '68.

Rus was caught in the same draft as Frankie and Ry, called the same month. And he came home considerably subdued. Not that he was wounded or deeply damaged by what he'd seen. He worked as a flight controller at Da Nang, and the only death he saw was an airman who walked into the propeller of a C-130. There was a sudden mist of blood and the next moment the body minus head and shoulders lay dumped on the tarmac—the raw stump of each arm tossed to either side. And there were occasional rocket attacks, mostly in the distance, along the periphery. Enough to keep you tense, but nothing really close and hot. Until Tet.

That night he woke to the flash and boom of grenades,

rockets and satchel charges mixed with the wrenching fire of a 1000 automatic weapons, men yelling, screaming, shadows running this way and that, no telling who or what—he jumped from his cot and ran barefoot across the tarmac in his skivvies, racing towards a bunker as a Marine tossed him an M-16 and barked, "Know how to use it?!"

"Sure!"—which wasn't quite true.

"Then follow me!"

Rus followed fast, fumbling with the weapon like a new recruit, hadn't touch one since basic and that was nearly a year before, and now pitch dark, under attack, panicked, running scared, he tripped at the entrance to the bunker and squeezed the trigger in his fall. The weapon fired on full auto and sliced an arc above the Marine's head as neat as Zorro slicing a "Z." The Marine spun around in fierce shock, saw Rus getting up, then glanced back to the bullet-stitched wall.

"You fuck!" he yelled and snatched the rifle from Rus's hands like a drill sergeant in disgust. "Git the fuck in there and stay the fuck down!"

Rus hunkered down in the bunker with a score of others listening to the sound of battle. Numb with fear and shame, cursing himself, *Dumb, dumb*—a wonder the Marine hadn't busted his jaw. Because he'd nearly killed the man, so close, an inch or two lower would have popped his head like a cracked egg. That's when Rus lost his confidence, the pure brash confidence that could seduce on a whim. Having nearly killed a man, he grew doubtful, and thereby changed. Like new pressed khakis losing their crease once they're worked in, soaked through with sweat and grime. Tempered by consequence. So with Rus, gone to seed since the war.

Subdued, yes—but "The Rustler" was in no way neutered. He lived with a fine slender blonde named Lori. They'd lived as man and wife for five years, his sole woman. She was a hard worker, good cook, and kept him on an even keel. He liked himself much better with one woman. Loyal like his one-man dog, Dig, a staunch German shorthair he'd raised from a pup that followed like a shadow, hanging on his every word and move—at the very moment standing on the porch with his nose pressed to the window screen, his eyes fixed on his master. Rus hunted and fished, worked off and on as a carpenter, grew a garden, grew a beard, and chewed tobacco. A Skoal man. Learned to fiddle and colored his speech with old saws and allusions to the old ways. An old-timer at 28. An old-timer who'd heard enough goddamned foolishness.

He shuffled forth in no great hurry with that glint in his eye aiming to make his presence known. He sat his spitcup to the table like a hard-struck gavel and said, "Now looky here. I been listening for nigh on an hour to you all rattling on like marbles in a tin can. Why I'd sooner fry a fart in a skillet than cipher all this talk 'bout shares, who gets what 'n why. Arguing back 'n forth, a'circlin' like ol' hounds gnawin' flees. I just got one question..."

"Shoot, Rus. Fire away!" Frankie said, he and the others eager to lend an ear.

"Then you answer me this"—Rus paused like a veteran showman with a shrewd sense of timing, knew he had them in the palm of his callused hand. "Just this one thing I wanna know. *What was paid the lad who held them horses for Frank 'n Jess?*"

Caught off guard, Frankie blinked like a fighter tagged on the chin.

"Well now, that's a tough one, Rus. Hard to say."

"Aw bull, Frankie, don't give me that. You know what you'd say and so do I. You'd say he got less. But I say he got *an even split!*"

"Suppose you tell me why?"

"Because when Frank 'n Jess come outa that bank they for certain wanted them horses to be there!"

"Oh Rus, you're getting lost in your own myth."

"Bull! You're gittin' greedy is what"—holding up his spitcup to drive his point, backing Frankie off. By now the women had edged in and crowded the arched opening to the living room to listen to the exchange. Siding with her man, Lori stepped up and waved a finger in Frankie's face.

"Rus is right, Frankie. You're just being greedy," she declared in a hurt tone like he was Simon LeGree trying to throw them out in the cold. "Rus works so hard when he cuts hemp. He comes home so doggone tired sometimes he falls in bed and doesn't move all day. He deserves as much as *you!*"

"Now honey bun, calm down," Rus said, smiling, patting her arm, proud of his woman standing by her man. "Just calm down. This is between us fellas."

"Well he thinks he deserves more and he doesn't."

"Lori, I didn't say any such thing"—Frankie doing his best to wiggle free when he noticed his own sweet Alice watching from across the way, giving him a knowing smile that said she'd like to take a bite out of him.

"What's the matter, Frankie?" she said, one hand cocked to her hip. "You feeling a little outgunned?"

"Oh no, not you too, Alice," he moaned like Caesar stabbed on every side. "Come on Russie, help me out," he pleaded. "Got the women ganging up on me."

"You dug the shithole, boy. Now you stand in it."

"Alright! Alright!" Frankie raised his hands in mock surrender. "Lissen up. Here's the deal. Best I can do. We'll make it a ten-dollar spread. We sell for forty, you get thirty. We sell for thirty-five, you get twenty-five."

"And not to fall below twenty-five," Will stipulated.

Frankie cringed as if forced to give his last dime.

"Okay...even if we sell for as low as thirty, you still get twenty-five. Agreed?"

A slow ripple of consensus rounded the room. The boys looked to one another and nodded, and seeing none opposed, in the pulse of a minute the compromise was forged.

"But! Under one condition," Frankie stated. "You'll each take a turn trucking the stuff down to the farm."

"No problem there," Lee said, answering for all. "We'll do our part."

"Okay," Frankie slapped his hands together, "then we're back in business."

"Hold on. What about weight?" Will asked.

"What about it?"

"Whose gonna keep tabs?"

"Jack, I suppose. He'll be drying and sitting on it in any case. Right Jacko? So he can weigh what comes in and what goes out.

Square all accounts. Does that work for everyone?"

"Fair enough," Will said, all trusted Jack to keep a clean slate.

"Anything else?"

"Yeah, one more thing," Will looked Frankie straight in the eye. "I want everyone to carry a running pack." Another contention between them, because Frankie had always pooh-poohed the notion.

"That's a good idea, Will. I agree. Everyone should have a running pack. Shoot, you can start by inspecting mine." Cheerful, conciliatory, delegating duties, trying to tap a sympathetic vein.

"No, you're a big boy, Frankie. You check your own underwear. But in case we have to run for it, I want everyone to have a change of clothes, ID, and forty to fifty dollars in cash. And it won't hurt to pack a bar of soap along, so you can wash the grim off in a creek or pond before you hit the road."

"Hell yes!" Frankie raved. "You want soap? We got soap! You bet. Mouth wash, antiperspirant, dippity-doo. Anything else, Wolfer?"

Will shook his head and laughed. Everyone laughing now, entertained by Frankie's bluff charm and their collective prospects.

"Alrighty then," Frankie said, sitting back down at the table. "Let's talk turkey. First thing, on the way back tonight we'll stop by Lee's place and pick up that ninety pounds. We'll get it all keyed and have Gabe on the road by Friday. If you're all ready, we can cut this weekend. Both Saturday and Sunday night. Work Labor Day weekend. How about it? All agreed? Good. We'll camp up by Lovell Lake and head out after sundown. I scouted a good patch right below the Nebraska border. Lays in between two pasture hills, clear and open, no brush or deadfall. Best to start there. Then with a decent moon in a week or so we can hit the creek patches and really rock 'n roll."

"That's right," Lee enthused. "By mid-September, with a harvest moon and the seeds set, we'll hit Burr Oak Creek and cut till the snow flies"—excitement building like in a locker room before a big game.

"Uh, I don't think we should go up there," Frankie noted.

"Why not?" Lee asked. Not like Frankie to skirt an advantage and they all knew it was the best patch in Kansas.

"Because we cut there two years ago. You and Will hit it last year. I just don't think it's a good idea. Third time isn't always a charm."

"Why the hell not? We hardly put a dent in it. There's ten to fifteen acres of hemp along that creek, all hidden down out of sight of the road. And not a soul within three miles. What's the problem?"

"I think Val's up there."

"Val? You mean Valentine LaReese?"

"Yeah, LaReese. He rented that old farmhouse about a mile off the highway."

"So what? He didn't rent the creek, did he? He doesn't own that land."

"No, but he's up there. He has four or five women working for him. Pays them a hundred dollars a night."

"Well that's just dandy. Got him some slave girls and moved right in. How in hell did he find out about it anyway?"

"Sammy told him."

"Sammy? Why'd he do that?"

"Look, Sammy didn't mean to, Lee. He feels real bad about it. But he deals with Val from time to time. And Val's pretty clever. You don't know him, but I do, and I've seen him work. One night last spring he laid out several lines of coke. Pretty soon they got in a pissing contest over who knew where the biggest hemp patch was. And Sammy spilled the beans."

"You were there?"

"No, but that's pretty much how it happened. It could happen to anyone."

Lee shook his head, felt really burned. Not betrayed, but definitely burned. Because that was sacred hunting ground to Lee—where he'd first explored the world and learned to ride. Where his father had staked his soul on farming and lost. And each time Lee went back to harvest he claimed something for his father and himself. Took the gain the land had failed to give and somewhat evened the score.

"We'll find other patches," Frankie assured. "You'll see. I just don't think it's wise going up there. You don't know Val like I do."

Lee got up from the table and left it at that. He'd keep his own counsel on what he thought was wise. And no, he didn't know Valentine LaReese and didn't care to. But he wasn't ready to concede the best hemp patch in Kansas either. Lee stepped out onto the porch. Rus followed. They stood letting their minds clear, their eyes adjust.

"Ya know," Rus said, shaking his head, "sometimes Frankie's so slick it scares me. All that snow about Val being so clever and you see what he pulled off. Gave up five dollars and kept ten. Got us singing his song right when we had him cornered. Like a dern coon leading a dog into deep water to drown. He still come out on top."

"He gave and we gained," Lee said offhand. "Don't forget, they did buy that farm."

"Well, guess so. Reckon you're right."

Rus put a pinch of tobacco under his lip and cast his eyes to the far corner of the porch where Diana knelt petting Dig.

"Hey now!" he grumped. "Don't be sweet talking that dog, Diana."

She gave a startled look, "I was only petting him."

"No, you were spoiling 'im," he answered in a more moderate tone as he walked over. "Goo-goo over him like that he won't be worth a hoot come hunting season. Now Dig! Git back in the truck where you belong!"

The dog lowered his head and trotted back down off the porch, then stopped and looked back up at Diana, reluctant to leave those soft hands and that sweet voice.

"Go on, Dig. Git in there!" Rus snapped his finger and pointed to the truck.

The dog promptly hopped up in the bed and stood wagging his tail. Anxious to please his master. Rus and Dig had lived together a full year before Lori moved in. During that time man and dog had formed an uncanny bond. Each still jealous of any third party that came between them.

VIII. CC HOLTZ

Beer didn't help him sleep. A six-pack usually did the trick to put him down for a good five or six hours. But the question kept spinning like a damn gyro in his mind while he laid on the mattress like a ship gone aground, the cargo sloshing in his gut-hold offered up anything but a clue of how to get back on course. He stared at the ceiling till the gray dawn filled the room, then he got up to face another day. Still dogged by the question: What had Joey seen?

Sheriff Hoss Wayne had spent most of the week meeting with Joey's friends, classmates, coaches, teachers, neighbors, and family, anyone the boy may have confided in and not a one had heard a thing, except Chris Boswick. On Wednesday Hoss had led the funeral procession with the line of cars stretching for three miles. A forest of people stood around the grave, heads bowed in silence, all sweating from the heat, most suited or veiled in the dark cloth of mourning. Surely one of them knew what had scared the boy so bad it made him vomit on his own shadow. Now Friday, two days since the boy was buried and not a word. Nothing.

On top of that he'd just heard Special Agent Reynolds of the KBI remark that if you don't get a break on these things in the first 48 to 72 hours, they almost never get solved. "Take it from me," he said, popping a stick of gum in his mouth before walking out, as nonchalant as if he'd been discussing the chance of rain.

Hoss was glad to see him go, him and his whole crew back to their fine building in Topeka to debrief and plan tactics for the next crime scene. They'd hit town like custom wheat harvesters in bright shiny equipment, ready to do the job in a day, but after taking a test run around several fields, they found conditions none too promising—too wet, too weedy, foresaw too many breakdowns and delays—and decided to move on to more favorable ground, something more worthy of their time and expertise. In leaving they gave Hoss a list of malcontents and n'er-do-wells as if all he had to do was check them off one by one to find the murderer. All he saw were the usual sore-heads, drunks, and fools he dealt with in his daily rounds. It was like dropping the header on a combine so low that the sickle and reel threw up more grit than grain in the threshing. Grit might suit the function of a gizzard, but it didn't set well on Hoss's stomach. He crumpled the list of names in the clinch of his fist and tossed it in the trash. He had indigestion so bad that morning he didn't even stop by the Downtowner Cafe. Wished he could do like the priest, wave a can of incense over the whole mess and bury it.

Thought of the priest gave Hoss an idea. The boy was Catholic and likely went to confession. Maybe he told the priest what he'd seen. Something so disturbing that it got him killed. And Joey had wanted to tell someone, for he'd nearly told Chris Boswick. So Hoss drove to the church, a place he seldom paid notice. While he was no church-goer, much less baptized as far as he knew, he shared the ingrained suspicion of most Protestants towards Catholics—their robes and rituals, their dark inner sanctums, their long dead language, all carried over from a darker age and time, somehow foreign if not downright evil. A suspicion borne in the blood through centuries of rivalry and endless bloodshed. Even their architecture was suspect, too massive, ornate, and graven.

Our Lady of Perpetual Mercy Church, a tall red-brick structure of ascending columns and recessed arches that housed various statuary and stained-glass windows, stood at the end of a long shaded street, surrounded by some of the grandest old trees in town. The steep roof and belfry towered to the sky, the copper flashing and bronze bells tarnished by time. On the far left the rectory nestled as quaint as a cottage though it rose a full three stories. And in the shaded acreage further back appeared the broad crenelated facade of the Sisters of Mercy Convent, the grounds enclosed by a red-brick wall topped by dark spears of a wrought iron fence that converged at a huge double gate to bare the entrance. Quiet, mysterious, closed off from the world and largely to the eye, it all set at the base of a prominent hill bordering on the south and west. Sheltered and remarkably cool even on a hot August morning.

Hoss welcomed the fresh pine scent of the tall Ponderosas that stood evenly spaced like guards throughout the environs of the church and convent. The day of the funeral he had waited outside the church and only attended the graveside ceremony. And the priest hadn't looked at all well, suffering from the heat, the press of bodies, dressed as he was in a long black robe and black silk gloves worn for reason of ritual no doubt. His face had paled, at one moment so faint he nearly fell as the casket was being lowered before he steadied himself and sprinkled a handful of dirt in final benediction.

No, apparently it was not all that easy to bury a lamb.

Hoss stepped to the porch and knocked. After a quiet moment the door opened. Again the priest seemed slightly faint as he held the edge of the door and motioned Hoss in. Oddly enough he still wore the black silk gloves. Hoss stared in question.

"I have a skin condition," the priest explained.

Father Michael Kairn was a slender man in his mid-thirties, with neat dark hair, fine features, and pallid flesh. He looked like a Latin ascetic in spite of his Irish name. But if interest in any way forms a man, he had a passion for the Spanish language and culture, particularly as it influenced Latin America, having spent his early ministry working in the villages and slums of Guatemala.

"What brings you to us this morning, Sheriff Wayne?"

Hoss stood gripping his straw Stetson, not certain how to address the priest, had never actually spoken with him before. Father Michael noted his hesitancy.

"You may call me Michael," he said. "I realize you are not Catholic."

"Right," Hoss nodded, didn't really want to call him Michael either. The man seemed too delicate, too pretty, like he wore a mask as he stood mute, motionless, his hands folded in wait. A general would have made him his aide-de-camp.

"Well you see, Mike...I'm still trying to make sense of Joey Connor's murder."

"I, too, Sheriff. At times, I confess, faith is hardly an aid."

That kind of statement made Hoss dizzy. He didn't care a whit for faith, doubt, or anything in between. His concern lay with the nuts and bolts of things, whether the nut fit tight or loose and whether the bolt was bent or missing, not whether they existed or what might be there in their stead.

"It occurs to me, since you were his priest, you may have talked with Joey."

"Certainly. I spoke with Joey. I speak with all my parishioners."

"Recently?"

"Yes. On several occasions this summer."

"What about?"

"He sought my counsel on a rather personal matter regarding Cathy Torres, the girl he was dating. Joey was a young man with natural urges and was somewhat conflicted by his desires. Very concerned that he act in accordance with his faith and his deep love and respect for Cathy."

Hoss hated the circle of words and again felt the dizziness coming on.

"Is that it?" he asked. "That all you talked about?"

"Yes, I counseled him. That's all. What is it you hope to learn, Sheriff Wayne?"

"I don't hope for a single thing, Mike. But I do aim to learn who killed Joey Conners and why. What I've learned up to now is that he saw something..." Hoss saw something too, a slight wince in the mask as the lips tightened. "Something that made him so scared he wouldn't tell the police. So scared he vomited outside Co-op Tire last Friday. So scared he might've told you in confession."

"Need I remind you, Sheriff Wayne, confession is taken in sacred confidence?"

"And I remind you that boy's life was taken *period!* In a most cruel manner. So if you know anything about what he might've seen or feared, I'd thank you to share it."

"Sheriff Wayne, I assure you, Joey Conners spoke to me of nothing other than his intimate concerns for Cathy Torres. Neither in confession nor otherwise."

"Right. Then I thank you for your time." Hoss still gripped his Stetson and didn't offer his hand. "I'll get back to minding the county and you can get back to your *re-fu-gees*." His parting shot was in reference to a series of articles then current in the *Salina Journal* that featured Father Michael's work with the Sisters of Mercy Convent in giving sanctuary to Central American refugees while appeals were made to the INS on their behalf. Most locals opposed the effort; a bare few were even sympathetic.

Father Michael held a tight smile in response, expected scorn and contempt as the price paid for doing anything of worth in this world. Even members of his own parish complained that he was trucking them north like cattle just to feedlot them. But he'd seen them slaughtered like cattle, and if he could save hundreds instead of a few dozen he would gladly give his blood. For they were not economic refugees, they were political refugees, and if not given sanctuary many would be killed. And in a most cruel manner as he had most certainly witnessed. He didn't expect Sheriff Wayne or few if any of the locals to understand, though many of their own ancestors had fled tyranny as well. If salvation awaited understanding, the world would perish.

*Be like Vi-et Nam...*Hoss thought walking down the steps. *Damn do-gooders got us in and screamed bloody murder till we got out. When Saigon fell I bet them Commies shot every Catholic bastard they could lay their hands on. And that do-gooder in there knows something he's not telling*—a further thought as Hoss walked towards his Bronco parked across the street. But the thought made him smile and eased his stomach, because he'd caught a scent of something. He rubbed his belly, feeling pretty good, ready to drive to the Downtowner Cafe and order one of Meg's giant chicken fried steaks with taters and gravy and four hot rolls.

In the near yard Hoss noticed Mrs. Wylett out watering her zinnias.

He walked over, tipped his hat and said, "Good morning, mam."

The old woman turned to the big gravelly voice, blinking through her bifocals in want of recognition. She had white hair and wore a blue print dress, her back bent from osteoporosis. But she suffered no palsy, kept a firm grip on the garden hose as she raised her free hand to shield the sun, squinting till she bared her dentures in a bright smile.

"Why it's Robby Wayne," she gasped. "Ilene's boy."

Mrs. Wylett and Ilene Wayne had been life-long friends. Though Mrs. Wylett was somewhat older, they'd had much in common, like sisters. For one thing, both were die-hard Baptists. They believed in full immersion and little else. Because no mere sprinkle of holy water and no amount of churchgoing would save a sinner. Though suffering might help. And they had suffered. Both had married rowdy men who made poor husbands, though Hoss never heard either woman complain. They saved their complaints for the Catholics:

"Do as they please Saturday night and come Sunday morning they're forgiven."

"That's right."

"And you know what them priests do with those nuns."

"Oh, you bet I do. That skirt and collar don't change a thing."

"A wolf in sheep's clothing. Sooner or later a man'll get what he's after..."

"That's right!"—both nodded after each comment, couldn't agree more.

In fact Hoss suspected that one of Mrs. Wylett's chief pleasures in life was living across from the Catholic Church, so she could stand in her front yard and give them hell.

"My lands, Robby. Either you're getting taller or I'm getting shorter."

"No, you're looking just fine, mam."

"Maybe so...but what are you up to today, Robby?"—like he was out playing and had stopped by for a cookie.

"Well, I been over talking to the priest about Joey Connors."

"Oh my yes," she said, pursing her lips in a frown, "the boy that was murdered. Him and the girl…" shaking her head. "You know I saw him run by here, oh…a little over a week ago. Wednesday evening, I believe it was. Yes, because the blamed paper boy threw my paper in the flowers there and I didn't find it till it was good and soaked. Made me so aggravated. I love to read my paper, you know, it helps me sleep. Anyway, what was it now…? Oh yes, I was out here watering my flowers and Joey ran by like the dickens. Then he winds up dead."

"You sure it was Joey?"

"Heavens, yes. They only live a couple blocks north, the Connors. Known him since he was born. His momma and daddy too. Pretty good folks for Catholics."

"Where did he run from? What direction?"

"Why, from over yonder, I imagine," she said, indicating the church. "And that's another thing. A minute or so after he run by here, a big pickup roared out of the alley there. Squealed its tires up the street and around the corner. Burning rubber something awful. You think they paid for them tires? I bet not. And I nearly called it in because my two cats Flo and Lia, they…" she gave an impish grin, "they like to cross the street and use that Catholic yard for their litter. I'm afraid they're gonna get run over one of these times the way people drive."

"You happen to see who was driving?"

"No, it was all black with those smoky kind of windows, you know."

"Black, huh? Did you catch what make?"

"No, just black. These new ones all look the same to me."

Hoss smiled. "Well, I'll keep an eye out for that pickup, Mrs. Wylett. You can count on that. And you take care now. Good seeing you."

"Good seeing you too, Robby. And tell your momma hello."

Hoss merely nodded—sometimes Mrs. Wylett forgot that his mother had been gone for five years now. He always enjoyed seeing the old woman; it somehow recalled his mother to him. Hoss drove off in a far better frame of mind than when he arrived. He not only had a scent, he'd glimpsed the rat's tail. Ready to start digging. But first he'd have that chicken fried steak.

CC Holtz sat in the den of his large stone rancher. The house rested on a sloping promontory of the Ionia Hills that rimmed the lower edge of Hill County. From the front porch you could view the sweep of Range County all the way to the Blue Hills thirty miles south. A quarter of a mile down from the house a paved road ran east and west, marking the county line. A paved driveway curved up past a shaded pond then looped full circle in front of the house. A shelter belt of tall spruce and cedar grew to the north and west, and to the east stood a big white barn with assorted pens and corrals commonly filled with stock in transit to or from a sale.

Immediately surrounding the house and barn lay a thousand-acre pasture fenced with stout hedge posts and seven strands of barbed wire—there grazed CC's prize herd of buffalo and Texas longhorns, kept in part for his amusement and to ensure his privacy. The herd numbered over a hundred head, and no intruder dared attract attention from either bull. Throughout the front lawn and lower pasture grew so many willows, Russian olives, and cottonwood that you could barely see the yard light from the road, only note the dark ridge of the house and trees beyond the glimmer of the near pond.

CC relished his privacy. Once he had finished with the day's business, he lived remote as a king. And he'd paid a kingly sum. The house was built of native limestone, custom quarried and laid up to his specifications, starting with the huge fireplace erected dead center and open to the den. "By God I want 'er big enough I can spit a quarter beef and roast it!" he'd told them. Same with his desk: *Big enough to butcher on!*

He sat back of the desk in a big leather chair of genuine cowhide with padded armrests and carved oak legs. The only light on in the room was a brass desk lamp with green enamel base and shade. A fat cigar lay smoldering at the edge of a black marble ashtray; the drift of smoke slowly swirled like the variegated veins frozen in the stone. To the far left a bronze stallion reared eighteen inches high. A gold-plated horse clock rested dead center. The time, 9:45.

The phone rang. CC slowly grasped the cow-horn receiver and raised it to his ear.

"Holtz here," he said in a low throaty voice, rich and worn as old leather from years of auctioneering. He wore a white western shirt and a tan suit, the jacket removed, shirt color unbuttoned, bolo tie hung loose. A large man in his late fifties of ample girth and jowl. His hair had silvered and thinned to a widow's peak and he kept it combed straight back. He had a ruddy complexion and an oddly pointed face for such a broad man due to his long slender nose and the narrow set of his eyes— tiny gray eyes made prominent by their sharp focus and gleam. A lidded gaze, not the least bit sleepy, but shrewd, reptilian, with only a wisp of hair on the brow. His reading glasses lay on the open ledger beside his pen. A glass of brandy set to one side. He went over the books most evenings. Kept his own records, like a coin gripped in the press of his palm.

"Yeah...yeah, I figured you'd call. But before you say one damn thing, you tell me where you're calling from..." CC listened and nodded. "Uh huh...pay phone in Salina. Good thinking. Ya know the Feds might be a little peeved at you and the Sisters stowing them people of yours in that convent. They just might tap your phone, find out how you been bringing 'em north..." He smiled, again listening. "Ohhh...so you're not worried about the Feds?"

—*No, Mr. Holtz. The worry is more immediate. Sheriff Wayne came to me this morning. He asked about Joey Connors.*

"Yeah...wha'd he say?"

—*He knows that Joey saw something. And that it scared him.*

"So the boy saw...so what?"

—*Joey's dead, Mr. Holtz. So is Cathy Torres...*

"Look priest, we had nuthin' to do with that. Not one damn thing."

—*I pray that is so. But I fear otherwise...*

"To hell with your fear. What else did the sheriff say?"

—*He asked if Joey had divulged anything. He even asked about confession. Naturally, I told him that Joey had said nothing. Which is true...*

"Good, then he's just sniffin' around like a dog out to scare up a rabbit. You lay low like ol' brier rabbit and that dog'll get bored 'n run along. Take it from CC."

—*I'll take nothing more from you, Mr. Holtz. I'm sorry I ever dealt with you…*

"Now lissen here you worthless pecker in a skirt. We got us a deal and by God you'll deal. You being sorry don't change a damn thing. I git 'em north and you give 'em sanctuary. How they pay for it's their own damn problem."

—*Spare me your vulgarisms. I know who I deal with and why…*

"I won't spare you shit!"

—*We paid you well and you accepted…*

"You paid me cost and I gotta have profit. We didn't force a one to carry. If they got cash, fine. If they don't, they gotta carry. You don't cross borders on a wing 'n a prayer. It takes planes, guts 'n money. So one mule died. It was the greedy bastards own damn fault. He shit four condoms in Dallas and claimed he hadn't swallered a fifth. Mex give 'im benefit of the doubt, didn't wanna go poking up his ass. But the fool up and swallered it again…shit, slime 'n all. You know the rest. It bust his gut and he died pukin' at your feet."

—*You have no idea how horrible it was. The man's agony, the blood…*

"Oh, I got an idea, don't think I don't. Hogs 'n cattle die on me ev'ry day. It's always a mess. We haul 'em off to the rendering plant where they churn 'em into soap. That's how ya clean up a mess. Soap, water 'n elbow grease."

—*But why the two kids? Why? I said I would speak with Joey…*

"Lissen, priest. You don't know who killed that boy and girl. You may think you do but you don't. And I don't either. Remember this. Mex helped you get your people across the border. He carried off the trash before it bloodied your hands. And from the get-go I'd a' never lifted a finger to help 'cept for you being there when his momma died. Why she asked for you then I don't know. That's women and religion for ya. S'pose she needed a priest. But you fuck with me or Mex, I'll fuck you and ev'rything you hold sacred. Send ev'ry lamb you saved straight to hell.

"You may think you made a pact with the devil, but I'm just a businessman cutting my losses and taking out insurance. Now I's raised on the Bible too. You can see me as the devil if you like, but I prefer you see me as Caesar. You pay Caesar his due, you can keep herding your flock home to heaven. So you lost one lamb, what's that against the dozen you saved? You wanna keep saving souls...? Yeah...uh huh. Good. And I'll help. But we best lay low for now. Just remember it was you as wanted the body gone. You called in a panic asking for Mex. So Mex come and hauled 'im off, wrapped like a pig in a blanket."

—*I wanted him to view the consequence...*

"Consequence, hell! You could've buried 'im somewhere on the grounds, there in the garden or under a thorny bush. But you wanted to wash your hands of it. And we took 'im off your hands. Too bad a curious John happened by. But it happened and it's done. That's consequence. Sorry won't change it. You can whip your ass bloody for all I care. Wail 'n moan and beg pardon on high. But go tell it to sweet Jesus 'cause I got work to do. *Bye!*"

Ten minutes later two hired hands, Red Mueller and "Straydog" McGill, stood in front of CC's desk. Both dressed in ranch-hand denim. Red was the taller of the two, angular, his brown hair tinted red by the sun, windblown and dusty from the day's work. Straydog was of average height with long dark hair and beard, and sky-blue eyes that shied from any word or glance directed his way. Both stood with their heads slightly bowed, their hats in hand, getting their butts chewed by CC.

"Don't I letcha hunt, Red? Where else can ya hunt and make good money? You too, Straydog, don't I treat ya right? Don't I? But you hunt, you hunt where 'n when I point. Got it? You run out ahead like a pussy-crazed hound I'll blast your ass to hell. Got it? And there's a limit to the hunt, Red. You bide my rules and mind the scent, ol' CC'll treat ya right. Got it?!"

"Yessir Colonel," Red answered with a tic of a smile. "But it weren't us...as done nuthin'. We...you need to talk to Mex. You just...just need to talk to him."

"That's twice I've heard that lame excuse. Don't lemme here it again. Who did or who didn't? Shitfire! Someone sure as hell did. Left two kids layin' there like roadkill. Run off 'n left one helluva mess. Talk...talk to Mex, ya say. Christ, I told you two to keep an eye on that boy. Not let 'im go off halfcocked."

Red and Straydog shifted about, uneased by his stare.

"Uh...Colonel," Straydog chanced to speak. "We...we just ride with Mex is all. Don't think I'd git 'tween him and what he's up to."

"Yeah, yeah, I know. He's a hothead. Thinks he's had it rough. Where in hell is he anyhow?"

"Said he'd be along directly, sir."

"Yeah, he knows *Sic 'em* but he don't know *Come!* Thinks he's had it rough. Like the two of you, I 'spect. Done your hitch in the Navy, served in Asia, a'whoring and drinking in ev'ry port. Come home to the land of milk 'n honey and land your ass in jail first thing. And ol' CC bails ya out. Sets ya up in a fine place with three squares a day. Money in your pockets. Nice trucks to drive."

"We ain't got no complaints, sir."

"Damn right you don't. And that damned priest thinks he's a saint. He'll be a damned martyr if he don't watch his step. Ev'ryone thinks they got it rough. Hell, growing up, the ol' man gone most the time, off running booze, gambling, half the time jailed. Yeah, and he served in a war too. The first big one, WWI. No cakewalk in them trenches. Went in 1916 at age sixteen. Come home with bad lungs from that mustard gas. They didn't give him ten years to live, and he didn't. Anyhow, he come dragging up one winter night there in the mid-twenties, a deep hacking cough, lungs all ate up with nu'monia. He took to bed and looked bad. There wudn't a doctor in fifty miles. Ma sent me to fetch the priest. Yeah, we was Catholic back then. Ol' Father Grady didn't much care for us Germans on account our kin started the war. But he come. Walked two miles through that blizzard. He stepped in and took one look at the ol' man and told Ma she better lay out his good suit 'n start digging the grave 'cause he wudn't gonna make it. She slapped that priest with her dish rag and shoved him right back out in the blizzard. She didn't weep, pray, or ever set foot in a church again. She went to nursing the ol' man, steamed 'im, wrapped 'im warm, spooned 'im chicken soup. Sat up three or four nights and saved his sorry ass so he could die in a shootout a couple years later. A big liquor bust down in Kansas City."

CC swirled his glass of brandy and took a swig, cleared his throat and continued:

"They'd married when he's nineteen, just back from the war. She's only fifteen. She said they courted on horseback and always told us kids that she got pregnant on horseback. I guess she loved that no-good sunuvabitch. With him gone things really got hard. Bad as he was, he always had money. And money's the saving grace, boys, don't think it ain't. Hell," he growled, shaking his head, "I's a ten-year-old boy when the Depression hit. The man of the house. Then my brothers Bob 'n John, our little sister Dory. The only thing that got us by was Ma's chickens. And I stole most the grain to feed 'em. Anything I could chuck to my shoulder and log home, I took it 'n ran. Ev'ry fall Ma would can them ol' hens not laying so good. We'd scald 'n pluck 'em while she sharpened her butcher knife on the mouth of the crock jar. Then we'd gut 'em, she'd bone 'em. I remember finding those little yellar eggs inside and we'd tease her 'n say, 'Hey Ma, why'd you kill this 'un, it's still got eggs in it!' She'd say, 'Shush and git to work.' We worked alright. 'Bout all we did. Hire out for any damn thing to scratch out a living. And just ol' greasy canned chicken for Christmas dinner, and each of us a new shirt Ma stitched together from castoffs and hand-me-downs. Popcorn on a string hung from a scraggly ol' cedar no greener'n rye grass along a dirt road in late summer. No, not much of a Christmas. And I hate chicken to this day. But hell," CC's eyes brightened, "we had us some fun with them chickens too."

"Wha'd ya do with 'em, Colonel? Ya fuck 'em?"

"Hell no, Red. You are one sick puppy, ya know that? No, we didn't fuck 'em or do anything of the kind. We'd hold 'em in our arms, tuck their heads under a wing and rock 'em to sleep like so..." CC gently swung his cradled arms back and forth like a hypnotist, holding his audience rapt. "Once they's asleep we'd climb up and drop 'em from the barn loft door. The chicken would wake with a squawk 'bout halfway down and hit the ground in a flutter a'dust 'n wings. Then run in a circle like their heads was chopped off. 'Course that happened lots too. Enjoyed wringin' their necks more than eatin' the filthy things."

CC reached for his cigar to take a puff, then spat in disgust finding it had gone out.

"Christ, where is Mex?" he said. "Lucky for him I liked his Ma so much or I'd wring his neck."

The one referred to stood in the shadows, having entered without their notice.

"Hey now, I'm glad you liked my mamma," came his soft languid reply. "Did you like my daddy too?"

"Red, Straydog, git on outa here. I wanna talk to Mex alone. And keep playin' dumb, you're good at it." CC lit a fresh cigar and watched the other move into the dim light, moving quiet as a shadow even in his boots.

"No, Mex," he answered once they were alone, "I didn't know your daddy. You know that. No one knew your daddy you little bastard."

"Well then, maybe you were my daddy, huh?"

"Naw, if I's your daddy you'd be a whole lot smarter."

"One sure thing, boss. I'd be a whole lot uglier."

CC pointed his cigar and grinned.

"That's another thing you got in your favor, boy. You're funny. Real funny."

The other grinned back, showing his fine teeth. He stood 5'9" in his stocking feet and weighed 190 pounds, with broad shoulders, short trunk, and long limbs—built supple and strong like a boxer. He moved with cunning and grace, like he could move forever; the same when he stood still, so relaxed like he may never move again. His black hair was worn in a long braid down his back. And his blue jeans fit snug as his belt, while his white t-shirt showed off his dark skin and biceps to firm advantage. From his neck hung a silver medallion stamped with the profile of an Aztec warrior. His face reflected the same handsome features—large dark eyes and sharply defined brow; broad cheekbones and strong chin; an aquiline nose and wide sculpted lips that bore the hint of a savage smile. Young women often asked if he was an Indian, he'd simply smile and say, "I'm anything you want me to be, baby."

He definitely had his mother's eyes. Fierce and beautiful. The prettiest woman CC had ever known. Another reason he loved her was that he could never own her. A dark angel he could never get enough of—only hold her for a night. And it did no good to threaten. She'd merely thrust up her neck and say, "Go ahead, use your knife. Let me taste death. I've had so many limp dicks in me I'd welcome a sharp knife."

She'd whored from age thirteen. Whored her way north from Juarez to Junction City, and kept on whoring till she died of cervical cancer a week shy of her thirty-ninth birthday. Andrea Corina Marquez Orvano.

As in all her doings, finding herself pregnant, she simply had the child and never shared her reasons. She named her son Javier. Which he latter shortened to Jay. But he was generally known as "the Mexican," and most called him Mex. He wore the name like an emblem, a proud brand—even had "Mex" tooled on his belt. CC never knew if the boy was his or not. The mother never said, and likely didn't know herself who the father was. But she asked CC to look after the boy once she knew she was dying, even signed the papers declaring him legal guardian. Having lost his mother, the boy hardly welcomed a surrogate father. CC brought him back to Hill County the summer he turned fifteen—never an easy age for a boy, and their relationship was far testier than most. In truth, it had never warmed. They remained more rivals than anything, both still vying for the woman's memory and affection.

That first summer CC bought the boy a new jeep, hoping to win him over. The boy wrecked it twice before driving it into the river. That fall he attended the Mankato high school. Strong and mature for his age, he was a superb athlete and popular with his peers, but that didn't keep him from getting expelled. He exposed himself to a group of girls in English class, then went *mano a mano* with the principal. Two coaches wrestled him down and made him lean to the wall while they applied a two by four to his back side. He just laughed at the bruising, then spent the remainder of his junior and senior year at a military academy in Salina. They shaped him up and shipped him out.

Straight to boot camp. He'd volunteered—anxious to prove himself a tough hombre.

Unlike many he enjoyed Vietnam, though he had a rocky time with the brass. Busted three times for insubordination and dealing on the black market. But Private Orvano could fight. Twice wounded and once cited for bravery. He received the purple hearts but no medal. His lieutenant was killed in the following firefight and the citation let to lapse. Perhaps in light of subsequent events. Recovering from his wounds, he commandeered a colonel's jeep on a weekend pass to Saigon where he sold it for $1000 in MPC—Military Police Currency, commonly called monopoly money, issued to keep the good old *In God We Trust* American dollar off the black market. No matter, in the end the colonel never recovered his jeep and Private Orvano never fessed up.

"Hell no," he said following his arrest, "I never drove no jeep nowhere, no way." And "sir" was no part of his vocabulary.

Still, he liked Vietnam, liked the action, both on and off the field. In his only letter home he sent a photo of himself smiling with his arm wrapped around a dead VC, signed, "Making friends, Poppito!" He even offered to re-up, but the Army said no thanks and discharged him. He shrugged it off. Shed his uniform and spent a year in LA chasing fast women and high times, then returned to Hill County to make himself known. He'd been back four years. CC saw potential. Doing his best to groom him.

"*My daddy's rich an' my momma's good lookin'...*" Mex smiled as he sang.

"Don't push it, boy. Your momma's memory is fading fast."

"Okay, boss. What you want with me?"

"First, I want ya to watch the coke. Deal it, don't use it."

"Hey, no sweat. I only hold a little back for the ladies. Once they git a taste you should see the things they do for another whiff."

"I can imagine. Just watch that shit. It can fuck your judgement."

"Hey now, I wasn't the one who bet the farm on a losing hand."

"You watch that lip."

"Yeah, lost big to *los Italianos*..."

"Okay, okay. You've had your fun, now shut the fuck up."

"Sure boss. I'm all ears."

Each waited, wary of the other's disdain.

"I thought you had things under control. Said you's gonna talk to the boy."

"I tried. But he ran. Only the guilty run."

"Uh-huh. So you run 'im down and—"

"Now I didn't say that."

"Bet it chapped your ass you seeing his gal was Mexican."

"*No problema.* I've watched putas fuck gringos all my life."

"Yeah, well here's a flash for ya, Mister *No Problema.* The Sky County Sheriff, Hoss Wayne hisself, had a talk with the priest this morning. He seems to think the boy saw something and was plenty scared. He pushed the priest on it. Didn't learn anything, but he pushed."

"That punk. That fucking priest. I'll fuck him like—"

"Easy Mex. He ain't said nuthin'. His dick's in this too. Remember that."

"Sure, boss, okay..." again relaxing, letting his muscles uncoil, his smile broaden. "So the sheriff picked up on a little rumor. So what's the problem?"

"Problem is...the boy musta said something to someone."

"Maybe so. But he only said a little. And *los muertos no hablan.*"

"You seem awful cocksure of that?"

"Let's just say a little bird told me."

"Same bird as killed that boy n' girl...?" CC puffed his cigar, eying the other.

"There's a bird of life and a bird of death. Many birds sing to me."

"Yeah, well, fuck your riddles. That still leaves us sixty to seventy grand in the hole. Even with the coke. And we can't truck no more damned refugees, not just now, not till the dust settles."

"No sweat, boss. Like I said before, my little bird Val has an idea."

CC laid his cigar in the ashtray and leaned back in his chair. "Okay. S'pose you tell me what you 'n LaReese got cookin'..."

Hearing the perfunctory click of the phone sent a chill down Father Michael's spine. He'd never felt more forsaken and alone. And trapped. Snared by his very effort to grant salvation in this world, this life. The Liberation Theology that had once buoyed his faith had been swamped by recent events, pushing him beneath a wave of despair. Returning late that night, he entered his room and knelt to the floor, folded his hands and attempted to pray—then he broke into tears and collapsed staring up at the darkened room like it was a dungeon, wondering, *What have I done?* He had thought himself clear-eyed and toughened by his experience in Central America, capable of charting a course that would make virtue of vice, thinking he could employ and direct any manner of man, use coarse yarn like a weaver at his loom to construct a pattern of God's will on earth, having lost all faith in a higher promise. But he saw it all unraveling and knew he was not nearly tough enough. Though strangely, in the cusp of his deepest despair, he'd never felt more in need of or closer to God. Yet he could not reach out and seek Him for the shame he felt. The Divine Presence so long vanished from his world like the sun swallowed into a void, taking its loving warmth and light, at last returned as the blazing torch of Judgment. And he could not bear to look at or reach to that fierce wrath. He buried his face in his gloved hands. No matter how tight he clinched his eyes he saw the victims' blood like a dread stigmata bleeding through.

Father Michael vowed to wear the gloves as penance every day for the rest of his life in quiet acknowledgement of his guilt like he'd worn them nearly every night since adolescence to deny himself the pleasure of the flesh. Yet even then, he'd removed them from time to time, trembling in fever to touch himself, stroking in fetal ecstasy till he achieved release and with that shudder and heat felt his flesh glow as if filled by the Holy Spirit, like a bright sword gripped by the Virgin. And as suddenly darkness would find him as he rushed to wash away the taint and shame. Refitting his gloves, he dared not remove them for a month or more till he could no longer deny the need, the temptation, the absolute province of the flesh.

Gradually he felt God turn from him like a stern father as his mind turned to the world and its suffering, its injustice and greed—and he questioned God for His cold, distant ways. And now, having played God, he questioned himself. If he could no longer believe in the promise of eternal salvation, he could readily perceive eternal suffering and torment. Wondering what pit in hell awaited him, quaking in the sulfurous vat of his own sweat and filth, reliving the murders over and over again. The worst of Purgatory was too blessed, and even then his only hope of release would be the prayers of those already consigned to dust.

How he missed them, those he'd tended, and all the little villages that bore and sustained such suffering. He missed the chickens scratching alongside dusty footpaths, roosters crowing at dawn, skinny half-starved dogs slinking to the shade, hungry-eyed children staring from the doorways of mud-walled *jacales*, all the rich, rank closeness of life—the rude heat and stale pools of rain mixed with the urine of sheep, goat, and man, and the smell of woman, her true scent, her deep sharp musk untempered by lotion and perfume. He missed the raw temptation, the constant need and fear in midst of which he stood central, beckoned to and called upon. In life and in death. There he was a priest, here he was a mere functionary, a custodian. And worst of all, he felt himself a fool.

Too proud, too ashamed to ask forgiveness, he would let no man absolve him. He was therefore damned. But he would continue down that path even as it led to perdition, for he would not forsake those to whom he'd promised succor. Not a one.

IX. LABOR DAYS

Saturday night. The boys piled into Frankie's '65 Ford Econoline van—an old warhorse painted army green, windowless, not a stitch of upholstery through the bare metal interior to buffer against the grind of the road and engine. Even on pavement it rattled and shook like a cargo plane at take-off, and turning onto the gravel road a mile below the Nebraska border, heading east towards their destination, it bucked and groaned with added vigor, the inside quickly filling with dust, leaving a thin film on every surface and a dry grit in the mouth. At the base of a long hill the van eased to a halt. The bones of a dead cottonwood reached to the starry sky like a skeletal hand to mark the drop-off and pick-up point.

The boys emptied out and with a slap of the back panel Jack cruised on.

They hustled down the ditch and one by one crept through the strands of a barbed wire fence held spread by Will's boot and hand. Soon six silhouettes trailed off into the pasture, led by Frankie who knew the ground. The patch lay north and south about the size of a football field. They made their camp on the north end, roughly 200 yards off the road. They'd leave the south half as a barrier and cut it the following night.

They spread the tarp and set to work—alert, zealous, in common effort to make their gain, each loath to let the other down, enlivened by the freedom of their act and the balmy night. The wind blew steady from the south, and while they carried mosquito repellent, they needed none for it was dry as a bone in the bowl of the hills. And isolated, not a light visible beneath the dome of stars except the faint glow of two towns on either horizon—Red Cloud to the north and Mankato to the south, and even their names evoked a sense of wonder and legend. Likewise each man carried his own myth in the making as he grasped his machete and hacked at the hemp as if tapping a deeper essence, a truer self, set apart from the world of time and machine, standing whole and elemental if only for the moment. They hardly spoke through the first hour, remaining watchful and wary, attuning their senses, mostly using a sign or a word or two, but gradually they relaxed and found the rhythm and began to banter and joke like trusty veterans.

"Reminds me of a night in the Central Highlands during the dry season," Frankie said, feeling flush, spirited, as he looked to Rus and Ry.

"Kind of," Ry answered, a shade more tentative. "Only this has the sweeter smell of home. And no VC."

"Sure, no argument there. But that's the beauty of cutting hemp. It's got the thrill and action of war, with some of the risk, but no horrible consequence."

"Don't know as I need any thrill or action, cowboy," Rus said, sending a spat of tobacco into the pile of leaves. "A quiet night on the lone prairie suits me fine."

"Aw now, Rus, don't be a stick in the mud. Don't you miss Nam? Even a little?"

"I miss the beauty. That was one beautiful country. And I'd like to see it without the war. But I shit my pants good during Tet and that once was enough."

"Yeah, guess so. Got pretty rough at times..." Frankie sheathed his machete and shook out a large plant. "I remember once up north, this big-shot general flew in to give us a pep talk. Told us how we were gonna stick it to the NVA, really kick butt. Like it was a big football game. When he finished all he heard was the sound of a thousand feet shuffling. But hell, they all talked like that...the generals and high brass. Always talking blocks and sweeps and body count like they were keeping score, collecting chips to cash in for the big win. Shit yes, and we won every last fucking battle. Tet too. Ain't that so, Ry? Beat 'em back and bloodied 'em so bad they didn't recoup for years. But we couldn't outlast 'em. We had the crack team, no doubt.

Big beefy boys, the best gear. And all that firepower. Man, it was awesome. Make you believe. And they were just a bunch of raggedy-ass little bastards, all undersized and ill-equipped."

"But they didn't play our game, did they."

"No Ry, they didn't." Frankie grabbed up another plant and continued stripping the leaves as if each sweep of his arm depicted another thought or action. "Hell, they moved the goalposts and boundaries every other night. It's the Oriental mind, fertile, tenacious, drawing you in like the jungle to cut you off. You never knew when they'd hit or where. And the score didn't lay in the body count. The only thing that mattered was who was willing to stand and fight. And they stood on their home ground ready to fight forever. Fuck it! Like Ry said, they played their own game. Made their own rules. Terrorized the refs, bribed the officials, slit the throat of any fool holding a yard marker. Shit, they even booby-trapped the ball. And you could be damned sure the end zone was mined. After seeing one body blown to bits, nobody wanted to rush in there."

Ry grinned at Frankie's summation. Had seen it all firsthand and replayed it a thousand times. From there the talk drifted on to other subjects—of women they'd chased, of fast cars and wild rides.

"Tell you the time I nearly shit my pants," Frankie said. "And this was way before the war, Rus. And still the worst scare I ever had. You know CC's boy, the Mexican?"

"You mean Mex from Mankato?"

"That's the one. It was my senior year and he was back up from Salina for the weekend, out fucking around. He had the Colonel's big tan Cadillac. I caught a ride with him and two other fools back from a dance in Arcadia. You know how many hills and curves there are on old Number 9? I swear he had that Cadie floored nearly all the way. Telephone poles zipped past like fence posts. I sat in back screaming for him to *Slow 'er down!* That maniac just laughed, didn't slow a lick. After that I couldn't bear to look. So scared I hugged the floorboard and prayed for deliverance. And you know me, I don't believe diddly-squat. Then I crouched up to take a peek right before we hit the big bump at Gilbert's Station. Shit, that Cadie went airborne, drifted sideways, and I saw my short life flash before my eyes. Thought that was all she wrote. Then we slammed to earth and those tires screamed like they're flat to the rims...the Cadie bottomed out and shot sparks up past the windows like a skier shooting spray. When I jumped from that car, I swore I'd never ride with the crazy bastard again. That boy had a major screw loose, and if you ask me, he still does. Wears a deep mean streak right down his spine."

Will looked up and nodded, "Yeah, I heard he nearly killed a guy over in Cawker last winter. In a fist fight. But can't say as I know 'im."

"Well, you haven't missed much. Unless you wanna ride with the devil. And get this, I stopped by the Parks brothers last week. Mex and Valentine had been out there asking to buy the 50 caliber. Offered $2000 in cash. Evin said he told them they'd been chewing too much peyote if they thought he had any such thing."

The boys all laughed at the notion of the old man staring down the no-good pair. The Parks brothers were local legends— gunsmiths and master mechanics, adventurers from another time. Evin was the oldest at 83; while Ellwood, four years younger, still bragged on and deferred to his big brother. They lived out in the Blue Hills in southern Range County on the homestead where they were born and raised. Lived there with their mother, Fay Parks, age 101, slowed and shriveled by the years, but nimble-witted and lively as her boys. She wore her white hair braided like an Indian.

When Lee drove Diana and Jesse out to meet them earlier that summer, the old woman was thrilled to see the young mother and child. She led them to a soft chair by the window and said, "Wait right here, I will show you something." She soon returned with a pair of beaded moccasins that Evin had worn as a baby. "In the old days before we fenced the land," she explained, her eyes twinkling at the memory, "the Cheyenne still passed through, following the old trails. They would ride up on their ponies and stare at the house until I came out with some biscuits or coffee. But if I had pancakes, oh...that was their favorite. One morning I walked out holding baby Evin, and this hard-faced old Cheyenne, he reached in his pouch and gave me these"—she dangled the moccasins in front of Jesse's eyes and smiled. Then she gave him a ginger cookie and patted him on the head and laughed as if she saw her Evin in the little boy.

Evin had fought in WWI as an Army Ranger.

"They attacked at night with nothing except bayonets 'n trench knives," Ellwood vouched while his brother sat grave and silent as an old warrior. And both had served in WWII. Wanting in the fight but deemed too old, they were assigned duty as gunsmiths. It was during this time they managed to smuggle a 50-caliber machine gun home to their mother, sent it through the mail piece by piece. And in the Roaring 20s they built their own bi-plane and barnstormed across the prairie. Later on they spent some wild years fortune hunting in old Mexico, and often wintered in New Orleans in high style and the company of women, evident from old photos tacked to the wall. Yet the brothers never married. Instead they'd shared a world of experience and had a thousand stories between them. Shrewd creekbank naturalists, they knew plants and their uses. And they were keen to animals, often drawing them forth— they could mimic the cry of the owl and the Red-tailed hawk among others.

"I kid you not," Frankie said, "when I drove in, Evin had a dang skunk standing at the front step, eating from his hand. Said he'd coaxed it up from the creek, a little closer each day. Now it comes up each morning to fetch a snack…"

Patient and enduring, the brothers were truly anomalous to that day and age. The boys admired their curiosity and wit, their maverick ways, and felt a special kinship to the pair, striving to be somehow like them. Especially Frankie.

The talk ebbed and flowed as the boys came and went, off to cut another bundle then back to strip. Unlike the week before, they had no problem distinguishing the plants. The females were in full bloom, putting on seeds, while the males were mere stalks, so dry and brittle they snapped at a sweep of the hand. By 1:30 they'd cleared the back part of the patch up to an approximate thirty-five yard line where the plants bunched and swelled, yielding like a stubborn defense. The boys took a break, sprawled out on the tarp and the nest of leaves, sipped coffee and gazed to the stars while coyotes yipped to the wail of a distant train.

"Look at that!"—Will pointed as a meteor streaked across the northern horizon, leaving a purple glow in its wake.

"Damn, that's a big one..."

To anyone looking, it made them blink, bright as a flashbulb that blinds the eye.

"Funny thing," Will said, turning to Ry and Lee, "we haven't even talked about it."

Lee raised to his elbow and said, "You're right. I woke Diana when I got home that morning. We watched it for awhile, just flitting there like a bee above a flower. But we haven't talked about it either. Hard to say much about a thing like that."

"What the fuck are you two talking about?" Frankie blurted, impatient at their vague tangent. Rus and Dixie both glanced around, curious as well. Ry couldn't keep it in any longer and started to laugh even as he spoke.

"You won't believe this, Frankie. But we saw a U...F...O."

"Oh shit the bed, Ry. Don't feed me that crap."

"No, it's no shit, listen..." Will said, sitting up to explain. "Last Sunday morning, we were loading out, just leaving the patch and we saw it."

"You saw it, Will?"

"Damn straight. Sure as I'm looking at your lying eyes"— adamance trumping doubt like a quarter slapped to a bar-top. "And if you'd been there...well"—words failing him before the inexplicable nature of it all. "Christ, the damn thing was as big as that meteor. And moved just as fast. Only it...it didn't leave a trail."

"No, it moved like a pure ball of light," Lee said as Will left off. "Like a ball hit hard to left field. Then it stopped on a dime. Didn't even slow, simply stopped. Then it swept east, then north again, like a ball thrown from third to first. And perfectly straight, without any arch. Sometimes it simply hovered in place, or skittered here and there like a water spider."

"And you saw it, Will?"

"I saw it, Frankie. You know me...I hardly buy the moon

landing. But I saw the damn thing. Me, Ry, and Lee."

For once Frankie sat speechless, stumped. If Will had seen it, he had to give it credence, because Will was too stubborn, too bullheaded and hidebound to go fruity over UFO's. Everyone had heard of sightings and heard various explanations. But to actually see one? He wondered whether the Parks brothers had ever seen such a thing.

"I still wonder what they're up to," Ry said, still suspected a "they" behind it all.

"Maybe they've come for us," Lee offered.

"What would they want with us?"

"Could be they want our thoughts...our minds," he answered, playing the notion, seeing where it might lead. "Not our brains so much as our awareness. Tap into our mind and memory to siphon off 'n add to their own. Or simply for a quick buzz, like a snort of coke or a hit of hash. They may see the earth as a mind garden or a big fruit tree loaded with brain berries ripe for harvest. And we're the sweet fruit. All three to four billion of us. Just when we start to reach out in quest and wonder, shooting off to seed another surface, they reach down to pluck us by the handful. Crush us in their vats to make their wine. Think of them as intergalactic gourmands."

"Whoa, I'd rather not"—this from Dixie.

"Think of it though. Their first course was soup 'n salad, all the lush swamps of the Devonian Age. Then they enjoyed the meat course with the death of the Dinosaurs, all fried to extinction in a grand meteor strike. Now it's time for dessert, choice fruit 'n fine wine. The fermented nectar of the brain stem."

"What would they plant next?"—Ry curious as ever.

"Hard to tell. We may be the last crop. The earth spent, used up. They'll find a fresh orb in a far galaxy. You know, the ol' slash 'n burn. Like us clear-cutting every last patch of hemp. Nothing ever changes. Just gets weird."

"Jesus, I'll say..."

With that thought the boys returned to their labor. Worked on till four o'clock then toted all the bags and gear to the roadside ditch and crouched in wait. Will checked the time with a penlight. Still ten minutes to spare, Jacko and the van not due to arrive till 4:30. It was very important that he arrive on time, a matter of trust. If he was early, the vehicle sat there like a beached whale, too conspicuous. If late, even by a few minutes, everyone began to worry about being stranded with a 1000 pounds of hemp come sunup. Worried too that the van may have broken down or wrecked—or that Jacko, who loved to drink and often passed out after three or four beers, may have felt compelled to tip a few to calm his nerves and was now dead to the world sixty miles away. But they soon spied a glow of lights from the road west; a minute later the van rose over the hill and headed their way.

Good ol' Jacko, right on time, his one eye clear and alert as the van rolled to a stop. The boys crowded around like they were greeting the ice cream truck, quickly loaded and jumped in. Not a minute had passed and the van again sped up the road. Frankie sat in front while the rest lay in back, talking and laughing, still high on the glorious night and their haul of hemp. In another hour fatigue and hunger would set in, but for now all was right with the world.

At a parking area at the west edge of the lake they switched to Dixie's little blue Valiant. Jack headed on down to the farm in Clay County.

Frankie and the boys arrived back at their camp at first light, feeling pretty ragged and could have cared less if the old folks across the way, early risers walking down to plop their lines in the calm green water, now stood wondering what that bunch had been up to all night. Each group looked to the other like wayfarers in a dream, or ghosts in the fog of dawn, soon to fade or burn away. The boys crawled into the tent they'd pitched the previous evening and curled up on air mattresses or foam pads and tried to claim a few hours sleep before the day turned hot and the flies came to feed.

In fact it was the heat and flies that woke them—steaming heat accompanied by aggressive black flies relentless in their hunger. The boys flopped and rolled in feverish sweat, slapping at the flies, covering their faces with a hand or an arm, trying to block out the day. Their faces looked worse than if they hadn't slept at all—eyes puffy and their skin scrunched and wrinkled like a work shirt pulled from a dirty clothes heap.

Lee dragged his air mattress out of the tent and wandered across the road into a plowed field. Still not a breath of air even in the open. He lay there in the blazing sun for about ten minutes before the flies again found him. No longer satisfied with blood, they bit like they wanted meat. He swatted one, leaving a red mush on his arm, then sat up and looked around.

He saw Frankie stumbling his way like a zombie in want of breath.

"It's no use," Lee called to him. "They're out here too."

Frankie merely nodded and about-faced. Both headed straight for the water like seekers of the true faith ready for full immersion to escape the plague of flies. They paddled out into the lake and lay on their air mattresses, cooled by the water and the soothing lap of the waves. At last free of torment. Pure bliss. Again for about ten minutes. Then Frankie's air mattress deflated.

"Fuck it," he said. "Let's drive to town and have breakfast."

"Sounds good to me."

They rousted the others out and all soaped up and rinsed off in the lake. Each felt tolerably refreshed shed of the filth and donning clean clothes. Rus had his big black coffee pot out preparing to boil some water on his camp stove, anxious to play "Cookie" on a cattle drive, when he saw them all heading toward the car.

"What's the big toot!" he hollered. "Doncha want coffee before ya go?"

"Save it, Rus. We can get coffee in town."

"Why, I never seen the like," Rus grumped, stroking his beard. "Passin' up good camp coffee for store-bought." Then he pointed to the old folks out frying up their morning catch beneath the awning of their Air Stream. "You gonna let them old-timers show us up?"

"Yes I am. Right now all I want is a cool restaurant and a big hot meal."

Everyone did. Rus too, but he was having more fun not admitting it.

"What a bunch of tin horns." He shook his head and stuffed the coffee pot back in a canvas bag.

"Don't fret, Rus," Frankie said. "We'll let ya rustle up some grub later on."

"Well, I'd hope. Can't be running off to town at every little hunger pang."

The boys drove into Mankato to enjoy a hot meal. High noon and The Red Rooster was filling up. A horseshoe counter centered to the kitchen and booths lined either side. The boys sat down at a booth presently being cleaned and began chatting up the waitress, a pretty brunette with a fetching smile. Ry fairly sang her name as she took his order.

"Lora Lee, what a pretty name," he said, teeth showing through his smile.

"You gonna order, or you gonna bite?" she teased.

"Think I'll bite on the roast beef special," he said. Breakfast having long been served, the rest of the boys pretty much followed suit, grins all around.

When the food arrived, Rus glanced up and frowned.

"Hey, can't we get more hot rolls?"

"Maybe…?" she said, arching her brow. "If you ask real nice."

"Wull, ain't I being nice?"

"Don't get me to lying, honey."

Rus warmed to being called honey.

"I take it you don't like being bossed."

"Uh-huh," she smiled, "I'm kinda ornery like that."

"Alright then, can we git more hot rolls, *please?* Don't aim to give ya a hard time."

"Now, if you could give me a hard time," she added with a wink as she reached to pour him more coffee, "you might not have to say please."

At those words and her maidenly form leaning across the table, the boys roused with a collective moan. Blood warmed, they watched her shimmy as she walked away. Her short skirt stretched tight while her perfume lingered by, mixing with smell of meat and gravy, butter and cream.

"You hear that?" Ry grinned.

"Yeah, and look at that ass, will ya? Just look at

that..."—Frankie gawked. "God yes, I'd give that a hard time Give her a wedding dick any day of the week."

"Rein it in, boy," Rus said with a nudge. "It was me she's sweet-talking'."

"Oh, Rus. That pencil dick of yours wouldn't even tickle her fancy."

"Hey! You can strut that long dong all you like. But this here dick has tapped more holes than a Texas wildcatter."

"Maybe so, Russie," Frankie laughed. "But ain't that a fine ass."

No argument there. A woman like that was bound to flame the urge, like summer and heat. Though Will felt far too conspicuous and wished his lusty compadres would keep their interest a bit more subtle. Might as well try to muzzle a trio of coyotes warming to the moon. By now they were drawing stares from several tables across the way—warning stares, as if the regular crowd had proprietary rights on admiring that ass simply because they left her a tip every day.

Frankie met their stares and hardened his own.

"You fellas got a problem?" he asked in challenge.

Several shook their heads, and all went back to minding their food.

The boys soon got a platter full of hot rolls and more sweet-talk from Lora Lee. And by the time they left Ry had her phone number, his sly smile winning out over Rus and Frankie. Meanwhile Will, Lee, and Dixie were happy to get the hell out of there, what with Frankie talking a mile a minute and a mite too loud, all but announced THEY'D BE CUTTING HEMP A MILE SOUTH OF THE COUNTY LINE TONIGHT!

"Jesus Christ, Frankie," Will said, ready to gag him. "Why don't you just call up Sheriff Hyland and have him join us."

"Aw fiddle-fuck, Will. Patch Hyland don't give a shit. All that old fart does is cruise Main once a day then sit by the phone and hope it don't ring. CC's had his balls in hand ever since we were knee-high to grasshoppers. Everybody knows that."

"Yeah, but everybody ain't as big a fool as Patch Hyland."

"Okay, fine. If it makes ya feel any better, next time I won't say a word."

"Yeah, well I won't hold my breath."

The boys were soon back on the road and back to joking about Lora Lee. They all felt fit and restored upon their return. The wind had picked up and shooed away the flies, and they dozed off and on through the afternoon in the shade of a forked Hackberry that stood on a grassy bank above the lake. They'd pop an occasional beer from the cooler and lay back and listen to the leaves flutter and sing as waves washed ashore in the surge of passing ski-boats. A troop of boy scouts camped across the inlet to the north with their scout leader and several other adults, most playing badminton amidst shout and laughter, racing about while a few fished.

Will sat cross-legged like an Indian and sharpened his machete on a whetstone, thinking his must be the quietest camp on the whole lake. Too quiet. Again he felt too exposed, like in the restaurant, like anyone could guess what was going on if they cared to look. About mid-afternoon a game warden drove around the curve, slowed to a stop, then backed up, apparently to take a second look at the license plate on Dixie's blue Valiant. A Douglas County tag, home of Kansas University and a notorious haven for hippies and the drug culture.

"Don't sweat it," Frankie said to Dixie. "I'll go have a talk with him."

Dixie and the rest of the boys tried not to notice but glanced from time to time as Frankie leaned to the driver's window, shook his head and laughed, swept an arm out towards the lake then pointed to the old folks camping south, shook his head again and laughed. The warden didn't appear wholly convinced by Frankie's bluster and bull, but he was amused. After a brief exchange he tipped his hat and drove on.

Seeing Frankie give a thumb's up, Dixie grabbed a beer and made ready to relax.

But not Will, he wanted the full story.

"What did he say, Frankie?"

"Oh, he just wanted to know if we'd caught anything. I said, Hell no, them old codgers caught every fish that was biting first thing this morning. Then fried their fillets and sat there smacking their lips while we got nary a bite. So we gave up. Hoped for better luck this evening."

"He suspicious?"

"Suppose he is? There ain't a damn thing he can do about it."

"Don't be too sure, Frankie. I don't like my ass hanging out like this. We've got the old folks watching. Boy scouts over yonder and now the game warden. And us with machetes and running packs—"

"There's no problem, Will. They can't arrest you for having a machete."

"No, but they can damn sure note a license number and call a sheriff or hi-po and relay their suspicion. Tell them what car to watch for."

"I agree," Lee said. "We are a little obvious, like in the cafe. But that's not what bothers me so much as all this running around. The logistics are gonna wear us out. No one slept much, not with the heat 'n flies, and we've still gotta cut tonight. Each time we're on the road, to or from a patch, or running into town increases our chance of being noticed and getting caught. But the worst part is it's a waste of time and energy."

"So what's your point, Lee?"

"Let's camp right in the patch. Stay there till we're done."

"No, that won't fly," Will said. "We can't do that."

"Sure we can. Me 'n Brolik did it two years ago. Frankie dropped us off and picked us up. We took out a ton. Two guys in two days. 500 pounds dry."

"I like the sound of camping," Rus said. By now all the boys had gathered round, listening. Dixie and Ry both shrugged, in favor of whatever was decided.

"What if they jump us?" Will was still opposed.

"We run for it, like always," Lee said. "We've got running packs. And I'm not saying we camp where we're cutting now. It's too open, too near the road. Nowhere to run, nowhere to hide. But the big creek patches are ideal. Didn't you say you had one lined out for next week, Frankie?"

"You bet. A nice big patch about four miles southwest of Oakvale."

"Anyone living on it?"

"No. There's an old farm couple on up the road. Maybe half a mile north."

"Then we can camp there. Drop in an hour before sunup and stay three days. Cut in the daylight and get more done. Sleep at night when it's cool. We won't need much for food. Some spam, bread 'n honey, some raisins, apples. A couple jugs of water."

"Shoot, I'm all for it," Rus said, taking a fresh pinch of Skoal and rolling it in his tongue. "We'd end a lot of foolishness and cut a-heckuva-lot more hemp."

"Yeah, it's a good idea. And that's a big patch. We could use another man."

"What about Bruce? He's back from grad school, broke. Said he'd like to cut."

"Brolik? Sure, okay by me." Frankie looked around; others nodded.

"Well I don't like it. We're getting too many hands in the pie."

"Come on, Will," Frankie urged. "We all know Brolik. He's cool. A little pompous, but he's alright. And with Gabe and Jack out, we need every hand we can get. The more cutting, the bigger the pie. Better the split…"

Will set his jaw and glowered, felt thwarted at every turn like an elder displaced by the young. Too many variables entering the equation, not like the old days when they kept it close-knit. Too many ellipses and surprise turns, and he didn't like figuring the area under a fast-moving curve. He didn't trust calculus. He liked things plain and solid, like in geometry, either perfectly round or in a nice neat square.

"Then answer me this, Frankie…"—he had one last question, too wore down to argue, but he'd make his point. "If Gabe's off to Detroit on a deal, and Jack's due back here to drop us off, sleep the night, and pick us up…who's minding the farm?"

"The Kid."

"The Kid…?"

"Yeah, CK. The Cannabis Kid."

"Who the fuck is he?"

"He's this wild-ass nineteen-year-old that Sammy and Pete dug up."

"That's great, just fucking great." Will shook his head and rolled his eyes in sheer disbelief—then set his jaw and said, "He better not be getting a full cut."

"No, he gets thirty bucks a day, board 'n room. And I pay out of pocket."

"How did this come about?"

"It's a long story, Will. Let's just say he's working off a debt. But you'll meet him in a few days. You'll like him. You'll see. He's funny. Dixie's met him. He's funny, right Dixie?"

"Yeah, he's funny," Dixie said with an edgy grin. "Only problem is you can't shut him up."

This hinted of a pretty big problem. The thought of a wild-assed kid who wouldn't shut up raised doubts all around. Will gained due sympathy on this point. But hopefully any problems with the Kid would be Frankie's, not theirs.

Jack rolled in a little past six. Rus fired up his cook stove and soon had everyone feeling better, even Will, as he served up hamburgers, baked beans, and camp coffee—a stout black brew with eggshells added to settle the grounds, so strong it both awakened and steadied the nerves. They chowed down, checked their equipment, then broke camp. As the sun set in the west, they piled in the Valiant and the van and headed out, ready for another night's harvest.

They worked more relaxed than the night before, being tired helped. They set a steady pace and never slackened. Their hands, cramped and blistered, soon warmed to the task. They each taped up the holes in their gloves or used an alternate set of fingers and kept on stripping. The night passed without event and by the time Jack rolled around to pick them up they'd all but cleared the patch, leaving only a few scraggly plants in the trough of the hills. They loaded the twenty bags they'd cut and rolled on, putting miles between themselves and the scene.

Frankie rode with Jack on down to the farm, while Dixie delivered the rest of the boys to Will's place. Ry dropped Lee off at the big house shortly after sunup and headed on home.

Coming in that morning Lee felt a keen relief. Diana met him at the door and kissed his scruffy face. Sweet on him again. Plus he was relieved to bring no hemp home, only his weary self.

"Missed you," he said.

She smiled. Her hair, lush and curly, auburn in the morning light.

"You been okay?"

She nodded.

"How about Jesse?"

"He's sleeping through the night again. And talks to the wee-oh bugs..."

"*Wee-oh* bugs...?"

"That's what he calls the cicadas."

Lee smiled. "Good. How about the dog? Did he come back?"

"No..."

"What about Sheriff Guy?"

"No, no one's been by except your mother. She brought out some tomatoes yesterday afternoon and asked where you were. I told her you were helping Will. Did everything go okay?"

"No problem, Dita. We cut a heap of hemp. We'll key it up Wednesday and collect on the first batch."

"I'll be glad when this is over."

Lee smiled. "Yeah, I know."

"Do you want anything to eat?"

"No. I just wanna clean up and sleep for now"—anxious to shed his clothes and drop his body like a dead-weight. Home, fatigued, nearly too beat to climb the stairs.

Diana led the way up, said she wanted to check on Jesse. Lee followed a few steps behind and soon fixed his gaze on the fine arc of her thighs as they rose to the frayed edge of her cutoffs where the lower curve of her ass peeked through. He felt his blood surge and his energy mount. And if there was a cold spot at the top of the stairs, neither of them noticed in their rush to share the moment.

X. INTERLUDES

Lee met with his old friend, Bruce Brolik, Monday evening at a bar off Main Street in Cibola City. The Smoker was a regular institution, part of local lore, the place where three generations of Range County boys had enjoyed their baptismal drink and then some. It had always served the coldest, cheapest beer around—currently one-dollar pitchers and two bits per draw. No one left there walking on one leg. An old-fashioned poolhall tavern. Used to be Pete's Smoker, a real quiet place, now known simply as The Smoker, and considerably louder.

Pete had died two years earlier and left the bar to his only son, Hank. Pete had manned the bar and drank beer from opening to closing time every day of the week expect Sunday for over forty years and died at the ripe old age of 67. But Hank never drank beer, he only sold it. He drank whiskey. Straight up. A big, red-faced, hard-core boozer, going downhill fast at age 31. Sure, he had his moments of terror and a flash of DT's before slamming his first drink each morning. But drying out was no option. In it for the ride. He had a running bet with two other hell-bent fools on who would drink themselves to death first, and Hank was the odds-on favorite. Most doubted if he'd see the far side of thirty.

"Bottoms up and keep 'em comin'!" he'd roar. Didn't take a damn thing serious, including his own demise. And he was certainly no hands-on manager, unlike his dad who'd been a permanent fixture behind the bar, Hank was mostly in and out. And he'd changed any number of things besides the name. Added a good dozen neon signs and some cheap paneling for décor, put a women's rest room in back and a jukebox up front, blaring out pop and country tunes. A current favorite was "Knocking On Heaven's Door" by Bob Dylan, which Hank claimed as his theme song; never maudlin, he'd laugh and sing along, *"That lo-o-ong black clo-owd is a'comin' da-o-owln..."* The sad thing was he'd sold off all the grand old pool tables with the leather pockets and replaced them with coin-operated versions. Of course there were pinball machines and a foosball game to add to the general din and clatter. Once a real quiet place, The Smoker, a haven for old men to play cards. But it was still a good place to meet for a beer or two.

Lee and Bruce had been friends since third grade, rival pitchers in little league and rival intellects through high school and beyond. Lee was the more athletic of the two. Bruce was more bookish and owl-like, longed for a higher plane but always fell a bit short by being too intrigued by the human, too tempted by the act. And therefore found himself drawn to the play and moment of cutting hemp. Besides, it helped defray his college expenses—the loans taken out to earn a BA and Masters in philosophy, with a doctorate yet to seek. He was a Wittgensteinian no less. Staunch, stolid, at times Puritan in his views, at least as things pertained to language.

"You can't say that!" he'd admonish in reaction to a commonly held sentiment, like for instance, *Time heals all wounds*, declaring it "a meaningless statement."

It struck Lee that Bruce wished to limit the language to a strict, logical, linguistic form. Leave it stripped like an engine laid bare piece by piece till it no longer ran, or a body so dissected and labeled that it no longer bore any sign of having lived. Whereas Lee loved the play of words—the simile and metaphor, all the color, cuss, and rhythm. He put it to music to make his songs. Sought a poetic truth that reflected the immediate world and experience. Something Bruce rejected utterly. He saw poetry as colorful bunk, a deceit, a snare to be avoided at all costs.

"That's just *downhill yoga!*" he'd declare. "You can't scrawl whatever color you like and call it truth. That's just kids playing with crayons."

So they clashed like matter and anti-matter, opposed and

negated each other's point of view. To Lee, Bruce was blind to
the ever-shifting play of life and emotion.

"And what if it just steps up and punches you in the nose?"
he'd ask—"it" being his very urge. Because Wittgensteinian
truth seemed as sterile and fixed as a ball-bearing suspended in
a vacuum, an absolute that would not tolerate the least friction
nor speck of dust—which merely harkened back to the purity
of eternal forms. Socrates himself had brooked no poets and
sought to ban them from the Republic. So there was nothing
new under the sun. Lee would listen, shake his head, and finally
fume, "What the hell does *Wi-gun-steam* have to say about a
single damn thing that people actually do and live by? Like
greed 'n sex. Or the price of hemp for that matter. Tell me that!"

"It's Witgenstein, *Wit-gen-stein...*" Bruce would groan at the
crass inability of most people to appreciate the man's unparalleled
genius—then shout: "For God's sake, Lee! Ludwig Wittgenstein
could whistle Beethoven's entire Ninth Symphony!"

"*Whoop-dee-do!* I'd be more impressed if he could whistle
Dixie!"

"You're a benighted blockhead, you know that?"

"Beats an ubiquitous ass..."

So on and so forth as each swilled their beer, so opposed in
temperament and predilection, no way they were ever going to
see eye to eye. But they were still good friends and enjoyed the
rant as much as anything. People listening, even the good ol'
boys in The Smoker that evening, thought they were about to
go at each other's throats. But the argument was more a game,
like mental handball, though the ball was oddly shaped and
often left the room once put into play. What they were really
doing was trying to understand themselves. And that was
hopeless. So they usually ended up drinking themselves sober
and agreeing on the matter at hand.

"Well? You wanna cut or not?"

"Shit yes!"—Bruce was sounding less like a high-minded
ascetic and more a hard-eyed realist by summer's end. Three
months of working in a grain elevator and breathing hot dust
while loading and unloading boxcars and trucks amidst the
rattle and grind of machinery had brought him back to earth.

And he'd been there before, high-minded but not highborn. His father worked in heavy construction.

Bruce's initiation to that world came his fifteenth summer, working on a road crew in southern Iowa. That's how he came to know Frankie, Rus, and Ry—three wild men four years his senior. Bruce was the kid underfoot, allowed to tag along, but only so far. He watched them race big earthmovers, chase after women, and pop pills to get by on little sleep—mesmerized by their strut and swagger, like sneaking into a Yankee dugout to see Whitey, Yogie, and the Mick up close. And the following spring when all three were drafted, he noted their exit; and two years later, he noted their return. No longer a kid, he was ready to voice his own mind when Frankie, fresh from the war, in the midst of an oddly radical-patriotic spiel, all passion and paradox, anxious to overthrow the government and set things right, asked:

"What's the matter, Bruce? Don't you have faith in the old country anymore?"

"No, none at all," Bruce answered with crisp certainty.

An existentialist by then. A reader of Sartre, of *Being and Nothingness*. He wore a brown leather jacket and smoked "Gualoises." A short while later he took up with one of the prettiest girls Range County ever produced, Julie Baken. They soon married, which left Frankie, Rus, Ry and many others wondering how he'd pulled it off. A mix of self-possession and cynic charm. He'd been to Paris and looked the part. Stood in semi-shadow, ever watchful, reserved, caught her eye and drew her in. Above beauty she had brains and a cynical core all her own—wore a thick shell around her heart, a nut that Bruce found harder and harder to crack, till it nearly broke his Wittgensteinian will. In their war of wills they kept a mutual respect and a wary distance. Hers was a classic beauty that wished to bear no children. And Bruce wanted a child as bad as he wanted Julie. That was the cusp of their dilemma; one in which Wittgenstein offered no help. In spite of his intellectual leanings Bruce was deeply human, and loyal; in his heart laid an intangible you could trust like bedrock. Lee knew this and suspected it was a finer truth than either of them could construct out of poetry or philosophy.

"So you ready?"—back to the question at hand.

"I said *yes*, didn't I?"

"Good. Then we'll meet at Will's place Thursday evening..."

Sheriff Hoss Wayne faced a dilemma of his own. He loved his daughter Sandy and his son little Rob, but not his wife. And she didn't love him, not anymore. He doubted if they'd ever been in love. He'd liked her at first, but now he couldn't even stand her name. Joleen. Though she went by "Jody." They'd met in '68 when he was home on Christmas leave, and married after a two-week romance. Tired of sticking it to Saigon whores, he liked her rosy cheeks and pleasing heft. Vietnamese women were somehow too delicate and frail, like their men—you could pluck their heart out. Trouble was the heart kept right on beating, regenerating, till it seemed like death only served to increase their will and number. In meeting Jody he felt a new need, something in him wanted to make life, to beget and somehow atone for the lives he'd taken. Three months later when he returned to Vietnam for his second tour, she was pregnant with Sandy.

At first being married had felt better than being a Marine. She admired his uniform, his size and presence. But their time apart was wrenching, and her resentment simmered. They never really hit it off after that. Initially lively and cute, in seven years she had ballooned and soured. He didn't smile all that much himself. Both waited for some outside force to make the split final. About all she lived for was women's bowling league. And maybe it was his fault, her growing sour and cool to his touch, because he wasn't the kind of man to sit and talk. Up most mornings and out the door by six, came home late, sipped beer and watched TV then went to bed. Married to his job, not his wife, almost as remote and distant as his father and he didn't know how to break the pattern. Didn't like to ask questions he couldn't answer.

Friday morning after speaking with Mrs. Wylett, he'd been sorely tempted to walk back over and put his hands around the priest's neck and ask what the boy had been running from and who. It might have worked to produce an answer. But not likely. He needed a direct link—a name, something that would make the priest sweat when he next confronted him. He went to the courthouse to check on vehicle registrations over the past few years, glanced at the sheer volume of paper and felt overwhelmed. He decided to try his luck with car dealers and service station attendants.

By noon Saturday he'd come up with a half dozen pickups that matched the general description—trouble was, given a closer look, none of the owners made a likely suspect. And he couldn't very well tell people why he was looking for the pickup in the first place, that risked tipping off the guilty party. So he'd hatched a story with Silas Jordan, an old farmer he knew and trusted. He'd tell them that Silas had been out mowing hay when one of his calves broke the fence and ran into the path of a black pickup. The calf bounced off the back fender and the pickup drove on.

"Silas feels bad about letting that calf stray," Hoss would note. "Feels he's liable and wants to pay for any damage done." Just following up out of routine courtesy. That was his cover. Plausible enough. He used it with everyone he met and had tracked down six—but lacking the one he wanted those six were like sand through the hourglass. He realized his method was too scatter-shot, too hit and miss.

Again Hoss drove to the courthouse to look at vehicle registrations. He thumbed through them briefly, then checked out several cases of files and took them back to his office. There he sat leafing through page after page, grudging as a kid shut in doing homework, yet gradually warmed to the task, carefully checking make, model, and color. He worked all day Sunday and Monday, and finished late Monday night. Returning home, he sat alone watching TV in the darkened room, sipping a "Bud," wishing he was as clever as Johnny Carson but feeling about as witless as Ed McMann. He hadn't found a thing. By Tuesday morning he was utterly stumped, panicked by the thought of losing the only thread he had to go on. While he'd told Sheriff Craig that they should together, his instinct was to go it alone. But he needed to cast a wider net.

Range County jail, 8:45 a.m., the phone rang. Guy laid his newspaper aside.

"Sheriff Craig speaking."

—*Sheriff. This is Hoss Wayne over in Sky County. You got any news?*

"Good to hear from you, Hoss. But no, not thing. People are shocked, ya know. Prone to jump at their own shadow after something like that. How about you?"

—*Got a little something I'd like to check out.*

"Sure. What is it?"

—*I have a hunch that a late model black pickup was somehow involved. A sporty type with smoked windows. I've asked around but so far I've drawn a blank. I need a name, Guy. Find me a bad-ass in a black pickup, we can start digging. But thing is…we can't tell folks what we're up to or we'll spook the one we're after.*

"Makes sense."

—*Good. Then we better use the same story.*

"Okay. What ya got…?" Guy listened. "Yeah, uh-huh. Silas Jordan." He jotted down the name. "Got it. Anything else?"

—*Nope. Just hope you have some luck.*

"Same here, Sheriff. See what I can do."

Guy hung up the phone, folded his hands and popped his knuckles. *A black pickup with smoked windows?* He'd seen several around and had one in mind. Things no longer seemed so… what was the word? *Random.* The thought stirred his blood like when May first kissed him back in 8th grade. He saw a world of possibilities opening up; a world in which he could have an effect. And today was sale day—the Range County Livestock Auction held every Tuesday at the sale barn on the southeast edge of town. The best auction in north-central Kansas, hosted by Colonel Holtz himself. Half the pickups in the tri-county area would be there along with cars, trucks, and stock-trailers, filling every parking space and both sides of the road for a quarter mile in either direction. Many people came simply to eat because the old farm women who worked the kitchen served the best food around. Guy often ate there and planned to do so again that day.

Shortly after 11 a.m. he turned in the entrance and cruised past the rows of dusty manure-splattered trucks. Casually indifferent as he wound his way to the west edge of the parking lot. There he spied a shiny red pickup parked in the space reserved for the black one he'd expected to find. Mex Orvano and his two sidekicks were just climbing out. Guy eased to a stop as Mex pointed to the hood and shouted at Straydog:

"Don't scratch the fucking paint, you moron!"

"Wull, it got bird shit on it," the other explained.

"I see that. I got eyes. So wash it off, don't scratch it off."

"Just git 'er painted?" Guy asked, still seated in his car, the engine idling.

Mex glanced around.

"Hey...my favorite sheriff. You come up kind of quiet."

"Yeah, no big hurry. Just out for lunch. So? Did ya just git 'er painted?"

"Why do you ask?"

"I thought you drove a black pickup?"

"Ah yes..." Mex flashed his signature smile, a mix of raw charm and threat. Then he snapped his fingers at Straydog and Red. "You two better get on up to the chutes and start running stock or CC'll have your ass. Go!" Again he smiled, turning to Guy.

"Yes, I drove a black pickup, Sheriff," he said. "But then I see Val LaReese gets one just like mine and I don't want to be mistaken for him, ya know. Besides, black is boring. Red is more exciting..." he ran his hand over the sheen, "the color of my blood, the color of my race."

"So you had 'er painted, huh?"

"Sheriff? Why are you so curious about my pickup?"

Guy's turn to smile, seeing that he had his interest.

"Oh, there's no problem, Mex. An old farmer over in Sky County saw a black truck hit his calf the other day. The calf had strayed, so he'd like to pay for any damages."

"Hey now, that's real nice of you, Sheriff. And real nice of that old farmer. But I don't think he'd want to pay for this. It's a brand-new truck."

"So you traded?"

"Yeah."

"Where abouts?"

"Up in Omaha."

"That's a long way to go for a trade."

"They got some great deals up there."

"I bet they do. See ya around, Mex."

"Sure thing, Sheriff." Mex watched Guy drive on. Then he looked to the barn and squinted hard, licking his lips as he smiled. "Sure thing, *motherfucker...*"

The sale barn had once been the Cibola Livery Stable. Built in the early part of the century, it stood north of the old highway and railroad tracks. On any given day it had housed over a hundred horses, but it had long since been converted to its present use. It had a two-tiered corrugated tin roof and received a fresh coat of white paint every few years. The entrance, dining area, and kitchen occupied the south wing of the former stalls. To the north the old haymow opened to the central roof, with bleachers built in a semi-circle like a crude theater around the fenced arena below. Nothing fancy in way of a floor, only rough-troweled concrete that crumbled into loose gravel and dirt where the animals paced and turned. Support posts and beams were worn smooth by time, and every surface had been painted white, same as the bleachers. Depending on the press of the crowd and the strength of the sale, anywhere from 250 to 300 people could be seated, with others standing in the aisle and doorway. Over the dominant odor of livestock and human sweat hovered cigar smoke and the lingering scent of old leather, as if scores of harnesses and tack still laced the walls and rafters. To keep the air moving window fans whirred from the four upper corners, secured as much by spider webs and dauber nests as by wire and nails. The sale wouldn't start for another half hour and the only ones seated were a few old-timers looking to claim their favorite spot.

Most people were still eating and carrying on out in the dining area. The tables and chairs were a clutter of chrome and wooden castoffs, though sturdy and durable like the people there gathered. Four denim-clad farmers, each in their mid-sixties and all wearing a feed or implement cap, sat at a red and white checkered-cloth table, receiving a mock scolding from their waitress, a hefty old matron with flush cheeks and dimpled arms. She wore a white apron as long as her pink polka-dot dress.

"Don't tell me you boys are full?" she joshed.

"Not me, Martha. I always got room under my bib for your sweet pie."

"Not till you have more meat loaf 'n taters, you don't."

"Oh mercy, Martha. Don't believe I could."

"Don't you *mercy me*, Don Henry. You git more of my good cooking in you or next week I serve dog biscuits 'n Gravy Trains and see how you like it"—the women always encouraging the men to eat, eat, eat, a holdover from the days of sunup to sundown backbreaking labor.

"Martha, you could sweet talk the devil into being good. Boys, I do believe I'll have more meat 'n taters."

"Over here, Martha"—the skinniest man of the bunch, Wendal, tapped his twice cleaned plate and said, "I'll be having that pie now. Make it black berry."

"How 'bout you, Jeff?" she asked the husky man opposite.

"Well, reckon so. If'n ya got cream to pour on top."

"Now Jeff, don't think I'd grain my horse without slopping my hog, do ya?"

"Ouch! She hit cha purdy hard with that one, Jeff."

"I'll say. Don't think I'd slam a shithouse door that hard."

"You have and you would. You 'n I both know it!" she declared, walking back to the kitchen. They grinned and watched her go.

"By gum, lookit her walk," Jeff said. "Quite a gal, still got that sa-shay."

"Remember those times dancing out back, huh?"

"Reckon I do. And remembering, I get the hankern. Think I'll go home and git some off the ol' lady tonight. Just toss my hat in through the front door 'n say, 'Does anyone in there wanna fuck?' If the hat comes flying out I might as well climb back in the truck and head for The Smoker."

"Save your breath. At your age you ain't gittin' none tonight. Or any night."

"No, 'spect not, Wendal. But I sure as hell git the hankern."

"Then save your hankering for beer. We'll hit The Smoker after the sale 'n grab a couple cold ones."

"When are you boys gonna ever learn," Don Henry said, laying his massive forearms to the table. "Beer ain't good for nuthin' but a piss bucket. Now I got some shine out in the truck. A couple snorts a' that'll send ya thirty yards backwards on your tiptoes right quick-like."

"Why say," Jeff's eyes lit up. "I might try summa that. And give the wife a snort. Set her toes right back behind her ears!"

Yessirree! They all slapped their thighs.

Lee and his older brother Garret sat at the next table, listening to the old men hoot and holler. Chuck Brindle, a friend of Garret's, sat with them. All three wore cowboy hats. Lee had on his tattered straw, tipped as usual to the back of his head. Garret's hat still held its shape but had wide sweat stain and dusty brim. Chuck's hat looked brand-new like the rest of him, fresh off the rack. He worked for the Farm Bureau and bred and raced Quarter horses on the side. He was presently telling Garret and Lee about a race he'd been to in Amarillo over the weekend.

"We were lucky to even place," he said with a nod of assurance. "They had some fine horses. Yessir, some great bloodlines down in Texas..." Chuck had been born and raised north of the Red River and carried an Oklahoman's envy for all-things-Texas.

Don Henry leaned over and tugged his sleeve.

"Brindle? Ain't you learned anything living up here?"

"Why, what do you mean, learned anything?" Chuck batted his eyes behind his glasses in wonder of what he'd done to draw the old man's ire.

"Texas this 'n Texas that," Don Henry scowled. "Don't you know Texas is like grandma's pussy. Everyone knows it's down there but no one gives a shit!" he barked, anxious to share his joke.

But the laughter was cut short as they noticed Martha standing by with their platter of food. Clearly, grandma begged to differ.

"Ready for your pie, Don Henry?" she asked as his big face reddened.

"Dagnabbit, Martha. You weren't s'posed to hear that."

"Uh-huh. I hear lots of things I *ain't* supposed to. Do you want your pie or not?"

"Yes ma'am." He looked to his big hands and sat quiet.

Both tables quieted for a time. The only sounds were knives, forks, and spoons striking plates as the men leaned to their food and smacked their lips. Once Martha had made her rounds and returned to the kitchen, talk renewed.

"I told you it was good," Garret said.

"Uh-hum…real good," Lee mumbled, wiping up his gravy with a hot roll.

"You need to come in more often."

"I know. Been kinda busy."

"Got anything going?"

"Oh, me and Will have a little project. Stand to make some money."

"A man gets a chance to make some money, guess he better go for it."

Garret and Will had been best buddies in high school and were still friends, so he had a fair idea what his brother was up to and simply chose to talk around it. He didn't approve, but he understood. Garret was five years older and about the same height as Lee, only built stouter. He kept his hair short and was considerably more conservative. While they cared a lot for one another, they were not as close as either would have liked. Sons of a suicide, both haunted and scarred in that moment, they walked closely parallel paths that rarely converged. Garret had been the man of the family since age 11 and still tried to keep an eye out for Lee. But Lee had always gone his own way and Garret had his own concerns. He'd married into a farm family and had his hands full trying to juggle the contending interests of his wife, in-laws, and himself. At every turn he shouldered the weight and shouldered the blame. When beef and grain prices rose, his disposition was sunny and he loved to laugh. When they fell, he grew sober and dreaded each day. Right now he was in a sober period.

"You be able to help us cut silage?" he asked.

"How soon will you need me?"

"Not till the first hard freeze, along in early October."

"Sure, I'll help out. Should be free by then."

Most people had finished eating and in the quiet lull CC made his grand entrance from the kitchen. He wore his Stetson at a cant and his suit coat open to the bulk of his belly as he strolled among the tables, letting folks know that the auction would soon begin. He'd lay his hand to a shoulder and greet everyone by name.

"Wendal, Griffith, Don Henry. How you boys doin'? Git a'nuff to eat? How 'bout you, Jeff? Good...good." Then he'd note someone across the way and swing up his arm and shout, "Talbert! You old skunk! Where you been hiding?"

Working the crowd, and it didn't matter who they were or if they answered, he let them know his was the voice to which all turned to learn the latest news and the current price. He modulated his tone and tact depending on whose ear he aimed to bend.

"Garret Clayton, have you bought me any cattle to sell?"

"No. Not at these prices. Think I'll keep 'em a while."

"You can't fatten 'em forever, Garret. Gotta move 'em sooner or later."

"Then I'll do like you. Come Christmas, I'll butcher 'em up and give 'em to the poor."

"Easy...easy there, Garret," CC chuckled. "You make charity sound plum cruel."

"It's the market that's cruel, not me."

"Tell ya what," springing right back, leaning his weight to the table in further confidence, knowing Garret's love for horses. "Mont Akins is selling that Palomino gelding of his today. Now he ain't a bad ol' horse. Put in a fair bid, ya might save 'im from the dog food factory."

"That might be," Garret said, not batting an eye. "But I know that Palomino, and from what I've seen, he'll make better dog food than horse."

"*Oo-wee!* You are a tough customer, Garret Clayton."

"Yeah, and I hear CC Holtz is an old soft touch."

CC threw back his head and laughed. Both men were shrewd horse traders and could drive a hard bargain, always circling, sizing each other up like two fighters testing their moves. CC decided to move on, now laying a hand to Lee's shoulder.

"Say, I hear your brother here is living out on the ol' Tannis place. Gonna buy that place, Lee?"

"Haven't…really decided," Lee answered, somewhat puzzled as he turned to CC. "Only been there a short time. How did you know?"

"There ain't much happens in this county I don't know, young man. And I hear you play a mean guitar."

"Not as mean as I'd like."

"Well you keep at it son. Range County might have its first star. Then by God we'll change that big sign out on the highway to read, Welcome to Cibola City, Home of Lee Clayton."

CC gave a wink and moved on. He knew how to work people, find their interest and make it his own. Lee didn't like being called "son" and he didn't like to have his aspirations bruited about. Still, he couldn't help feeling flattered by CC's notice, though he barely knew the man.

Chuck Brindle sat fidgeting with his napkin then laid it to his plate.

"Lee," he said, "I've been wanting to ask you something."

"What's that, Chuck?"

"I saw the painting you did of Mrs. Wilkin's husband, 'The Major.' I was impressed and wonder what you'd have to have to paint a horse scene?"

"That depends…"—Lee showing interest, it beat painting portraits of dead husbands. "Anywhere from five to eight hundred, I suppose. What do you have in mind?"

"I'd like a Kentucky scene," Chuck said, leaning forth to share his vision. "A horse standing up by a white panel fence. A bluegrass meadow with a red barn and a big white house in the background. And some big leafy trees and a blue sky. The colors I like are red, blue, yellow, green…"

Lee's interest faded as fast as Chuck's excitement grew, but he played along in deference to this brother. No doubt Garret had fed Chuck the notion, trying to drum up a commission for Lee and do him some good. But it was the kind of good Lee didn't want because that kind of painting was like Don Henry's

view of Texas. About that exciting, and Lee wasn't interested.
"Those are all fine colors, Chuck," he said. "Primary colors,
best of the bunch. But we're a long way from Kentucky. I don't
think I could pull it off. Now if I could interest you in a Kansas
scene. Say, a view of the Colonel's pasture up there in Hill
County. A fine spirited horse with windblown mane trotting
up to a rock-post fence. Buffalo and Longhorns grazing on the
hillside. Prairie grasses all tinted gold and russet in the autumn
sun. Red-leafed sumac lacing up a draw to a growth of juniper.
And a huge thunderhead rising in the sky like a mountain of
clouds. That I could paint. Though you're probably looking at a
thousand dollars."

"Gosh, I don't know, Lee. I kind of had my heart set on a
Kentucky scene."

"Well, a man should get what he wants. Hope you find you
one."

Garret sat silent, staring at his plate, heard his own
stubbornness in Lee's voice and didn't know how to counter
it. He couldn't understand why Lee wouldn't simply paint the
picture and take the money, because Chuck would pay $1000, no
problem. But he'd heard Lee's refusal. No use trying to saddle
a dead horse.

Men began to stand and leave their tables, most shuffling
on into the sale. Sheriff Craig sat at the counter, sipping a cup of
coffee. He nodded at Lee's approach.

"Any more trouble with that greyhound?" he asked.

"No, Guy. He hasn't been back."

"Good. I had a talk with Earl and told him I didn't think he
ought to let a coyote killer run loose, 'specially round a kid. Earl
said he hadn't thought of it like that. Said he was real sorry."

"Well, he waved when I drove by this morning, so things
have smoothed over."

"Good. I'm glad to hear that."

"Yeah, well...thanks for stopping by and helping out."

"Just doing my job, Lee," he smiled. "Trying to keep the
peace. You take care."

Lee said he would, then drifted on in to join Garret on the
upper bleachers. He wanted to stay for an hour or so and listen

to the cadence and observe the scene. The Colonel certainly had
a musical voice. It started like a low drum roll then kicked in like
a lead guitar with snappy clean notes, all in the mid-range—a
golden baritone that edged to a tenor at a moment's urging.

"That's a fine set of animals," he said of three hogs as they
ran in a circle, squealing at the prods. "There ain't a finer cut of
pork served in Martha's kitchen, and that's a fact. Who'll start
the bid at thirty? *Who'll gi'me thirty? I got thirty, got thirty, now
thirty-one, thirty-one. Got thirty-one, now half, now half. Gotta half,
who'll gi'me two? Okay a quarter, give a quarter, gotta quarter, now
half, now half, gotta half. Who'll gi'me two, gi'me two?* Give me two...?
Come on boys," he ceased his cadence, "you're sittin' on your
hands awful early today. *Gi'me two, gi'me two...?"*—scanning
the audience in search of another bid, studying each face, each
nuance and idiosyncrasy, for each bidder had his or her own
sign—and there were women among them. Some reached up to
tug an ear, other's simply furrowed their brow or gave a slight
nod. A few would actually raise their hand, but not very far.

"*Got thirty-one 'n a half.* Going once...going twice. Sold!"—he
banged his gavel, "To Clive Anders, you ol' pig thief, for thirty-
one and a half." CC only paused once he'd made a sale to take a
drink of water or check the time, then moved on. Worked a sale
like a dealer drawing everyone to the game. Mex stood by as a
spotter with a whip in hand, which he'd raise, yelling "HUP!"
to call out the bid. But he only sensed movement like a snake
in the grass, while CC held the entire crowd in his gaze like a
hawk hovering above a field and most always noted a bid before
he heard it called.

Red and Straydog worked in the arena, using cattle prods—
"hot-shots"—to sift and sort the animals and keep them moving
in a circle to give prospective buyers a better look before
herding them out. Hogs and sheep sold early on, then cattle and
calves, and last of all, the horses. Many of the animals had shit
themselves from the trauma of being taken from their pastures
and trucked to strange surroundings, there crowded into pens,
herded through chutes and jabbed with prods. And if you
ignored man's logic and need and looked solely to the animals
amidst the riot and shout, the scene took on the crueler aspect

of a blood sport with the arena the pit and Red and Straydog the handlers. But you didn't drive frightened animals weighing hundreds of pounds through a rude maze to their auction and death with kind words and gentle taps.

Hard to believe that in the past century men had actually sold men in a similar fashion—a notion that left Lee wondering what man wouldn't do for money. And he wondered of his own acts and where they would lead? Though his were nothing to what he imagined, he felt himself and his friends verging closer and closer to the pit, and he wondered what he would do faced with the choice of his blood or another's? Yet even now, focused to the arena, to the Colonel's cadence and the caller's whip, to the animals' desperate fear, he was all but blind to the depths before him.

Of all those gathered only Guy had a clue. But he had witnessed the feast of violence, or its aftermath, having seen the boy and girl left murdered along the road. And he sensed that violence in Mex. He knew the young man had a past and the past could bleed through to the present like an image lost in a mirror, unbidden and mercurial as the quicksilver backing melted in the heat of a moment.

As he drove out a half hour later Guy noted the license on the new red Chevy Apache. He wanted to check title records and contact the dealer in Omaha where Mex had traded and see if they still had the black truck. There was always a chance it had sustained some damage in the chase or retained some other clue. And there was another angle to consider, Valentine LaReese. Though Guy saw him more as a crook than a killer, you could never be sure—even a coward made desperate would kill. Guy hadn't seen much of him lately. Heard he'd moved to Hill County and wanted to know just where. That Valentine now drove a black pickup only deepened Guy's interest.

But if Guy had a scent, so did Mex. All that day, cracking the whip, calling out the bids, his nostril's flared in anger of Guy's suspicion. And he would not wait a day to act. Late that afternoon, following the sale, he drove to Salina. He went to a fine restaurant and ordered tenderloin cooked rare. He usually flirted with his waitress, but he said little, remained remote and self-contained. He ate slowly and left a 20-dollar bill. From there he drove to the airport, parked his truck and called for a rental car. Asked what kind, he said any dark colored sedan would do. Fifteen minutes later he was headed up Highway 81 in a navy blue Chevelle. He arrived in Arcadia an hour after sunset. He cut the lights as he drove in back of the rectory and parked next to the priest's gray Buick. Finding the back door open, he gave a sharp knock. Father Michael soon appeared beyond the screen; each man stood briefly mute to the other.

"What do want, Javier? To bring more blood to my door?"

"No Father, I have a problem. May I speak with you?"

"Very well," the priest said, letting him in.

As Father Michael ushered him through the kitchen Mex switched off the light. Father Michael turned in question—the next instant he saw the flash of a stiletto and felt the point enter his nostril, tipping back his head. "What...are you doing?" he stammered weakly, trembling from the pain as blood ran to his lips.

Though slightly taller he appeared a frail boy next to the powerfully built Mex.

"Be patient and you'll see," Mex smiled. "And hey, you might enjoy it."

From the wall peg by the door Mex grabbed the silk rope, or cincture, used to gird the priest's robe. "Come Michael, follow the knife," he urged, employing the familiar, his voice soft and caressing as if theirs was a gentle passion about to unfold. "Come now, don't be afraid." He led him into the living room and made him kneel. "Careful Michael, the blade is very sharp, and your brain is only inches away. There now, that's it...kneel before the Savior."

The priest knelt like a shadow attended by a shadow. The only light on was the shaded bulb at the base of the crucifix marking Christ's tormented gaze.

"Now put your hands behind you," Mex said; then insisted, "Give me your hands!"

Feeling the knife edge deeper, the priest did as he was told. Mex quickly bound his gloved hands and pulled the rope taut, raising his arms. Then he gripped the priest's chin and wrenched back his head and wrapped the rope twice around his neck, securing it with a half-hitch. The tension of the rope and the leverage of his raised arms worked to choke off his air, while by arching his back Father Michael could just manage to breathe.

"Now we can relax and get to know each other," Mex said, kneeling beside the priest, speaking to his ear. "You have a pretty face, ya know..."—wisphering now as he slowly drew the flat of the blade down one cheek to the veins of his throat. "Your skin so soft and smooth, nearly as pretty as mine. But too pale. You need more blood, Michael. Maybe I can get your blood up. Get you hot. Would you like that?"

Father Michael tensed and rolled his eyes to the threat as Mex moved closer.

"Feel my breath, my teeth..."—he bit the priest's neck and ear. "Did that send a shiver down your spine? A thrill, an expectation? Are you warming to me, Michael? Yes, I see you're sweating now. Your breath coming short and quick...like a bitch about to come. Careful now, you must breathe. Now get ready. Are you ready?"

Father Michael arched and groaned as he felt a sharp jab to his lower ribs.

"Don't worry. It's only my knuckle. If it was my knife, you would hardly feel a thing. So sharp, so quick...you could not even draw a breath to scream. You would simply weaken and lay like a willing puta as I made you mine. Would you like that, Michael? Like to feel my hands raise your skirt...draw down your pants...spread your ass as I shove my dick in you. All you could do is whimper and squirm till I finished. Then I would pull out my knife and let you bleed to death. And if I have to... that is exactly what I will do. I promise."

Mex stood and leaned over Father Michael, staring into his eyes.

"This is my problem, Father. Someone saw my truck. I don't know who or when. But they suspect something, I know that. And I know that big ugly Sheriff has been to see you. If he comes back and asks about me or my black truck, you tell him that I make deliveries every month or so. Charitable donations of beef and pork to the Sisters of Mercy Convent. Fresh from the Colonel's own locker. Got it? Can't have your bitches eating nothing but fish and smelling like fishy whores, can we?" Mex waited, watching the rope tighten. "So…will you help me, Father? Can you do that?"

Father Michael managed a throaty *"ye-e-s"* in reply.

"If he comes, you better make him believe, Father. Or I swear before the Savior I'll shove my dick in you. But first, my knife. You understand?"

Again, Father Michael wheezed *"y-e-e-s"*—straining to breathe as his face turned purple and his eyes bulged from the tightening rope.

"Hey now, that's a good boy."

Mex stepped around and cut the rope with a flick of his knife, pitching the priest to the floor where he lay choking for breath. Mex offered no further aid; he glanced to the crucifix, then turned and left quietly out the back.

Father Michael listened to the car start up like a cruel breath to his ear. Again he felt a chill down his spine as the tires crept slowly over the rocky drive and faded into the night. Only then did he work his hands free and gingerly remove the rope from around his raw cramped neck. His hands shook; he could not think. His assailant's image still hovered like a shadow, yet he wanted to hold him, clasp him to his breast and call him "Brother." In his torment he had no thought of guilt or blood, or stigmata, only a deep urge for union and release. Gazing to the crucifix, his eyes moist with despair, he slowly removed his black gloves and reached for his flesh.

XI. FRANKIE'S FARM

High noon at Frankie's farm in Clay County, the sun hung like a giant sunflower face down in a blaze of heat. Along the ditches and fencerows stood legions of its seed in bloom. Nothing stirred except the ripple of heat waves and the grass and leaves combed by a meager hot wind. The boys were busy keying up the hemp in a hog shed on back of the house—the door and Dutch window propped open to catch what wind came through. The shed was shaded by several box elder trees and an old elm, and all but hidden by surrounding sunflowers and pigweeds.

"Next year, just you wait," Frankie declared, not the least diminished by the heat, "I'll plant that whole bottom forty acres to marijuana. Colombian, by God. Drill it in with the milo." Already making plans, already buying seed.

Everyone was feeling flush. Gabe was back, having made the sale, putting money in everyone's pocket. Even Will was smiling, felt he had every nickel coming to him, gripped a wad of 20s and 50s that totaled $700. With the harvest of two more nights soon ready to sell, each stood to make another $1500 minimum. And the season was barely under way. Mental gears were spinning fast, calculating money to come.

"Who says crime doesn't pay!" Gabe voiced their collective glee.

"Where you gonna sell this next batch?" Will asked, acting the rudder, keeping things on course.

"Already got a deal set up for this weekend. Gonna meet with some California boys down in Kansas City"—he slapped Will's back with firm assurance and added, "Relax, ol' Pard. We'll

soon have some real money in our pockets." The ex-Hegelian
Marxist was already dreaming of a sports car and a motorcycle,
proof positive of materialistic determinism. All you had to do
was recognize the process and your part in it. The truth would
set you free.

Greed and friendship harnessed to a cause, each lending
a hand as they placed the hemp in a paper sack to weigh on
a balance scale, sprinkling in a few more leaves till it tipped
at precisely 2.24 pounds—equal to one kilo, or "key." Two
sacks ready, they stuffed the contents down either chamber of
a double-barreled iron contraption that stood like a headless
robot about four feet tall. The lid bolted, hydraulic jacks were
placed under each chamber and pumped to the max. After it
set a minute, they popped the lid and proceeded to kick out
two fresh keys. At a nearby table the bricks were wrapped in
butcher paper neat as a Christmas present at Macy's, minus
only the ribbon and bow. Finished, each key was packed tight in
a cardboard box then doused with talcum powder to disguise
the sharp green scent. A regular assembly line formed to key
the hemp, and they were proud of their product.

Like Frankie said, "The best damn worthless weed ever
made!"

The boys took turns at the various tasks to break the
monotony. Dixie and the Kid were presently manning the jacks,
by far the hardest work of all. Both stood shirtless and lathered
in sweat, waiting for the next batch, sharing in the banter fired
back and forth to keep all entertained.

"Now Kid, don't be slacking off," Frankie warned.

"What d'ya mean, *slacking off?*" the Kid answered, flashing
his baby blues in shrewd innocence, his voice made husky from
all the dope he smoked. "What d'ya call this?" He slapped a
hand to his sweaty belly.

"I call it baby fat, Kid. The fruit of soft-living and sloth. Oh
yeah, groan all like. You think you've got it rough, you should've
known my old drill sergeant. A big black bastard, tough as nails.
Sergeant Gus Rostum. Now I loved that nigger. He always said,
'Ah hates a sneakinish woman an' a la-a-zy man!'"

"Sure, Fascisto. Don't sweat it. You get your thirty bucks

worth"—the Kid giving as good as he got, sore at his measly wages amidst all that plenty and had even tagged Frankie with his new nickname, *Fascisto*.

"Go on Kid, try 'n break my cold, cold heart. And don't forget, you also get board 'n room."

The Kid's mouth gaped open as he shook his mop of dirt-blonde hair.

"Board 'n room? You kidding? I might as well drink muddy water and sleep in a hollow log. All I get is scrambled eggs 'n old biscuits. And lookit these...." He pointed to the bug bites covering his chest and arms, and the big red welt on the side of his belly that he claimed was caused by a brown spider—all received from sleeping on the floor.

"I'd be better off outside!"

The Kid had a point, the house wasn't much. It mostly just stood there like a dead thing waiting to fall. The next high wind or clap of thunder might do the trick. A living testament to the very song—"This Ole House"—a narrow two-story facade of loose siding, torn screens, and broke windows that stood at the top of a rocky drive, facing west towards the road. Closer up the paint flecked off like dry scabrous skin. Inside, the pine floors were warped and splintered, while remnants of linoleum lay in jagged blotches through the kitchen. The framework had sagged and heaved, forcing the doorjambs out of plum. The wallpaper had faded and pealed, leaving patches of exposed lath showing through like rib-bones where the plaster had fallen. Except for the outhouse in back, the place was more or less modern. Several bare light bulbs dangled from the ceilings, and there was running water at the sink—brown water disgorged from corroded pipes. A galvanized tub that served for bathing was kicked to one corner.

All and all it was adequate and livable for a gang of creekbank boys. But when Frankie's new sweetheart Alice had passed through, she took one look inside and said, "See you in Lawrence, Frankie." She wouldn't even stay the night. The place literally crawled with bugs. An entomologist's dream, but a nightmare for anyone trying to sleep, laying on an old mattress in the rank heat, staring into the dark, listening to the

skitter of roaches and flees, spiders and bugs of every sort, not
to mentions rats and mice. Hornets and wasps nested inside
and out, governing every nook and awning, claiming much
of the air space. And the walls virtually hummed with bees.
Frankie and Dixie had scoped it out the previous evening,
examining the exterior in wonder of how best to get at all that
honey. Finally they decided to wait for cool weather when the
bees weren't so active, then smoke them out and harvest the
combs.

Frankie was perversely proud of the place—the more others
complained, the more he liked it. Definitely no citified country
getaway, a real down-home weed-patch outlaw haven. He saw
potential in every aspect of the place, loved the house, the land,
the creek and surrounding hills. The very remoteness. For years
he'd wanted land and now he had it. His own realm. And he
had his own jester to liven up the court. All he had to do was
crack the whip on occasion.

"Just remember what got you in this pickle," he said as Kid
showed-off his bites, still complaining about the fact of no bed.
"At least you've got a pot to piss in and a window to throw it
out of."

"Aw sure. Rub it in, Fascisto. And all I did was take a shit…"

"Right! A two-thousand-dollar SHIT!"

"Okay,· but so? It could happen to anyone. Get this," he
said, turning to the others. "Here's the scene. It's midnight. A
windblown rest-stop off I-70…" The Kid squatted, re-enacting
his crime. "I had to shit, man. I mean *really* shit. All cooked up,
ready to serve. And Pete says, 'You got two minutes. If you're
not back out, I leave you.' So I grunts and I groan…" The Kid
puffed out his cheeks and bugged his eyes in pantomime.
"Then BOOM! I shit the whole monkey in record time. I rips off
the paper, do my stuff…and stuff it. Pull up my pants 'n spin
around like so…flush it with my boot. Then I start out the door
and feel my hip pocket. Aw fuck! The dope is gone! I look to the
floor. Nothing there. I rush to the stool and reach in just as it
swirls away. I git shit all over my hand trying to grab it."

He held out his hand in disgust like it still reeked.

"Agh! Get it away!" Dixie cried.

"Dixie, look? See? It's okay," the Kid laughed. "I washed it off, ya know."

"Right, Kid. Just keep it out of my face."

"Alright, alright..." the Kid shrugged, then looked around and said, "See? It could happen to anyone."

So that's how the Kid came to work for Frankie. Flushed $2000 worth of coke down a roadside shitter. Pete was a small-time dealer and had fronted him the coke. When the Kid came out and told him what had happened, Pete wanted to neuter him or worse. But castration wouldn't bring back the money or the coke. Besides, Frankie liked the Kid and interceded, said he'd buy the debt and let the Kid work it off.

"Time to get back to work, jack-off," he said, seeing the Kid ignore his task.

"What? Can't I tell my story?"

"You told it."

"So...?"

"So, you want me to sell you back to Pete?"

"No!"

"Then get back to work. Remember, Kid, there's a special place in hell reserved for the lazy and the slothful. Shoved to the lowest pit where they lay frozen in ice at the base of Satan's thighs. Denied all movement and warmth to the end of time..."

Kid rolled his eyes, knelt down, and started pumping the jack. It was their game, master and slave, all in fun. For the most part. But the debt was real enough, and at the rate of $30 a day it was going to take a while. Still, things weren't nearly as bad as the Kid made out. Many days he hardly worked at all, and Frankie fed him well, took him out to restaurants and bars. Plus, he had all the *sinsemilla* he could smoke, which for the Cannibas Kid was a major bonus. And he got an occasional free line of coke. Like later that day after they'd finished keying the hemp.

"Come on, don't I git some more?" he asked, looking to Frankie like a starved pup.

"Do you want paid for today or do you want another line?"

"Oh well, crap, gimme another line," the Kid groused. "What's one day added to a thousand? But I better get more than one line for thirty bucks. I ain't stupid, ya know, I can add."

"Sure, Kid. You're a real math whiz," Frankie said, passing him the plate and a rolled twenty. The Kid leaned down and started snorting the white powder through the rolled bill. "Tell ya what, Kid," Frankie grinned like a carny to a mark. "This line's on me if you can explain the Pythgorean Theorem."

The Kid stopped in mid-line and looked up.

"Criminee, Fascisto...gimme a break. I don't even know what you said."

"Okay, I'll make it easy. How do you find the hypotenuse?"

The Kid grimaced in thought then smiled like a winner.

"I got it! Find a rope to hang a hippo, you gotta hippo-noose, right?"

Frankie laughed. "Kid, you crack me up. Go ahead and finish your line," he said, "you earned it." Then he tried to explain. "Look Kid, the hypotenuse is the long side of a right triangle. You square the two shorter sides then add them together to find the square of the longer side. *'A' squared plus 'B' squared equals 'C' squared.* That's the Pythagorean Theorem. You should know this, Kid. It's fundamental. A key to our understanding of the world."

"Wait a minute...you use a square to find a *triangle?* You're confusing me here, Fascisto. The only triangle I know is the patch of hair around a girl's pussy. Man, when I put a lip-lock there I always git the right answer!"

With that the Kid had them all in stitches—a real class cut-up.

Frankie shook his head like he was tending a hopeless cause.

"Good God," he groaned. "Kid fucked a fat girl over in Manhattan the other night. Now he thinks he's Lothario."

"So...? Least I got laid. *I takes 'em, I rolls 'em, I gives 'em a good time, smears 'em up in butter, licks their pussy till it shines...*"

"Was she a virgin, Kid?" Ry asked.

"How should I know?"

"Did she scream?"

"No. She yelled, *'Ride 'em, Kid! Ri-i-de 'em...!'*"

"Then she was definitely no virgin," Ry said with a wide grin.

"It's a good thing, too," Lee added soberly.

"Why's that?" the Kid asked.

"You might've caught sex bile."

"Sex bile...?" The Kid looked dubious, but Lee was hard to read.

"Yeah, sex bile. Didn't you have health class in high school?"

Frankie nudged Ry and said, "He had retard health along with retard math."

"Okay Fascisto, so I got a little learning problem. A little dyslexia."

"Poor, poor Kid. You 'n Picasso both. It makes 7's look like noses and triangles look like pussies. Right?"

"So? It doesn't mean I'm stupid." Then he turned to Lee and said, "Sure I had health class...but maybe I was sick that day or fell asleep or something. So tell me about this sex bile thing."

"Well, there's not much to tell..." Lee began slowly, doing his earnest best to tutor the lad. "They know it's transmitted by virgins. They're not certain why, but they think it has to do with the power and make-up of new hormones. That initial surge held back by the hymen, if you follow..."—the Kid nodded like the most attentive student in class. "Which means you damn sure don't wanna be eating any virgin pussy. Because that's how you catch it. Sex bile. It enters through your mouth."

"Mouth? Then what?"

"You know how it is when you've been out all night drinking and smoking, you wake up with cotton mouth? It's like that, only it doesn't go away. As it gets worse it gets harder 'n harder to breathe. Then the bile enters your spine, bending it like a bow, only backwards."

"Can they straighten you out?"

"Oh, they've got methods, but they're pretty crude. More or less like medieval torture. They stretch you on a thing similiar to the rack. Leave you like that for days on end. But if they don't catch it in time, well..."

"What? What happen's then?"

"It works its way down to your scrotum and the infection creates this terrible pain and swelling. The spasms further contract your spine. And eventually..." Lee paused and looked him in the eye, sober as the wages of sin.

"Well...?"—the Kid lingered in wait of the prognosis.

Lee winked to Ry. And right on cue Ry sat up and grinned.

"Kid, you bend over and *fuck* yourself to death!"

"OH NO!"—the Kid clinched his eyes, knew he'd been had as Ry and Lee both slapped the table and the boys all laughed. But the Kid took his hazing in stride and laughed loudest of all, relieved he hadn't contracted sex bile. And he meant to keep their attention now that he had it, kicked back his chair and stood.

"Listen," he said. "I gotta new song. Made it up yesterday." He spun the lyrics in his usual singsong while strumming air guitar—"*I didn't play football, didn't play in no band, didn't sit on the sidelines or cheer in the stands...I learned to smoke dope an' drink whis-key, an' play mouth-harp on a girl's pus-sy....*"

The Kid delivered a few more lines then stopped and glanced around like he expected applause. Finding none, he continued undaunted. "Hey, I got more. No, really," he said, again strumming air guitar—"*I can rhyme all day, I can rhyme all night, got rhythm in my jism, I can make ya feel right...* Ya see? I got the gift."

"Your gift and our curse"—Dixie tried to check the flow.

"No, really. I got dozens of songs. And get this. I gotta name for my band. *Jimmy Joe Jesus and the Nashville Hopheads!* What d'ya think?"

"Great, Kid. Fantastic!" Frankie cheered him on. "All you need now is a manager and a bus, then you can go coast to coast 'n collect fat-girl groupies!"

The boys were carrying on in such manner with the Kid spewing out raucous lyrics when Rus and Jack returned. They'd driven into town directly after keying hemp to buy more beer. Both looked a little disappointed seeing the party had started without them, the plate being passed, half the coke already gone. Rus was the first to react, shuffling in lugging a case of beer.

"Why I never saw the like," he grumped, shaking his head. "Send us off to town, then snort all the coke. Hope it rots your nose chimney."

"Don't fret, Russie. Ol' Frank saved some back for the lad who held the horses."

"Well I'd hope to Christ..."

Rus plopped the case of beer to the table and pulled up a chair as Frankie laid out a liberal dose. Meanwhile Jack remained poised at the door, focused dead center in an all-but-accusatory stare, certainly one of deep scrutiny, slowly turning his good eye to each with a tilt of his head and a cocked smile. Their talk and laughter soon subsided, held in suspension as each felt the glint of that eye and waited for him to move, or at least say something.

"Gonna spit it out or not?" Ry finally asked, wanting in on the joke.

Jack's smile broadened as he slowly raised his hands.

"Oh, it just struck me," he said, rubbing his good eye with his palm, leaving the glass orb free to pursue his thought, "what a perfect bunch of proles we are. There's not an aristocrat among us," he laughed. "Just take a look around. Look at your noses..."

At that moment it was easily their most prominent collective feature, made more prominent by their very activity. They looked around, wiped their noses and sniffed, suddenly conscious of the numbness setting in along with the elation and keen awareness. Most of their noses had been bent or broken in some manner, and all were slightly large or appeared so the more they looked. The effect was nearly hallucinatory, for the nose is perhaps man's most animal-like feature, and when focused on, it more resembles a muzzle or snout or a long beak. No two were the same or even similar, like each represented a different tribe, yet all were made one by that difference, a mongrel tribe of creekbank boys made one by their common effort and region of birth. Jack had definitely hit on something, though the trait was actually more democratic than proletariat in spirit. And no, not a one showed any sign of aristocratic lineage.

"Hey Fascisto, think I can have one more teeny line?" the Kid asked, wheedling for more. "I mean, I think it would do a lot for my nose, ya know."

"Go ahead, Kid. Knock yourself out."

The boys all laughed and reached to pop a beer. Yeah, the

Kid was alright. Like Frankie said, absolutely irrepressible. By now even Will had to admit as much.

"Just keep him here at the farm," he told Frankie. "I don't want 'im in the patch."

Ry and Lee seconded the motion.

"Come on. How come I can't go?"

"Because," Frankie said, a pillar of patience, "you're needed here."

"Aw sure, I know the real reason. Someone's gotta stay 'n feed the bugs."

Then the Kid leaned back and launched into his current favorite:

"I don't wanna work on Frankie's farm no more
Don't wanna work on Frankie's farm no more
I wake up in the mornin', fold my hands 'n pray for pussy
Got a head full of some shit that makes me feel all goofy
It's a shame he makes me sleep down on the floor
AW-W-W, don't wanna work on Frankie's farm no more..."

While the boys whooped it up down at the farm, Guy spent most of Wednesday placing phone calls, trying to locate the black truck. By mid-afternoon when he finally reached Luger's Chevrolet in Omaha, he learned less than he'd hoped. They still had the truck on the lot, but according to the salesman there was no body damage.

"No, none at all," he chirped. "A real sharp truck. There's a few gravel specks on the hood that we touched up and buffed smooth. But no, it's a dandy," he continued, never missing a chance to make a sale. "We cleaned the interior, shampooed the carpet, tuned 'er up. Shucks, it's got less than twenty-two thousand miles on it. You ought to come up 'n check it out. We can make ya one heck of a deal."

Guy said no thanks and hung up. One thing he did learn was that the truck had been traded the Monday following the murders, fairly suspicious but hardly proof.

By evening he'd also learned that Valentine LaReese had

rented a farmhouse about three miles northwest of Oakvale. Rumor had it that he lived there with two other men and six women, making for a regular hippie commune, which caused quite a stir through the region. Though town folks allowed that Valentine seemed right friendly and always paid hard cash—and yes, he did drive a big black pickup with dark windows.

"A Dodge Ram," one old boy vouched, seated in the lone downtown cafe. "Know for a fact 'cause he was in for lunch 'n parked right yonder. Got a bright hood ornament big as my fist. Blind ya to look at it." So declared, others nodded in assent.

Guy thanked them and walked out. Even though it was a whole different county, and strictly speaking beyond his purview, he aimed to keep tabs on Valentine LaReese. But his suspicion still centered on Mex Orvano, and he shared his suspicion with Sheriff Wayne in a phone call the next morning.

"They still have his black truck in Omaha," Guy said. "It's been gone over and cleaned up. Doubt if we'd find anything. But Mex got mighty curious in his cool way when I asked about his black truck and where it had gone. Of course I fed him our story, but don't think he bought it. Him trading on Monday... well, that still ain't proof. But he could be our man."

Hoss listened and wrote "Mex Orvano" on his notepad, then circled and stabbed it with his pen. "No, we can't arrest on that," he answered. "But you got me a name, Guy. And I appreciate it. I'll see what I can do. Be in touch."

Hanging up the phone, Hoss smiled like he hadn't in months, not since finding his wife's dildo hidden under the mattress— the thought of her preferring that to the real thing had sobered him. But just then he didn't give a tinker's dam about her or the dildo, he had a name and was anxious to see if he could use it to pry something loose.

From his office Hoss drove directly to Co-op Tire, one of the few places he hadn't checked when asking about the black pickup. He turned down the side alley, hoping to catch Chris Boswick in back and avoid sharing his suspicion with the manager and any customers up front. Through the shadowed interior he spied Chris bent over working a tractor tire off its rim. Hoss honked once and motioned him over, kept the motor running to ensure their privacy.

Chris dropped the roach he'd been toking behind the tire and let the smoke drift slowly out the side of his mouth as he stood and wiped his hands on his jeans, always somewhat anxious at seeing the Sheriff appear due to his marijuana habit—in fact he grew some on the side, good smoking pot, mostly for his own use, but he wasn't above selling it to the right party for the right price. The last of said smoke left his lips as he approached with a tentative smile to see what the Sheriff had in mind. Relieved to hear Hoss ask if he'd seen a black pickup.

"Sure, I've seen a few around," Chris answered, suddenly animate, curious.

"The reason I ask," Hoss explained, "is Silas Jordan, there south of town, saw a black truck hit one of his calves and feels obliged to settle up."

"Old Silas, sure. Lemme think…" Chris rubbed the back of his neck. "Well, the Mexican was in a while back."

"You mean Mex Orvano? The sometime son of Colonel Holtz?"

"Yeah, that's the one. A full-time sonuvabitch if ya ask me. Real cocky in a real bad way"—Chris speaking freely now, shaking his head and doing a fair shuck and jive for a big sandy-headed white man. "Funny thing, he wanted new tires all around. And he needed new tires like I need two heads. But the man wants tires, we give 'im tires. So he goes up front for a Pepsi while I shoot 'er up on the lift, ya know, kinda laughing and scratching my head about the tires, when Joey walked in. I told him about the tires and he didn't so much as crack a smile. Never smiled all that day."

"Was that the day we talked about? When he said he saw something?"

Chris merely nodded, suddenly quiet, recalling Joey's fear and subsequent events.

"You having any luck on that, Sheriff?" he asked.

"Could be," Hoss noted, absorbed in his own thoughts. "But about that truck," he promptly added. "I'd keep it between us. Old Silas doesn't want every truck owner in the county trying to collect on a bent fender."

"That's cool," Chris answered, rubbing his neck in wonder at the odd request.

Hoss touched his hat brim and drove on. He knew he made Chris nervous and he knew why, having long suspected him of growing marijuana. And it didn't take a blood hound to smell it on him. But in light of what he'd just learned, Hoss could care less if Chris lit one up and blew the smoke in his face. Still smiling as he drove across town to confront the priest.

What surprised Hoss was the priest's utter lack of concern at seeing him.

"Please come in," Father Michael said, opening the door. "It's much too hot to be standing in the sun."

And his answers were so matter-of-fact as if rehearsed the night before.

"Mex Orvano? You mean, Javier. Yes, I know him. Why do you ask?"

"A black truck driven by him was recently seen leaving these grounds."

"Certainly. He delivers meat every so often."

"Delivers *meat?*" Hoss was caught off guard by his own question.

"Yes. Colonel Holtz was raised Catholic. He makes generous donations to the Church. Including pork and beef to the Sisters of Mercy Convent. I believe the last delivery was…just a minute"—Father Michael looked to the calendar hanging in the foyer—"Oh yes…Wednesday, the twenty third. Two weeks ago yesterday."

Hoss didn't like the answers. Too pat, too prompt. He narrowed his eyes and focused hard on the priest, inspecting every nuance, every movement of his flesh. He noticed the red welts above the white collar.

Father Michael raised a gloved hand in reflex.

"A rash from shaving," he hastened to reply.

"More skin problems, huh? Like with your hands?"

Father Michael smiled faintly and remained silent.

"Suppose you tell me why, on the same Wednesday you got your meat, my witness saw Joey Connors run from the church grounds down the street here? And a short while later saw a black truck driven by Mex Orvano in pursuit? Why is that?"

Father Michael flinched at the question. His lips tightened then parted as if awaiting a prompter.

"I...uh... I have...no idea," he stammered, pressing his lips in an awkward smile. "Perhaps your witness is mistaken."

"No, my witness is damn certain."

"Then...perhaps Joey and Javier had words. Javier is...a passionate man."

Hoss didn't understand "passionate" in that context. And he didn't trust the priest's pretty face. To him "passionate" and "pretty" implied a woman, not a man.

"How do you mean, *passionate* man?" he asked in disgust.

"I mean simply that Javier can be hotheaded."

"Hotheaded huh? Hotheaded enough to have words with a high school boy. Then chase him down the street with a pickup. Maybe hotheaded enough to hunt him down and kill him."

"I did not say that, Sheriff Wayne."

"No, I said it." Hoss glared down like a drill sergeant, forcing the other to blink away. He watched the sweat form on the priest's upper lip and temple. He could smell the stink of fear in him, like rank urine in his sweat.

"Got anything more you'd like to add, Mike?"

"Are you accusing me of something, Sheriff?" Father Michael glanced up, again composed.

"No. I'm asking you a question."

"I've told you all I know."

Hoss stared another moment, tempted to reach out and wring that pretty neck.

"See you around, Mike," he said, then turned and walked out the door.

Stepping down off the porch, Hoss secured his hat and smiled to the sun. Smiled like someone who's found the light after a long darkness. No, he hadn't found proof, but he had something better than a hunch. He knew in his gut that Mex was his man. And he also knew that Mex had a hold on the priest. Hoss had to find a way to up the pressure and break that hold. Because he needed a confession from the priest. The only question was how?

XII. CREEK PATCH

Paired headlights rolled down the road through the night, here and there reflecting a highway marker or a stop sign. In turning off the pavement the low beams caught the sharp-lit eyes of a coyote before it leapt to the sanctuary of a shadowed ditch. The boys also soon emptied out of the van and joined the night. A skiff of clouds drifted beneath the stars as the van rolled on. The red taillights blinked faintly through the trail of dust then merged with the darkness.

Early Friday morning, an hour before sunup, their breath visible in the damp cool air, the boys entered the winding creek patch southwest of Oakvale. They followed a fence line that bordered a cornfield to the south and encountered little in the way of marijuana till they dropped down into the broad creek bottom. There they discovered a lush stand of tall plants—fairly weedy towards the creekbank but clean and nicely spaced further back. Happy to find something worthy of their long hike in, they quickly unshouldered their burdens. Lugging equipment in and hauling the harvest out was a grudging task. And a three-day camp meant packing along sleeping bags, food, and extra water—the water carried in two large plastic jugs.

Their burden was eased somewhat by an idea Lee had hit upon while helping his brother chore Tuesday after the sale. Garret had stuffed an armful of alfalfa into a rope hay net then hung it from a nail in the corner stall, allowing the horses to feed without stomping the hay underfoot. The utility was immediately apparent—if it could hold hay it could hold a bag of hemp. Lee drove straight to town and purchased four hay nets. By hooking a pair to either end of a pole, you could balance the load across your shoulders and any two men could carry what had once taken four. They could use the same method whether loading in or loading out. And over a long haul it was much easier than gripping the weight by hand.

"They look like Vietnamese farmers, don't they?" Ry observed, watching Lee and Dixie descend the slope.

"Yep, keep a'humping boys," Frankie laughed. "Bwana likes his native porters."

"I got news for Bwana," Dixie answered through gritted teeth as he eased his burden down. "Bwana gets to carry next load."

No doubt they'd each have ample chance to tote hemp over the next three days. And the hay nets would prove their worth. Only one of many refinements added over the years. From time to time each of the boys had a better idea to move the whole. Likewise alone they might hesitate to act, but one dared and moved the others, and yet another probed where each had stalled, and in such manner they split the atom of restraint and induced a chain of action and reaction that led to the desired goal. Or in some cases to misadventure. Which was Will's prime concern. Because he still didn't like staying in the patch or working by day.

All that first morning while the others busied themselves cutting, he'd edge up the bank every half hour or so and have a look—note a tractor working in a distant field or the occasional traffic along the road that left nothing but dust in the wind. And in this instance he drew comfort from the wind as it blew steady from the west to blanket any noise. Finally, along about noon, he left off looking altogether. Apparent the rest of the world paid them no mind. And he had to admit they could cut twice as much hemp by day as by night. Plus the seeds were starting to mature, adding to the weight. Even the college-boy philosopher, Bruce Brodick, who could get under Will's skin like a rash, was keeping quiet and keeping pace. Proving likable. So Will had no complaints. They were cutting more hemp than he'd ever dreamed. By the end of the day they looked to have 35 to 40 bags.

This brought on a fresh concern.

"How the hell we gonna get all this shit in the van?"

"Don't you worry, Wolfer," Frankie assured. "We'll stuff it in if I have to run back and body slam it!"

And next morning at 4:30 when Jack arrived, they loaded the van with room to spare, but not by much, and not nearly enough space left to load themselves out when the time came. They'd still be okay Sunday morning, but come Monday they'd need two vehicles. So they'd have to improvise: either use the Kid, or better yet if Gabe returned by then he could drive. In any case there was no crisis, merely a further hitch to consider and adjust to. And they'd slept well in the patch, relatively speaking, much better than by the lake amidst the heat and flies and all the scrutiny. The spam didn't taste any worse after the fourth meal, and it didn't taste any better either. But placed on bread smeared with honey, followed by a crisp apple, it wasn't bad fare. And their water was holding out. By Saturday afternoon they'd worked themselves a half mile further east, still finding plenty of hemp, each holding steady.

Too steady for Frankie. Like they were all working a job— too diligent, too quiet and earnest for his taste. He wanted to put a spark into things. Light their fuse.

"There's eighty acres of pasture down at the farm," he said. "I'd like to stock it."

"Might as well," Rus answered indifferently, knelt before his machete stabbed in the ground, cutting end buds off the stems. No one else said a word.

"I mean, we should start rustling. What's to stop us?" This got their attention, Frankie acting the instigator, trying to rev them up. "Nothing real big, you know," he continued. "Just a dozen heifers give or take, enough to start a herd. And a few steers to keep us all in meat. Maybe sell the calves off in the spring," he suggested with a big smile, definitely selling himself on the idea.

Rus pointed to Frankie with his rough leather glove and said, "You do any rustling, boy, you do it by your lonesome."

"Aw Rus, where's the ol' *Rustler* gone?"

"Don't pull that crap with me."

"That's right," Will added. "You can cut that talk right there."

"Hell I will. What about you, Ry? Up for a little rustling?"

"Not really," Ry answered. "We nearly got caught stealing pigs"—recalling the night back in high school when he and Frankie had stuffed four squealing piglets in a gunny sack, jumped the fence and ran for their car, the farmer's dog hot on their heels. But they made their escape and fattened the pigs for an FFA project and sold them for good money. "Besides, cows are a darn sight bigger than pigs. Plus, we'd need a truck. And no, I'm really not interested."

Frankie slacked his jaw in disbelief—couldn't light a fire under a single one.

"Look Frankie," Lee added the final straw. "My brother fattens cattle, you know that. He loses four or five out of a hundred due to sickness or what-have-you, there goes his profit. Right now he's not breaking even. And there's a whole lot of others in the same boat. So I don't wanna hear about rustling period."

To Frankie this sounded a shade sanctimonious, every last bit. He narrowed his eyes and looked from one to the other of his friends. What angered him was that they wouldn't even entertain the notion. Even for the sake of entertainment. What was the use of free will and freedom if you couldn't at least examine the option of each and every act? Including rape, murder, incest, torture, depravity of every imagined sort, compared to which rustling cattle was a mere prank like stealing apples. And not that you would ever do any of those things. No, that wasn't the point. To be wholly alive you had to consider the vastness of the world and human experience and not react like a bunch of hidebound puritans. Feeling thwarted, Frankie lashed back.

"Christian *guilt!*" he declared. "You're all chained by Christian *guilt!* Heads bowed, working like a pack of dutiful slaves. How do ya think all the great wealth came about? Someone *stole* it, that's how. Alexander plundered Persia! The Romans robbed Greece! The Huns sacked Rome! The Vikings ravaged every damn coast they set foot on. The English corsairs sank the Spanish galleons once those bastards had gutted the Aztec 'n Inca. Hell, the very land we stand on was stolen. Every last stinking inch. The Indians slaughtered, starved out, and shoved off by men just like us. There's not one lick of difference. And you stand there in the prison of your own guilt, afraid to act to your own advantage."

"No. There's things we'll do and things we won't."

"Sure, Lee. I know. You've got scruples. Like the other day you wouldn't even take a snort of coke."

"I didn't want any, Frankie. It's that simple."

"Christian guilt. Deny yourself pleasure. Scorn life. Be humble and suffer."

"No, I don't like to suffer. And I don't like coming down off a cocaine high."

"*Christian guilt!*"—stating his case.

"Okay, Frankie. But I'd call it something closer to shame. I had to drive home that day, and I don't want to stand ashamed in front of my wife and son…"

Following his last big bender, Diana had found him passed out on the floor like a spilt bottle while Jesse looked on in question of what was wrong with his Daddy. When Lee finally woke, her silence was worse than any accusation.

Frankie let them have their little victory, took his machete and went back out to cut another pile of hemp. Whirled his machete like a dervish dancing in a hot wind, hated constraint, hated being lectured, his own buddies acting like stodgy old men or worse, like his grandmother wagging her finger in his face, saying—*See, I knew it would come to this!* He took his spite out on the hemp, cutting plants this way and that, regardless of their height and foliage, simply because they stood.

The wind had died down towards evening and the "gling" of his blade on the stalks carried through the creek, sounding to the boys like a sharp chime. In the near distance a dog started barking and they wondered if it could hear the "gling" as well.

"Think you could hold it down?" Will cautioned, a stickler for quiet.

"What! Think I'm too loud?!" Frankie shouted with a laugh. "Think someone's gonna hear up through all these weeds and trees?!"

"Well shit. At least use my old corn knife. That thin-bladed bastard of yours rings like a bell." Another contention between them: Will preferred old-time corn knives over machetes for the fact that their thick blades only gave off a dull "thunk" in cutting.

"Aw hell!" Frankie raised his voice another decibel in answer. "The crickets are so loud I can't hear myself think!"

"That's the trouble. You're not thinking. You're too full of bull."

"You damn right! Pure bull! And I've got a nine-inch dick to prove it!"

"Watch it you don't trip over that dick of yours and land in your own shit."

"Yeah, and it'll be pure gold! Pure gold!"

"Save your breath, Will," Rus advised. "Best thing to do is put the boy back on a rubber knife."

But Frankie wasn't listening, he flailed on undiminished, undeterred, hacking the hemp in a hot tantrum—"*gling! gling! gling!*"—syncopating with the crickets in a widening swath. Eventually he tired, drenched in sweat, having exorcised the demon. And he'd worked up a sizable bundle of hemp, which he shouldered back and plopped down as if in evidence to some unspoken truth.

No one said a word, including Frankie, all content to quietly strip for a time.

As the sun sank low, they bagged the last of the hemp. Again they barely spoke, weighed by the thought of all the bags they'd soon have to carry. The problem was they were camped approximately halfway along the diagonal of a mile-square section of land; the creek cut from the southwest corner to the northeast tip before passing under a bridge. Either direction posed a mile-long hike out to the road. While to the north the road ran only a quarter mile away. But an old farm couple lived in a house along that stretch, and their dog was still barking.

"We better get started," Lee said, broaching the subject. "Need to break a trail before dark. You all wanna head east or west?"

"Neither," Frankie said. "Let's check up north. See if there isn't a way in."

No one objected to taking a look, not even Will.

Frankie and Lee waded the creek and headed up the sloping bank. Bruce tagged along. At the rise they crouched by the foxtail and fireweed that grew along the fence to look the situation over. A milo field lay directly north while a row of trees bordered the field west all the way to the road, partially blocking the view from the house. A narrow lane ran along the near side of the trees next to the field, providing access from the road to the creek. The vein at Frankie's temple bulged and pulsed, his instincts focused as he noted the lane and determined his path.

"Looks kind of dicey coming in," Lee said, guessing his intent. "I don't mind toting the stuff."

"Don't be a glutton for punishment, Lee. We can drive the van in and load right here. No problem."

"What about the dog?"

"He'll be asleep by then. He's just barking at evening shadows."

A brief lull in the wind revealed the chirp of birds waking through the trees as the baked earth settled and the sun slipped west. The grasses stirred in the gathering calm.

"Makes sense to me," Bruce said in an eager whisper. "I vote bring the van in."

The logic of fatigue outweighed any doubt in his mind. And silence confirmed the decision. Nor did anyone else voice the least objection upon their return. Two days of cutting had worn them down. Grungy from layers of sweat, dust, and insect repellent, they ate their meager fare, rolled into their sleeping bags and slept.

Will rousted them out at 3 a.m. and by a quarter past four they had forty-odd bags stacked along the fence. Meanwhile Frankie had trotted on east to intercept Jack beyond the bridge and lead him in. The wind blew to their advantage, steady from the west. The boys could see the yard light at the house blinking through the shift and sway of the trees. They looked to the east in wait of the van and finally saw headlights approach and slow by the bridge, then vanish. They stared through the night, straining their eyes to glimpse a shadow of the van as they listened for the dog. They saw nothing and heard nothing.

Then a light came on in the house.

"Up early," Will said. "Hope that dog doesn't start barking."

They watched and waited and listened to the wind. Each trying to catch sign of the van, a dash light or a profile. Moments passed and still they saw nothing and began to wonder. Had something happened? Maybe the engine stalled from a chance vapor lock? Then suddenly, not ten feet away, without any inkling or sound the van loomed up out of the night like an apparition from the deep.

"Like a goddamned genii," Lee announced as the boys gathered around the van in greeting. Not a one had sensed it coming down the lane. "That was slick, Frankie, real slick," he said, breathing easy. Frankie granted a faint smile—showed them once again how to thread the needle.

They formed a chain and quickly loaded the van, then gently latched the door.

"We'll need two vans tomorrow," Frankie said as Jack prepared to drive out.

"Yeah, we guessed as much. Gabe contacted a rental in Manhattan."

"Then he's back. Did he make the sale?"

"It's a done deal. Cash in hand."

"Good. Then you two meet us tomorrow morning down by the bridge. We'll cut straight through and load out at one. Got it?"

"One o'clock. Got it. We'll be there."

Jack took a slow breath and eased off the clutch. The van rolled into the night, all but silent, as if taken out by the tide. A minute or two later, safely beyond the bridge, the lights beamed on and the van headed east. The boys drifted back to camp to catch a few more hours sleep. All quiet at the nearby farm.

*Everything running smooth...*Jack thought to himself as he touched his cigarette to the coiled glow of the dashboard lighter. Merely routine, like driving a delivery van. Only problem was the van lacked a radio and the hours were rotten. He couldn't do any serious drinking, not and be awake and alert at two in the morning. Always a drawback to any job he supposed, smiling as he smoked his cigarette. And the boys were definitely on a harvest roll; the van could barely pull a hill at 45 mph. No hurry, an easy sixty miles and home free. At the next stop sign he got out and checked the headlights, taillights, and turn indicators. All working fine. Piece of cake. He jumped back in and turned east onto Highway 36.

A half hour later still heading east, a few miles past Bellville in the first glow of dawn, watching the day come alive, the land bloom in color, he glanced to the side mirror and saw a highway patrolman zoom up from behind like a demon in a bad dream. No lights, no siren, the cruiser simply latched to his bumper and hung there. Like a tailgating jerk. What could be the problem? Jack knew he wasn't speeding. And if a taillight had burned out, what would it matter, it being day? He kept glancing from the road to the mirror and the constant shift of focus back and forth with his one good eye was making him dizzy. He caught the van drifting left towards center.

"Easy, easy now..." he muttered, reining it back like an old horse. Felt himself getting rattled and knew he'd better watch it.

Apparently the trooper suspected something, but couldn't pull him over without probable cause. Then again the bags were piled past the back window. Maybe that was sufficient? All Jack knew for certain was that the interior reeked to high heaven with green hemp, and if pulled over what could he say when asked, as he surely would be, *What's in those bags?* He decided he'd just smile and say they were grass clippings. Yeah, he could say he used them as mulch in organic farming. "Just grass clippings, officer..." He practiced saying it in a casual way and it didn't sound at all convincing. Damn, he needed a cigarette bad and had a hard time holding the lighter steady in his shaky hand, and an even harder time plugging the lighter back in its hole. The shakes lessened somewhat as he smoked, though his left foot kept tapping the floorboard like a hopped-up jazz drummer working a hi-hat.

Suddenly the trooper whipped out and sped on past. *Great to see him go!*

Then just as suddenly he whipped back in and hung there less than a car-length away. *That can't be safe*, thought Jack. "Get the fuck outa here," he cursed under his breath, careful to maintain a smile, all but certain the trooper's laser eyes could read his lips even in reverse through those mirrored sunglasses.

"Go on dammit. Go catch a speeder. For sweet Jesus, get the fuck on..."

Whatever the trooper's game it was wearing on Jack's nerves. But Jack held steady at 50 mph and didn't slow. Bumper to bumper for another two miles. At last the trooper pulled away. Hit warp speed and left the van like it was standing still. When the cruiser disappeared over the far hill, Jack took the first turn south and followed country roads in a wary zigzag all the way back to the farm. So relieved once he got there, he had three cold beers for breakfast. Told the Kid to unload the van and had a couple more while he fried up some ham and eggs and hash browns. Food in his belly made him feel solid again. But after tomorrow Frankie could find someone else to drive. Because from then on Jack wanted off the road and in the patch!

Diana hated the long, lonely nights. If Lee were only gone during the day she wouldn't have minded. By day the old house was spacious and friendly and invited exploration. But at night it was dark, cold, and vast, haunted by a thousand shadows. The upstairs hallway seemed to stretch on forever, and the diamond-shaped window glowed in the moonlight like a red eye looking in. And the chill before Jesse's room never warmed. She'd stand in the chill and try to fathom its cause. She touched the plaster wall, the wooden floor. She looked to the window, the door, then to the servant stair directly behind her. Perhaps the stair acted as a natural flue to create the chill—so she reasoned and returned to bed in attempt to read herself to sleep.

But with the cats gone the mice had reclaimed their domain, defecating in every corner and racing up and down the hall in frenzy to nest and breed. Occasionally one would pause by her door and rail like a native at her intrusion. Sometimes she'd hurl a book at the upstart while the rodent danced aside to jeer in even greater defiance of her clumsy throw. More often she simply grew disheartened and closed her eyes. Maybe she didn't belong there. Maybe the house had been empty for so long that it only wished to harbor mice and shadows and the ghosts of those who'd first walked its floors.

Sunday morning as she sat on the front steps in the warm sun, watching Jesse ride his pedal tractor in the circle of the drive, she had a far different perspective. Looking to the many windows, the large porch, and the screen door to the kitchen, she felt at home. Wanted to live there forever. Dreamed of planting a garden and flowers in the spring. All the house needed to come alive was someone to fill it with life. It would take time and patience and maybe another child or two, once Lee settled down. She smiled, for she enjoyed being a mother even if it meant being an outlaw's wife. Though Lee was not really an outlaw, not to her thinking, he was simply a young man with a dream. And Diana wasn't one to issue an ultimatum: *It's either me or painting, either music or me.* She wouldn't do that to the man she loved. No, she merely hated the long nights he was away. And the worry.

Around noon she took Jesse into the kitchen and fixed him his favorite lunch of peanut butter, jelly, and toast. She urged him to drink all his milk, but he shook his head "Huh-uh." So she made a silly face and said, "Quick now, better drink or Mommy's face will get stuck like this." He giggled and slurped it down, didn't want his mommy to look like that. In the living room they sat together on the couch and she read from Mother Goose while he looked at the pictures and listened. Finally he leaned to her breast and fell asleep. She gently laid him to the couch, tucked his baby pillow under his arm and covered him with a blanket. She returned to the kitchen to wash the dishes.

While putting a dish in the pie cupboard, she heard someone softly knock.

An old lady stood on the porch, smiling as Diana opened the door. Her lavender dress reached nearly to her ankles and was adorned with tiny white flowers, a laced collar and cuffs. Her silver-white hair was rolled in a bun and she wore a lady's wide straw hat banded with a blue silk ribbon. White gloves covered her hands. Dressed so dainty and quaint, a holdover from the day when a lady dare not let the sun touch her skin. And still pretty. Her watery blue eyes full of nostalgia and question as she looked to Diana.

"I hate to intrude," she said in a frail yet pleasant voice. "I was passing by and we used to have such marvelous parties out here. I was wondering," she glanced aside then asked, "would you mind terribly if I came in and looked around a bit?"

"No, not at all. I'd be delighted." Diana showed her in, intrigued by the sweet little lady who carried the breath and aura of another time. So gracious as she entered and removed her gloves to slowly trace the woodwork and the walls. In passing through the living room, she observed Jesse asleep and said, "Isn't he precious..." Then she walked into the foyer, her low-heeled shoes barely sounding on the broad oak floor. She stopped before the grand staircase, laid her hand to the banister and gazed up its length.

"This brings back so many memories," she said, turning to Diana. She feasted her eyes on the floors, ceilings, and walls. The three adjacent rooms had sliding double doors of which two were open and one was closed. "They would place the band right here," she smiled, indicating the curved wall of the stairs. "Then they'd open up the doors and we'd dance through all the rooms." Her eyes misted at the memory and seemed to follow the couples dancing as she mused, "Such a long, long time ago..."

Jesse began to fuss in his sleep and Diana glanced to the couch.

"Oh, I'm so sorry," the old lady said. "I fear I've disturbed him."

"No, it's quite alright," Diana assured her. "His naps are fitful."

"Well, you should tend to him, my dear. I'll be going now," she said, smiling sweetly as she walked to the kitchen and added, "No, no...don't bother. I'll let myself out. And thank you for allowing me to look. You are most kind."

Diana acknowledged with a slight nod as the old lady left quietly out the door.

Kneeling by Jesse, Diana whispered, "There, there..." trying to coax him back to sleep. His hair was matted in sweat and she brushed it from his forehead; seeing that he was wrapped too warm, she pulled his blanket to his waist. His eyes rolled half open as he asked, "Is old woman here?"

"No, honey. Just a nice lady who wanted to see the house."

Jesse closed his eyes and muttered "...*old woman*..." Again he slept.

At those words Diana felt a sudden chill and rushed for the door. The car was already gone. She hadn't noticed one when she let the old lady in; but hadn't looked for one either. She stepped out on the porch and scanned the road both ways. She saw nothing. Of course it had been a minute or two. Again she thought of the old woman in Jesse's dreams, then had to smile at such a ridiculous notion. No, just a sweet little old lady. As real as day.

"I had the strangest dream," Lee said as he tossed the last of the stems into a gully where Will stood stomping them down. They'd stayed behind to police the area while the rest of the boys moved camp closer to the bridge. Will didn't want to leave anything too obvious in case the old farmer happened to check his field that day.

"When was that?" he asked, glancing up. "Last night?"

"Actually this morning, right before I woke. Maybe that's why it was so vivid."

"What was strange about it?" Will took a keen interest in dreams.

"You remember my cousin...killed in the car wreck a couple years ago?"

"Yeah. He spun off that hill west of Gilbert's Station."

"Right, hit a patch of ice. Anyhow, he was in my dream. We were both standing there in a place about like this, a wooded creek at twilight, night coming on. We didn't say much. We both knew he was dead and I was alive, and that put a gulf between us. Still, we acted familiar, casual even, as we approached. I asked him what he was doing there in the creek, though we both knew I was the intruder. He said, *I hunt the deer.* He always loved to hunt, ya know. Next thing we're both running at a tracking pace as if in hunt, down a winding path through the trees, under overhanging limbs all stark and bare like every leaf had fallen. We came to a small clearing and he stopped next to an old bedstead...one of those ornamental iron-frame jobs, all lopsided 'n bent, sinking into the ground, with a rusty set of springs and no mattress, just a mat of molded leaves. He pointed there and said, *This is where I lay*. Didn't say 'rest' or 'sleep,' just said, *This is where I lay*. Then a hound brayed off in the distance and he turned his gaze as if called, and said, *I've gotta go*. Then he disappeared, lost in the shadows, gone before I noticed. The strangest dream. Not like a dream at all. Like it was real."

"Some dreams are real," Will said. "And I'd bet you met 'im. Hard to make sense of, but I bet so. Like I met my Grandpa once," he slowly nodded. "Laid down and slept right by his grave. Good thing I had my sleeping bag along or I'd of froze to death from all the whiskey in me." He gave a quick laugh. "Yeah, it was the winter following my back surgery and I's feeling pretty low. Wanted to be close to Grandpa, I guess…

"It had snowed in the night and put a good thick blanket on everything. And the mound of me laid next to the mound of him, somewhat like I'd joined the dead. And I swear he came up from his grave and entered my dream. Sat there and talked to me like when I's a kid. I could never recall what he said and it doesn't matter, it was just good to hear his voice and feel him near. 'Course only one of us woke next morning. I stood and shook off the snow, looked to his grave and thanked him. Glad to be alive and no longer felt so damn sorry for myself. Funny thing, I haven't been back to his grave since. And in a way I'm grateful he's dead."

"How's that?"

"All the changes in the last twenty years, he just wouldn't understand. It would kill his faith in things and he never lost that. And I don't know if he could keep it anymore."

Keeping faith was a struggle they all shared.

"But those dreams are real," Will declared as he stomped the last stems. "I have no doubt. Like your cousin and my Grandpa, they reach out and touch us in our dreams to remind us they're still around and that there's a spirit in us. They probably tag us when we're awake too, but we're too busy to notice."

Will gazed to the trees a moment, listening to the wind as if searching for the link in things. A creekbank shaman, always keenly alert to danger and to meaning as well. He cut hemp with his grandpa's cornknife in part to maintain his attachment—the wooden handle stained by the sweat of both.

"Yeah, I do miss that old man," he said.

They soon headed on up the creek to join the others.

As the boys worked on through the day into the evening, it became increasingly difficult to find good plants. They either had to wander off in search or settle for meager cuttings close by. But they carried on, eager for every last pound they could get. In three days they'd harvested the length of a mile-long creek, and it was apparent they'd need an even bigger patch next time to keep cutting to the end. An hour past sundown a quarter moon edged above the trees to aid their search for worthy plants. The first decent moon they'd had in two weeks.

"Got another patch in mind?" Will asked more out of curiosity than concern.

"No, but I'm thinking on it," Frankie said. "Wednesday, while you guys key the hemp, I'll head out west and take Lee along to help run the creeks. We'll scare up something."

"Be nice to hit the big Burr Oak patch," Lee was still angling for his home place.

"Sure it would," Frankie allowed, at once sympathetic and dismissive. "But that's not an option. Val's got it. So we'll have to find another. You'll see, we'll find one just as good."

Frankie, confident as ever. And that was certainly the hope, because with a patch like Burr Oak you could lay into it and never stop. Here the hemp grew intermittent in a series of scattered plots. There it grew full and broad through the entire creek bottom. A river of hemp compared to a piddling stream.

But they left the matter lay without further speculation and continued working, mostly silent, their arms weighed by fatigue, going through the motions, slogging at the task, adding to the pile. So weary they let their minds drift, unfocused from scant food and little sleep and the strain of searching through the darkness as the wind bent limbs and leaves, forming unexpected phantasms where moon shadows merged with shades of ancestors and prior forms more primitive and perhaps less friendly, till at times their own flesh seemed to shift shape and meaning. Even a mind honed on rigorous thought grew susceptible and began to waver, cut off from the familiar comfort of lights and buildings and placed in a distant wood in the company of the night, the wind, the moon and stars, soon felt logic and reason weaken like a crude wall crumbling to the effects of nature as old fears and superstitions wormed in and took root.

Bruce shed his philosopher's skin and loosed his mammalian senses. He saw his pile of hemp fast disappear and knew he'd have to search for more. He felt his stomach knot in dread. Across the night came a long, harsh shriek—something between a cat's cry and a colt's whinny.

"What the hell was that?" he asked, peering into the dark.

"Probably a screech owl," Lee said.

"Oh no"—Bruce shook his head with a nervous laugh. "I know what an owl sounds like. That's no owl."

"Maybe not," Lee conceded. His first offer scorned, he upped the ante. "It could be a spirit bird. Though they're pretty rare."

"A spirit bird?" Bruce flinched as he heard the shriek again.

"Yeah, I think so..." Lee nodded in mock earnest, then slowly smiled. "Some lost soul fluttering limb to limb."

"Jesus, Lee. Knock it off."

"Why? You spooked by a little spirit bird?" Lee asked, having fun with his old friend who always insisted on firm meaning as if each phenomenon could be laid bare and you could actually choose your fears and dreams.

"No, I'm not spooked," Bruce answered indigent. "I just want to know what the fuck that is."

"Could be a cougar," Will said, joining in the fun.

"Holy shit, surely not a cougar."

"Oh yeah, they're around," Will vowed. "Don't think they aren't. And they'll mimic a woman's scream or any number of cries to flush their prey."

Will sounded convincing, having witnessed the very thing, and Bruce, though doubtful, was far from certain. He gripped his machete and studied the night, his breath coming short and quick. Ry noticed and took mercy, knowing what a night in the jungle could do to the mind and how the terror of a lone insect could rattle your nerves.

"Wouldn't let it worry me, Bruce," he said with his usual grin. "There hasn't been anyone dragged off and eaten in the wilds of Kansas in over a hundred years."

"You're forgetting that old farmer south of Jamestown," Frankie noted.

"Christ, yes," Ry laughed. "That's right, the same summer we got back from Nam. His danged hogs ate 'im."

"Yeah, they figured he had a heart attack or stroke. All they found were his overboots and belt buckle. Hogs ate him hide, fur 'n all."

"No, Frankie, I think they found a bone or two."

"Believe you're right, Wolfer. I stand corrected. They did find part of his pelvis."

"That's one helluva fate." Ry was still laughing. "Eaten by his own hogs."

"Sounds like a lost chapter out of Animal Farm," Dixie said.

"Well, he definitely went to hog heaven, that's for sure!"

"I just hope that poor old bastard was dead before the hogs started in."

"Speaking of hogs. I could use me a porkchop about now."

"Shit yes. A whole platter full..."

The boys traded quips while Bruce marched off determined to show he wasn't buffaloed by the night. Maybe he wouldn't go all that far or find the best plants, but he would cut an armful. Besides, he held a rational advantage in face of any threat: a long knife. And he fully intended to slash the heart-throat-spine of any cougar, hog, or other beast that charged his way. Instinct armed with reason. A few minutes later he noticed Rus off to the west, cutting by the creek, and Lee to the east. His flanks protected, he forged ahead and began selecting his plants with greater care. Focusing on his task helped calm his nerves and he soon gathered a fair bundle, pleasantly surprised by his effort, though still relieved to make his way back to the others.

He'd no more than dropped his load when Rus came running up from the creek.

"Everyone here?" Rus asked, breathing hard, his voice urgent.

"Lee's still out," Bruce said.

"LEE! *LEE-E-E!*" Rus called. Hearing a "Yo!" in answer, he yelled, "*Get in here ASAP!*" No old-timer drawl, each word crisp and clear.

"What the hell's up?" Will asked, like everyone curious of the sudden alarm. But Rus didn't answer, still doing a head count with his eyes, making certain everyone was there as Lee came sprinting in, machete in hand, ready to grab his running pack and hightail it. "What's up?" he asked in echo of Will.

"I just saw a pack of wild dogs," Rus explained. "Big mean looking cusses down by the creek. They catch a man off alone no telling what they'll do."

What few people realized was that wild dogs killed more livestock than coyotes. And once wild, dogs proved extremely vicious, having no fear of man. The boys cast their eyes about— the shadows no longer tricked the mind with play and fancy, but cloaked a real and cunning danger.

"Where were they headed?"

"They were following the creek on around the bend. Could be coming back."

"Let's take a look," Frankie said.

Rus and Lee followed, threading a path through the spindly hemp till they stood on the bank above the creek. The moon lit the rippled water like a sheen of dimes as the dogs trotted up the shallow creek bed. In the lead a large white shepherd paused and pricked his ears, gazing up at the men, his narrow eyes glinting like bright copper in the moonlight. He took their measure, assessed no threat and moved on followed by a burly hound with a torn ear. The rest were mostly mongrels of collie mix, heads lowered and shoulders hunched like rude marauders in a line of march, numbering eight in all and all surly and indifferent to man. Hardly a one looked their way except for a tall wirehaired beast that brought up the rear and appeared crossbred with a coyote from its sharp nose and mangy tail. It stopped and gave them a hard look to let them know it was no friend of man, then joined the others trotting on under the bridge.

"You can bet they're up to no good."

"Like I say, Rus. It's our own kind we've gotta fear."

The boys loaded out at one o'clock. Packed all the hemp in Jack's van and packed themselves into the rental driven by Gabe. Will, the last one in, latched the door, hit the side panel and said, "Let's roll"—relieved like the rest to be free of the patch and back on the road, headed for a warm bath, a hot meal, and a long sleep. But Will most of all, he slapped his knee in a rush of excitement and shouted, "Hot damn, boys! This is great. Counting tonight, we've taken over a hundred bags out of that patch. You know that, Ry? Lee? By my guess that's close to eighteen hundred pounds dry. At thirty bucks a pound that's... Shit, that's $54,000! Right Gabe? You get that sold we've each got at least five to six grand coming. What do ya say to that, boys? Fuck'n A, not bad for three days work, eh? Not bad at all..." Will was in a fever, high at the prospect, infectious, kept them talking and laughing all the way back to his place.

Meanwhile Frankie rode shotgun with Jack. And Jack was not about to count his chickens before they hatched. His immediate concern was how to make it back to the farm without being pulled over.

"I dunno," he said, approaching the highway. "I don't like taking 36 again."

"Why is that?"

"A damn trooper tailed me yesterday for a good ten miles. Laid in back then pulled in front. I mean *close!* Like he was playing bumper cars."

"Sounds like he was trying to rattle ya, alright. Well, if you want, we can take the county road south to Number 9...ride it east to 16 then cut down to 24. That is if you don't mind crossing Sky County and chance running into Sheriff Hoss Wayne."

Jack shot his good eye to Frankie and said, "Long as it keeps me off 36, I don't mind. And I swear...after this run I don't wanna drive for a while. I'm ready to work in the patch."

"Whatever you say, Jacko. No problem. I'll drive the next round."

Frankie drew a hand over his eyes and yawned, too tired to worry about a trooper or sheriff or anything but sleep. Already nodding off as he laid his head back.

"Where do I turn east?" Jack asked a few minutes later.

Frankie jerked awake and blinked to the road like he was on an alien planet.

"About five miles below 36," he said in a vague monotone. "You'll see a sign...if you get lost just wake me..." A moment later his head rolled to the side and bobbed to the rhythm of the road.

Jack crossed 36 and cruised on south. Felt like he'd put the devil behind him as he lit a cigarette and smiled, settling in for a long quiet ride. The flat-nosed van perched the driver directly above the bumper so it seemed you were sitting on the bow of a speedboat and could reach down and touch the pavement passing underneath. The illusion was enhanced by the headlights locked on low beam to assure a low profile through the night. Jack checked the odometer—they were now four and a half miles below 36. He kept his eye peeled on the road ahead, trying to discern the telltale sign.

On low beam the lights barely reached a hundred feet, and it was a good thing he was intent on the road or he wouldn't have noticed the wide-set eyes of the shaggy form looming his way. His first thought was a deer. But it was much too big and coming fast. He slammed on the brakes, throwing Frankie up against the dash as the van skidded to a halt, bumper to eyeball with—"*A goddamned buffalo!*" Frankie declared.

"Hey man...I'm sorry." Jack sat raising his hands off the wheel, his heart pounding so fast he couldn't grip. "But that, that buffalo, he was...man, I had to brake hard."

"It's okay, Jack. Just bumped my head a little. No harm done," Frankie laughing now; "But *shit the bed!* Look at the *size* of that sucker! If you hadn't stopped, he'd have taken us both out."

The big spike bull sniffed the radiator then raised his head in full profile to the windshield, blanking out all else as he turned a lone black eye on the occupants in a manner that mirrored Jack's own. Then he gave a perfunctory snort and sauntered off into the ditch.

"I mean I never..." Jack was still agitated. "A buffalo? Where the devil did he come from?"

"Over there," Frankie said. "That's Colonel Holtz's big

pasture to your left. He's got another hundred head in there plus longhorns. Once we turn onto Number 9 his place is only a quarter mile or so east. We better head on up 'n let 'im know his damn buffalo is out."

"Think we should? I mean…we're hauling a lot of hemp."

"Hell Jack, he's an old crook himself. He won't give a shit. Besides, if someone comes along and hits that buffalo, they're liable to wind up dead. You saw the size of him. He'd wreck a train."

Frankie for all his cuss and swagger often acted the good Samaritan—and at the oddest times. Jack gripped the wheel and drove on. In a short while the van crept up the drive and stopped in front of the Colonel's large stone house.

"That's some place."

"Yeah, he's top dog around here. I'll only be a minute."

Frankie got out, walked up to the door and knocked. Waited a few seconds and knocked again, only louder. This time lights flicked on and a voice growled from within, "Hold your horses! Christ, I'm comin'.…" The door swung wide and CC stood in his boxer shorts and tee shirt, pistol in hand, asking, "What the fuck you want?"

"Careful you don't blow your foot off with that thing," Frankie said.

"Why hell! It's Justin's boy. Frankie Sage." CC eased the hammer down and chuckled. "Shit, don't mind this thing. I don't answer the door after dark without my pistola. But I swear, boy, you look plumb rough. What you been up to?"

"Nothing much. Been helping a friend clear some brush out west of here."

"You don't say…"

"Yeah, we were taking the cutoff from 36 down to Cibola and damn near had a head-on with one of your buffalo. A big bull."

"Oh shit. That'ud be Brutus. That cagey ol' bastard. Tell you, he'll test a fence till he bulls on through. Never goes far, but I better git the boys and round 'im up. Where'd you see 'im last?"

"About a hundred yards north on the county road."

"Uh-huh…southwest gate," CC allowed. "Say now, I'm obliged to you, Frankie."

"Don't mention it, Colonel. Well, I better be going—"

"Whoa now, hold up a minute. Don't be running off. A man does the Colonel a favor, by God, I show my thanks." CC disappeared and soon returned, handing Frankie a fifth of Kentucky Bourbon. "That there's some of the finest sippin' whiskey you'll ever put your lips to. But I reckon the son of Justin Sage would know as much," CC chuckled. "Yessir, me 'n your old man tipped a few in our time."

Frankie accepted the bottle with a slight nod and even slighter smile.

He didn't like whiskey and he didn't need reminded of what had killed his father and lost their farm. He'd watched his dad go through a hundred cases of the stuff, seen him in every stage of drunk—hand on the bottle, reeling with laughter, full of bluster and bull, then turn mean, hard, and vulgar, stumble to the floor, wake in his own vomit then crawl to the bathroom to slug another drink and wretch again, or worse, slur a few weak words in sorry attempt to make amends, at last a walking skeleton, dead at age 40. All the same Frankie wouldn't shun the offer.

He gripped the bottle and said, "Sure, Colonel. Good luck with that bull."

Then he turned away and walked to the van.

CC stood at the door and eyed him like a shrewd coach eying a prospect. He'd known Frankie since his birth. Watched him grow and knew something of his turmoil: how Justin had once tried to kill the boy and later on the boy had nearly killed him. The "why" was between them, father and son, but the tale was generally known. CC admired Frankie's fight. Knew he was tough and smart. And he also had a good hunch what Frankie and the boys were up to. *Yessir, might need to talk business...*

Frankie climbed in and handed the bottle to Jack.

"There you go," he said. "A little treat for ya, Jack. It's even got your name on it. Just don't uncork it till we hit the farm..."

Jack held it to his eye and read the label. Sure enough, *Jack Daniels*. Good stuff. He stashed the bottle under his seat, backed the van around and rolled down the drive. Frankie folded his arms across his chest and closed his eyes—found his father's ghost even as he found his sleep.

Jack only glanced down to light an occasional cigarette, otherwise he kept his eye on the road. And it wasn't a waiting trooper or sheriff he watched for, it was the wide-spaced eyes and looming shape of another buffalo, one of thousands he sensed in thunder and rush like a ghost herd running just beyond the headlights.

Far below the hanging moon the van crept steadily through the night, down blacktop highways past farms and sleepy towns, finally crossing the lower sector of Sky County to reach the farm by 3 a.m.

The last thing on Sheriff Wayne's mind was a vanload of hemp. But the lone trooper on highway 36 wasn't the only one playing a hunch, crowding a suspect. Up early as he had been most every day of his life since joining the Corps, Hoss showered and dressed and was out the door by six. He took a light breakfast at the Downtowner then drove straight to the Catholic Church. Parked his Bronco directly across from the entrance a few minutes before early Mass, sat there and stared as parishioners walked up the front steps and were greeted by Father Michael. Now Monday—he'd followed the same routine four days running. People started to notice and glanced back in wonder. Hoss met their gaze and said nothing. He could not serve warrant, but he could damn well serve notice, and he meant to let the priest know that he knew and that he would be there again each morning. Like a bad conscience.

Hoss set his eyes and let the anger boil up in his face till the deep lines of his cheekbones and jaw darkened like scars. He knew he looked mean and used it to full effect—pitting the will of a soldier against the will of a priest. And only after they all had entered and the door had closed did he drive on.

When asked by one parishioner or another why the Sheriff was parked there each morning, staring at them, Father Michael would simply say, "Perhaps he seeks an answer and hopes to find it in the Church. Who knows? One day he may enter and stand among us." Then he'd smile faintly as the questioner, usually quite old, would quietly nod, recalling their own long struggle with faith and how it came easily once the flesh began to fail. Of course Father Michael knew his subtle role, the part he played, as well as his guilt. But he knew as well what no one, including Sheriff Wayne, even suspected.

He was his brother's keeper.

XIII. SCOUTING

The green van spewed out road dust like a jet trail dispersing in the wind as it rounded one section then another, following the erratic course of a high plains creek. Viewed from a distance the van might as well have been pulling a plow for what little progress it appeared to make. Occasionally it would stop and the rider would jump out and run into the creek while the van cruised on and returned in ten to fifteen minutes to fetch the rider, then off again. The hunt precise, methodical, and so far in vain.

This was the fourth creek Frankie and Lee had searched that day, now at the far edge of Smith County facing nothing but dry gulches west to the Rockies, and they still hadn't found a likely patch. The only one of promise lay in the open directly downslope of a large hog operation with no safe line of approach. A nice patch of tall hemp so lush and green you'd think it was irrigated, and was in part, catching the overflow from the hog lots rich in nutrients. So tempting a prospect that they drove past several times trying to figure a way to work it without being seen, but they finally gave up.

"Stinks too damn much anyway," Frankie said in disgust, though worse than the smell was the thought of leaving such a prime field untouched. Other than that they'd spied nothing but weedy growth along fence lines and ditches.

Frankie had picked Lee up before dawn and they reached the heart of Hill County by sunrise. The mist still lay in the low draws and swales. The first creek Lee entered, three doe stood poised at the tree line like sleek ballerinas. They bolted at his approach, and he read in their presence a favorable sign of what lay ahead. Yet he found nothing but dew-laden grass, bird song, and the bloom of clover in the air. A fit harvest for a poet's pen, but not for a machete.

By noon the birds were silent and a hot wind blew from the west. The grass appeared so dry and dormant you'd think it hadn't tasted moisture in a year. Along the roadside a rotted deer carcass lay half buried in the dust like crumpled cardboard, cast off and broken, without hope of life or movement. And out across the fields whirled scores of dust devils like relic spirits haunting the land—as if in every gust there spun the ghost of another drought-blown dirt farmer replaying his fate, still trying to cleave a furrow and cast his seed.

Lee leaned his head to the open window, tasted the hot dust and wind as the land swept by. His eye caught a cowpath meandering through a pasture to a wooded creek and in his mind he was a child again running barefoot through the dust.

Watch it for them sandburs!—the voice calls. Texas sandburs littered the ground like miniature longhorn skulls, long and sharp as tacks. *They'll jab ya to the bone!*

He never checks his stride, veers away and skips free of the sticker patch, on past the buffalo burrs, his feet light and nimble as his shadow. So he remembers that day as he ran, his father's voice calling after. And he longs to answer, *Watch it for that bullet!*

Or so he preferred to think, and told others, that his father died from the self-inflicted gunshot one fine spring morning. But no, he'd wrapped his legs in a log chain and jumped in the river. A horrid thought, drowning in that deep dark current. Lee was six at the time and had sifted it through his memory till he could taste the very water. Much preferred thought of a bullet—hot lead piercing the flesh, like in a Western. For it was the West after all, the very rim of the high plains. Hot, dry, and merciless, with rude omens in the air howling after every shadow under the sun.

Watch it for what lies ahead!

"Yeah, *I know*..." Lee mumbled in distant thought.

"What's that you say?" Frankie asked, jolted from his own silence.

"I said I been looking and haven't seen a thing." Lee pulled back to the present and added, "Maybe that buffalo was trying to tell you something the other night."

"Yeah, like what?" Frankie didn't care for portents, positive or otherwise.

"That there's too many hunters and not enough buffalo. It's like a hundred years ago. We're at the last of the hunt and the great herds are all gone."

"Fuck the buffalo," Frankie scoffed. "If I'd lived back then, I'd of been a scalp hunter."

"That's just hot air," Lee said, looking to his friend. "I don't believe that for a minute. Now you might've been a rustler. But not a scalp hunter."

"Look, Lee. Indians raped, killed, burnt, and raided whenever it struck their fancy. I wouldn't have shed a tear or hesitated one instant to hang their hides up to dry."

"Granted, a number of them did. And I wouldn't begrudge any man defending himself against marauders or hunting them down. If they scalped mine, I'd have scalped theirs. But that's a far cry from setting out to be a scalp hunter."

"So...do you really think I'd rustle from your brother Garret or anyone like him?"

"No, no more than I think you'd have been a scalp hunter. But back then you might've been a rustler. And back then I might've helped you."

Frankie smiled and shook his head, silent a moment as he turned onto a paved road and headed north to scout the environs of the Republican River Valley.

"Okay Lee," he said. "You want to find justice in every equation, keep your soul clean. Go ahead and be the last of the buff hunters. But I'll be the last of the realists."

Though Frankie could wax romantic at times, he more often broke the spell with a slap of words to wake his listener to the hard facts, because to know the world and your part in it you'd best not pretend. He heard nothing in the wind. No word, no warning. And would heed no voice but his own. And when he recalled his father, he seldom did so fondly. Remembered being shoved outside the trailer while his old man bedded a tavern whore one night on a run through the Dakotas, harvesting wheat. Frankie turned fourteen that summer and listening to their grunt and wallow did not warm his heart. He soon grew more insolent and took his beatings till he could beat back. Battling in a rage of love and hate. Rarely a day passed that his father didn't drink himself drunk. Eventually the bottle finished him. And there's nothing romantic about death by the bottle. Slow, wretched, it numbs and warps all feeling and any feelings for—leaves a man empty and broken like a bottle shattered in a ditch. And that's how they found him, froze to death in his truck along a lonely stretch of road in eastern Colorado. He said his last goodbye and drove into the sunset.

You could find romance even there if you were fool enough.

But the heart is tough and tenacious and endures like a sandbur in a drought. And even a sandbur flowers and only wounds when stepped on. While Frankie seldom spoke of his father, he'd kept his old coffee thermos and carried it along in the seat beside him. A big metal thermos, dented and chipped, fixed with a handle Frankie had fashioned out of copper tubing. He kept that much attachment at least and even told Lee in a quieter moment once that it had been his father's. And like his father he took his coffee black and sweetened with heaping spoons of sugar. Though it was his mother who always told him, "You catch more flies with sugar than with vinegar." Frankie was a curious mix of both the sugar and the vinegar. He could play the Good Samaritan, the bold Captain, and he could play the devil. Liked to keep it real. Attentive to the deep glue in things, all the spidery threads connecting the web.

"They were both cowards, you know. My old man and yours. Couldn't hack it."

Lee had to wonder where that came from, the sudden belligerence towards their fathers. More of the realist, he supposed. They spoke of their fathers from time to time, but never in those terms. Lee wouldn't let it pass.

"Easy for you to say, you never walked in their shoes."

"No, but I've walked in my own aplenty. And I think they were cowards."

"I don't buy that, Frankie. They weren't cowards. My dad was tough. Tougher than most. And I've heard the same about yours. So it wasn't that they were cowards. Maybe they took too many hits early on and didn't care for how things turned out. Life didn't hold any more promise. Lost its shine."

"Like I said, they were cowards."

"Well speak for yourself. Mine had busted every finger on both hands from fighting anyone who spoke against him or his family. I think a man only has so much fight in 'im then he's lost. We haven't used up ours yet, that's all. We don't each have five kids and no good choice left us."

"You always have a choice, Lee."

"Not a good one. Not one that offers any real freedom and lets you live the way you're meant. Most men live to a ripe old age because they accept whatever rut they're born to or fall in. Fighters die young. Damn near every time. That's what I think."

"You may have a point there..." Frankie relented somewhat. "But not by much. It's your fatal flaw, Lee. You always look for the poetry in things."

"Well, there is poetry in things."

"Right. Noted, footnoted, then tossed to the trash heap, whether leather bound or scrawled on the page. All those fine sentiments and golden thoughts at last gnawed on and nested in by mice. Refuse for rats. There, that's poetry for ya!" The sharp slap, the spite of the iconoclast—that was Frankie for ya. "Give me metal, something I can forge and use. Something real I can trust."

Lee couldn't help but note the poetry in those words, how the slap and spite drove its point like a hammer driving a nail.

"Something you forget, Frankie. Man is not molten metal. Each heart has its own reasons. We may share a like moment, a similar experience, but we're not all stamped by the same die. Sure, there are cowards who kill themselves, and there are drunks who are pure fools. But there are good tough men that end that way too. Some part of them fated, formed like cast iron. And hammered on, it don't bend, it breaks."

"There! That's one thing certain, *they broke!* Your old man and mine. I still say they had a choice and you don't wait till you hold a losing hand to make it. You choose as you enter the game and make your play."

"Sure. They had their choices. And we may wonder about the choices we make before we're through." Lee was already wondering if his main choice in life had already been made or still lay ahead. "Our fathers were born in a different time, Frankie. Dealt different cards and didn't have half the options we do. We can never know their story. Only guess."

"Maybe so..."

Frankie knew his father's story like a tree he'd climbed on and fallen from. Knew the trunk, upper branches, and exposed roots—anything deeper had long rotted so there was no use in digging. Whereas Lee knew only parts of Justin's story, mere fragments, like limbs scattered in a storm. He'd seen him once in the late fifties sitting up in the cab of a big wheat truck, looking distant and haunted, like Lee recalled his own father, as if each was shadowed by something they dare not mention. And he remembered the time several years later when Justin, in a drunken rage, had taken out after Frankie with a gun. The summer of '62. Lee's older sister Janice, home from her first year at college, worked for Frankie's aunt and uncle that summer, cooking and cleaning house. But that day she was saddled with the job of looking after Frankie's younger brothers and sisters while the rest of the family rushed out in search of Justin, hoping to head him off. They left Janice armed with a pistol, in charge of six kids, and told her if Justin showed up at the door to shoot him. Pretty rough assignment for a babysitter at seventy-five cents an hour, but a sure motivator to return a girl to college. Luckily, the crisis passed with no one harmed. Once again they sent Justin off to a sanatorium to dry out, and once out he returned forthwith to drinking. Made his choice and stuck to it.

Lee also knew the part Will had told him. The same part Will had told Frankie to remind him why his father drank. Will had heard the story off a man who'd known Justin and Reba all their lives, part of common lore shared in confidence over a beer. It was in the early years of their marriage when Frankie was still a baby, and whether Justin had been out drinking or working late in the field was never made clear, not part of the story, in any case he came home one night and caught Reba with another man parked near their farm. Justin ran the man off at gunpoint and chased Reba back to the house. When he reached the door, she held a gun of her own—a 12-gauge shotgun aimed at his chest. She told him in no uncertain terms that she would do what she pleased with who she pleased, and if he ever tried to stop her again, she'd kill him.

As with any standoff there were partisans to both sides. And whatever the truth of the story, on two points there was no dispute: Justin drank hard and Reba played hard. She was out dancing most nights and engaged in more affairs than a Hollywood starlet, beautiful and headstrong, made her own choices. The question was like the chicken and the egg, which came first: His drinking or her messing around? It flicked on and off like a neon above a dark empty street. Again, the why was between them and carried to their graves. Only the tale was known.

Lee had to wonder what he would do if he came home and found Diana with her legs spread to another man. It would tear him apart. And out of love and rage he'd want to tear her apart. But what would he do? What kind of choice could you make once you had a child, a son? Could you abandon him and walk away? Deny what you still loved? Or would you damn it all and turn to drink and try to drown the rage within?

Justin too had been a son, the son of Julius Sage. Julius had died shortly after Frankie's fourth birthday, and while Frankie barely knew him, he'd always admired his grandfather. Saw him as part man, part myth, much like Lee viewed his own father lost in the early years when a child's innocence and fancy colors the world in shining knights and dragons with little shading in between.

So the dead often loom larger than life.

But many people admired Julius. He was the grandson of immigrant pioneers, a veteran of WWI, well-liked and tough, chiseled out of the old rock. Even during the 30s when many were losing land, Julius managed to buy more. Not by crooked dealing but by sheer will and constant labor, a stubborn fortitude bequeathed by his German forbears. Stories abounded of his hard-bitten frugality. How he worked from dawn to dusk

seven days a week and wrestled rocks out of his fields by hand.
How in winter he wrapped his feet in gunny sacks and walked
five miles to town to sell butter denied his own family. They ate
their bread plain. On return trips he shouldered deadfall three
miles back from the river to fuel their stove. And one fabled day
in the mid-30s when most were selling out or barely holding on,
Julius walked into the land office and purchased another 160
acres, paid for in cash, every last red cent.

You had to admire that kind of pluck and determination. At
the same time you had to wonder about the son of such a man
and its effect on him. Maybe the son didn't want more land.
Maybe he just wanted to butter his bread and grew up craving
all the butter denied him. When Julius died, Justin buttered his
bread both sides of each slice and did so in like manner with
everything he touched—ate fresh salmon, prime rib, kicked in
the door of frugality and held a banquet, a feast, kept spreading
butter till the whole loaf and land was gone.

Frankie wanted land. And he wanted butter too. One thing
he had to grant his father, the man had a prodigious appetite. No
slouch there—improvident, prodigal. Where most men found
satiation and backed off, Justin kept right on churning, roaring
through the night, feeding his fire till it burnt to ash. At times
Frankie even boasted on his father's gargantuan appetite, his
month-long binges, his inordinate ability to lay siege to his own
soul. But his admiration of his grandfather remained absolute,
untainted by irony. Like his love for his mother. He knew her
faults, her sharp tongue, her unbridled desire, but he loved her
no less.

"Here's some poetry for ya," he said, glancing to Lee.
"I dreamt of my mother one night, several months ago. She
appeared before me as clear as day. Then she turned into a long-
stemmed red rose. She loved roses, you know."

Full of surprises today, thought Lee as he listened.

"Yeah, that sort of thing's hard to figure. I had a similar
dream last week, there in the patch. Saw my dead cousin. It was
like he came to visit."

"That's it," Frankie said. "A visit. Like she came to see me.
Looked directly into my mind and formed a red rose. And I

could smell the rose when I woke up..." Frankie reflected on that strange fact, then asked, "You ever see your dad in a dream?"

"No, not even once," Lee answered. "The odd thing is I sometimes sense him near. Mostly when I'm alone at night or on a vague, windy day. And I hear his voice. Not like us talking. But voiced in my mind. And it's not something I imagine because it always catches me unaware."

"What does he say?"

"Oh, just little things like, *Be careful...*"

"That's sound advice."

Talk of his mother had softened Frankie's edge and calmed the cynic. But he still preferred the tangible, something solid underfoot. Though he'd dreamed of his mother, her form and essence emergent from a red rose, weren't dreams simply wishful notions as guessed by Freud? Either bunk or anxious echoes of daily doings? Yet that dream was so vivid, so mystically real that he had to doubt his own doubt in wonder of its meaning, and of her, of her flesh and spirit present in him. What did such dreams or visits signify? Some truth, or nothing? No one could say. The mystery was absolute and left no path to follow or explore.

And how could he not doubt, raised as he was? People were ruled by their need, deep selfish needs; no matter what they claimed of virtue, they would slither like snakes to taste satisfaction. All the grand excuses and false scaffolding disguised the fact that social order and civilization hung by the merest thread. Vietnam had taught him that. Clerking body bags with a sullen old sergeant who pointed down and said, "Take a good look, boy. Them's the true believers. Look where it got 'em..." When the shit hit the fan, you hit the ground, and those not as lucky landed in body bags. And no commander's glib talk about grabbing rifles and charging up the Ho Chi Minh Trail to take Hanoi would wake a single one. The luckless dead were zipped away to lasting silence, their cry for another chance at life fallen deaf to every ear. Those were the dead Frankie hated to see visit his dreams. And when they did, calling out to him, he woke more determined than ever. Because he wanted land, land in Kansas, the land of his father and grandfather. In land he saw warrant against mortal loss. Permanence. Even as the flesh turned to dust it endured in the land. And the little plot in Clay County was only a beginning. He wanted land and would take considerable risk to get it. Working the one angle he knew.

"I'll tell you someone who's tough," Frankie said, downshifting on a long grade, "that's the old Colonel. CC Holtz. There's one tough sonuvabitch. Started out with nothing and clawed his way up. Now he owns a big chunk of land and a fair share of everything else worth a damn around here. No question he's a crook. Crooked as a dog's hind leg. But it's not that simple. Look at his buffalo. He doesn't make a dime off them. And he's helped a thousand people. They'll never nail 'im. He's devious, smart, and tough."

"Yeah, he's quite the operator," Lee allowed, a bit shy of an endorsement. "No arguing that. I saw him at the sale barn last week. I didn't think he knew my name. But he knew I's living on the Tannis place and asked if I was gonna buy it. Even asked about my guitar playing. Makes you wonder what else he knows."

"That shrewd old bastard knows plenty," Frankie said. "The other night when we stopped by to tell him his buffalo was on the loose, he could smell what we'd been up to. That old dog's got a nose on 'im. And one helluva cannon!" Frankie laughed and Lee knew by his laugh they weren't going to be talking poetry for a while.

"Did I ever tell you about the time CC fucked this gal at the sale barn? Smack dab in the middle of the arena?"

"No, I guess not." Lee had heard a version of the story from an old carpenter while still in high school, but never one from Frankie.

"Stumpy was there and saw the whole thing," Frankie began. "Stump was this little peg-leg drunk that worked for Dad. Hell, you had to be a drunk to work for Dad. He'd bail them out, they'd bail him out. Anyway, late one night, years ago, all the bars had closed and CC and a bunch of local hellions still wanted to party. So they all headed down to the sale barn. CC had a young gal along he claimed he was fucking. Someone said they doubted as much. CC stood and slapped down a hundred-dollar bill 'n said, 'By God, I'll prove it! Fuck 'er right here in front of y'all! Right out in the arena, by God!' Then said, 'C'mon!' Grabbed the gal and headed in. Everyone followed and gathered at the railing in big hoot n' holler, making bets on whether he'd actually do it.

"Stump said he thought it was all a joke. But CC threw down a couple of horse blankets there on the dirt and told the gal to strip off her clothes and lay down. CC dropped his drawers and stroked his cannon while she posed doggie style and wiggled every which way, but he couldn't get it up. By then everyone had a fistful of money in the air, shouting, laughing, egging him on. According to Stump, CC finally jerked the gal by the hair, held it to her mouth 'n said, 'Suck it, bitch! Suck it like a bottle calf!' At those words the whole place hushed, the gal went to work and in short order she had his big cannon standing straight out, ready to fire. Then CC laid into her like a raging bull. Stump said it was ugliest fucking he ever saw. Worse than anything in a barnyard."

Frankie took a measured breath and added, "That's CC in a nutshell. One way or another he'll get what he's after. Use charm, money, or brute force."

Nothing delicate in the story or its telling, all hard facts as vivid and vulgar as its protagonist. The version Lee had heard was not nearly so graphic and fudged on many details. This one spoke more of violence than of sex. Of a cruel hunger latent in all who watched or listened, including himself.

"CC might be tough," Lee answered. "But he's also downright mean."

"Yeah, maybe. Maybe so…"

Frankie too was sobered by the telling. Disturbed by something depicted in the scene. And something else he hadn't counted on, his own scruples perhaps.

They ended their talk and resumed their search for hemp.

The van soon crested the long hill, granting a broad view of the valley beyond. The sun glistened off the sandbars and shallow waters of the Republican River as it laced here and there like a fine blue ribbon edged in mother-of-pearl. The valley was lush, irrigated, and planted mostly to corn—a rich

farming region and former haunt of the Pawnee who had raised
corn there long before the settlers came. The Indians dwelled
in villages along the river and hunted the buffalo further west.
A tall fierce people feared by neighboring tribes, the Pawnee
were in a sense still evident in the bright tassels and feathering
silk of the satin green corn that stood in marked contrast to the
dusty hue of the surrounding hills, as if their spirit and vitality
enriched the very soil.

Frankie and Lee focused on the hemp that lined the fields
and ditches, as tall and prime as the corn. Problem was it didn't
grow in any one place, but all strung out, to harvest it they'd
need a truck and a crew working either side of the road, tossing
in the plants to haul off and later strip. This was neither wise
nor practicable. The only patch they found grew around an old
windmill and didn't hold enough hemp for two men, let alone
eight they were now planning on with Pete wanting to cut.

"Let's try down by the river," Frankie said.

"Yeah, might be something back in there..."

They drove in through several fields and found nothing
but Indian grass, willow shrubs, and plum thickets scattered
under tall cottonwoods that shaded the banks. Great spots to
camp and fish, but nothing to harvest. Further on, winding
up an irrigation lane, they spotted a truck antenna beyond the
tassels, coming their way like the lance of a mounted sentry.
Frankie threw the van in reverse and sped back onto the road.
They didn't want to be caught trespassing by an irate farmer
especially when every side trip had proved a dead end in a
running maze.

They followed the road as it curved south out of the valley
and back up into the hills. Lee cast his eyes over the plains. He
noted clouds grouping in the west—below the high cirrus that
often laced the sky appeared a broad pattern of muscular dark
cumulus, slowly massing in their march east as if called by all
the dust devils whirling through the fields that day.

"Looks like we might get some rain," he said.

"Wouldn't hurt a thing." Frankie eyed the clouds. "It's been
awful dry."

Lee smiled. If he had a dollar for every time he'd heard that

phrase, "been awful dry," he'd be as rich as CC Holtz. Heard his
father, grandfather, uncles, and brother say those very words
and gaze to the sky in want of rain, standing supplicant to a
higher will to draw its favor. Always looking to the sky in vague
or urgent hope as if God and all His benevolence and wrath
were present in a looming thunderhead.

"I hate to be the one to break it to you, Frankie," Lee finally
said as he sifted his thoughts with the passing terrain. "You
being a realist and all. But we've been looking everywhere but
the one place we know there's hemp. The one real patch where
we can cut and make money. And I know LaReese is up there,
but the thing is…he might not be *in* there. It's still not prime
season."

Lee watched as Frankie mulled it over.

"I don't know, Lee," he said, still wavering. "If you want, we
can check it out. But if Val's in there, we pass it up."

"Sure, I understand. Bird in the nest, leave it be. Squatter's
rights. But LaReese doesn't own that land and he doesn't rent
that pasture. I know because I asked Garret and he said a fellow
named Corbin rents it. If we get there first, it's up for grabs.
We hit it next week, Monday through Thursday. Four hard days
would make our season."

"Okay, Lee. Like I said, we'll head down and take a look."

They took the next road east into Hill County and followed
it to North Branch, a tiny ghost town gone to weeds, then they
turned south. In another few minutes the van slowed and Lee
jumped out at the western edge of the disputed patch—a broad
creek pasture of predominant oak mixed with walnut that
revealed only a trace of hemp near the road. Lee's home place.
While his father had never owned the land, merely rented, to
Lee it was the womb of life. The world's center. After crossing
the fence into the pasture, he ran along the edge of the trees and
felt an inner peace and surge of breath as if entering the only
time and place he truly belonged. The same trees he used to run
under and climb on, cattle paths as familiar as the lines of his
palms. Pristine and pure as in his memory. Like nothing had
changed in twenty years. Like he could top the next rise and
find his father mending a fence.

What he saw caught his breath. More hemp in the creek bottom than ever before. A broad swath a hundred yards wide running southeast as far as the eye could see. Oak and walnut interspersed throughout but otherwise no brush or weeds to hinder the harvest, and every plant and stem fully leafed, weighted with seeds like a hybrid crop. Lee raced down the embankment, his heart pumping fast as he ran along the field of hemp like a wolf running at the edge of a vast herd of elk, in a fever of plenty. He continued for a full half mile till he came to a cross-fence that divided the property. The far side was heavily pastured and the hemp grew scant and thin. Lee had seen all he needed. A dream patch, replete and hidden.

He returned at a slower pace to scan for sign of anyone cutting. He didn't spy a single plant down, no telltale stubble, no stripped stalks or stems. The pasture left fallow, wholly ungrazed. The hemp stood wafting in wait like a virgin forest.

When Lee jumped back in the van his exhilaration was unchecked.

"It's unbelievable," he said in a rush. "There's three times the hemp I expected. And no one's been in there, Frankie. Not one footprint. Not even a cow paddy. It's the mother lobe."

"You looked it over real good?"

"Well not every square foot. But I ran the whole length to the cross-fence 'n back. Hell, Frankie, we can lay into the back half of the patch and cut till we drop. If Valentine shows up, we'll give him the front half. He can't bitch about that. There's enough hemp in there for two crews to work a month without butting heads."

"So he's not been in there?"

"Not to cut he ain't."

"Well, well, well…" Frankie said, at last warming to the notion. "Looks like Val's been sitting on his hands. If ya snooze, ya lose. He oughta know better. And serves him right, using women in a patch. They're probably all waiting for their time of the moon or some such crock. I know several in that bunch and I wouldn't trust them to gather eggs. Now don't get me wrong. There are women who are fairly capable, a few can still cook. But not a damn one can stand next to a man and do a hard day's work…"

Frankie was off on a favorite rant, a dyed-in-the-wool chauvinist, and often angered women over the very point. Especially back in Lawrence at various parties where he'd have all the feminists lined up waiting to take a punch at his gut as he baited them.

"Come on girls," he'd laugh. "Give it your best shot. Face it, a man is stronger. The bull mounts the cow every blessed time. Bitch about it all you like but you'll play hell changing one damn thing..."

He'd hold out his arms and let them punch away, laughing till he was blue in the face. Wear them down till they had to take vengeance by dousing him with beer. Then all had a good laugh. And later, as the evening waned, a certain one might loosen his belt and take his hard pulse between her thighs. Fuck him limp to prove her worth. That *she* could outlast *him*. An old game between man and woman. Which suited Frankie fine. The first to admit, women definitely had their finer points.

By evening, when Frankie dropped Lee off, the clouds had shouldered forth and bunched up to blacken the sky. Raindrops left dark splotches in the dirt like cast pennies while others hit cold against Lee's flesh as he ran and leapt to the porch, greeted there by Diana and Jesse. The pitter-patter on the roof grew steadily louder and then the heavens burst open with a crack of thunder and lightning. They stood on the porch and watched and listened as the rain poured down in driving sheets so thick at times they couldn't see the road or yard, only the blurred outline of the pickup parked forty feet away.

Jesse reached his hand out to catch the overflow from the eaves and giggled with excitement as Lee lifted him high so he could catch it by the handful and splash it to his face. Then Lee ran with him out into the yard and tossed him in the air and swung him around and around, whopping and dancing in the rain, tasting the fury of the storm. Both were drenched when they returned to the porch a minute later.

"There now," Lee grinned, handing him to Diana, "he's been baptized."

Jesse, still laughing from the thrill, pointed to the rain and said, "Look Mommy. Ka-sun go pee!" Jesse put a "k" sound on many words, particularly nouns. Diana suspected it came from her asking if he wanted to *"ta-ka-bath?"*

"Go big pee!" he repeated.

"Yes, I see, honey. But look at you," she said, cuddling him. "You're soaked. *Brrr!* We better dry you off."

"At least he won't need a ka-bath."

"Hah! Maybe he won't, but you will."

Lee smelled pretty ripe from running miles of creek banks.

"How 'bout supper? I'm hungry."

"You're too late," she teased.

"Aw Dita...have a heart. I've been hunting wild hemp all day."

"Okay. Maybe I'll fix a little something," she smiled. "If you *ta-ka-bath.*"

"It's a deal."

Lee ran up the back stairs, stripped off his clothes and drew his bath. He lay in the warm water and listened to the rumble of the storm and the buffeting wind. The house was amazingly solid; it didn't quake in the thunder; the windows barely rattled in their frames. The storm had all but ended once Lee had dried off and dressed. A sudden cloudburst that dropped an inch or two then rolled on east. The setting sun was already breaking through, reddening the sky in the west by the time Lee returned to the kitchen. Diana had the table set with pork chops, potatoes and gravy, corn and fresh-baked bread.

"Is this what you call a little something?"

"I found it warming in the oven," she slyly offered, her green eyes bewitching as her smile. And she'd also changed her clothes, now wearing a close-fitting, long cotton dress of variegated color and pattern like gold and scarlet leaves of autumn, with about twenty buttons down the front that Lee loved to unfasten one by one.

"So you just said that to trick me into a bath. What else you gonna trick me into?"

"You'll have to wait and see," she said, toying with an upper button. "Tricks are secret stuff."

"Uh-huh." Lee winked to Jesse and said, "Your Momma's full of tricks, ain't she?"

Jesse smiled like he was in on every trick, but not about to say.

"Did you swing in your swing today?" Lee asked.

"I swing! I swing to ka-birds...in tree. And bump Rue..."

"We swung all afternoon," Diana said. "You know the dogs, they have to be right there with Jesse, whatever he's doing. So they got in the way a time or two."

"Rue cry..."

"Yes, honey. But Rue will be okay," she assured him.

Lee had built Jesse the swing the previous day. They hunted out a special limb together, choosing a stout bough on an old hackberry that stood next to the cedars in back. Lee climbed up and secured a length of new hemp rope. Then he fashioned a wooden seat with a "V" notched at either end and set it about a foot off the ground, at the right height for Jesse. And Jesse swung to the altar of the sky—cast himself to the trees and clouds and watched his shadow sweep back across the ground then he reached to the sky again in a smooth pendulum from sky to earth.

"*Ee-e-e!*" he sang with laughter, loved the swing like he loved the rain.

They took their time with supper, savoring the food. Jesse liked the bite-sized pieces of meat Diana cut for him, and ate part of his corn, but drank all his lemonade, which he called "*Wice!*" for its sweet-bitter taste. Then he toyed with his "ta-toes" while his mommy and daddy talked about the day and various other things. Diana told Lee about the old woman who'd stopped by Sunday. When Lee asked who she was, Diana answered, "I don't know. She didn't say and I forgot to ask."

"Hope she wasn't working undercover," he joked.

"No, Lee. She only wanted to see the house. She said they used to have huge parties and dances out here."

"I bet so. It's big enough to invite half the county."

While Diana cleared away the dishes, Lee and Jesse played guitar. Lee would finger the chord and let Jesse strum as they slowly sang the song. They were working on Jesse's current favorite, "The Ballad of Billy the Kid:"

*"There's guns across the river aimin' at ya, lawman on your trail
like to catch ya,*

*"Bounty hunters too are out to get ya...Billy they don't like you
bein' so free..."*

Jesse would attempt some of the lyrics, but mostly he
strummed along and listened, loved to hear a song about a
kid. Sometimes, when off alone, they'd hear him sing it in part,
making up new words while keeping the refrain, *"Billy they
don't like you be so free..."* But not tonight. He'd had a full day
and was ready for bed shortly after dark. Diana and Lee both
tucked him in and covered him with a warm blanket, for the air
was cool in the wake of the storm.

They too went to bed early. Lee carefully unbuttoned
Diana's dress, then peeled it from her shoulders, past her hips,
and let it fall as she stepped free of its foliage, clothed solely in
her silk-smooth flesh. They made love slow and easy, like time
and the world was theirs to weave in any pattern they willed.
Later, they lay entwined in a tapestry of hair, limbs, and flesh,
listening to the last of the storm fade in the distance.

Diana's eyes moistened with tears—one wet her cheek as
she looked to Lee.

"I wish you wouldn't go back out," she said. "I hate the
worry and being alone."

"I know," he answered softly, wiping away her tear. "Just
one more week, Diana. Four more days and nights, that's all I
ask. And if it sells, we can buy this place if you want. Besides, I
already told Garret I'd help him cut silage in a week or two. Just
hang tough a little longer, Diana. Can you do that?"

"I guess so," she said faintly. "Just so it ends."

They said nothing more and listened to the night. To the
breeze rustle the mulberry limb against the roof outside their
window. To the sibilance of their own breath mixed with the
occasional creak of the house easing into slumber. Otherwise it
was quiet and pleasantly warm as they lay amidst all that space
like a lifetime waiting to be filled.

XIV. SPACES

Sheriff Guy Craig sat at his desk, puzzling over all the blank spaces. He had a suspect, the recent owner of a black pickup, M e x, three spaces down; and O r v a n o, six across. But no lateral connection. So even there he felt stymied, less certain than a week before. Then Saturday night he'd arrested another three down and six across for assault and battery, Tod Little—a surly 17-year-old who also drove a black pickup and already had a prior assault, a drunk and disorderly, plus multiple traffic violations. His father bailed him out Monday morning and took him home. And it wasn't that Guy suspected the boy of the murders, it was simply the matching number of spaces in his name and the fact of his pickup that left things muddled.

Guy hadn't worked a crossword puzzle since that fateful Sunday, now out of habit of mind and concern he created one from the murders, trying to connect motive to event, establish relationships as clear and precise as the letters of any word or name and so provide an answer to the haunting question—*Why?* Also out of habit he always worked the puzzles to completion, one way or another filled in all the spaces, like in tic-tac-toe, even when you saw there would be no winner, you played out your option. At least Guy did. Yet here he had a maze of spaces left to fill, and beyond three down and six across he couldn't guess a single one. Nothing but the unknown and nameless revolved in a mental void, and reaching for a dictionary wouldn't help without a further lead. Nor had he heard from Sheriff Wayne in the past week. Other than the one name, Mex Orvano, he was facing a complete blank. Guy realized that many murders were never solved even with a suspect in mind. Or only eventually

solved, after putting your suspicion on hold for years awaiting
a break in evidence or a witness to step forth. And he hated
the idea of Mex crisscrossing the county like a young prince,
flexing his muscles, flaunting his pride, his women, often gone
to Mexico or California, leaving the why and wherefore of his
comings and goings like so many spaces to be filled in.

At 10 a.m. Friday morning Guy's phone rang. He answered.

It was Special Agent Ron Tyllis of the KBI. Another three
down and six across. And a "special agent" no less. Guy had
to wonder if there were any agents who weren't "special." But
he said nothing in that regard, always cordial unless given
cause. Besides, he'd dealt with the man during the bureau's brief
investigation of the murders and found him tolerable.

"Agent Tyllis...sure I remember you. What prompts your
call?"

—*We're investigating a Valentine LaReese. His parole ended in
July and his last known address was there in Cibola City. While we
have no current address, we have reason to believe he's still in your area.
Certainly, we could send a man up, but if you know of his whereabouts
it would save us some legwork.*

"Yeah, I know where he's at. I make it a point to keep an eye
on Valentine."

—*Great. That's good to hear. And where exactly is LaReese at
present?*

"Suppose you tell me exactly why you want to know?"

—*Sheriff Craig, surely you understand, this being an ongoing
investigation, we prefer not to divulge anything at this time.*

"Well, I prefer otherwise. Because I have an ongoing concern
of my own. And since this involves my people and my county,
I want to know..."

There was a considered pause. Guy waited.

—*Okay then. But I rely on your discretion and trust you'll keep
this to yourself.*

"I wear a hat and keep it on."

—*Okay, fine. Just so you know this is for your ears only. We
have LaReese involved in several drug transactions in Lawrence and
Manhattan. All recent. As well as a federal firearms violation. We*

have undercover agents working the case and could've made an arrest, but we think we'll have a broader case and better evidence if we nail him where he lives. We hope to cast a wider net and link him to other crimes, even a possible tie-in to the murders of the young couple, Joseph Connors and Cathy Torres.

"I see. In that case Agent Tyllis, I'll tell you what I know. Valentine is living in a rented farmhouse northeast of the little town of Oakvale, up in Hill County. You take Highway 28 north out of Oakvale for two miles, then head west a mile and a half. You getting this down…? Okay. It's a two-story white frame house on the north side of the road with a row of cedars to the west. You can't miss it. He lives there with two other men and five or six women. So it's rumored."

—Alright, I think I've got it. Two miles north, a mile and a half west… Anything else?

"Yeah. When do you move?"

—No date definite. But soon. We're in the process of getting warrants. We'll keep you posted.

"Good. Because I want in on it. And here's some free advice for you. Don't let Sheriff Patch Hyland of Hill County know till the last minute."

—Why is that?

"Let's just say he doesn't keep his hat on."

—Thanks for the tip, Sheriff. We appreciate the info.

"Don't mention it. Good luck with the warrant…"

Hanging up the phone, Guy felt a greater certainty than when he'd answered it. He quickly jotted the name: V a l e n t i n e L a R e e s e. Nine down and seven across, intersecting at the "l." And he began to see vague outlines of other words and letters filling in the blanks, not entirely, but starting to emerge like ghosts in question, giving hints of an answer. Soon, when the hammer fell on Valentine, it could bust things wide open. Reveal all the missing pieces like leaves taken up in the wind and whirled before the eye while a few fell into place in sufficient number for Guy to discern the rest of the pattern. Fill in the blanks and tie the murders to M e x.

Whereas Guy was somewhat diffident in manner and spare of speech, he was far more open and approachable than Sheriff Wayne who was invariably taciturn, cool and severe as his hard chiseled face. Neither of them had been elected due to their affable nature, people respected their competence, and with Sheriff Wayne this was strictly the case. Hoss, while firmly polite, was never more social than duty required. He had no real friendships and sought none. A true loner. And as of Friday morning, back on his own. His wife Jody had asked for a divorce. Not that it surprised him and not that he really cared, her standing there in an orange housecoat, plump as a pumpkin, her hair in curlers, her face caked in beauty cream, looking about as unattractive as a women could be. She'd already seen a lawyer and said if they kept it friendly, she'd only ask for child support.

"Can I still see the kids?" That was his main question.

"I don't see why not," she answered. "They can go with you anytime you're not working." Of course Hoss never took a day off, she knew that. But he did occasionally take them out for ice cream, or to a movie, or to the swimming pool. Hoss loved his kids, Sandy and little Rob, and still wanted to be their father in his distant way. Still wanted to take them out for an afternoon or evening, same as now.

"So you have someone?" he finally asked.

"Yes. Darlene Kadle."

"Darlene…? Oh yeah, your bowling partner," Hoss noted matter-of-factly.

"She's more than that, Hoss. She's my… I really don't care to explain. Let's just say she'll be moving in, and you'll be moving out."

This was a surprise. Not him moving out, he expected as much. But a woman? Hoss stood dazed, like he'd been punched, didn't know what to say. A woman going for a woman lay outside his reckoning. Like the UFO he'd seen, it belonged to another realm, beyond his grasp. He had no thought on the matter, no idea what to say. Simply registered the comment and remained grounded, practical.

"Will you give me a day or two to find a room?"

"Sure Hoss. Take a week, whatever...there's no rush," she said wearily. "And don't worry, you can see the kids whenever you like."

Hoss nodded and started out the door, then paused a moment.

"Just toss my stuff in those two duffels," he said. "I'll be by and pick 'em up."

Jody merely shrugged. She knew the routine—whether overseas or across town, all he needed were those two duffels. He owned a half dozen khaki pants and shirts, wore the same uniform every day. It wouldn't have surprised her if he chose to sleep on a cot in his office. Nothing had really changed. Still married to his job.

And what with all their talk that morning Hoss's immediate concern was that he wouldn't make it to the church before the priest closed the door. But he arrived with a minute to spare and parked directly across the street. The priest was welcoming the last of the parishioners as Hoss stared stone-faced, once more registering his suspicion. Though Father Michael maintained a placid veneer and solemn composure, deep down the effect was telling. He felt a chill at the sheriff's presence, his stern look of judgment. Relieved to close the doors and return to the peace and sanctuary of worship. If only he could shut out the world forever.

Hoss didn't drive on that morning as usual. He saw Mrs. Wylett out in her yard, leaning to her walker. Every few steps she'd kneel down and dig up a dandelion with a butter knife she carried, then stand and edge on, unhurried, determined, like an old hen slowly pecking for worms. Hoss walked over and doffed his hat.

"Good morning, ma'am."

She gave a brief start at seeing his shadow and hearing his voice.

"Dear me," she said, looking up, "you made my heart skip a beat."

"I'm sorry, ma'am."

"Oh, don't fret yourself, Robby. I was hunting these danged

dandy lions and not thinking of another living thing. I've gotta keep after 'em. And you know I only use my walker when I have to dig. It helps me to kneel. Otherwise I get around fine."

"Yes ma'am, you do an admirable job."

"Why, that's sweet of you, Robby. I see you've been keeping an eye on those Catholics again this morning. And like you asked, I've been watching for a red pickup but I haven't seen one. Nor that black one either."

"That's quite alright, ma'am. You just call if you do. But there's another thing," Hoss said as Mrs. Wylett looked up and waited, gripping her walker, curious of his change in tone. "I uh...was wondering if you might rent out that upper room."

"Well I haven't for a while. You know my last renter was such an odd duck. A Jehovah Witness and they're the absolute worst. He was such a dreary man, I'd rather live with a drunk... and I *have* lived with a drunk. Anyhow, after he left, the Jehovah fellow, I didn't care to bother myself. But for the right person I suppose..."

"Then I'd like to rent it, ma'am. Because me 'n my wife, we... you see we're getting a divorce. So I...I need to move out."

"Oh...I'm sorry to hear that, Robby. Did she find her a new fellow?"

"No, it's...not quite like that. We just have our differences."

"Well you're lucky you're not Catholic," she said, raising a gnarled finger to make her point. "'Cause they don't allow divorce, them Catholics don't. They try to run your life every step of the way."

"Yes ma'am, I know that. Then you'll rent me the room?"

"I don't allow no entertaining up there."

"No ma'am, there won't be any. I come in about eight or nine. Have a few beers."

"And I don't allow rowdiness."

"No ma'am, I just have a few beers and watch Johnny Carson."

"Why, so do I," Mrs. Wylett beamed. "I never miss Johnny. He's a Nebraska boy, you know. My Herbert was a Nebraska boy, born and raised up around Kearny he was. And rowdy, my lands he was full of the devil, rest his soul."

"Yes ma'am. I should tell you, I'm an early riser. But I'll try to keep it quiet."

"Oh, you won't wake me, young man," she said, waving off his concern. "I'm up at four thirty every day. Have my breakfast and wait for my paper."

"Mind if I move in this evening?"

"No, suit yourself, Robby. Be my pleasure to have Ilene's boy upstairs. But I tell you I don't climb those stairs no more. So you'll have to do your own cleaning. Now I do have plenty of sheets and blankets up there and I will do the laundry if you carry it downstairs, but that'll be extra."

"Yes ma'am, I understand. Then what'll you need in way of rent?"

"Oh now, you get yourself settled in. We'll think of something..." she answered vaguely, already heading off with her walker in search of dandelions, as intent in her hunt as Hoss was in his.

His domestic situation all but ironed out, Hoss stopped by his house at noon, picked up his duffels and told Jody he'd sign whatever papers once they were ready. Walking out the door, he felt a breath of freedom stronger than he had in leaving the Marine Corps—and he felt some compassion for his wife as well. She wasn't a bad woman, he simply didn't care for her in that way, and now that he didn't have to lie beside her and pretend affection, he could better appreciate her good points. For she was a sensible and caring mother. Nor did he feel at all jealous in losing her to a woman. Because to him, Jody and Darlene were more like sisters and he couldn't really picture them as lovers, simply best friends. The kids stood to get twice the mothering, though he'd have to watch and make certain little Rob didn't end up too coddled.

At the Downtowner a short while later, he noticed Meg the waitress had a nice smile. And watching her walk away, he liked the way she moved, the way her hips filled out her skirt, the way the skirt brushed her knees. He liked her frank expression and her fine legs. Things he hadn't let himself notice, and noticing, he realized he wasn't dead below the belt after all. In a flush of generosity Hoss left her a two-dollar tip instead of his usual one.

Hoss returned to his office and put his mind in his work, letting the gyro steer him clear. Took no more thought of Meg than he did of Jody. Wouldn't chase the first skirt that crossed his path the second time around. He'd learned that much at least. Looking forward to the little room above Mrs. Wylett's. Better to live alone like a monk than in grudging dread of someone who wasn't truly at fault. He pushed women from his mind and filled out several reports. At 3:15 Mrs. Wylett called, sounding a little agitated. His first thought was that she'd changed her mind about renting him the room, but it was something else entirely.

—*Robby, I just seen a red pickup pull in behind the church. Now I...*

"Thank you, ma'am. I'll be right over."

Hoss hung up, grabbed his hat and was out the door, headed for his Bronco with no real plan in mind other than to confront the pair. Stand tall and cast his shadow. He knew he couldn't arrest anyone. But he aimed to catch them face to face, the priest and Mex Orvano, look them in the eye and let them know that he knew and that he would dog them till one or the other slipped up.

Hoss turned in the church entrance and circled around back. The red pickup was parked in the shade of the rectory. Mex stood in the truck bed handing an ice chest to Father Michael as Hoss drove up and got out.

"Hey now," Mex smiled, greeting Hoss like they were old friends. "If it ain't the big bad Sheriff riding in on his big white Bronco. How's it going, Mister Wayne?"

Hoss didn't bother to answer. He and Mex were prior acquainted. A couple of years before Mex had put a local tough in the hospital. Raymond Jake Hall, or "Mad Jake" as he was known. A notorious bully, always looking for a fight, and found more than he bargained for when he tangled with Mex. No doubt he deserved a whipping, but Mex took special delight in beating the man half to death. Both frequented a tavern on the north edge of Arcadia known as The Cave. And frequented the same woman, Jenny Johnson, a sprightly redhead. Jake landed the first punch, and Mex finished it. So there were no charges. Jake and Jenny married once he got out of the hospital and confined their squabbles to themselves. Though rumor still placed Mex in the picture.

And much as Hoss would've liked to, he couldn't very well reach out and jerk Mex into line. Not with the pack of pedigree lawyers CC kept on call in Kansas City. Earlier that summer when Hoss wanted to subpoena livestock sales records in response to the rash of cattle theft, the prosecutor said, *Forget it.* He couldn't buck a Kansas City law firm on mere suspicion. Hoss would either have to catch the culprits red-handed or use subtler means. Hoss hated subtle.

"What you got in here?" he said, tapping the ice chest.

Mex grabbed a bottle of beer resting on the cab, tipped it up and guzzled it dry.

"*Owweee,* let's see now, Sheriff?" he laughed and tossed the bottle to the ground. "Could be some nasty contraband. A little something for the Sisters, you know, to liven up their day." Then he squatted down and popped the lid. "But *nawww,*" he said while holding a package for Hoss to inspect. "It's just plain ol' grade-A beef. One of my little charity runs. I'm sweet on the ladies, ya know. Even the good Sisters gotta eat."

Hoss glanced to the priest who was standing back, oddly diffident on his own turf. Father Michael nodded faintly, meeting his gaze.

"Good afternoon, Sheriff Wayne," he said. "How are you today?"

"Fine Mike. Just fine."

"Mike? Really Sheriff, you should show more respect to Father Michael."

"No, it's quite alright, Javier."

"Javier?" Hoss could play the name game too. "Where did you get a fancy name like that, Mex?"

"Hey, careful now, Sheriff. My mother gave me that name. Some of us had a mother, ya know."

"No shit"—drawing him out like a DI working a wise-ass recruit. "Never guessed you had a mother."

"You fucking bet I had a mother. A magnificent whore, beautiful. I was lucky. Unlike some who are born of sows and cows and grow up ugly as a horse."

"A whore? I buy that. But not a mother. Not a real mother. Or she'd have used that mouth of yours to mop the floor."

"Stop it! Now!" Father Michael injected angrily, shed of any deference, assuming the role and authority of a priest. "Of course he had mother, a very real mother. And I'd thank you both to cease the ridicule."

"You knew his mother?"—Hoss now pushing both of them.

"Yes, I...attended her death. Administered last rites. It was many years ago."

Hoss noted the defensive tone and stood silent as he looked from one to the other. Seeing them side by side, his scrutiny deepened. Father Michael was tall, pale skinned and slightly built, while Mex was muscular and bronzed. Yet they shared the same dark eyes—beautiful eyes, as even Hoss would admit—with long lashes and defined brows. And the same lips, full and sensuous, though one quivered in faith and doubt while the other curved in a sharp smirk. Their features so similar, they were like two halves, the good and bad, of one soul. Whether Hoss thought in those terms, he clearly sensed as much. And based on what he saw he would have named them brothers.

Father Michael grew unnerved under the hard steady gaze. "If you're through, Sheriff," he said, "I do have other duties."

"Got a couple questions for Mex. Then I'll be gone."

"Questions? I like questions. You ask real nice, I'll answer the magic three."

Hoss ignored the sarcasm and cut straight to his question.

"Until recently you drove a black pickup with smoked windows. Correct?"

"Yeah, so? I traded it. They're like a woman, they get a little clunky after a while. Especially if you drive them hard."

"I have a report of a pickup matching that description leaving this church in reckless pursuit of a young man down Ninth Street. All happened several weeks ago. The young man was Joey Connors. A few days later, he and his girlfriend Cathy Torres were brutally murdered. Were you driving that black pickup, Mex?"

Mex leaned back and laughed.

"You're funnier than I thought, Sheriff. Real funny. Ask

yourself, why would I chase a young man?"

"No, I'm asking you"—firm, unsmiling.

"You know me, I only chase young women."

"Be careful they're not too young, Mex."

"Oh, I'm careful, Sheriff. I'm always careful who I fuck."

"Right. And it's my job to see that you are."

"Hey, you do a good job, Sheriff. You keep everyone on their tippy-toes."

Mex leapt over the side of the pickup with a laugh. Then he grabbed the last ice chest and started up the steps of the rectory. "See Sheriff, I'm real careful." He tiptoed in his boots, still laughing as Hoss got in his Bronco, started up and backed out.

Once inside, Mex dropped the chest to the floor and looked to Father Michael.

"There now, that's how you handle a big bad sheriff," he said. "You laugh at him. He can't do a thing. He can't prove a thing. All he can do is ask *stu-pid fuc-king ques-tions!*"—with each harsh syllable he stabbed his knuckle in the priest's sternum.

Father Michael cast his eyes to the floor in silence. What could he say to this man he knew to be a murderer? Who showed no remorse or guilt? Who had threatened his life, and in a gross manner threatened to violate his person? What could he say? *Tú es mi hermano*—my brother. How could he ever tell him?

Despite Mex's laughter Hoss was the one smiling as he drove away. He'd learned more than he'd hoped. Gained a further suspicion. And if it proved true, he could grab the priest by the short hairs and make him talk. Blood was thicker than water, even holy water. And Hoss had an inside angle: he knew Father Thomas Crohn, though he always addressed him as Captain Crohn, a Marine Corps chaplain that Hoss had gotten to know in Vietnam—a tough Jesuit who could cuss and drink like a soldier, address their needs and fears. He served his faith and country and had shed his blood, still carried shrapnel in both legs and a purple heart in proof.

Hoss had a deep respect for the man. Both on duty and off. They'd shared many nights in the seedy bars lining Tu Do Street in Saigon, rife miasmas of soldiers, sweat, and smoke

where they drank round after round of Ba Mi Ba beer while
bar girls drifted past, pressing to their flesh, even the priest's,
saying, "Show me money, honey, I show you heaven." Father
Crohn would quietly point to his collar, worn even then, and
brush them away. The men waited to see if he'd take one of the
tiny beauties up on it. But he remained true to his vow and oath.
Semper Fi, ever faithful.

Father Crohn had left the Corps in '71 and now worked in
a tough inner-city school in East St. Louis. "Still trying to win
their hearts and minds..." he'd say to Hoss, for they kept in
touch, exchanging Christmas cards and an occasional phone
call. Hoss called that very afternoon. They traded their usual
pleasantries, still addressing each other by rank out of old
habit.

"Captain, I got a problem here," Hoss announced abruptly
after a minute or so, his voice suddenly more formal and urgent.
"I could sure use your help."

—*You've got it, Sergeant, you know that. Is this...a personal
matter?*

"No sir, nothing personal. It's official. I need background on
a priest. A Father Michael Kairn. That's Kairn with a K. K-a-i-r-n.
He's with the Sacred Heart Catholic Church here in Arcadia. We
also have a convent, Our Sisters of Mercy. You may have heard
of them, they've been in the news some."

—*Yes, certainly, I know of them and their work with refugees. In
fact I respect their effort. So I must ask, since your question is quite
irregular, Sergeant, is there any friction between you and Father Kairn
over this issue?*

"No sir, I'm mostly neutral. If he can help those people, so be
it. My concern is murder. A double murder here in late August.
Two teenagers, a boy and a girl."

—*You suspect Father Kairn?*

"Negative, sir. But I think he knows who did it and I think
he knows why. Hell, I've got a good idea who, but I need proof.
And I need to know why he won't tell what he knows, because
without that I can't dig any further. At first I thought it had to
do with confession, why he wouldn't tell. Now I have a deeper

hunch. I think he's trying to protect the murderer because of something old between them."

—*You mean sexual?*

"No sir. I mean blood ties. It's just possible they may be brothers."

—*I see. So...how can I help?*

"Like I said, Captain, I need background. Where he was born? Who his mother and father were? Where he went to school? The basic poop."

—*That should be doable. Too bad he isn't Jesuit, that would expedite things, but being up that way, he's probably Dominican.*

"Sorry, Captain. Other than Catholic I don't know what he is."

Both chuckled briefly.

—*Yes, it can get confusing. But never mind. I can reference that in a few minutes. The rest may take a while, possibly a week or two. And you understand, Sergeant, there are lines I can cross, and lines I can't...*

"Yessir, I understand. Thanks for your help."

—*Save me a cold one, Sergeant. And make it a Ba Mi Ba.*

"Sorry, Captain. All I got is Bud."

—*Then by God, Bud will do. See what I can dig up. Semper Fi.*

"Yessir, Captain...semper fi..."

Dinner was like a bad date, everyone wished it would end. And it wasn't the food. Diana had cooked up a delicious vat of curie chicken and baked three loafs of French bread. There was plenty of iced tea, red wine, and beer to wash it down. They'd invited Will and JoAnn, Ry and Kara, and Bruce and Julie out for the evening. Friends to fill up the space and warm the house. Will brought along a kitten from yet another litter, a little black male that he gave to Jesse, showing him first how to hold it.

"No, no, not around the neck," he explained, ever calm and patient with kids and animals. "That might choke him. Here, put your arm under his chest. There, you've got it." Jesse smiled and went to show Diana his new "Ka-kitty."

"Ah, look at him," she said softly, peering to the blue almond eyes. "What do you want to name him?"

"Ka-kitty," he answered without giving it another thought.

Things had started off well enough. Everyone was in a festive mood from the harvest—the latest batch had totaled 1,920 pounds, a hair shy of a ton, and once sold it would put nearly six more grand in each of their pockets. And four more days in a prime patch should yield another ten grand minimum. It looked like their initial hopes were panning out. And sooner than expected. But halfway through dinner what should have been a celebration was turning sour. Soured in part by the very prospects. Bruce, buoyed by the wine and the thought of all the cash coming to him, declared his intent of moving to Oregon and pursuing a doctorate in philosophy. Julie declared otherwise.

"Then you'll be going alone," she said with an icy smile. "Because I'm staying here."

"For crying out loud, Julie, what do you have against Oregon? You haven't even been there?"

"I don't need to go. I like Kansas. It suits me."

They'd been having pretty much the same argument all summer. He looked hurt. She looked determined. And they continued to air their difference, ping-ponging back and forth with slight variation as if once set in motion neither could desist, each either indifferent to those listening or hopeful of gaining a sympathic ear. But so aired, their resentments fell like a wet blanket on the table. No couple there seated was immune to trouble, each had problems brewing over the cash to come, whether to quit while ahead or chance getting more. Pulled together in lean times and pulled apart in face of plenty, each harboring their own hunger and fear. And seeing displayed what could so readily devolve their way made them doubly uneasy.

Will excused himself and went upstairs to use the bathroom. Soon after, Diana, JoAnn, and Kara began clearing away the dishes. Ry raised his brows and gave Lee a surreptitious look that said, *See what I mean?* Because Ry had once dated her. Julie. And why not? She was a brown-eyed beauty with long dark hair, smooth coppery skin softly hued as if in twilight, and

formed to the Mediterranean ideal—turn any man's head past
90 degrees. Ry asked her out to a movie. And it was a disaster.
Not the movie, the date. Actually they both enjoyed the movie,
Planet of the Apes. Again things had started off okay. They shared
an interest in science fiction, both liked Asimov and Bradbury.
It looked to be a pleasant evening. But immediately following
the movie, the ice age descended. The moment they reached the
car, she dropped her smile and said, "If you think we're going
to fuck, you can forget it."

"That was pretty blunt," Ry later told the boys. And it wasn't
that the thought hadn't crossed his mind, but he was keen to
requisite ritual, patient, respectful, willing to let nature and
sensibilities take their course, and if the flesh so urged, great—if
not, fine. But hearing her rude comment he had nothing more
to say and drove her straight home. She definitely had her man
repellent on and the stuff was strong. As effective as DEET. Toss
her in a jungle, nothing would touch her.

And this evening she had her kid repellent on as well.
When Jesse came around to show her his kitten, she said, "Sure
kid. I see it." Curt, dismissive, cold. She flashed a false smile
then went back to smoking her cigarette and staring daggers
at Bruce, letting him know that if he still wanted a child he
could forget that as well. Not that she was at all heartless or a
bad person; she was often friendly, engaging, and warm. Quite
simply she didn't want to live anywhere but Kansas; she didn't
want to have children; and she didn't fuck on the first date.
Fair enough. And certainly, living with a man who claimed to
have a lock on the truth, particularly a logical positivist who
deconstructed every other sentence, could bring out the demon
in anyone.

"Just listen to yourself, Julie," Bruce continued to plead his
case. "You're not making any sense, not even being logical. You
say you like to hunt for rocks in creek beds. Jesus Christ, they've
got rocks in Oregon. A rock is a rock!"

"Isn't that what you call a tautology?" Her answers
occasional and terse, though this time she rose from her sulk to
elaborate. "By the way, I hate that word. *Tautology*. It sounds like
a tall thirteen-year-old geek with pimples. *Disgusting.*"

"You're evading the point, Julie. Always evading the point..."

So their hearts unraveled as their tongues sharpened, leveling charge and countercharge, adding debits to the growing list of IOUs that would never be forgiven.

Ry and Lee left the grudging pair to their domestic fate and followed Jesse out into the kitchen where he'd found Kara, she of the long blonde hair and winsome ways. She knelt down to pet the kitten, letting Jesse stroke her hair as he loved to do. Next to his momma, she was his favorite.

"Watch it he don't steal your gal," Lee said with a wink. Ry had a good chuckle, he and others glad to focus on something more playful. Will had returned from upstairs and presently stood at the door to the kitchen.

"Is it just me?" he asked with a puzzled look. "Or has anyone else noticed a cold spot up in the hall...there by the bathroom?"

Diana turned with a tentative smile.

"Why yes," she said, "it does seem cooler there. But I think it's because of the stairs. They draw the air like a chimney."

"But warm air rises," Will noted. "You'd think it'd be warmer, not cooler."

"Must be the ghosts," Lee laughed. "Waiting there to scare the piss out of ya." He'd walked through the spot a hundred times and thought nothing of it. There were cold and warm spaces in every house due to doors, windows, airflow, any number of things.

"Oh, I didn't mean anything like that," Will said. "It just... struck me as odd."

Diana listened and said nothing more, played it off with a smile.

Will, Ry, and Lee went on outside and walked into the yard. Will lit up a joint, took a hit, and passed it on. He slowly exhaled and watched it fill the night air and fade.

"Gabe'll be heading to California tomorrow," he said. "Wish he could've done a quick deal like in KC. I don't envy him driving a tone of dope to Santa Rosa in a rental van. They check 'em going through the sierras, I hear. Check pretty regular."

"There's always a risk," Lee answered evenly, passing the

joint to Ry. "And I agree, I wouldn't wanna drive all that way. But at least he gets to fly back. And if all goes well, he should be here with a bag of money about the time we leave the patch."

"That's another thing giving me bad vibes."

"What? The Burr Oak patch?"

"Not the patch. It's that fucking Valentine being up there that worries me."

"Yeah, I don't like it either," Ry nodded. "He's kind of gun happy."

"Look, I ran the patch and he wasn't in there yet. And we'll have Pete along. They're quasi-buddies. If Valentine shows up, Pete'll talk with him. Hash things out. It'll be cool. You'll see."

"I don't know," Will answered, still doubtful. "So far so good, but I hate to push it. Things can change. And Hoyt Brothers gave me a call this week. They want me to come back to work as superintendent. A bridge job."

"I thought you were through with construction?"

"Yeah, I know...thought so too. But maybe if I'm in charge I can keep the next poor bastard from getting killed. Plus it pays more money and I can pick my own crew. Make Ry foreman and put you to work if you want."

Lee's heart sank hearing those words. He wanted no part of it. The whole reason they were taking the risk was to change their lives and not fall back into the same old rut. Hadn't Will said they were all dead men if they did? That life was nothing more than a prison if a man couldn't choose his own way? And hadn't that always been the problem in the past, pulling back instead of forging on? Lee wanted other options and he was willing to push.

"Maybe so," he said, for the moment noncommittal, not wishing to slight a friend. "But we should cut next week for certain. All of us. I mean it. You guys should see that patch. It's the mother lobe. We'll cut more hemp in four days than we have so far. Double our money. Make sixteen thousand dollars each. That's more than you can save in ten years working construction."

Lee spoke as much to encourage himself as his friends, for he had qualms of his own. First, there was the nagging thought that Frankie wasn't telling all he knew about LaReese. And something more, he'd had the same dream two nights running: a surreal dream in which the landscape surrounding the Burr Oak patch was transformed into a broad patterned chessboard of rolling hills, creeks, fields, and pastures, while the boys were shaped as various pieces standing like cigar store Indians tall as trees in the middle of the patch. Threat was inherent in any game—a series of options to pursue as well as obstacles to avoid or traverse. Same with the dream. What Lee couldn't understand, waking from the dream, was whether the boys were positioned to advance or already in check. His anxieties were shared with no one, least of all, Diana.

"Sixteen thousand dollars," he repeated, using it as the prod and the prize. "That's enough to buy a house and land."

"Yeah, that's a helluva lot of money," Will agreed, tempted once more. "Guess I better cut. Just feeling some bad vibes is all. Pregame jitters."

Will snuffed the joint between his thumb and forefinger then placed it in his shirt pocket. He glanced to the overcast sky, stars mostly obscured; he rolled up his collar and hunched his shoulders, feeling a chill nearly everywhere that evening.

XV. BURR OAK

"Jesus...Frankie! You on the road or in the damn ditch?"

"Wanna ride the ridges, gotta cinch your saddle, Wolfer."

"Right...!" Will was not amused.

The roads were gashed with ruts left from the big rain. Frankie tried to straddle them but the tires occasionally caught in a deep swerve of whatever vehicle had first cut through the mud, tossing the van hard right or left. Beyond a low bridge the ruts angled to the ditch and the tires struck broadside like hitting a sudden speed bump, pitching the boys every which way—heads, elbows, and shinbones struck against the roof and side panel. Coming down, Will landed on a canteen, wrenching his lower back. Even in the dark you could see his face grimace in pain.

"Fuck, I'm fucked..." he moaned—then cried out, "Dammit, Frankie! Think you could hit the next one a little harder?"

Frankie shot back a dour look and said nothing.

No one in a cheery mood, 5 a.m. Sunday morning, the van crowded with the boys and gear, all set to drop off at the patch. The sky threatened rain. Everyone reluctant, feeling doubtful about the wisdom of going in, but no one willing to call a halt. A few minutes earlier when they turned off the highway, raindrops hit the windshield.

"Holy shit," Rus said as they formed into streaks, "hope it don't rain."

"Aw, it's just spitting." Frankie flicked on the wipers. "If it rains, I'll bend over and you can kiss my ass right there in the middle of the road."

"You keep dreaming, boy. The only thing you'll get from me is boot leather up your ass. Remember, it comes a rain, you got four miles of mud to plow."

"I'll plow it, Russie, don't you worry. If I have to bring a damn tractor."

That settled it, rain or shine, they were going in.

All except Will. He tried to reposition and was checked by the pain.

"My back is fucked, boys," he said. "Afraid I'll have to sit this one out."

"What the heck, Wolfer, I'll cut for ya," Rus offered.

"Sure, and we can tote your stuff," Lee added. "All you have to do is strip."

"No. When it's this bad there's no way. I'll play hell getting out of the van, let alone cross the fence. I need to see Doc Bryant and have 'im pop it back in place."

The boys left it at that and rode the last mile in silence. Halfway down a long hill the van slowed to a stop. Lee stepped out and checked the roadside.

"It's too mushy here," he said. "We better drive on to the next hill, it's a bit rockier up there...won't track so bad."

"Tracks? You worried about tracks?"—Pete's turn to scoff, riding shotgun and playing a pint-sized Frankie, griping about running packs and the lack of beer.

"You bet I am. And you better be too," Lee answered, a bit testy. "You ain't the big bad wolf out here, Pete, you're just a rabbit. We all are. And any farmer sees tracks leading into his pasture, he's gonna check it out. If they scare us up, we get hunted."

Truth was the moment the boys left the road and entered the patch they passed through a keyhole into another realm, a self-imposed exile where the margin of safety severely narrowed. Their presence unwelcome, their action illegal, they had no phone, no vehicle, and to contact anyone for miles around would likely get them jailed. All they had were their wits and caution. And mutual trust. So Pete's bravado was wholly out of place and damned irritating. Though likeable enough, impish looking with a sly charm and an impish grin, he was still a rookie in the patch and had to earn his stripes. And typical of a rookie he showed more bluster than good sense. He sported a new tattoo of a fire-breathing dragon and thought hemp-picking was all a lark. He even insisted on wearing a white straw cowboy hat that would show up like the proverbial whore in a barracks. If it had been the army, they'd have set him straight. But you could only go so far with a freeborn creekbank boy. Lee said no more and hoped for the best.

The van cruised down over the bridge and stopped near the crest of the hill. Solid ground. The boys piled out—Ry, Rus, Pete, Dixie, Bruce, Jack, and Lee. They formed a chain and quickly hustled the gear and themselves over the fence.

As the van rolled on Frankie lit a cigarette and passed it to Will.

"You gonna be alright back there?" he asked.

"Yeah, I'll make it. Long as you don't hit another fucking bump."

"Your back's really fucked, huh?"

"Yeah, it's really fucked," Will answered wearily; he could care less what Frankie thought. "But I'll say this—back or no back, glad I'm not going in there. Got bad vibes about that patch. And I notice you're not going in either."

"No. But going in there was Lee's idea, not mine. That's his call."

"Right. But you know how he is about that place. Thinks it's sacred ground."

"Yeah, well, we'll see how it plays out…"

The boys watched the van turn east towards the highway, soon swallowed in the night as they toted their gear on through the pasture. Faced with four days of cutting and sick of spam from the week before, they carried along two coolers of real food. Dixie and Pete, Jack and Bruce doubled up on the coolers while Ry, Rus, and Lee led the way. Clouds totally blocked the moon and made it slow-going through the darkness. They humped over gullies and down the slippery banks, threading their way to the depths of the creek. In the chill air about all they could see was one another's breath. A steady mist fell and the damp grass quickly soaked their pant legs and boots.

Rus packed along his camp stove slung over one shoulder. Lee wasn't exactly keen on the idea, but Rus assured him that it gave a smokeless fire and he'd only use it during the day.

"You'll see," he said, nudging Lee. "Along after sunrise I'll brew us up some coffee. It'll taste great." Lee had to admit, already soaked to the bone from breaking the trail, coffee at sunrise sounded pretty damn good.

But there was no real sunrise that morning, merely a gradual coming of the day. Utterly still and no longer misting, the dew lay heavy on every stem and leaf, marking time with a steady drip, drip, drip. The boys situated their camp about a half a mile from the road, unburdened their gear and began to explore the near environs of the patch. The plants were all nicely spaced, tall and full, the stems so heavy with seeds they hung like snow-laden boughs. Water leaves at the base of the stems were starting to change color and drop to the ground. Most turned a pale yellow, though one occasionally took on a dark purple hue.

Ry reached up and plucked a leaf, releasing a sprinkle of dew and falling seeds.

"You're right, Lee," he grinned. "It's the mother lobe. You could park a thresher in here and cut hemp till you filled a silo."

Further on they found the largest plant they'd ever seen. All alone in a grassy radius, it stood at least fifteen feet high and spread twelve feet at the base. Dixie paced it off then stepped back and looked it up and down as if estimating board feet.

"Hail Mary!" he exclaimed; "It's not a plant, it's a tree."

They all gazed to its spire in wonder of how it had grown so big.

"Boys, I think we've found the queen," Rus declared. "And we ought not cut her. It'ud be a sacrilege, a crying shame, not to let her seed another crop."

"Oh fuck that noise," Pete sneered, wasn't going to listen to any superstitious pap. "We're here to cut hemp and that's the first one I'm gonna cut."

He drew his machete, crawled in under and began hacking at the base.

Rus shook his head and walked away. He'd found him another candidate to put back on a rubber knife. Not that Rus or any of them really believed in such taboo. But once voiced, a notion was generally respected among the boys—as had been the custom among bands of men through the ages, because taboo spoke to instinct and encouraged self-restraint. And to flaunt it nearly always carried risk.

The boys left Pete to topple the queen and returned to camp. It was still too wet to cut. While they let things dry in the stirring breeze, Rus brewed some coffee then dug out his skillet and laid on a dozen strips of bacon. He soon had their mouths watering to the sound of popping grease and the sizzle of frying eggs. The boys gathered around, sipping coffee, eager to partake. The hot food tasted delicious in the crisp morning air. Within a half hour they'd all eaten and rinsed their pans in the creek. Their pants and boots had mostly dried. Leaves and stems fluttered in the breeze.

The boys grabbed their machetes and scattered out and began to cut.

Meanwhile Pete had wrestled the queen to camp and stood by stripping to the tarp, master of his fate like all men about to fall, laughing at the others for their lack of savvy.

"Look at this!" he called out. "I won't need to cut for a good two hours."

No idle boast there, that one plant equaled any dozen. But in trimming a lower stem, his machete glanced off the hard stalk and sliced a three-inch gash across his left knee. At his sharp cry the boys came running. Rus got there first and found Pete squatting down, turning pale as the blood soaked up through his jeans like syrup poured over a pancake. Rus quickly noosed the leg with a red kerchief to stanch the flow.

"Easy now, breathe easy…" he urged as he helped Pete lay back, then elevated the leg. He gingerly ripped open the jeans to examine the wound. The kneecap was visible through the raw flesh.

"He's cut pretty bad," Rus said, looking to Lee.

Lee's first thought was "tough shit," and while he didn't say it, he didn't express much sympathy either.

"It could be worse, it's only oozing blood. He can tough it out. Right Pete?"

Pete didn't answer; he lay rolling his head from side to side, feeling faint. Lee knelt by for a closer look, grateful the blade had missed an artery or they'd had no choice but to run for help. But the bleeding had already slowed. They could manage.

"Look, if we keep it dressed and clean, he'll be alright. He can ride out with Frankie Wednesday morning."

"Guess there's no real choice is there?"

"Nope. Not unless we wanna turn ourselves in. But we can make do. We've got duct tape, and I've got a clean pair of white socks. They'll make a decent bandage."

"Okay then," Rus said. "Best boil some water 'n clean it first."

The boys pitched in, lending advice and encouragement. They soon had the wound cleaned and bandaged nice and snug. Ry picked up a dark water leaf, slapped it to Pete's chest and said, "There, you've got the first purple heart of the season."

Pete raised to his elbows and smiled, his face flush, relieved now that they'd stopped the bleeding. He wanted to stand and they helped him up.

"Feels pretty good," he said, testing his leg. "It'll work, long as I don't bend it."

Rus offered to cut for him, the same as he'd offered for Will. Pete waved him off, saying, "Naw, I'll be alright..."

To his credit he went back to work, hobbling around like a peg-legged little pirate. Shed his cowboy hat and wore a blue bandana. Beginning to earn his stripe. More sober now and showed greater respect for the fallen queen, careful to chop away from rather towards a hand or knee. And thereafter he took only moderate-sized plants.

By mid-morning the clouds began to break, the sun shone through and the day warmed. While Pete proved himself game by attempting to cut, they helped keep him supplied, dropping off a few plants each time they returned. All worked in good humor. The hemp in prime season stripped with a simple motion of the hand, leaves and buds dropping off the stem like ice-cream off a ladle in July. Weather clearing and Pete on the mend, the boys honed to the routine, relishing the golden days of early autumn, leaves turning yellow, the air as warm and sweet as ripe plums, their flesh vigorous with youth, each felt himself the author of his own enchantment. Puffs of clouds floated through the southwest like flecks of popcorn in a bowl of blue. The spell lasted through the morning, till the noon whistle from the distant town reminded them that they were not entirely separate from the world and man and that things still reached out to touch them.

And there soon came a more poignant reminder. Bruce and Jack had jaunted west to try their luck and dashed back a few minutes later empty-handed. Both looked like they'd seen a panther.

"We're not alone," Bruce said, trying his best to stay calm.

"What do you mean?" Ry half expected word of another UFO.

"There's someone else in the patch."

"You see 'em?" Rus asked.

"No, but we found their gear. Two big army bags full of hemp. And a lantern."

"But you didn't hear or see anyone?" Rus asked again as Lee returned with a bundle of hemp and eased it to the ground.

Each one thinking the same thing: *Time to grab a running pack.*

"No. Just those two bags," Bruce answered to their immediate relief. "They're stashed near a small clearing about fifty yards straight west. We checked but couldn't find any tracks. And the grass had turned white under the bags, so no one's been there for a few days."

"That's right," Jack said, still wary. "I doubt if they've been in there since the big rain. But I dunno, it stays dry, they're bound to show up..." He cocked his head and cast his glass orb through the foliage like he could see trouble coming, wondering why the hell he'd traded the highway for the patch.

"Back in the clearing...did you see any plants down?" Lee asked.

"No. No plants down. It looked like they'd been snipping off end buds. Which seems awfully tedious," Bruce noted, beginning to relax and poke at the logic of things, "just doesn't make much sense to me."

"It does if you know Val," Pete smiled. "He'll fucking lace it with angel dust and pass it off as Thai-stick."

Lee now understood why he hadn't noticed anything during his scout through the patch the previous week.

"What strikes me odd is why they left those bags behind. Makes me wonder if they weren't run off. Maybe busted. Hey, Pete, when did you last hear from Valentine?"

"Oh, about two weeks ago. He was in Lawrence and stopped by. But tell ya what," Pete added with a cunning grin. "When we get ready to load out, if he hasn't showed, we can take those two bags as well."

"The hell we will." This time Lee was insistent. "We'll take out what we cut and that's all. We won't touch those bags, you got that? We're here to cut hemp, not start a range war."

"Lee's right," Rus said as others agreed. "Don't trouble trouble."

"I second that." Dixie was a good union man, didn't cross a picket line or hijack anyone. "I hate job disputes. Which work is whose, and iron workers are the worst. And I hear Valentine packs iron."

"You boys are way too worried about Val," Pete laughed. "He's all bark."

"That's good. Then maybe we can hear 'im coming," Lee said. "Let's keep our eyes and ears peeled. We'll steer clear of that area and cut back in this direction. If he doesn't show by the time we load out Wednesday, we can skip on west and cut closer to the road the last two days. If he does show, we'll have a quick parley and make peace. Right, Pete?"

"Aw, there won't be no problem…"

The boys took little comfort in Pete's assurance and returned to work mindful of caution, kept their voices low and worked in a tighter radius. They listened for traffic along the road and every half hour or so one would climb the near rise and check for sign of anyone coming through the pasture. Noting all clear, they'd return and resume their task. In such fashion the day slowly faded.

By the time the sun dipped to the horizon the boys had settled down for their evening meal—seated on a dead log or sitting cross-legged near the stove, they chowed on hamburgers and pork and beans and sipped Rus's signature coffee. Their bellies fed and warmed, all felt pretty good about the day despite the earlier alarm. The wind died at sundown and the birds quieted in the hush of falling shadows. The boys hardly spoke. They laid back and listened to dogs barking in the distance, a tractor working late in a field, and miles to the south the slow moan of a train rolling west.

In wait of the moonrise the heavens shone in full splendor, vast and aglitter to the eye. A short while later the wind rose and clouds again shouldered forth, blocking out the greater number of stars till only a few appeared through the low stratus like minnows in a fluid stream. To the east the moon waxed full and cast its dusty light, intermittently defining the terrain and trees like a soft etching, then once more obscured as if smudged with charcoal. The boys lay in their camp beds and listened to the hypnotic swirl of the wind and leaves as the night deepened and cooled. At last fatigued, they slept like primal sons unburdened by language, unplagued by dreams.

The cry of a calf carried through the night, followed by a cow's deep bawl. Lee sat up. Rus and Ry were already awake and standing, staring east from where the distress came. Lee slipped on his boots and joined them. The wind had calmed and the sky again threatened rain while the low overcast amplified every sound. Along with the cow and calf they heard the hollow clank of metal and a yipping dog.

"See them lights?" Rus pointed to the haze of shifting spears cast beyond the trees, perhaps a quarter-to-a-half mile away.

"Yeah…something's up," Ry said.

"We better check it out…"

They didn't bother to wake the others, left them dead asleep and filed off through the hemp and trees, carefully making their way to the cross-fence as curious as they were anxious of what they might find. They moved easily through the adjacent pasture, the ground open and heavily grazed, but they took greater care proximate to the source, crouching to where the light dimly hovered as if an alien craft may have landed in the bowl of the hill beyond. And they might have expected as

much but for the hue of cattle and man-curses that were most
definitely of the earth. Near the summit they lowered to their
hands and knees and crawled forth through the damp grass till
they lay on the rim of a limestone outcropping.

On an upslope about seventy-five yards distant, a truck
directed its lights into a makeshift corral formed in part by a
pickup and a stock trailer parked at a cant to the pasture fence.
An old house established the far wall of the corral, while the
remaining passages were blocked by metal stock gates. Lanterns
hung from various fence posts, the trailer, and along the side of
the house, marking a lit perimeter around the truck's central
beam. Four men worked the cattle, using whips and prods and
a small stout dog that darted in and out among the kicking
hooves. Two stock gates formed a chute along both sides of the
ramp to the trailer, with the far gate braced to a fence post and
the near gate left free to pivot.

After driving an animal in, two men pressed the gate closed
while another blocked the path with an iron bar wedged waist
high between the front verticals. A fourth man then pulled a
branding iron from the red coals of a portable forge and jabbed
it to the left rump, singing hair and hide as the rank smoke
curled to the damp night air like a dread perfume. The victim
bawled and other animals looked on in fear. Another three
cattle and two calves huddled up against the outer wall of the
old house in wait.

The house was a one-story gray shell, hollowed out and
abandoned since the 20s, isolate, void of light and life, roof
collapsed, the yard and outbuildings gone to pasture. Lee
recognized the place. Remembered the day he and his brother
had ridden there on horseback—Lee was about five years old
and Garret ten at the time. They'd been herding cattle on the
spring wheat and grew curious of the house; it lay to the north
on a neighbor's land. They rode over for a visit, sat inside and
ate sardines and crackers and imagined themselves camped
in an outlaw den. They dug through the rubbish but found no
hidden gold or weapons, only a bent pot or two and some old
bottles.

Lee felt a nudge from Ry.

"Pretty weird, huh?" Ry grinned in a low voice. "Branding cattle by lamplight. And kind of ironic, us cutting hemp in one pasture and them rustling in the next."

"Yeah, like a scene out of the old west, except for the trucks. Think they're hauling in or loading out?"

"Looks to me like they're loading out," Rus said. "Either way, they're up to no good." Another pack of wild dogs in his estimate.

The boys lay there watching it like a movie. Free entertainment, like sneaking into the Cibola drive-in theater without paying. Ry chewed on a blade of grass, still grinning in wonder at the things men do to make money.

The rustlers were too distant to identify and the boys couldn't hear anything more than a stray cuss or shout. Try as they might they couldn't catch a single name, and to move closer risked notice from the dog. Though they could tell that the truck was an old Chevy by the shape of the cab and anyone could see that the pickup was a recent model, dark in color. The stock trailer was about mid-sized and mud-splattered. Otherwise all was as vague and grainy as a silent movie cast on a far screen.

In another ten minutes the last of the cattle were branded and loaded into the trailer. The stock gates were stacked in the bed of the truck. The lanterns doused and collected. The dog whistled into the cad. The pickup led the way out with lights on dim, pulling the trailer. The truck followed. They slowly wound up through the pasture and back onto the road. The pickup turned north; the truck headed south.

The boys stood and watched them go.

"Wonder where they're taking 'em?"

"Some distant pasture or sale barn, I'd guess," Rus said as if asking the question himself. "Or maybe the Sand Hills. Or Omaha or Saint Joe. Hard to say what you do with stolen cattle these days."

"Any thought who they might be?"

"Nope. Wouldn't hazard a guess."

"Could be Frankie out moonlighting," Ry offered for a laugh.

"Oh hell no," Rus scowled as they turned to make their way back. "That new pickup ain't Frankie's style. He'll blow a thousand dollars on tools to fix a hundred-dollar junker. I swear that boy, he'd rather grease his hands than grease his dick."

"Think so?"

"Why, I know so..."

In like manner they bantered and joked crossing the pasture, relieved to find the intruders gone and themselves alone again in their rude haunt. Though they quieted by the time they entered the creek and approached camp. A light drizzle accompanied their return. They crawled into their sleeping bags and drew ponchos over their heads as the drizzle turned to rain drumming on the fabric next to their ears. They listened to the rain mix with the hum of the earth and were soon asleep.

The rain continued through the night, though never hard. The boys slept warm if not entirely dry and woke in no great hurry to roll out, again facing a gray wet dawn. They pulled away from a puddle or stirred to adjust their bedding and slept on till roused by the sun breaking through and the sweet smell of coffee.

Rus sat by his camp-stove, humming "Soldier's Joy," a favorite fiddle tune, and wishing he had his fiddle. Feeling spry and ready to jig.

"Shake a leg, boys. Rise 'n shine," he announced, banging a spoon on the side of the kettle. "You can miss the late show, but not the day show. Come on now, we got a whole herd a' hemp to slaughter."

Ry sat up, blinked his eyes and winced.

"Criminey, Rus, lay off that kettle, will ya? You remind me of Whitey Hunter."

"Aw hell, I'm a far cry from that ol' fart. Here it is past eight o'clock. He used to kick us out at five-thirty. Drag us down to the cafe and make us listen to his bull for a good hour a'fore heading on to work. Ol' buzzard could've let us sleep till six."

"Could have, but didn't," Ry grinned as Bruce rolled over and moaned remembering the very thing, waking to the old man's stomp and shout the summer they worked on the road crew south of Des Moines.

Whitey Hunter was a one-armed heavy equipment operator

who ran graders. "A blade man" as he called it. And a damn good one. With that one hand he could drive a car and roll a cigarette. He'd steady the wheel with his forearm, open the pouch and pour the tobacco with his teeth, then roll, lick, and light it, rarely looking at the road the whole time while glancing over his shoulder and talking nonstop to whoever was riding along. A sociable old gent and self-appointed custodian of the young fellows—made it his duty to see they were out of their motel rooms and at work on time. Their nemesis at dawn, then he'd corral them in a bar any night they weren't out chasing girls, buy round after round and drink them under the table. But damned if he'd let them sleep it off.

"Remember that morning we left 'im hanging?" Rus noted, arching his brow.

"Yes indeed...like it was yesterday. You told him we'd follow to the restaurant. And there he stood in the parking lot..." Ry explained to Dixie as he squatted by to pour some coffee. "The ol' devil was waiting for us to pull in. Rus just honked the horn and we blew on by. Left ol' Whitey wondering what the hell...?"

"It was a Friday morning and we'd worked every blasted day for two weeks straight," Rus told the story while Jack and Lee took turns at the coffee and Pete sat bandaging his leg. "I got a wild hair up my ass to go see this little gal, Betsy McClure, down in Carthage, Tennessee. Sweet little blonde, fresh as a lily, she was fine I swear. I'd met her on a swing through there a year before while I's still with the band."

"Did you ever get it out?" Dixie asked.

"*Out*...?" Rus gave a vague shrug and continued. "Anyhow, so we hit Nashville that night. And yeah, we headed on out to Carthage next day. Found her place and hung around on the porch for an hour or so like a couple stray dogs."

"Rus was sweet-talking her pretty good, too. Till her boyfriend showed up."

"Whoops..."

"You better believe it. A big sucker in a black GTO. He thunders in 'n gets out looking like Judgement Day. Who's that? I ask. And she says, '*That's mah fee-awn-say...*' Bo, Buck or some

such name. I say, See ya later, Betsy. We head down off that
porch past Bo, Buck or whoever the fuck he is, and I say, Sure
some pretty country here along the Cumberland. Then I wave
back 'n holler, Thanks for the directions, Miss!"

"It really was pretty country down through there."

"Pretty country 'n dern glad to be leaving it."

"But did you ever get it out?"

"What...? Get what out, Dixie?"

"That wild hair up your ass. Did you ever get it out?"

The boys all laughing as Rus shot back, "Hell no! I's savin' it
for your sweet lips."

"Whoa now, you got that wrong," Dixie wagged his finger in
quick protest. "I play mouth harp, not ass harp. Which reminds
me, you still up for Winfield next week?"

"Up? You dern tootin'," Rus slapped his knee. "Saddled up
'n rarin' to go. Ready to hear some hot fiddle 'n flat-pickin'."

"Great! We get outa here Friday morning we can rest up,
drive down and still catch half the show. Be there all of Saturday
and Sunday. They've got New Grass Revival and Doc Watson
playing back-to-back."

"Next to a hot fiddle I'll take Doc on guitar anytime. You
going Lee?"

"I doubt it. Not this year. Don't think Diana's into it."

"Heck, bring her along. Lori'll be there. Tell her I'll do the
cooking."

"That might work."

"Speaking of shows," Ry declared. "You boys missed the big
event last night."

"How's that?"

"Cattle were raising a ruckus in the next pasture. Rus, Lee,
and I went over to check it out. Topped that near hill and Lo 'n
Behold...spied some rustlers at work."

"No shit?"

"I kid you not. Honest-to-god rustlers. They worked from
around midnight to one. Branded about a dozen head, then
loaded up and rode out."

"Damned if I heard a thing," Jack said, looking to Dixie and
Pete. They both shook their heads.

"Well I...thought it was a dream," Bruce said. "Sounded like a calf being killed."

"Yeah, they'll bawl to high heaven you lay a hot poker to their ass."

"Worse than a fucking tattoo, I bet." Pete grimaced as he stood, his leg stiff and swollen through the night. "Any idea who it was?"

"No, they had a dog along, so we didn't get too close."

"Could be that fucking Val. He only lives a mile or so east. But crazy as he is, I wouldn't think he'd rustle in his own back yard."

"They headed north with the cattle. So they might be from Nebraska. Still pretty weird though, seeing 'em out there rustling in the night. We've seen some weird sights this season, right Lee?"

"Right, first night out a UFO. Then the wild dogs..."

"And there's that big buffalo me 'n Frankie nearly hit..."

"Yep. Now we've got midnight rustlers. Pretty weird stuff, I'd say."

"And who knows," Dixie laughed, adding to their potluck of experience, "we have a good day, maybe catch a few wood nymphs out tonight."

"I could go for that."

"Oh yeah..."

The boys having fun living in the thick of the moment, oblivious to further motive or need, for it was as much their own story as money they sought. The clouds parted and drifted on east in promise of another golden day. The boys hung their bedding from tree limbs to dry, same with socks and other articles of clothing. Rus again peeled off slices of bacon and cracked eggs in the skillet. Bruce squatted by, first in line, hunger driven. He picked up a tin plate and noticed something green caked to the edge.

"Is this plate clean?" he asked.

"Shoot yes. Washed it myself..."—Rus took and held it to the sunlight. "Clean as a baby's butt."

"Then what's this?" Bruce pointed to the green crud.

"Aw hell, that's just moss. Used it to wipe 'em clean. Don't be such a fuss bucket. A little creek lettuce won't hurt ya none. Here, have some eggs..."—Rus plopped on a pair sunny side up, sizzling hot with bacon grease.

At the sight and smell Bruce forget all about the moss. He leaned back on the log and downed his fare with a slice of bread. A pure moment in a pure morning. The boys all enjoying the simple pleasures of food and friendship. The hum of the fire, the crackle of grease, their lips smacking on juicy bacon. The air fresh, pregnant with odors. The peace of the morning broken only by a mob of crows that landed in a tree to the north with a furious squawk as if protesting a theft they had no part in.

"I wonder what gives with them crows?" Ry asked.

"If I remember, there's a plum thicket up that draw," Lee said. "Might be a coyote or raccoon in there. If it was a jay or some other bird, they'd run it off."

"That squabble would run me off. Pretty incessant." Ry gritted his teeth. "Like monkeys in the jungle. Wake you every morning with their shriek and chatter. Mean little cusses, they'd throw shit at you like a horde of VC. We had this big tough kid from Chicago in our platoon, named Bolinka. He got pissed one day, took an M-79 grenade launcher, popped a round into the trees and splattered monkeys to kingdom come."

"Monkeys were good eating," Rus said as he leaned to his plate.

"Yeah, the villagers usually had one roasting over a fire. And monkey on a stick wasn't half bad. But I couldn't abide anything with a hand or foot attached. It looked too much like a child. Made me queasy. Weird, too, how they caught 'em."

"Why? They use grenades?" Dixie laughed.

"Afraid not. That wouldn't leave much to eat. No, they'd weave a basket and leave a hole in the lid just big enough for a monkey to stick its hand in. Then they'd place an apple inside and set it by a trail. Sooner or later a monkey would happen by and reach in to snatch the apple. Then they'd have 'im."

"How so?"

"Craziest thing, once it grabs the apple, a monkey won't let go. Won't even think to let go. And the hole's too small to retrieve the apple. So he sits there all day trapped by his own want. Till some villager comes along and knocks 'im in the head."

"Whoa, that's a frightful thought," Dixie said. "Clobbered by your own fool urge to grab something. Makes you wonder if we don't all have a little monkey in us."

"Sure, why not? There's women for one. Eve used an apple..."

"Christ yes, always ready to grab for tits 'n ass..."

"Or a fistful of dollars..."

"Right again..."

"Then there's cocaine..."

"You tell 'em brother..."

"My God yes, leave you kicking like a poisoned cockroach wanting more."

"Tell me about it," Pete said in mild disgust. "Had a guy come by last week and offer me his girlfriend for a quarter gram. I said, Look fella, just bring me the money, I've already got a girlfriend. Jesus..."

"Definitely a dangerous drug..."

"No doubt. Good thing it's high-priced and illegal..."

"Hey Pete"—Rus gave wink—"If ya ain't got a boyfriend, I might could fix ya up with Dixie for a little snort..."

The boys laughed again at their want and folly. But finished with breakfast, they soon quieted and began sharpening their machetes on pocket stones, each focused to their blade and separate in thought of what might betray them. Each was subject to a pending urge, drawn by a flame that if touched would burn—like cattle lured by sweet alfalfa to their branding in the night.

Their day reflected the paradox—all were playful in work and mood, yet plagued by doubts. Wondering if Valentine would appear and why he hadn't, of who the rustlers might have been, and most of all whether more rain would make the roads impassable, leaving them stranded with a ton of hemp? Though the sun shone with a warm wind, clouds continued to pass overhead. And clouds and rain were like smoke and fire, given one there was a good chance of the other. But worry wouldn't change a thing. The boys forged ahead and put their faith in the sun and their own effort.

"Got your hand on an apple, boy?"—or offshoots thereof

became their byword, their hedge against aggravation and worry as they glanced to the sky and checked the road, till by evening their sole concern was all the hemp they had to carry out. Forty-eight bags split seven ways with each man carrying two at a time meant three trips plus. A full mile per round trip, totaling four miles in all, and half that distance toting eighty pounds of wet hemp presented a load of work even with poles rigged with hay sacks to ease the burden.

Luckily Pete's leg had limbered through the day and wasn't bleeding, so he was ready to do his part. A little too ready, perhaps. They'd eaten supper and still had a half hour before sundown. Lee and Rus thought it best to wait till dark. Ry agreed.

"Fuck it!" said Pete. "Who's gonna see us? Hasn't been a car or truck down that road all day." He had his cowboy hat back on, jeans stuffed in his boots, hell-bent to drive the herd to market. And Bruce, Jack, and Dixie were leaning his way, none too anxious to stumble through the dark. Pete shouldered his pole and bags and started off, striding like a stiff-legged little Prussian. And just as boneheaded.

"Pete!" Rus hollered. "If I had a litter out of you, I'd stuff 'em in a gunny sack 'n drown every last one." But Pete marched on, wasn't listening. Short of knocking him down and sitting on him, he wasn't going to stop. And with the others prone to follow, Rus muttered, "What the hell..." decided to throw caution to the wind.

The boys soon humped up over the rise and began the long trek across the broad grassy slope towards the road west. A deep ravine lay about a hundred yards shy of the road, running parallel as it fed into the creek. The boys angled down to the dry bed and climbed up the far bank. They'd stash the bags there and wait till dark to position them near the road. By now Pete was bringing up the rear, out of breath and out of shape, his body more inured to beer and cocaine than long exertion. Still, he managed to stutter-step to the base of the ravine, but gave up trying to climb.

Rus scuttled down to fetch his load.

"How ya doing there, buddy?"

"Aw...not too bad," Pete gasped. "I'm good for another trip. After that...I don't know"—somewhat less willful, slowly giving in to the pain and weakness of his leg.

The boys ambled back in listless fashion, bobbing their empty poles, all weary from two days of harvest and burdens yet to carry. Back in camp they slacked their thirst and once more secured their loads, trudging off like pack mules in a line of march—heads bent, mute in their labor, watching their boots scuff the grass with thought of nothing more than bedding down like the sun now vanishing in the west. Rus took the lead while Pete kept a fair pace thirty yards back. In the dimming twilight they reached the ravine and again descended to make the steep climb up, their legs tiring under the weight and effort. Rus and Bruce were first to the top, followed by Lee who knelt thereby and dropped his load. He'd no more than taken a breath when he noticed his companions draw tense and alert.

"There's someone up yonder," Rus said.

"Yeah, and more over there..." Bruce glanced off towards the road.

And now Lee heard it too—a car door slammed, frightfully distinct in the quiet evening. Then he scanned back south as a black pickup followed by a red jeep sped through the gate and skidded to a stop at the head of the ravine. From the road came the hard static of a two-way radio echoed by the same north across the creek as more car doors slammed in sync with shouts from both directions, surrounding them in a dizzying swirl.

The next instant two men exited the lead pickup, each armed with a rifle or shotgun, otherwise vague figures in the gathering dusk. One quickly circled east in a flanking maneuver while the other sent a hail of automatic rifle fire through the trees, hitting with a dread zip and thud, severing limbs and leaves.

"Why the fuck don't they identify themselves?" Lee voiced in anger and fear, his heart beating twice for every quickened breath. "They could at least say we're under arrest before they start shooting."

"Don't think they're the law," Rus said as they hunched down behind the bags.

"Then who the fuck are they?"

"I don't know and I'm not sticking around to find out."

"Me neither!"

Lee grabbed his running pack and looked to Bruce edging back towards a cedar thicket. Bruce shook his head and said, "No way. I'm not moving..." Lee glanced across the ravine and saw Pete frozen in shadow behind a tree. Below, Dixie and Jack raised their heads like startled deer and raced off after Ry already heading for deeper cover like he was again running through the jungle as more gunfire ricocheted across the creek answered by a crisp burst close by.

Rus and Lee exchanged a quick nod and took to their heels, dashing across thirty yards of open ground, registering the crack and whiz of hot lead as they leapt the fence and hurtled a bramble of gooseberries. They slid down a sheer bank to the waiting creek, a scree of dirt and rocks tumbling in behind as they hit with a splash and regained their footing. Both stood knee-deep in murky water.

"I'm headed for the bridge," Rus said between deep breaths. "You gonna come?"

"You think it's wise? No telling how many are along the road. They could have the whole section surrounded like coyote hunters. Better to lay low."

"Well, do what you want, Lee. I'm gonna run for it."

"You sure?"

"Yeah, I'm headin' out. You comin'?"

"No, not just yet. But good luck."

"You too..."

Rus shuffled on through the water and soon rounded the bend.

Lee waded on out, his boots slurping in the deep mud. He gripped a root and pulled himself up the near bank and disappeared into a dark cluster of hemlock and hemp.

XVI. ON THE RUN

Nightfall. Clouds scudded below the moon, sometimes blocking it from view, sometimes weaving a veil, depending on their density and dispersal. Lee had observed the movement of the moon and clouds for nearly an hour, uncertain of the time, having no watch. The gunfire had ceased, slowly abating like the last kernels of popping corn, followed by scattered shouts and the mumble of distant voices carried off in the wind. Now silent.

Lee had heard several gunshots in the vicinity of the bridge shortly after Rus left and more to the southwest where Ry, Dixie, and Jack were headed. For several minutes he feared the worst and was gripped by grief, but hearing nothing more, he let it pass. And what of Bruce and Pete so proximate to the gunmen? There was no way of knowing. He only dared hope that his friends were either on the run or being carted off to jail, that all were safe and none harmed. A hope so fervent it verged on prayer, wondering what god he could appeal to. The god of the moon and stars? Of the desperate moment? Of the very creek where he had once felt so secure and blest? Now hunted?

All he heard was a quiet inner voice say, *Buck up, you can't lay there forever...*

In his initial panic he'd wedged his body under a fallen tree trunk, half expecting a hundred men to sweep the creek in search. But short of using dogs they would not have found him. From his own experience he knew that flushed game was more easily hunted than game holed up; the latter could only be smoked out and that entailed knowing where they were. Lee would not be easy prey.

For some time he'd watched the moon, determined not to move till it reached the outer limb of a dead tree that stood in the direct foreground. And gazing to its cratered surface, he discerned The Sea of Tranquility—that men had actually ascended there and returned struck him at that moment in the midst of his own paltry venture as a feat so incredible as to inspire awe and a wilt of shame. And so shamed he stood and shook off his fear. Aside from making his way clear of the area and escape arrest, his sole hope of redemption lay in intercepting Frankie before he too fell in a trap.

Surely someone in Oakvale, not three miles distant, had heard the gunfire in the quiet dusk and notified authorities. Which to Lee's mind eliminated Valentine as the likely aggressor—no way he would risk such a rash show of force. Though he was very likely the cause. Lee could well imagine him doing some fool thing to rouse the local citizens, like selling drugs to a boy or girl or threatening a neighbor, and so roused they decided to rid the county of him and his kind and in the process happened on the boys. "Armed vigilantes" was Lee's surmise. And if too few to search the creek, they had likely posted sentinels to watch through the night.

After taking a couple of steps and hearing the slosh of his boots, Lee sat down on a log and pulled them off. He wrung out his socks then eased them back on, his feet raw and blistered from two days of being wet and worked in. His boots had stretched and were breaking over at the heel; he laced them tight for a better fit and set off once more, angling towards the road north of the bridge. He had a canteen of water, a running pack, a penlight, and a compass—though he felt no need to check, confident he knew his way. His main concern was to watch for any sign of man and avoid sticks that would snap underfoot and betray his presence. Threading his way carefully past trees and brush, he soon emerged into open pasture and moved at a brisker pace.

He covered a couple hundred yards before realizing something was wrong. The ground didn't rise and the road was nowhere in sight; he should have reached it in half that distance. He scrambled up a small bluff that edged the creek to get his bearings. He still saw no sign of the road, but in the midst of the dark foliage of the creek flickered an island of light. Two men stood by a lantern checking assorted equipment and bags of hemp. Lee suddenly realized he was staring down at his own camp. So they had left men behind, while others were likely still out hunting.

He crouched down lest the moon cast his silhouette, then crawled under the fence and took refuge in the adjacent milo field. He ran a good hundred yards before kneeling between two leafy rows. Well-distanced, he popped open his compass and cupped the penlight to get a reading. He held the compass to the north, but the needle kept pointing south, or at least in the direction he thought was south. He repositioned the compass to read north, then aligned his body and glanced up. The land, the sky, the compass—all appeared in reverse of what he sensed. He closed the compass, flipped and caught it like a coin, thinking it somehow subject to random malfunction, that at a toss it might read heads or tails. Again he popped the lid. This time the green fluorescence glowed of its own as the needle floated in delicate quiver then held steady, again pointing in the opposite direction of what Lee thought was north.

Whether it made sense or not, he had to trust the compass. Because nothing made sense just then. Being shot at and flushed like a rabbit from your childhood home made no sense. And typical of any addled prey he'd ran full circle, and that definitely made no sense. Having played the fool enough, he followed the compass northwest across the milo field and in a short while reached the road. From there he headed north instead of south for fear of someone stationed by bridge.

The road presented danger as well, but he had no real choice if he hoped to head Frankie off because it was midnight or past and he had miles to go. He planned to take the next road west a mile then head south. To skirt the intersection and to save time he cut northwest. Not knowing the terrain he soon found himself slogging through a plowed field, his legs weighted and slowed by the effort. When he reached the road, he scraped off his boots and noticed a split in the left sole. He realized why soldiering was so hard on the feet. In hope to spare his good boots, he'd worn his old ones. A foolish choice. And the one thing missing from his running pack was running shoes. Still, he had a change of clothes, wallet, ID, and cash. Plus a canteen of water—though he'd drank nearly half already, his mouth so dry from the initial fear and panic and the long trek toting hemp. He took a single swallow to wet his mouth and headed on at a shuffle-jog, bearing west, gaining distance from the scene. In a few more minutes he turned south, moving with greater assurance and ease. By now he reckoned he was four miles north and three miles west of Oakvale, and to intercept Frankie south along the highway, he needed to cover at least eight or nine miles. Not such a problem given better shoes; he cursed his boots and lengthened his stride. His one advantage was adrenalin coursing through him like a hot drug.

The first farmhouse he came to stood back from the road, dimly lit, remote and sleepy in the damp night. He gave it little notice, merely slunk down in the ditch and passed on. But the next house stood immediately west of the road in the bright glare of a yard light with two large dogs guarding the porch. Across the road sat a series of hog sheds with various farm implements parked along the north, the entire area overgrown with weeds. Lee crossed the ditch and circled east, picking his way through the tangled weeds and junked equipment. He tripped once, tearing his jeans on a snarl of barbed wire. Further on he struck his shin against the iron hitch of an old corn planter. And crossing south he waded through a hog lot, sucking mire into his boots, not the best poultice for bleeding feet. He sloshed through a ditch of standing rainwater to clean them somewhat before regaining the road. What should have taken mere minutes had taken a quarter of an hour. He cursed the place, downed a gulp of water, and despite the condition of his feet, quickened his pace south.

Here and there the moon shone through the veil of clouds like an ancient tower clock fading west. Fortunately the road was free of inhabitants over the next two miles and Lee made good time, pausing only once in scrutiny of a hunched form in his path that looked for all the world like a basketball wrapped in fur. At Lee's approach it sprang to life, leaping one way while he leapt the other. Most likely a raccoon from its humped back and loping escape. Lee laughed and ran on to the next hill. From there he noted the meager lights of Oakvale camped in the broad creek valley east, while south of town the lights of a lone vehicle crept along the highway. His only chance of reaching that point before Frankie passed through was to leave the road and travel cross-country.

He followed a long sloping pasture into the low valley, again making good time. But the bottom ground was planted to milo, and while not as muddy as the plowed field he'd crossed, it was still gooey. No longer able to run, he tromped through the milo in headlong stride, kicking off clumps of mud every few steps only to gather more. In the grass and timber near the creek he found better footing, but was hardly relieved. The White Rock flowed more like a river than a creek and he had no idea where to cross or what lay ahead. He simply plunged on, soon battling a forest of hemlock and stingweed; he couldn't see his own hands grasping to break a way through—bindweed wrapped his legs and torso, so willful and resistant it made him wish he was back in the mud. Which he found soon enough crashing through the snare of weeds as he took one blind step and slipped down a muddy bank, ending chest deep in a swirl of cold black water.

The creek was swollen from recent rains. Lee edged into the current, briefly touching bottom before he began to breaststroke across, carried swiftly downstream as he sought the far bank and footing, legs numb with cold and fatigue, fighting the weight of his boots, feared he'd drown like his father, arms weakening, knew he couldn't swim for long, envisioned his body half-buried in silt, crows and coyotes squabbling over the plums of his eyes. Suddenly he nosed into the muck of an earthen wall. He wiped his face and glanced up. A cut bank rose above him nearly as high and steep as the one he and Rus had escaped down. Lee reached forth and clawed at the mud, gained some footing and began to kick and dig, slowly stair-stepping his way up, grasping at rocks and roots for any handhold. Finally he gripped a low-hanging brush and pulled himself up over the rim. He plopped to the grass and rolled over, gasping for air.

Thoroughly winded. He lay there watching his breath steam to the sky, warmed by his effort but chilled by the water. And the chill soon deepened in the night's brisk wind.

The yellow moon peeped through the clouds as if tempted to hatch its light, then sealed once more in its embryonic void. Cold and wet as he was, Lee too wished to curl up, close his eyes and sleep. *Crumble into dust like a mud-formed doll...*the inner voice chided. The next instant he kicked himself up and staggered on. Had to keep moving. Had to stop Frankie. And he hadn't gone ten steps when a sharp blow struck his legs and knocked him to the ground. Stunned. Didn't know who he was or what had hit him. The world and self fogged in a fluid haze then slowly focused. His mind cleared. He sat up and squinted his eyes, noted the faint line of an electric fence attached to a short insulated post. There were other posts spaced down the way. He'd hit electric fences before and always got a jolt but never had one slam him to the ground. Of course he'd never hit one while soaked head to foot, which likely added to the shock. On the brighter side he now felt fully awake, like having drunk a pot of thick black coffee, dregs and all.

Lee found a forked stick nearby and used it to depress the wire like the head of a snake, then carefully stepped over. He continued on, following the stick like a blind dowser till he located the perimeter wire and likewise crossed again. He kept the stick for a walking staff as he entered the mile-wide stretch of land that lay between him and the highway. All plowed ground over which he plodded and trudged like a plow horse, dragging his accumulated effort and exhaustion like a plow, too weary to kick the mud off his boots, simply leaned in his traces and plowed on.

Closer to the highway he drifted on south to avoid the headlights of a sedan that kept cruising halfway up the hill then turning back to town like a nervous proctor pacing a hall. Always the same sedan, judging by its profile and missing taillight. Probably the town constable, an old whiskey sipper hired to keep an eye on the main drag and usually passed out with his feet propped up in the window by that hour. But due to occurrences north of town he may have felt compelled to monitor the road leading in and out. So Lee reasoned, extending his trek south.

At the crest of the long hill he drank the last of his water and clicked the canteen into its canvass holster. Clear of the patrolling lights, he cut straight for the ditch, his lone concern being how to signal Frankie. He tested his penlight; it still worked, but seemed awfully faint to cast a beam across the sea of night. Armed with a peashooter when he needed a shotgun. But he would have to make do and chance moving closer, wait in the ditch till he recognized the van then rush onto the road.

He presently observed a set of headlights coming north. Lights on low beam, possibly Frankie. But as it loomed, he saw it was a large truck; he crouched down and watched it pass. Immediately thereafter another vehicle appeared, lights on high beam, so he knew it wasn't Frankie and he edged back into the field beyond view.

There was no more traffic for a time as Lee continued south, and he began to wonder if he'd arrived too late. Then a third vehicle appeared, still distant, but lights on dim. He knelt in the ditch and waited. Strained his eyes to define the shape against the curtain of night as the headlights beetled forth. At last he discerned the box-like van and sprang up from the ditch with a wild shout, waving the penlight. But the lights were cast to the far ditch and the driver didn't see the frantic form dancing at his side—Frankie sat in profile at the window, hunched over the wheel, numb to all but the wedge of light on the road ahead, lost in the dim realm of the psyche that neither sleeps nor wakes.

Lee stood in the middle of the road and shouted long and hard, arching his penlight overhead in desperate hope that Frankie would check his mirror and stop. But the van continued on indifferent as if passing a shadow in the night. Lee stomped the road and cursed himself and his caution—if only he'd jumped out a second sooner he might have caught Frankie's eye. Might have stopped him from going over the edge like a doomed sailor into the dragon's mouth. He stumbled off the road and slumped down by the fence. Seeing Frankie lost like the rest of his friends, lost due to his own fool scheme, and seeing the night's long effort, his run prove futile, Lee hung his head and cried like a baby. Muddy, wet, beat. Cried like briar rabbit tarred in the night.

Again he heard the inner voice urge, *Buck up, can't be wasting tears when you're out of water.* Lee wiped his eyes and answered, "Yeah, I know..." as if the voice were there beside him. His father's grave lay on a hillside only a few miles northwest and he sensed him near. Not that he wished to beckon him in any wise or form, ever wary of the ghost as life and death stand separate and opposed. Yet he felt connected by the very air and did not fear as the voice again urged, *Better get going...*

Lee stood and hobbled on, crippled by the state of his boots and feet, no longer in a hurry, simply prompted by the voice. And he wondered in the vagueness of his mind, was it his father's voice or the other, the shadowing spirit that calls all to account? Or was it the darker soul quietly insinuating, following in his footsteps, waiting for him to weaken then pounce and offer a hand up for a price? Trailed by ghost, god, or devil, he had no answer to the question that had haunted man from the beginning. He simply trod on, somewhat aimless, had no real plan other than to reach the railroad, and no real urge other than thirst, hunger, and sleep.

In another mile the land began to lighten, revealing the pattern of distant trees and vegetation, and a hint of color in the fields washed with umber and shades of gray. The sky was completely overcast, the air cool and misty. Soon the faint line of the railroad appeared, and on an embankment a quarter mile west he noticed the purplish tinge of what looked to be a plum thicket. Lee cut across a pasture, once more heartened, striding in hope to allay his hunger and thirst. And he found plums, but the railroad had recently sprayed the right-of-way, shriveling leaves and all. Though some still looked plump and tempting, he left the poisoned fruit for the coyotes and crows, climbed the embankment and staggered on down the tracks.

Mankato laid another six or seven miles further east. His only thought at present was to cross the highway and find a place to hole up for the day. A farmhouse sat just south of the crossing beyond the fence, but he was too tired to circle around and it being first light, he chanced to pass. Two spaniels with briar-tangled fur rushed out from the yard and took up a yip and howl, following on his heels, more curious than vicious. Lee paid them no mind, but kept a furtive eye on the house, watching for sign of anyone at a door or a window. Still early, all abed he hoped. He walked on, casual and unhurried, trying to look the typical bum passing down the rails at dawn—but the typical bum had passed from the scene thirty years before. In any case the spaniels soon tired of following and turned back with a parting bark or two to send him on his way.

Directly east of the barn lay a field of cane sorghum that stretched for eighty acres along a gentle slope and adjacent pasture. Excellent cover for a fugitive. Lee trotted on another hundred yards then checked back to make certain no one was watching. The coast clear, he crossed the fence and slipped into the field. The enveloping cane towered eight to ten feet and grew dense and leafy as a jungle planted in evenly spaced rows. Lee ran to the very depths of the field, selected a relatively dry area, broke over a number of plants and stomped them into a nest. There, down out of the wind, he lay listening to the crisp swirl of leaves and tasseled heads. He split open a stalk and chewed its sweet pith in attempt to slake his hunger and thirst. Then he balled his fists and drew up his knees, shivering for warmth in his crude nest, hidden from the world like a ragged foundling in want of sleep.

He dozed fitfully for a couple hours, battling the damp chill until the sun broke through shedding a blanket of warmth. He sat up briefly and peeled off his boots and socks to air his blistered feet, then lay back spread-eagled beneath the sun and let it soothe his aching flesh. He draped a forearm over his eyes to shield the rays and in that faintly violet realm he slept.

When he awoke the sun centered the sky. He glanced from the wall of cane to the distant blue, flexed his toes and fingers and otherwise barely moved, continued soaking up the sun, had no food or water, pressed by no urgency. At last he roused, sat up and crossed his legs, took a razor from his running pack and dry-shaved as the blade tugged and scraped at three day's growth. Luckily, he was thin whiskered and achieved fair results at the price of only a few nicks. He ran his hands through his hair, smoothing it some, working to improve his appearance for entry into Mankato that evening. Then he shucked his mud-caked clothes and donned fresh jeans and a warm flannel shirt, both kept dry in his running pack. And pulling on a pair of clean socks, it felt like new skin drawn over his sore feet. But his old skin balked at pulling on his damp boots, rubbing each blister like salt in a wound. He decided to simply scrape off the mud and let them dry through the day. Put them on later. He stuffed his old clothes in the running pack, slung it over his shoulder, picked up his boots and walked in stocking feet down a soft earthen path between two rows of cane.

A broad pasture with scattered timber bordered the field to the south. Beyond the fence stood a grove of young cottonwoods; Lee crossed over and sat down against the largest one, its trunk about the width of his head. He gazed back towards the field and glimpsed a chirping meadow lark perched on the fence and watched a trio of butterflies perform their fluttering ballet above a pile of seasoned manure. Nearby, a monarch lit on a flowering milkweed while through the pasture bees buzzed and droned, harvesting the nectar of various other flowers—from stately golden rods and purple crested ironweeds to common prairie clovers. He had no thought of his situation or circumstance, content for the moment to simply drift with the immediate scene. Feeling warmed and rested, he reclined in the shade of the cottonwoods and listened to the singing yellow leaves. From time to time one spiraled down and landed in the grass. He closed his eyes and breathed easy, lulled by the day's deep orchestral hum.

In the midst of his reverie came the low clank and groan of a vehicle motoring up through the pasture. He bellied to the ground, his heart drumming as he peered around the base of the tree then jerked his head back. Two men in a faded blue pickup forty yards south headed his way, front tires astraddle a winding cattle path. Lee hunched his shoulders and shimmied around the radius of the tree like the second hand on a watch, keeping himself opposite the truck as it passed by. Only then did he notice his running pack and boots left in plain sight—he reached out and snatched them back and tucked them under his chin. He lay tense and still as the truck disappeared over the near rise and stopped by the field. A door opened, then another. He didn't move; he barely breathed. A minute later the doors banged shut and the engine revved. The rear axle made a high whine in backing up. Again they came his way. This time he reversed action, shifting counterclockwise around the tree to keep himself hidden. The truck passed so close he could have spit on a tire. But it kept rolling south, bouncing along the cattle path. And again he chanced to peek. On the gun rack in the back window hung a lever action rifle and a pump shotgun; yet the men merely glanced to one another and talked, apparently oblivious to his presence.

Lee wondered if someone had seen him that morning at the railroad crossing and mentioned it to a neighbor and were out giving the area a cursory look. Or maybe not. Surely if they were looking, they'd have seen him, and having seen him they'd have stopped, there being two of them and both armed. At the very least they'd have chased him off their land. And that they hadn't seen him was a minor miracle—the tree being so narrow his ears stuck out either side. Seeing them gone, he breathed easier. Still, he pulled on his boots and laced them tight, ready to run in case they returned. Numb to the pain of his feet, focused solely on the men, their threat and motive.

Then it dawned on him that they'd probably driven up to check the field and see if the cane was ready to harvest. Given another few days to dry, they'd likely be in there with a field cutter and trucks. The same with his brother Garret thirty miles south, likely doing the very thing, checking on his fields and fine-tuning equipment, preparing to cut silage any day now. Right then the notion struck Lee as highly attractive—sitting at the wheel of a big farm truck following a field cutter down rows of cane while it chopped and spewed stocks and leaves over the cab into the bed, nothing to do but hold steady at five mile an hour and listen to the radio, a jug of iced tea jostling in the seat, go to a restaurant at noon and eat your fill of fried chicken, potatoes and gravy, all the while earning $2.50 an hour, not to mention the bonus of going home each evening to Diana and Jesse and sleeping in a soft bed. It all sounded pretty damned good compared to being shot at and running the length and breadth of a far northern county till you were so dog tired and thirsty you could gnaw a bitter root, all on the chance of easy money, the desirability of which now ran directly counter to attendant consequences.

Sometimes *easy* was just way too hard.

With that thought the day darkened as Lee turned to see a massive thunderhead eclipse the sun, coming up from the west as suddenly as the pickup through the pasture. Jagged splits of lightning etched the horizon like fiery cracks in a deep-gray bowl that magically fused in the blink of an eye. Then a blinding strobe lanced a hillside no more than half a mile away. Thunder quaked and boomed like a large tonnage of sheet metal dropped to the near ground, followed immediately by a dense wall of rain marching down over the hill into the pasture. The wind whipped up, bending the trees and riling the cane before the onrushing storm. The temperature dropped as Lee felt the splat of cold rain. So recently dry and warm, he dreaded the thought of being wet and chilled. The cane field offered no shelter and there appeared no culvert or bridge to duck under. His only option was an old tree trunk fallen to the grass and bleached by time like the remnant bone of a dinosaur. He ran thereby and kicked and wedged himself in till he lay snug and dry at the hollow center. Carpenter ants, riled at his entry, crawled over his hands and face but remained oddly at truce with his skin, so he let them be—and their focus soon returned to the bone of things as they burrowed back into the rotted wood.

In the next instant the storm hit in a riot of rain. Lee uncapped his canteen and set it in the grass to catch what little he could. Then he reached out and cupped his hands and trapped the water to his mouth and continued to sup greedily for the minute or two it poured. So brief and meager was his refreshment and so deep his thirst that he was ready to shake his fist in angry want of more when it started to hail. Marble-sized balls of ice dropped rapidly over the pasture, rattling off the tree trunk, bouncing through the grass. One ricocheted near and he picked it up and popped it in his mouth, rolled it with his tongue to relish its cool wet joy. Better than any fruit he'd ever tasted. Within seconds the hail tapered off and Lee rushed out mindless of the few still falling and grabbed up handfuls to stuff in his canteen, racing here and there like a kid at an Easter egg hunt. His canteen full, he popped several more in his mouth while the storm quickly passed on east. In the quiet aftermath the wind died down and the sun shone through. The remaining hail stones soon faded in the grass as if they'd been only an illusion.

Lee sat on the hollow log and watched the colors surface in the fresh varnish of rain and the bright sunlight. He clutched the canteen to his chest and every once in a while, as the ice melted, he'd take another swallow. A lean ration considering his thirst, but so dear and welcome that he smiled in gratitude to whatever god or devil had sent the storm.

At evening's approach he ambled north across the pasture towards the railroad. The last rays of the sun reflected off the rails as he headed east on the last leg of his journey, in no great haste, stepping gingerly from tie to tie, feeling the bite of oak, iron, and cinder through the thin soles of his boots. He drank the last trickle of melted ice and covered all of two miles in the first hour, glancing up now and then to note the lights of Mankato so tantalizingly near yet seeming to draw no closer in his sluggish advance. The moon was already well up at sundown and now rode directly overhead, casting its light on the rails shimmering in eerie parallel till they converged in the distance, rails so highly polished by the friction of passing freight that they captured the very starlight in their sheen.

From the west sounded the low stern whistle of a train at the highway crossing. Soon its lone eye beamed out of the night. At its approach Lee crept down along the fence and watched it pass. He envied its passage and longed to hop aboard and ride to the rock and sway—dangle his feet from an open boxcar and gaze into the night. But the train rumbled on like a great iron beast and left him to walk the empty rails.

Over the next two hours it took him to reach town Lee reflected on events from the night before. Though he still harbored deep concern for his friends, given time to think it struck him more as a reckless prank than a violent attack. So it may have been Valentine after all, staging the drama—and the gunfire and shouts like the flash and thunder of the recent cloudburst had simply passed, leaving no one harmed, merely dazed and scattered. That was his hope, while dread of darker happenings plagued every step.

At the north edge of Mankato he left the railroad and walked south past the grain elevator and the empty corrals of the sale barn. His presence soon announced by barking dogs as he continued down a dark street past sleepy houses and arching trees towards the lighted stretch of highway that ran east and west. The sole of his left boot scuffed the pavement as he limped along like a weary straggler in a long march. At the highway he waited for a car to pass then crossed to the Sinclair Station.

It was still open. The clock in the window read 11:10.

The attendant was a thin haggard man of indeterminate age, his mouth sucked in like a deflated ball from lack of teeth. He perched on a stool behind the counter, holding a Pall Mall in his greasy fingers, the ash set to fall as he thumbed through a battered issue of *Field &Stream*. He wore stained coveralls and a soiled cap pulled low to his caged eyes, and he looked more suspicious than friendly as Lee stepped in and said, "Howdy," making straight for the water cooler where he slurped for a good minute before filling his canteen from which he gulped some more. The attendant stared at him drinking all that water, but Lee offered no explanation, shameless in his thirst, great to feel it gurgle down his throat to his belly. Finally sated, he topped off his canteen.

"That's good water," Lee said. Then he asked if there was a phone booth nearby.

The attendant stubbed out his cigarette and jerked his head east.

"'Bout a half mile on yonder there," he rasped, his voice clogged like a carburetor in need of cleaning, "I reckon they's one…at the motel."

Lee thanked him for the water and stepped back into the night. He walked with a slight shuffle to keep his boot sole from flapping and hadn't gone a full block when a patrol car eased to the curb and stopped. He'd hoped to escape notice but was none too surprised and waited as the officer got out and walked his way. "Officer Mitchell" from his nametag—a typical small-town policeman in his mid-thirties, heavy set, with sandy hair, black-framed glasses, and a pleasant smile as they exchanged greetings.

"Is there a problem, Officer?" Lee asked.

"No, we just like to check folks passing through. You headed east?"

"Actually, I was headed west. Hitching out to see some friends around Norton. But I kinda gave up on the notion," Lee shrugged. "Got caught in a thunderstorm between rides. Then night came on. So I decided to walk back into town. Hope to hitch a ride on home."

"Where you from?"

"On south of here. A little east of Cibola."

"Then we're practically neighbors." Officer Mitchell's smile broadened. "But I still need to see some ID if you don't mind. Just routine..."

Lee took out his driver's license and handed it to him.

Officer Mitchell looked it over and noted, "Clayton, huh? Seems like I've heard that name."

"Probably so," Lee answered with a tentative smile, wondering in what context and how recent.

Officer Mitchell said he'd be right back, walked to his car and called in on his radio to make certain there were no outstanding warrants and such. Several minutes passed as Lee tensed in wait, trying to fathom what was being discussed, ready to declare his right to silence and request his one phone call if arrested. But Officer Mitchell soon returned and handed Lee his license.

"Sorry it took so long," he said sheepishly. "The dispatcher was in the john."

"Sure, no problem," Lee smiled. "That happens from time to time."

"Right it does. Anyhow, Mr. Clayton, you're free to go. But I'd advise against hitching on. Might be a long wait before you catch a ride. And there's another storm due from the west. We could put you up in the jail overnight?"

Lee grinned and shook his head.

"Thanks, that's a kindly offer. But I've got money. Think I'll try a motel."

"Well, the Buffalo Inn on east here has decent rooms at a fair price. Harvest crews usually bunk there. I can give you a lift on over if you like?"

Lee accepted, not to appear rude; and tired and foot-sore he was glad of the ride.

"They keep you pretty busy around here?" he asked in a casual way as they cruised up the street, hoping to glean some word of his friends.

"Oh, can't complain. Mostly routine stuff. The worst part is working nights. We did have a rape a couple months ago. A little high school girl picked up by a stranger. No idea who he was. So many cars passing through, he could've been from out of state. Anyhow, he used her pretty bad then dropped her along a road about ten miles on east. Lucky she wasn't killed like those two kids over in Sky County. Hate to think of that kind of thing happening around here. I've got a daughter myself. Can't be too careful these days."

"No, I guess not…"

They rode on in silence, passed through another intersection, then pulled into the motel parking lot. Officer Mitchell circled around and Lee got out, thanked him for the ride and watched him drive off, still in the dark as to his friends and happenings around Oakvale. He walked into the motel lobby and rang the bell. He waited a minute and rang it again. A middle-aged bleach blonde emerged from the back room, squinty-eyed and plump as a pillow, dressed in a red and white polka-dot housecoat and fluffy pink slippers. Lee asked for a single room, then filled out the requisite form and handed her the money. She gave him change, glanced at the form and frowned.

"You forgot to give make and year of your car and license number," she said in a dull peevish tone.

"Don't have a car," he smiled. "I'm afoot."

Her frown deepened to a scowl as he picked up his room key and headed out. He crossed directly to the phone booth, inserted a dime, and placed a collect call to Diana. Hearing her sweet voice was like water to his soul.

—Lee! You alright?
"Yeah. Sorry to surprise you like this..."
—No. I was hoping you'd call.
"How's that? I'm not due back till tomorrow?"
—Will told me what happened. Him and Ry...
"Ry? Ry's okay?"
—Yes. He and Will were driving back roads all afternoon looking for you. Bruce was out too.
"Bruce? What about Rus and Jack, Dixie...Frankie? They okay?"
—Yes, Lee. Everyone's fine. They were all worried about you.
"And you? Were you worried?" he smiled, now free of concern.
—Some. But not too bad. You always said if something happened to give you a day or two.
"Well what *did* happen?"
—It's pretty complicated. I don't know the full story. But it was Valentine that shot at you guys. Then the next morning he was caught in a big drug bust. Him and his whole bunch, while you guys got away.
Lee couldn't make heads or tails of such a scenario, or such luck. He didn't try.
"How about you, Dita? You 'n Jesse, you okay?"
—Sure. We're fine. Just a little lonely.
"Yeah, me too..."
—Are you through now, Lee? Is this the last of it?
"Yeah, I think so, Dita," he laughed. "Time to hang up the ol' machete."
—Great, I'll find a nail... But where are you anyway?
"The Buffalo Inn. A little motel at the east edge of Mankato. Right off Highway 36. You might call Will or Bruce or somebody and have them fetch me in the morning. I'll be in room eleven. Got that?"
—Buffalo Inn. Room eleven...
"Right. And be sure to send someone. I don't want you up here. A little while ago a policeman stopped and checked me out. Everything seems cool. But I don't want you or Jesse around in case they decide to ask more questions. Understand?"

—*Okay, sure. I'll call Bruce or Will.*

"Good, that's my girl. Give Jesse a hug for me. And you...I'll deal with tomorrow. We can celebrate my retirement."

—*That sounds great!*

They said their sweet goodbyes and hung up. Lee walked to room 11, inserted his key and entered. Locked the door and latched the chain. He eased off his boots, shed his clothes, and took a hot shower. After toweling dry, he pulled back the covers, fell into bed and slept as if his bones lay deep in mud.

XVII. AFTERMATH

Bam! Bam! Bam! The racket at the door mixed with the pain of his feet, blistering his ears. His eyes cracked open like mud caked dry in the hot sun. He sat up sentient, yet unaware, like he'd risen from the mud, self and surroundings utterly foreign. Again the knocking. Lee squinted his caked eyes, gradually remembering who and where he was. *Bam! Bam! Bam!* Somebody knocking.

"Alright, alright..." he groaned. "I hear ya!" He pulled on his jeans and hobbled to the door. He unlatched the bolt and there stood Bruce with a big incredulous smile.

"Didn't you hear me?" he asked. "I about gave you up for dead."

"No, not dead." Lee rubbed his eyes and grinned. "Just bone-tired and feet half rotted off. But you're looking good." Good to see his friend, good to see him fit and smiling after fearing him shot. "What happened anyway? Everyone okay?"

"Everyone's fine. Let's get your stuff. I'll tell you in the car."

A few minutes later they were loaded up and heading down the highway.

"You'll never believe what happened," Bruce said, the excitement of events still flavoring his words. "After they jumped us, and you and Rus took off, I scooted back under a low cedar and tried to bury myself in the nettles even though they itched like crazy. I listened to the gunfire taper off. It was completely dark by then. And I could hear those guys walking the perimeter of the creek looking for us. Two of them stopped about four feet from me, I mean close. They lit cigarettes and stood there talking. I was in high panic, scared shitless. My mind flooded with thoughts of whether they'd hear or smell me even, then aim their guns and blow me away. I seriously considered jumping them before they had a chance. But I didn't move, despite the mosquitoes. Then the moon broke through the clouds and shined down through the trees like a spotlight. I hunched back trying to claim the shadows, all but certain they'd see me or hear my heart thump. And I think they would have seen me except for their own shadows cast my way, covering me. Finally, they moved on. And I still didn't move.

"I waited for what seemed like hours before deciding to edge through the pasture to the road. Even then I moved real slow, fearing any sound would give me away. I felt so proud once I made it to the ditch. I didn't think anyone was there and was a little careless in crossing the fence. I tripped and stumbled. Suddenly I heard voices and footsteps coming up the road. I crouched down, but their pace quickened, and I knew they had me. Then I heard a voice call, *'Bruce! Bruce! Is that you?'* It was Pete, and I was so glad to hear him say everything was cool and that I could come on out. Christ, what a relief."

"So it was Valentine and his crew...?"

"Yeah. Pete recognized them as they drew near, still blazing away. He stepped out and waved his arms and yelled for Valentine to *Quit fuckin' shooting!*"

"That was ballsy."

"I'll say. But too late, by then we'd all scattered. They were real apologetic. Said they never would have jumped us like that if they'd known who we were."

"I doubt that. I bet they knew...or had a good idea."

"Yeah, me too. Still, they bandaged up Pete's leg real good and helped us round up Ry, Jack, and Dixie. They were down hiding in the creek, but came out once they heard Pete give the all clear. We tried, but couldn't find you or Rus. We figured you two were long gone. So Valentine and his guys helped us gather the rest of our stuff and pack it to the road. We waited there till Frankie picked us up around five and headed on. Jesus, were we crushed in tight, I mean loaded to the gills."

Lee hadn't realized till then how lucky it was he hadn't

stopped Frankie or they may have all been left stranded and caught in the dragnet.

"What about Rus? Where'd he get to?"

"A highway patrolman picked him up along 36 shortly after sunup. I guess he made it to the highway then collapsed in the ditch, totally exhausted."

"Then he's in jail?"

"No. They let him out around noon yesterday. They didn't have anything to hold him on. They were real suspicious and asked a lot of questions. He didn't answer or say a word. Just bided his time till he got a chance to call Lori. She came and got him. But he was still in there when they brought Valentine and the rest in. He saw them being fingerprinted. Of course we didn't know any of this until we made it back to the farm around eight-thirty or so. The Kid came running out and said, 'Holy shit! I thought you guys were had!' 'What do ya mean?' we asked. Then he told us there'd been a big bust. 'It's all over the news,' he said. 'They got Valentine and his gang in the Mankato jail. Ninety cop cars in on it!'"

"Ninety? You sure? Or is that just the Kid talking?"

"No, no kidding this time. It's in all the papers, on the radio...TV. Seems our illustrious Attorney General Vern is out to grab headlines."

"Ninety cars...?" Lee shook his head. "Damn! That's a major funeral procession. Why in hell would they need that many?" Sheriff Craig asked himself the same question standing in the midst of the very scene—6:05 a.m. the previous morning. Cars jammed ditches and fields on both sides of the road, their tires spinning while they fish-tailed through the mud, engines revved, blowing blue exhaust to the chill dawn air, and a good dozen mired in the muck around the barn and shelter belt by the time the suspects were corralled and cuffed. Four men and six women stood half-clothed and shivering, barefoot in the damp grass, most of them still in bed mere minutes before and all but flattened by the press of authority.

Guy himself felt underfoot and shunted aside like a third-string freshman let to suit up for a big varsity game. Only it looked more like a sheriff's sale with every vulture in three counties picking through the gleanings. Furniture and household goods lay jumbled and strewn over the porch and yard in the search for contraband. An old UP railroad safe with gold arabesques swirled on black enamel had been dragged out behind the house and was presently being readied with explosives. Valentine sought to delay the inevitable by claiming he'd lost the key. But it was shortly blown open. That's when they found the plastic bags of white powder, hypodermics and vials, and over $30,000 in cash, mostly 20s and 100s. All highly suspicious. Not to mention boxes and clips full of high velocity rounds for two Mini-14s, both fully auto, and an AK-47. In addition, from the house and vehicles they confiscated a 30-30 lever action rifle, two 12-gauge pump shotguns, both sawed-off, plus a good dozen pistols, including, curiously enough, a tranquilizer gun. Which all in all made for an impressive arsenal, especially in light of Valentine's sorry claim that he was simply a hard-working farm boy trying to eke a living off the land.

What was more disturbing, at least to Guy, was the suspicion that many of the guns had been fired recently, evident from the scent of powder and fouled barrels, but most of all from the fact that during the initial raid a tough little brunette named Kate had hissed at Valentine—"*I told you not to take guns after those guys!*" He stared back daggers and she shut up. Didn't say another word even when prompted, "What guys you talking about, little lady?" The officer merely smiled and let it slide, there would be ample time to question her once all were sorted and faced the consequences.

Guy stood at the kitchen door and noted the exchange and chose then to sort himself from the throng. He walked out towards a makeshift corral that held an odd assortment of stock—goats, hogs, cattle and calves of different breeds all penned together, feeding from the same trough. The cattle wore fresh brands and most suffered from the scours, a common symptom of transport and trauma. Guy checked the stock trailer and found more patches of manure. He scuffed one with his boot and it gave way like dusty grease, still fresh. Hardly proof of rustling, but enough to prompt the officer in charge, Special Agent Tillis, to request bills of sale.

The corral merged with the northeast corner of the old barn. There, up against the wind-etched siding stood three fifty-gallon drums. The paint had rusted through, leaving faint ghosts of brand name and content, likely old fuel barrels. Guy idly tapped one with his boot and discovered it was full. Curious, he pried up the lid and immediately stepped back from the rank odor. He hadn't expected it to smell like sweet molasses, but it stunk like death. He dipped a rake handle and realized it was curdled blood about the color and consistency of black crude. The other two barrels were full as well—one hundred and fifty gallons of rancid blood. Securing the lid, he hardly knew what to make of it. He thought of the mutilated bulls drained of their blood and left to rot. He noticed a winch and hoist on the truck bed and began to form a picture in his mind of the "how" if not the "why." Again, it was hardly proof. Still, it would give Agent Tillis a further prod to use on Valentine.

Guy walked back towards the road and met the Hill County Sheriff Patch Hyland getting out of his car. Patch sauntered over, hands jammed in his coat pockets either side of his pot belly—otherwise a tall angular man, though slightly stooped and looking cowed like an old hound kicked aside at the start of a hunt. Not even notified until the raid was under way.

"Hey there, Guy," he said, tipping his gray Stetson to the back of his head, his pale blue eyes, watery and sad as an old hound's, appealing to the world in want of a place.

"Good morning, Patch."

"How'd you git here so quick?"

"Oh…I was out early. Saw 'em coming up the road. Thought I'd tag along."

Patch nodded vaguely, blinking his eyes at the sheer scope and magnitude of it all, more puzzled than disconcerted by his role, or lack of, in events unfolding. But proud nonetheless to have one card to play, and eager to share it with Guy.

"Say now, they didn't catch 'em all. We got us one, by golly."

"Oh? And how's that?"

"Well now, Jim Everly, our patrolman up here," Patch began

with a quick sniff of his nose, "he weren't let to know either. Anyhow, 'bout ten minutes ago, he picks up a feller hoofing along 36. A bearded feller by the name a' Rus Berret. Say now, ain't they some Berrets down your way?"

"Yeah, I know the Berrets. And I know Rus..." Guy also knew that he ran with Frankie, Ry, and the rest of the boys, but he wasn't saying. "So, what's the story?"

"Jim just said he's on foot and all done in. Miles from nowhere and won't say how or why he got there. Just sits there mum. Though he did ask for water. But he's part a' this bunch, you can bet."

Guy shook his head. "I hardly see how," he said, glancing to his watch. "It's been less than twenty minutes since we drove in. Even if he jumped the coup and managed to slip past all this, there's no way he could cover that distance. He might make two miles in that time. But it's twelve miles to 36."

Patch pursed his lips and studied the notion. He could imagine a deer running that far and fast, but not a bearded feller. "S'pose you're right," he nodded slowly, rubbing his whiskered chin. He hadn't had time to shave that morning. Let alone eat. He felt his belly groan on empty.

"Have any reports of gunfire in the past day or two?" Guy asked.

"Why yeah. Yesterday evening in fact. Along past sundown. Several folks from Oakvale called, one right after the other. Couldn't put down the phone to finish eating. Said they's some shooting up north a' town."

"And? Did you check it out?"

"Why no. Told 'em it was pro'bly dove hunters or fellers out shooting skeet."

"After sundown? Isn't that a little odd?"

"Say now. That is surely odd, ain't it?"

What Patch lacked in mental quickness he more than made up for in being genial and compliant—elected time and again due in part to the contrary urge in people to place someone in authority that no one needs to listen to or respect. So he was mostly ignored or brushed aside as he puttered around the courthouse and sat in cafes feeding on gossip. Even dogs barked and snapped at his heels the instant he stepped out of his car. But Patch never kicked a dog or raised his voice to a single living thing, his sole effort and concern was simply to please and no doubt he did some good in that regard. It certainly pleased CC to keep him in office and under his thumb.

But Guy was not presently concerned with CC or Patch Hyland. What did trouble him were the rumors of gunplay, because he didn't want to find any more bodies. And later that day after discovering several hundred pounds of dried hemp stashed under the hay in the barn, he and about twenty other men searched the nearby creek where he feared they would find a body. Walking in under the trees and up the muddy banks, he scanned the shadows—observed flies feeding on manure, and further on a faint stench that led to a calf carcass picked clean by coyotes. At each rise and bend he dreaded the worst. But all they found were two army duffels stuffed with hemp amidst evidence of a much larger harvest. One that should have yielded several tons.

As Guy headed home towards Cibola that evening, he watched the sun redden the far horizon and the earth slowly darken. Witnessed another day end with more questions than answers. What had become of all that hemp? And why the shooting?

The big question among the boys was whether Valentine would talk and point to them to ease his own predicament. Highly probable. So in spite of their luck, they weren't out of the woods yet. Frankie and Jack moved the hemp off their place to a neighboring pasture. They also cleaned the house of drugs and related items, anything that looked incriminating swept up and burned. They even hid the key press in a gully and covered it with brush, again in the neighboring pasture. Frankie sent the Kid to dry the hemp. Tossed him a canteen and a sleeping bag and said, "Go!" Didn't want the Kid around running his mouth in case the law showed up.

"What? You mean I gotta sleep out?"

"That's right, Kid."

"Aw Fascisto, what if it rains?"

"Find a hollow log."

"But..."

"No buts. Here"—Frankie handed him a tightly rolled $100 bill, the one they used for snorting cocaine.

"Gee thanks," the Kid groused, holding it to his eye like a spyglass. "What'll I do with this? Watch the birds?"

"Sure Kid. Sing to 'em all you like. And count the stars while you're at it. But if you see the law coming, you hightail it north to Vining. Check into that little motel and stay put till I come fetch you. Comprenda?"

Kid didn't like the sound of this at all.

"Come on, Fascisto, it isn't fair"—making one last appeal, reluctant to leave the bug-infested hovel and the company of the boys to go sleep alone in the wild.

"You're breaking my heart, Kid."

"But..."

"Here! Take the canteen and get going. Jack'll bring you some food later on. Meanwhile, you tend to that hemp." Brisk, efficient, good-humored, resolved. Frankie stood firm, tightening down all the hatches in wait to see if the storm would hit. Not one of them ready to toss off the hemp and forgo further prospects. Not with Gabe due back anytime with $60,000 in cash. And while their current harvest had been cut short, the haul would total at least as much, what with the seeds fully mature, adding to the weight, which should bring the boys another sixty grand to divvy up. For that kind of money you could shed a lot of worry. The boys braced for come-what-may.

"Looks like we'll buy this place," Lee told Diana, basking in the rosy comfort of being home, thrilled at his escape. "Get this batch sold, we can buy the house, barn, and pasture with cash to spare. What do ya say to that?"

Of course she said yes and hugged him like he would disappear if she let him go. Ready to put down roots. Loved the place, even with its eerie cold spaces and Jesse's nightmares. With Lee home and finished working hemp she knew those spaces would warm and the nightmares cease.

"Start of next week I'll help Garret cut silage, then milo. A legal harvest," he said, winking to her sweet smile and relieved to be free of the hemp. For Frankie had sent word that the boys should steer clear of the farm; the fewer birds in the nest the better. "It'll take maybe a month or so, depending on the weather. Then we can really settle in. I'll buy canvas and good brushes. I want to paint all winter. Try to get something going. And I'll need a good model—"

"You've got it!" she answered brightly.

"Who knows," he continued, "I may even do portraits of the dead. Bring 'em to life. Or try that blue-grass scene that Chuck Brindle's got his heart set on." Feeling magnanimous, giddy, part of something, at last able to give Diana a home. "You'll see, living here, it's gonna be *mag*-nificent."

Lovely was her word. "It'll be lovely," she said, her voice soft and warm, aglow with the thought of the garden she would plant in the spring, of the fruit trees she would tend and prune, of all the vegetables she would can, and most importantly the hope that Lee would end his ramblings and finally settle down and paint. For he was quite talented and could make a living if he would only take commissions and meet people halfway. This was the life she longed to live, and it lay in their grasp. Despite all the worry, she was proud of him and his efforts. Grateful he was home. Safe.

Throughout the evening Lee bounced Jesse on his knee, loathe to set him down even though his feet ached, home with his wife and son, thinking of all he might have lost that was still his. And later in bed with Diana, flesh to flesh, her nipples firm in promise like sun-warmed berries, her breasts smooth and soft as risen dough, they merged their breath and flesh, full of love and promise. All their expectations about to bear fruit.

But life follows a twisted path edged with surprises.

Bam! Bam! Bam! Someone on the porch, pounding at the door.

Lee and Diana both sat up. Jesse stirred awake in his crib, eyes to the night, clinched his pillow and supped his fist. *Bam! Bam! Bam!* More pounding.

"What time is it?" Lee asked.

"Nearly two-thirty."

"Christ! Who in hell…"? He slipped out of bed and pulled on his jeans, irritation giving way to anxiety as he descended the stairs and entered the kitchen. Through the window he could see it was Bruce. He opened the door in question.

"Sorry to bother you so late," Bruce explained, plainly worried. "But Frankie said not to call for fear you were on a party line."

"Okay, so what's up?"

"Frankie called and said Valentine is down at the farm. Guess he's out on bail. Frankie says he's got the idea you turned him in."

"Me? That's crazy?"

"I know. But Frankie says he's pretty hopped up and you'd better come and tell your story. Help calm him down."

"What the—" Lee gritted his teeth. "Can't it wait till morning."

"No. Frankie was pretty insistent. He said you'd better come tonight. Said you'd be doing him a big favor."

Lee had to wonder if Valentine held a gun on him. Had to wonder about a lot of things. One moment everything coming up roses, the next filled with dread. Dark and leaden. Like a light had gone out. Sick with dread.

"Okay…" Lee answered faintly. "Tell Frankie I'm on my way."

Bruce nodded, sorry to bear bad tidings. He could read Lee's reluctance and understood—would hate to be in his shoes, off in the middle of the night to talk sense to a mad man who'd shot at them only two days before. No, not a welcome prospect. And not the least rational.

While Bruce drove back to town to call Frankie, Lee slowly climbed the stairs and finished dressing. He told Diana that he had to drive to Frankie's farm and meet with someone and clear up something—trying to sound matter-of-fact.

Then she asked, "Meet with who? About what?"

"It's that Valentine fellow," he answered, his voice dry and edgy. "He's…he thinks I might have turned him in. So I gotta go down and…set 'im straight. Put his mind at ease. Understand?" Lee leaned down and kissed her and this time Diana knew that his worry matched her own.

"Be careful," she said.

"Sure. No problem. See you in the morning..."

Lee thought to take along a gun but decided against it; if
Valentine was in fact armed, the situation called for sweet
reason, every ounce he could muster. And Frankie wouldn't
have called unless he needed help—a little timely persuasion.
Still, during the hour-long drive to the farm, Lee was plagued
by doubt, wondering why Frankie who was such a nimble
talker couldn't convince the fool himself. Further, he sensed he
was being used, somewhat as a decoy or a pawn, pushed forth
to confuse an opponent and preserve an option. Suddenly all
motives seemed suspect, everyone walking a fine line, anxious
of what lay ahead. Lee gazed to the headlights blurring the
night—no matter how fast he traveled or which way he turned
he faced a dimly lit cavern amidst a greater unknown, with
every option a fragile space, barely perceived, surrounded by a
dark void where at any time an asteroid or comet could impact
like a stray bullet. Which was still his main concern: Whether
Valentine held his friends at gunpoint? His lone thought as he
arrived and got out, stepped to the porch and knocked.

Frankie opened the door and smiled, oddly quiet and
solicitous.

"I knew you'd come, Lee. I had faith in you."

"There any guns?" Lee asked before entering.

"No Lee, everything's cool." Frankie's smile broadened, a
little too broad to Lee's thinking. "We're just having a little talk.
Me and Pete, and Val here. That's Val's wife Jan, and his buddy
Fred, over yonder"—indicating the man and woman who stood
in the doorway at the far end of the room. The woman wore a
long buckskin dress, slit up the thigh. The man wore a vague,
stoned expression. Valentine, who Lee had never met, stood in
the middle of the room, looking askant—a lean wiry man of
moderate height with bristly black hair, deep-set eyes, a gaunt
unshaven face, wearing a soiled Hawaiian shirt and dirty Levis,
exuding all the charm of a rat. He gripped a pair of dagger-
sharp scissors he'd been using to snip buds off a marijuana
stem. Nervous, fidgeting, even as he stood there he never ceased

to move, flexing his arms and shoulders, popping his neck.
Definitely hopped up, blood racing, high on amphetamines.
Eying Lee as Frankie finished the introductions.

"Val, this is Lee Clayton."

"So you're Clayton, eh?" he scowled, mouth twitching. "Well
I ain't slept a wink since I got out," he said, drawing his lips
back like a grinning skull, "and I won't sleep a wink till I find
out who set me up. If you did it, boy—" he vowed, pointing the
scissors directly at Lee, "I'm gonna put a bullet right between
your eyes!"

So much for introductions.

"Hey Val! Enough!"—*"Knock it off!"* Frankie and Pete both
stepped forth in protest. "Lee doesn't need this crap," Frankie
continued evenly. "He'll tell you what happened."

Even Janice tried to calm her man. "Ease up, Val," she said,
rubbing his neck and shoulders. "Let's see what he has to say."

Lee entered warily and sat down; he didn't like the fact of
those scissors gripped tight and held ready. The threat was
palpable. Worse than any hazing he'd faced as a cadet. But no
getting around it, no turning back, in too deep. He had to steel
himself, remain steady, unemotional, direct. He locked eyes
with his accuser.

"Did you ever stop and think that firing those guns likely
got you caught?"

"No way!" Valentine stuck out his head like a hissing snake
as he paced back and forth. "No one was even near."

"No one except the whole town of Oakvale," Lee countered,
his voice firm but tense. "I grew up on that creek. Summer
evenings when the wind died down, you could hear cars honk,
people cheering at ball games. You can bet they heard those
gunshots."

"No fucking way. Don't play me for a fool. Because I'm
bettin' YOU walked into town and called the LAW! That's what
I'm bettin'. I might be a country boy, but my mamma didn't
raise no fool. I got an IQ of one forty-five. You HEAR me!" he
declared, tapping his chest. "ONE FOUR FIVE! That's a genius
and DAMN sure smart enough not to get myself caught. But
YOU! I say YOU called the LAW!"—again, jabbing the scissors

at Lee. "And unless you convince me otherwise, boy, I'm gonna put a bullet THOUGH YOUR HEAD!"

"Not if I put one in yours first," Lee vowed, losing his cool, as Frankie and Pet jumped once more from the sidelines crying foul.

"You fuck with one of us, you fuck with all," Pete warned.

"We've got guns, too, Val. You remember that."

"Yeah, yeah. You've got guns. Big fucking deal…"

"Look, Val," Frankie said, "I called Lee over like you asked. He came in good faith. The least you can do is hear him out."

"Sure, sure. Let's have it, the whole *stor-ree*…" he mocked, pacing back and forth, brushing off his wife, indifferent to any view other than his own boast and threat.

Lee waited in a mix of rage and fear that produced a sour foment in the pit of his stomach. Didn't want to say another word. Hated the part he played, offered up to tell his story. What was really going on, the thing on everyone's mind that no one mentioned was the possibility that Valentine would tell his story, tell all he knew about Frankie and the boys, about the farm and who they dealt with. That was the very real overarching concern that left all their efforts hanging by thread. So Lee wasn't simply acting in his own behalf, he was speaking for them all. Trying to calm a snake.

"Before I start, suppose you tell me," he said, addressing Valentine, "just how you got the idea I turned you in?"

"*Sammy!*" Valentine pounced, accenting the fact with his scissors. "He told me that was your old home place. And that I'd better be careful 'cause you still had some strong feelings there."

"That's right. I do have strong feelings," Lee allowed. "But if I was to turn you in, do you really think I'd wait till me and my buddies were caught smack dab in the middle? Hell, we had to run for it. We thought it was the law or vigilantes. We had no idea it was you. It was almost dark. All we saw were men with guns. Then we lit out, me and Rus. And everyone scattered…"

Lee told his story in detail to weigh Valentine down with the fact and burden of circumstance and so prove the sheer absurdity of his suspicion. He told of his trek to intercept Frankie. How he skirted around the houses and dogs. How he climbed the cut bank and hit the hot wire, leaving him dazed and confused like when he'd first emerged following the ambush and circled back into the creek, confused as to direction.

"Thought that was your *home* place?" Valentine jeered, casting doubt, as if cross-examining a witness. "Hard to believe you'd get lost?"

"We'd just been shot at," Lee noted. "Plus it was dark and overcast. And I'll frankly admit, I was scared. Ran in a circle like a damn rabbit. That's when I spied the lantern and several men there in the belly of the creek. I guess that was you and your bunch. Isn't that a little careless? Cutting hemp by lamplight?"

"Careless? Who's to see?" Valentine flung out his arms, utterly without fault. "No one's gonna be out there in the middle of the night. And when I leave a patch, man, it's clean"— asserting his superior method with a brief lecture. "We don't cut down a single plant. All we do is snip the buds. No one's the wiser. But you guys, man, YOU mow it like a fucking combine and leave the WHOLE place looking like a WAR ZONE!"

"Ain't that the point?" Lee answered. "Skip the fuss and cut all you can. Get in and get out and be miles away before anyone notices."

"Yeah, but you didn't skip away so easy, did ya? I sent Freddy over to check on things. See if it was dry enough to cut. And Lordy Lordy, he spotted ol' Pete in his big cowboy hat bopping up through the pasture like Dumbo the Elephant with his big ears flapping in the breeze. *Heh-heh-heh…*"

Lee looked to Pete in wry reminder of him wearing that hat and setting off before sundown. Pete offered a quiet nod—then he cocked an eye at Valentine.

"Hey Val? Thought you said you'd never of come in on us if you'd known who we were?" Tables turned on the accuser and Pete wanted answers. While Frankie, who'd been leaning back on the sofa, feigning sleep, cracked his eyes in warm interest.

"Look now! Freddy saw a guy in a cowboy hat, that's all I meant. Fuck, I didn't know it was you, Pete. I swear by my mother, I didn't…"—Valentine jumping back from his own stink, trying to kick it off his boots. "Didn't I help you, Pete? Didn't I fix up your leg and haul your stuff to the road? Look what it got me. You get clean away and I get busted. Fuck!" Valentine cursed his luck and stomped the floor, his movements all herky-jerky as he paced about like a spastic puppet.

"What a mess! What a fucking mess! Look guys, I could use some help here. I mean, they got all my money, my drugs, my truck. I even had to borrow a fucking car. And I can't do time, man, I mean it. Not again, man...I gotta have my drugs. And my momma? Shit, she had to mortgage her house to pay my bail. You know that? Man, it breaks my heart to see her wiped out. So I could use some help"—pleading his case, all his anxieties spilling forth in an incoherent jumble. Clearly a desperate man.

"What are you driving at?" Frankie asked, sitting up now, wholly roused.

"Fuck it, man? Are ya blind? I gotta pay for a *lawyer!*" he declared, shifting his eyes from Frankie to Pete, anxious, hopeful, scraping at his whiskered beard with the scissors. "Look man, I could use some help. That's all."

"We're not giving you any money, Val," Frankie answered flatly.

"I'm not askin' for money, man. I just..." Valentine felt himself slipping, being sucked down a drain. Only minutes before he had them all on edge, keen to his every word and gesture. Now he faced disdain, indifference. "All I want is some hemp. You've got plenty. Give me two hundred pounds."

"What can you do with hemp, Val? You've been busted. You can't sell it."

"But I know someone who can"—flashing his skull grin at Frankie. "I know the *Mez-zee-can*"—stressing each syllable with a heavy, south-of-the-border accent. "And he can sell it pronto. For good money too."

"Who? Mex Orvano?" Frankie observed, unimpressed.

"Hey, I didn't say that! I said the *Mez-zee-can.* There's more than one, ya know. And no one knows the *Mez-zee-can* but me. Not Jan, not Freddy. Just me. He's my connection, man. And I'll tell you something else, Mister Frankie 'n Pete"—regaining his swagger, like his card trumped theirs. "You don't fuck with the *Mez-zee-can.*"

"All the same," Frankie said with a yawn, "you're not getting any of our hemp."

"Why not? You've got a ton. Can't you spare a couple hundred pounds?"

"No. In the first place it's not mine to give. It belongs to them that cut it."

"Sure, sure. Tell me you're not the one in charge."

"No one works for me, Val. They're all big boys. They don't take orders."

"That's right," Pete said. "Our hemp belongs to a dozen different pickers. We can't just hand it over, Val. Besides, it's long gone. Long gone and far away..."

Frankie and Pete were driving a hard bargain to Lee's mind in refusing to deal. At this point two hundred pounds of hemp might prove a good investment. One that he'd gladly make to placate the fool. But it wasn't his call.

Valentine, reading their firm denial, narrowed his eyes and slowly nodded. He stood silent for a time, working his jaws as if assessing odds and options. Finally he gripped his scissors and turned to Lee.

"That wasn't a half bad story you told, Clayton. And I'd like to believe you," he added with a sly smirk. "After all, you had the guts to come face me. And the guilty almost always run. So that counts for something. But see, I gotta have proof..."

Lee sat listening, waiting—had dared hope the issue was settled, but now found himself back in the hot seat, being toyed with.

"Know what else?" Valentine flashed his skull grin. "There's nothing like truth serum to get the truth. And I got me some right here..." he said, tapping his shirt pocket. "*So-di-um Pen-to-thal.* The best little truth teller a'goin'. Results *guaranteed!* I shoot you up. Ask a few questions. If it all jives, we shake hands, and no *problemo.*"

The offer of an easy deal. Finality. A devil's bargain. Lee was half-tempted, all he had to do was surrender his free will and self-respect and let this mad man stick a needle in his arm. He drew a deep breath and shook his head.

"No way. I told you my story. And I told the truth. I'm not

letting you stick a needle in me."

"Why not? I gave it to all my people. Jan and Freddy too. I had to make sure no one stooled on me. It's no big deal. They took it. What's your problem?"

"I don't trust you," Lee answered. "You're no doctor or medic."

"What? Scared of a little needle? It's *clean*. And I can tap a vein, man, no problem. I know what I'm doing. I can put a bull to sleep like a baby."

"Right. That's my worry. You might put a man to sleep for a long, long time."

"Hey, it's just a drug," he said, taking out the vial. "Perfectly safe. Like putting sugar on your cereal. You take this"—he held it forth—"I ask a few questions. Then I'm outa here. Or maybe it's the truth you're scared of...?"

Lee weighed the option once more. He looked to Frankie and Pete—they each offered a neutral shrug, nothing more. Clearly he was on his own, his choice to make. Would he take a chance and put the matter to rest? Yes or no?

"Listen. I told you the truth. You can believe it or not. But you're not sticking a needle in me."

"Sweet, sweet, ain't that sweet..." Valentine sighed in exasperation, playing the good cop, bad cop, knew the routine. "I try to be reasonable, I really do. But you throw it right back in my face. Now YOU listen to ME"—staring hard as he tensed his body and thrust the scissors. "I'm gonna be askin' lots of questions, Clayton. Sooner or later I WILL find out who ratted on me. And if it WAS you, I'll find out WHERE you live! Hear me good, 'cause you WON'T hear me comin' when I COME HUNTING YOU!"

XVIII. ON GUARD

C *ome hunting you! Hunting you! Hunting you!*
     The words echoed in Lee's mind as he drove home, his
blood pulsing in fear of how he'd protect Diana and Jesse. And
when he'd asked Frankie, "What do you think?" once Valentine
had left, his answer, "Think I'd keep a gun handy," offered little
assurance. Having a family made him feel twice as vulnerable,
especially living in the country as they did. So much could
happen with no one around to witness or intervene. In this
instance Lee wished he was a lone wolf like Frankie and Pete
with no one to watch out for but himself. Not that he regretted
his wife and child, not for a second. It was his actions he
regretted, and the consequence that might bring them harm.
But regret was neither sword nor shield, and wishing would not
make the threat go away.

Nor were things so easy back at the farm as Lee imagined.
No one had gotten any sleep that night, not while playing host
to Valentine and his mania. And even with him gone they were
still haunted by his visit. All that morning Frankie and Pete
watched the road with grim concern for fear Valentine would
finger them and the law come roaring in any minute. Every
vehicle that rumbled over the wood-plank bridge produced a
drum roll of heightened alarm. And when Jack returned from
Kansas City around noon, having driven down to fetch Gabe
who'd flown in from San Francisco in the wee hours, they had
more bad news.

"I only got half of it sold," Gabe said right off as he flicked
the ash from his cigarette. "Had to stash the rest."

"What the fuck you mean, *stash it?*" Frankie demanded, on

edge, out of patience. Disappointed at seeing all their prospects unravel. "Why the hell couldn't you sit on it awhile? Or did you lose your nerve?"

Gabe passed it off, wouldn't be baited.

"Look Frankie, I could sit on it till Christmas for all the good it would do. My nerves aren't the problem. Valentine's the problem. Him getting busted brought the curtain down on the whole show. Really fouled the pot. He deals with the same people we do, you know that. And they say nothing doing. No one will make a move. Won't even take a phone call. Everyone's afraid of being named. Sweating it out. They won't touch a thing from Kansas. Not for a while. Not till the dust settles."

"Great! Then why didn't you bring it back?"

"You know better than that. They've got fruit fly infestation. Bad enough coming into California, but they're checking every truck and van headed out. The stuff is locked safe in a rental shed. I paid three months in advance. Scattered rat poison all around to keep the mice out. It'll be there, ready and waiting, when I make the sale." Giving a full report, confident of his game, covering every angle.

"Okay, okay. You're right..." Frankie conceded, gazing off in blank acceptance. Fatigued. The bags under his eyes were once more the size of half dollars. He rubbed his face with both hands and groaned, "The last thing we need is more hemp to sit on."

"You didn't ditch the hemp? You still have it?"

"Yeah. Got a ton dried and stashed up the pasture. Kid's keeping watch."

"Then we'd better key it up and move it out."

"Believe me, I'd love to. But where?"

"Take it back to my place in KC," Gabe offered. "Valentine doesn't know me. And he definitely doesn't know where I live. I'll sit on it till things cool off. Then we'll work up another deal."

"You'll take it out of here?"

"Why not? It's my hemp too," Gabe said. "I don't wanna lose it"—looking right spry for "*An asthmatic fat boy*" as Frankie liked to call him due to his aversion for hard work or physical activity of most any kind. No doubt he preferred thought to action, but

Gabe had his strong points and plenty of nerve. "Cheer up, Frankie," he smiled, his eyes alive to chance and probability, "we're over halfway there and haven't lost a thing. Still ahead. We've got another thirty thousand in cash and it's a big country. If we move fast, we can have the hemp keyed and out of here by sunup."

"But that sorry-ass apartment you live in—" Frankie grimaced, still doubtful. "Hell, it's smack in the middle of nigger town."

"Their *blacks*, Frankie. Blacks. And don't sweat it. The blacks and me get along fine. They don't bother me and it's a good place to do business."

"Oh, I dunno as I'd walk the streets at night," Jack allowed in nod to Frankie. "But you should've been there this morning. We helped this fellow jump-start his car. And I gotta admit...it *was* a Cadillac. But you'd have thought we were Tonto and the Lone Ranger the way he thanked us. A big ol' boy. I nearly lost my arm in his grip."

"And where do you think I scored this?" Gabe grinned, holding up a packet of coke. "A good deal too. Only a hundred a gram and still uncut."

"Well hot damn!" Frankie slapped his hands together. "The day's a wasting, boys. Let's crank up the ol' key press and start cookin'!" Energized at the sight of the coke and happy at the prospect of ridding the place of hemp.

But no one was happier than the Kid coming in from a day and a night in the wild. Happy as a puppy lost and found. All but wagging his tail and licking their faces.

"You won't believe the shit I heard out there!" he gushed, relating his experience alone in the night. "There were these two coyotes, no lie. I was in my bag and they come up 'n sniffed me. And I don't think they liked my smell, ya know, because they were talking crap as they walked away. No, really! And listen! I learned to speak Hoot Owl. Wanna hear me hoot for a toot?"

"Hell yes, Kid, have a blast! Hoot 'er up!"—Frankie laughing, back in the swing of things. "God, speaking of hooters. How 'bout those tits on Val's wife. Lil' Jan, was she dressed to kill or what? Looking fine in that buckshin dress slit clean up her creamy thigh, I swear. You should've feasted your eye on that stuff, Jacko."

"Uh, I dunno. Think I'd sooner pass with Val around."

"Yeah, him I could throw to the fishes. But her I'd like to toss across my bed and give her a big *you-know-what*—"

The boys yukking it up, keeping themselves distracted, entertained, as they worked feverishly to key the hemp and move it to safer pasture.

Lee worked all that morning securing the windows around the first floor of the house, turning the grand mansion into a fortress. He stood on a six-foot ladder, using a brace and bit and a Yankee screwdriver to sink three-inch long screws through the lower sash and screen, making certain no one could gain entry without considerable effort, leaving only the east door and kitchen windows free to open. Rue and Keeps sat at the base of the ladder, shifting their heads with his every movement, curious of any event outside the common routine.

Early on Diana had stepped out, also curious of Lee's activity, wondering why he hadn't come in for breakfast and why he hadn't said a word since returning. She noticed his rifle leaned against the siding and hoped it was meant to warn off the greyhound and nothing more.

"Is everything okay?" she asked, looking up, shading her eyes from the bright sun.

"No, things aren't a bit okay..." Lee paused and glanced down, not certain how to tell her. "Where's Jesse?" he asked, recalling her vow to stick by him as long as nothing threatened Jesse.

"He's inside, eating his Cheerios."

Lee nodded, feeling dazed and burnt from lack of sleep and cumulative anxiety, hadn't even recovered from his run out of the patch and now this. Diana still stood looking up in wait of an explanation.

"First off, Valentine threatened to shoot me. Or as he said, put a bullet through my head"—nor was Lee mincing words, wanted her to understand the full threat. "Frankie and Pete

got him to simmer down some. And no, he didn't have a gun,
just a foot-long pair of scissors he kept waving about. Anyway,
I told him my story and how it wouldn't make much sense me
turning 'im in when we'd likely get caught too. He seemed half
convinced. Then he and Frankie got to arguing over the hemp.
He said he needed a couple hundred pounds. Frankie 'n Pete
said no. After that he turned back on me, said he'd take my
word if I took sodium pentothal and answered his questions.
He had a needle and vial with 'im, wanted to shoot me up then
'n there. I said no. He didn't take it too well, said he'd be asking
around and if he didn't like what he heard, he'd find out where
I lived and come hunting me."

Hearing this, Diana didn't flinch.

"You know that kind, Lee. Full of big talk and always
blowing smoke."

Lee admired her pluck, but no, he didn't know that kind and
neither did she.

"You may be right, Diana. Just big talk and full of smoke.
But he's not exactly rational and I don't think you can appreciate
the fact without meeting him. And I'm not taking any chances,
not with you 'n Jesse to consider. And say he does come here,
just for argument's sake, say he shoots me. Do you think he'll
stop at that and simply walk away? Now, I'll gladly shoot the
bastard if I see him coming. But I'm afraid of what he might do
if I don't see him first. Like I say, he's not exactly rational. He's
more like that damn greyhound with human legs. Sly, shifty,
and mean."

Lee waited for his words to sink in. But Diana remained
calm. Her green eyes betrayed no panic. Her auburn hair,
combed and curled by the wind, wreathed her face in the warm
sunlight.

"Look, Diana. I want you to pack a bag and go to your mom's
place. Take Jesse and go to Oklahoma till things blow over."

"I'm not going. And you can't make me."

For all her soft beauty she could be tough and stubborn.

"Okay then," he said, noting her tone and stance. "But I
want you to get the shotgun out, the twenty-gauge, and take
a few shots at the tin can nailed to the post yonder. That way

you'll be ready to pull a trigger if you have to."

Diana said nothing and went back inside.

A few minutes later Lee noticed her out by the pasture gate, taking aim with the shotgun, Jesse and the two dogs standing back in rapt attention as she fired. At the first blast the can jiggled loose. At the second it went spinning through the air. Keeps ran to fetch it with Jesse close behind. Diana glanced back at Lee to ascertain her shooting. And dressed in blue jeans, boots, and red flannel shirt, she looked like a regular Annie Oakley. Amazingly poised and calm. She chambered another shell, put the gun on safety and returned to the house. Prepped and ready. Seeing her determined, Lee still wished she'd go to her mother's for a while, yet proud she wanted to stay.

By noon, with the house secure, Lee relaxed enough to eat a meal. Finished, he sat at the table sipping coffee, and kept an eye to the road while Diana washed the dishes. Around one they heard a car coming. Lee stepped out with his rifle and spotted Bruce's light-gray Plymouth cruising beyond the fence line, turning up the drive. Lee leaned his rifle by the steps and stood waiting. Bruce parked beside the pickup and got out.

"So? How did it go?" he asked, curious of the night's happenings.

"Not so bad and not so good. Valentine was full of threats. Hard to reason with." Lee gave a faint smile, thinking of all the times Bruce had accused him of the very thing: *Hard to reason with.* "He still thinks I turned 'im in. There's not much I can do but wait it out. Like Frankie said, keep a gun handy. Can't very well call the law."

"No," Bruce quietly agreed, no logic in that.

The two friends stood silent. They usually had plenty to say, points to argue, but at present they faced a dilemma neither poetry nor philosophy could solve.

"Hate to say it," Lee began, baring his concern. "Truth is I'm plenty scared. What with Diana and Jesse here. If Valentine does come, and if he nails me..." Lee paused as if struck by a bullet. "Look Bruce, I gotta ask and I hate to draw ya in, and I understand if you say no. But if you'd come back out tonight and back me up, I'd be grateful. Just stay in the house there. If

Valentine comes, I'll go out 'n deal with 'im. But no matter what, I don't want Diana or Jesse hurt."

Lee waited, watching his friend, asking him to stick his neck out. Sorry for asking but hopeful all the same. Bruce was never one for bravado, and he didn't offer any. Nor did he blink an eye.

"Sure," he answered, "I'll come..."—his voice somewhat tremulous like a blade of grass that leans in the wind, yet remains firmly rooted. "I need to drive back to town and tell Julie. I'll be back around five. Okay?"

"Sounds good. Thanks, thanks a lot."

"Do I need a gun?"

"No. I've got a twelve-gauge you can use. Diana has the twenty-gauge."

Bruce nodded and said nothing more. Got in his car and drove out.

Good to his word Bruce returned that evening. They ate a quiet supper, careful of the silence, knives and forks scraping their plates amidst the muffled sound of chewing, all being extra attentive to Jesse, as if the child represented a vulnerability in each, or perhaps a talisman, as if innocence might forestall an evil. And Jesse, who would have normally taken their silence as an invitation to perform, noted the guns and their grim faces and remained subdued, softly humming *"Guns 'cross the river aimin' at ya..."* while pushing his peas around his plate with his spoon, reluctant to eat, sensing their anxiety like he often read his mother's mind. Lee caught his eye and gave him a wink and a smile. Jesse smiled too. But the smile was brief as he turned his deep brown eyes to his mother in wonder of her thoughts.

The sun lingered on the horizon, bleeding through the veil of trees, hesitant to leave the day, slowly vanishing beneath the chill of stars. Even the wind blew cooler, mournful like a soul uneased. All took their positions in wait. Diana upstairs with Jesse. Bruce behind the couch they'd shoved into the kitchen to block the front door and the path to the stairs. Lee stood watch outside, pacing the yard and fence line. Part of him declared the threat absurd and himself a fool for over-reacting, but the greater part remained mindful of every sound, the dry rustle of a leaf, the creak of a branch, examining every shadow and movement, sensing threat at the periphery like a cat stalking in the night, fully expecting it to arise any moment and claw his face.

Diana sat in Jesse's room, rocking him to sleep. She smoothed his hair and brow, trying to clear her mind of present concerns, aware of his uncanny sense, wishing him a peaceful night and sweet dreams as she tucked him in.

"Where are *wee-oh* bugs?" he asked, more troubled than usual by the deep silence.

"Oh honey, they've gone to sleep for the winter. Now you go to sleep too."

At her touch he curled up and closed his eyes, cocooned in his soft blanket in want of the cicadas and their fond chorus. Dianna went to the bedroom and sat by the window, cradling her shotgun in watch of the road.

Meanwhile Bruce lay down on the couch, his shotgun leaned against the armrest. He'd brought along a copy of Wittgenstein's *Investigations*. But attempting to read he made little progress, his instincts aroused by the night, the wind, and the spacious old house with its dark interior and uncertain forms that lurked to mock his reason till he gave up trying to read altogether. Still, he took heart in Wittgenstein's words and held the book even as he concluded that apprehension and logic were in no wise correlative. He lay listening to the wind voicing down the flu, to his own breath, his heartbeat, and the clock ticking on the mantle. Only 10 o'clock and still a long night ahead.

Outside, Lee continued to scan the shadows, looking to the road close by and to the highway a mile distant. He noted several cars pass along the highway, one heading east and a couple heading west to Cibola. And no traffic at all after 10:30 or so. Rue and Keeps followed along, curious of his vigil, sniffing at the wind and the grass, marking the fence posts, strictly attentive to wherever Lee cast his eyes. But they finally tired of the game and returned to the porch to lay and watch. Around midnight Lee also returned to the house. As he walked into the kitchen, Bruce looked up in question.

"There's not a thing stirring," Lee said like he'd just been out to check the weather. The past few hours of pacing the environs of the house and barn had helped allay his fear. "I'll turn out the light and keep watch. You go ahead and get some sleep."

Bruce lay back down and closed his eyes, glad of Lee's presence and renewed calm. Emotions were contagious and carried a ripple effect. Lulled by the wind, the blanketing darkness, and the ticking clock, Bruce soon found his sleep.

Lee sat at the table and sipped a cup of cold black coffee, sifting the dregs in his teeth before he swallowed. He'd left the door open and gazed out through the screen towards the yard light and the play of shadows cast by the windblown trees. At times they appeared to sweep forth like wings in descent or a hand reaching to cup a flame, then recede and grow furtive and vague, producing a hypnotic ebb and flow. Lee was too tired to reflect or consider, he merely observed and occasionally nodded off, then jerked awake to slowly nod again, till at last his head lay across his arms on the table. The night deepened while the wind moaned through the trees and buffeted the door.

Lee heard the dogs barking and stood, instantly alert.

"What is it?" Bruce asked, also awakened by the sharp incessant howl.

"I don't know," Lee answered, grasping his rifle as he edged to the door. He heard Diana coming down the stairs and said, "You two stay put. I'll check on the dogs."

Stepping down off the porch, he spied Rue and Keeps at the far end of the drive, circling and yipping at something along the ditch. Lee clicked his rifle off safety and quietly approached. Halfway across the yard he discerned the threat curled at the edge of the road and cradled his rifle.

"It's a possum!" he shouted with a laugh. Bruce and Diana stood watching from the porch. "Just a damned ol' possum!" Lee laughed again as he headed on down to shoo the dogs away.

"Go on, you two. Let that possum be. Go on, get!"

Wary of Lee's boots, the two dogs turned tail and trotted for the house. The possum hadn't moved, still lay there playing dead. Lee knelt by to give a closer look—an oddly appealing creature with pinkish skin, feathery white fur, and bright black eyes, yet the rat-like nose and tail made it more loathsome than cuddly. Lee nudged it with his rifle, and it still didn't move. He thought of himself curled in the depths of the creek, waiting out the threat. Even a possum faced a poor percentage in that regard. "You better scat," he said, kicking dirt on the possum as he stood. "You might fool two pups, but that greyhound will toss you to high heaven..."

As ever, morning saw a brand-new day and they felt encouraged at seeing the sun and feeling its warmth. Jesse had slept through the night, and everyone else, including Lee, had gotten a few hours sleep following "The attack of the killer possum!"—as Lee dubbed the event, all laughing about it over breakfast. All except Jesse, listening in wide-eyed wonder of the beast in question.

"Ka-killer-possum? He come?" he asked with rapt concern, for the possum had assumed the proportions of a giant in his mind.

"If he does," Lee grinned, "we'll have your momma cook 'im in a stew."

But Diana read Jesse's unease, leaned to him and said, "Don't worry, honey. The possum is only a little animal. He was so frightened of Rue and Keeps that he rolled into a tiny ball and pretended to be asleep." A notion that struck Jesse as so funny, anything afraid of Rue and Keeps, that he let out a belly laugh worthy of a young Viking.

"Go see ka-killer-possum?" he asked brightly, curious of the formerly mythical beast shrunk to the size of a Teddy bear.

"No, Jess. That possum's long gone by now," Lee assured him. "Probably curled up in a tree, sleeping the day away." Which painted a cozy picture in Jesse's mind, a nest of leaves warmed by a dusty shaft of sunlight, and posited the question of what a possum might dream.

Soon after breakfast Bruce gathered up his book and prepared to leave.

"You need anything, just call."

"Sure, and thanks for coming," Lee said. "But doubt if I'll need any more help against the varmints." At a day's remove concern for Valentine no longer edged each moment like a cat clawing a screen. As Lee noted, "Him coming here is about as likely as a UFO landing in the yard"—though they both had to smile at the possibility.

Bruce felt relieved driving back to town, glad nothing had happened beyond the comic and absurd, looking forward to a quiet evening of study and detachment. Perhaps even a sweeter moment with Julie. Though at this juncture that would be a surprise. No longer looking for logic in love, simply hopeful of further moments.

Lee sat outside on the porch through the morning and the early afternoon, enjoying the sunlight, picking his guitar, keeping his rifle handy while Jesse roamed the yard at play with Rue and Keeps. Diana stepped out several times to ask if he wanted anything, some coffee or tea. He shook his head, didn't want a thing. Felt utterly content relative to the past few days. Happy to pick his guitar, watch his son run and play, and see his pretty wife standing at the door of their home-to-be. Feeling content. And contentment was something he had never desired or expected. Still young and anxious to make his way in the world, forge his own path. But for now—basking in the sun, his sore feet clad in soft moccasins—contentment seemed more than enough.

About mid-afternoon he heard another car coming up the road, through the trees, past the old haunted house, soon into view. Ry's light-green Wagoneer. Will and Rus both rode along. All greeted as they got out by Jesse and the two dogs. And Ry wasn't wearing his usual smile; in fact he wore a holstered pistol clipped to his belt and looked rather serious.

"We were down at Frankie's this morning," he said, glancing to Lee's rifle. "Heard about your trouble."

"That's right," Will added. "Gabe's back. We went to fetch our money."

Will also carried a pistol: a stub-nosed 38 stuffed in his jeans. Rus was unarmed.

"You doing okay?" Ry asked.

"Yeah," Lee nodded. "Valentine made a lot of noise. But mostly hot air, I think."

Ry tightened his gaze.

"Could be," he said. "But he's not through making noises."

"No, not by a long shot," Rus observed dryly. "Now he thinks it's me that turned 'im in." He stood at a slouch, so full of dread his skin sagged. "Gotta admit, it looked bad me sitting there in jail when they marched 'em in and all. I even slunk down in my chair. Him staring at me with those beady eyes. Like a dern skunk raising his tail to take aim and you don't know when or where he's gonna fire. Aw, hell with it! You know what his game is," he said, trying to shuck his worry.

"Was he down there? Valentine?"

"No. But he phoned shortly after we pulled in. Like he'd been watching the place. Frankie yakked at 'im a spell, trying to sweet talk things. Might as well try'n pet a mad dog. I heard 'im rant on the other end. Then I heard my name 'n wondered, What the hay? as Frankie handed me the phone 'n said, 'Here, see what you can do…'" Rus stood like a mime holding the phone, never one for sweet reason and prone to hardheadedness himself. "For crying out loud, what was I suppost to say to the dagum idiot. Hell, after me n' you split up I lit outa there like the devil's on my heels. So spooked I head up the wrong way. Made it plum near to Red Cloud a'fore I got my bearings. That's near six miles north. And I forgot to grab a canteen to boot. Had to drink pond water till my guts cramped. By the time I hit back to 36 my legs was done in. I dropped like a shot horse. Right there in the ditch. Sat 'n watched the sky slowly lighten. Then a patrol car pulls up and I still didn't move. Didn't give a hoot in hell. And when he asked what I's doing there, I didn't say a thing. Same back at the jail, didn't say a word. Knew if I tried to make up some yarn, the next question would prove me a liar. And that's purdy much how I answered Valentine when he claimed I turned 'im in. I just said, 'You damn fool, how in hell could I? Why, they hauled me in not ten minutes a'fore they hauled you in!' Then he wants proof! Wants to shoot me up with some kinda crap for Christsake…"

"What did you say to that?" Lee asked, curious of his answer.

"I told him he could stick it up his ass. Just as soon he shoot me as give me that shit. And he said he just might do that very

thing. Look me up 'n put a bullet through my head..." Rus
looked to the others, each of them armed. "And I ain't about to
start packin' no gun," he vowed. "I don't care, I just ain't. So I
said you just come 'n shoot me then if that's what you think you
gotta do."

With those words Rus glanced down and saw Jesse staring
up at him as all four men realized they'd overlooked the fact of
the boy standing there listening.

"Christ, I'm sorry, Lee..." Rus shook his head, feeling
bad about scaring the boy. For Jesse, young as he was, had
understood the gist of their exchange and looked as pale and
frightened as if he'd seen a twenty-foot snake uncoil and crawl
his way. Lee didn't need a mother's intuition to read his fear and
knelt down to calm him.

"It's just a movie," he said. "Like Billy the Kid. Only pretend."
But Jesse wasn't a bit convinced; he tore away and ran for his
mommy standing on the porch. He didn't like the sound of this
movie. He didn't want anyone putting a bullet through Rus, his
daddy, or any of them.

The men followed inside as Diana took Jesse upstairs. At
this time of day he grew moody in any case and needed a nap.
She read from his favorite book, *Sam I Am*, and soon had him
smiling. Meanwhile, the men sat in the kitchen sipping iced tea,
quietly rehashing events.

"I knew you'd make it out," Will said as he slapped Lee on
the back and sat down. "You had us pretty worried, but I knew
you'd pull through."

Lee nodded, grateful to Will and others for searching all
that next day.

"Did you have your running pack?" Will asked.

"You bet...and glad of it. I walked into Mankato in clean
clothes like a true citizen. A policeman checked my ID and sent
me on."

"He didn't ask about Burr Oak or anything?"

"Not at all. In fact he was downright friendly. Even gave me
a ride up the road."

Will grinned as broad as his jaw, proud his idea had proved
out. Then he plopped a stack of 100s and 20s on the table in front

of Lee and said, "There's your money. Three thousand dollars. You might want to count it."

Lee glanced up in question—he'd expected six.

"Yeah, I know," Will answered with a frown. "Same ol' Frankie. Can't seem to deliver more 'n half."

Same old Will, seeing the glass half empty when it was half full.

Ry went on to explain how all deals were off following the bust. How Gabe couldn't even make contact. Like everyone, Lee was disappointed at only half the money. Still, they had the hemp and there was always a market. Somewhere. Like Frankie told them, "Be patient, boys. Things will swing back our way."

So Lee was still hopeful. And deep down relieved to learn that he wasn't the only one taking heat from Valentine. Though he hated to see Rus or any of his friends under threat, he suspected the list would lengthen till it included half the county. Yet gasoline watered down still burned.

"You know something?" Lee said to Rus. "Valentine even made his wife take sodium pentothal. Made her and his whole bunch shoot up. Did you know that?"

"Why, I never..."—Rus stroked his beard in disbelief. "He's a lower down skunk than I thought."

"Here's another thing," Lee added with a laugh. "You've gotta wonder about his poor mother. Because he said she had to mortgage her house to pay his bail. I mean, you've gotta wonder if he didn't shoot her up too, saying, *Momma, I know ya love me, but I need proof!*"

By now they were all laughing, even Will.

"Yeah, yeah," he chuckled. "Gotta really wonder about his poor ol' mom."

From time to time each of them had worried their mothers sick and they had to wonder about that too—god-forsaken sons filled with remorse one moment and the next crowing about their deeds like swaggering roosters with fistfuls of money. But they would worry about their mothers later on, once they'd collected all their money and squared things up.

At supper that evening Jesse was back to normal, plowing his mashed potatoes with his spoon and making motor noises, grinning up at his momma when she urged him to try a bite like he had better things to do than eat. He'd taken a good nap that afternoon, his mother's voice, rhythmic and musical, had worked to smooth the men's rough talk of guns and shooting. All but blanked it out. There were lots of blank spaces in the big people's world, like a picture puzzle with chunks of missing pieces, and what did appear seemed mostly illusory. Still, Jesse knew what was real and what was dangerous, if not by experience, then by instinct, for reality could barge in like a monster plunging its head through a wall to eye you—or come quietly creeping up like a ghost neither ugly nor monstrous, but all too real, pleading from the hallway and crying in the night. But Jesse was not concerned about monsters or ghosts that evening, ready to be tucked in following his bedtime story as he hugged his pillow and curled up like a little possum, smiling as he nestled down. One thing he knew for certain, he wasn't afraid of Rue or Keeps.

As Diana descended the stairs and crossed into the kitchen, she felt a wave of gratitude like a blush of warm air wafting from the oven. Grateful for the house and the fact that Jesse was sleeping through the night—and grateful that Lee was in the next room playing his guitar instead of pacing the yard with a gun or out in some far creek swinging a machete. She leaned to the screen door to breathe in the night air and in that instant her serenity froze.

"Lee?" she asked, her voice trembling. "Were you down at the barn today?"

At her question Lee felt a surge of panic like ice water in his veins. He grabbed his rifle and rushed into the kitchen. Diana stood clasping her shoulders as if chilled.

"There's a light on down there," she said, glancing to the barn.

Lee switched off the kitchen light and gazed out. Through the barn loft door a dim light shone in a warm nimbus like an invitation to come view what lay in wait, perhaps an innocent born and licked clean, or some jagged form perched on a rafter or crouched in a stall. The barn had been empty for several years and Lee couldn't recall whether the loft door was open the last time he was down there or not. But the bigger question was the light. Lee was certain it hadn't been on the night before. Nor had old John been by lately for a load of hay.

"All right, here's what we'll do," he said, gripping his rifle. "This time you take the double barrel." He handed her the shotgun and led her out. About twenty paces beyond the porch they stopped by a small cedar big enough to cloak a silhouette. "Now listen, Diana. I want you to pull back both hammers and wait right here. I'll go down and look things over. If anyone comes back this way and it's not me, you blast 'em. Got that?"

She nodded and watched him disappear into the night, his form merging with the interspersing brush and corrals. Further on, she saw him re-emerge like a shadow at the base of the ladder that led to the hayloft. He climbed slowly, grasping each rung with one hand while the other held the rifle ready in the crook of his arm—scaling with quiet intent, his senses alert and prepared to react. Rifle cocked, finger to the trigger.

Lee eased up over the last rung and swung his rifle left then right. Nothing. He stood and scrutinized the shadowed interior, the cobwebbed corners and mud-daubed rafters. A forked hay-buck dangled from its trolley like a waiting gallows. Straw spilled from a heap of broken bales in the far corner and lay strewn over the rough plank floor. Overhead a pigeon fluttered from its nest and landed on a cross-beam sending motes of dust before the smudged light of a lone socket nailed about eye level on a middle rafter. The bulb so encrusted with dust and pigeon droppings, it emitted only a mist of light. Lee walked up and tapped it, and it flicked off. Tapped again, it flicked on. In lieu of a switch the bulb was left partly screwed into the socket, to be turned on and off at a slight twist. Any small vibration, the scurry of a rat or the brush of a wing, might have caused contact. Lee unscrewed the bulb a half turn and watched the filament glow and fade as darkness filled the old barn like a deep sigh, putting the mystery to rest.

But in Diana's mind the question only grew. She'd observed the light go off, then on. Then off again, leaving total darkness. She waited, hoping to hear Lee yell an all-clear. Again, nothing but silence and the question of what had happened. She braced the two barrels in the fork of a limb and held steady, her finger pressing the cold metal of the front trigger. She couldn't see a thing. She heard footsteps. She took a deep breath and tensed, waiting, her finger poised to the trigger.

Then a voice, vaguely indistinct though the drum of fear...

"*Diana...?*"

Her blood pulsed as her finger edged away.

"Dammit, Lee!" she cried out. "Why didn't you say something sooner?"—using strong language in the anxious moment, literally shaking as she lowered the gun barrel and eased the hammers down. "I nearly shot you. You know that?"

"Well I'm glad you didn't," he laughed, giving her a brisk hug. But he stopped laughing when he noticed her lips start to quiver. "Aw now, Dita," he said, holding her close, gently soothing her. "You're right. I should've called out. I'm sorry. But I got to thinking..."—and he laughed again at the thought of a pigeon triggering the light, of being spooked by a possum, of all their false alarms and comic endings.

"Heck, it was just an old bulb left loose in the socket."

"Well it's not funny," she said. "I almost shot you."

"I know, I know. But you didn't. That's the main thing." He clasped her shoulder as they walked slowly to the house. "And like I said, I got to thinking. The rest of the stuff might sell, and it might not. Right now we have a little over six thousand dollars. Not enough to buy this place but plenty to move on to Nashville or Austin. You know, get away from all this and give music a try."

Lee smiled like it was the best notion on earth.

"I don't want to move, Lee"—her answer as strong and adamant as her voice.

"No worry, Diana, no one's going anywhere. Just a thought."

But she knew Lee and his wanderlust. They'd moved nearly twenty times in the past five years—to Colorado, Canada, New England, plus a dozen other little places in between, at times holed up at his mother's or hers to face the *I told you so's*, which she hated most of all. And him saying that he wanted to move scared her more than anything in the past five days. Because she didn't want to move. Ever again.

XIX. HOG HEAVEN

Valentine LaReese was due for arraignment the following Monday morning. Slated to appear before the Fifth District judge at the Saline County Courthouse at 9:30 sharp and face charges of felony drug and firearm possession as well as conspiracy to transport stolen cattle across the state line. Not to mention a litany of lesser charges. But Friday night he stood before a sterner judge. Even as Lee Clayton climbed into the hayloft in answer to a perceived threat, Valentine stood before CC Holtz in answer to his summons. Not exactly under duress but given no real choice in the matter either. Pulled over to the side of the road a mile south of the county line and told to get in.

"Look man, I got shit to do," he said in protest. "I'm facing prison."

Mex just smiled and said, "Come on, Val. Time to see the boss."

A short while later he stood silent before the huge mahogany desk, flanked on either side by Red, Straydog, and Mex. The room was dark except for the green shaded lamp. CC leaned back in his big leather chair, puffing a cigar, his eyes two gray embers in a veil of smoke. Subject to their squint and scrutiny, Valentine glanced down and fingered the raised hoof of the bronze stallion.

"Don't touch that! Makes it tarnish!" CC grumped, leaning forth with a kerchief to wipe it clean, making no effort to put his guest at ease, concerned only that one of the charges might lead back to him. Like rustling, for instance.

"My God," he said, disgusted. "With beef prices sucking hind tit, beats me why a man would rustle in the first place?"

"You rustled in your day," Valentine asserted. "Everyone knows that."

"No! They *think* I did. And they can think all they want. But they don't *know*. Can't prove a thing. Never could. But you! They got you with a cow 'n calf from your neighbor's pasture penned up in your own damn yard. Damn fool..." CC shook his head and eased his tone. "What were you thinkin'? Messing with them bulls like that?"

"Look man," Valentine perked up at the question, "you gotta appreciate the finer points of terror. You see," he said, waving his hands, eager to explain his tactics like a salesman showing a new product, "I mean, it's like this, you plant a little mystery, and it spreads fear. Pretty soon they're afraid to even look your way. It's like war, man. You terrorize the enemy. Like in Viet—"

"Stop right there!" CC abruptly leaned forth and pointed his cigar. "Now you appreciate this. We lost that war, you best not forget it. And folks round here are our neighbors, not our enemy. You scared 'em all right, sure as shit, did you ever. Why, they brung a whole army up here to flush you out. You messing with them bulls got folks more riled than the fact of your guns 'n drugs. And what's the business of all that blood in them barrels, anyhow?"

Valentine fidgeted with his fingernail a moment, looked to Mex, then answered.

"We...planned to grow high-grade domestic. Ya know, with heat lamps inside a barn or Quonset. Grow year around. And blood...blood makes good fertilizer."

"Shit yes! Anything ya shit out your ass is gonna make good fertilizer. That's just the thing, you been shittin' too close to the house. *Too damn close!*"—CC slapped his desk in anger. "And them bull dicks they found hanging in your barn. Five of 'em!" he said, holding up the spread of his right palm for emphasis, then clinching all but a lone finger to drive his point. "There's one more dick should be hanging there, by God. That squirrel dick between your legs."

CC held him in the grip of that thought a moment then lowered his hand and smiled.

"There's three more swingin' dicks I'd like to hang up from time to time…"

Red and Straydog braved a chuckle while CC laughed himself into a hard cough.

"Watch it you don't choke, boss," Mex warned as CC cleared his throat.

"Uh-huh, I appreciate your concern, Mex. Truly do. But it'll be a good long time before I choke, boy, a good long time."

Valentine chose the moment to regain some favor.

"Say, Colonel…thanks for helping fix my bail."

"Think I'd let 'em throw ya to the hogs?" CC laughed, then added. "Just you keep that under your hat. Your ol' mom played her part, puttin' up her house. Best they think it was all her doing. And best she never knows who sent that lawyer, you hear?"

"Sure, sure, I understand"—Valentine jerked his head in quick succession. "Mom doesn't know a thing. She thinks someone from the church must've hired 'im."

"The church, huh? Well bless her heart," CC grinned, then drew himself up and leaned to the desk, his face full in the light and fully sober. "Thought you were gonna have Mex a load a' hemp by now?"

"Look, Colonel, that…that's not my fault. Someone stooled on me. I've been looking, I swear"—raising his right hand like a good scout—"when I find out who, they're gonna pay. I mean big time."

"Yeah, I know. You been blowing like a hot wind 'cross three counties. Stirring things up. Word gits around and that worries me. You see, you got a problem, you solve it quiet-like so nobody knows…" CC opened his jacket, revealing a pearl-handled pistol tucked in the inner pocket. "See this. It's just a twenty-two. Small, but sufficient. And I never show it unless I have a mind to use it."

"Look, I's set up, like I said…" Valentine raised both hands, pleading. "Listen, I got a hot tip…" He licked his lips like a rat about to share a tasty morsel. "Frankie Sage and his gang. They've got a ton at least."

CC took a long puff on his cigar and let the smoke drift

slowly away, all the while fixing his gray eyes on Valentine.

"Ya don't say, I'll keep that in mind," he noted, tapping his cigar. "But you haven't thought of talking to the law, have ya, boy? Maybe trying for a deal?"

"No! I swear by my mother!" Valentine declared, mindful of that pistol. "I know the rules, man. I don't talk. Let the lawyers talk, that's what I say."

"Uh-huh, and dog shit can outrun a rabbit!" CC growled. "I checked with that lawyer a' mine...looking into your case. He knows all kind a' folks, got friends in the prosecutor's office. Yessir, and he said you ain't talked. Yet. He also said that you look to do ten years in Lansing if ya don't talk. But let's say you feed that prosecutor a little something that hooks a bigger fish, why you only git a year or two. Maybe even walk. And I hear you been saying you can't do no more time. So I gotta wonder..."

"Hey, Colonel, that don't mean I'm gonna talk. That's...that's just—"

"I know, I know. Don't go pissin' your pants. There's always an out."

Valentine stood at a loss for words, visibly shaken at this point, hands trembling, badly in need of something to calm his nerves. He reached to his shirt pocket, didn't have a thing, not even a joint.

"Yessir," CC leaned back and smiled, "there's always opportunities in this world for a clever feller. A real go-getter. Me 'n Mex got us a little game brewing in Mexico. We could use a good man down there. 'Course you'd need to learn the lingo?"

"Shit man, I can do that," Valentine assured, finding his tongue. "I mean, I got an IQ of one forty-five. I can learn quick as that!" he said, snapping his fingers.

"Good, good. That's the spirit. Then you'll leave tonight."

"Tonight? But? I need to talk to my wife, my—"

"Don't fret your wife, boy. She ain't facing hard time, you are. Her we can git off. You we gotta git outa the damn country. Them senoritas down there'll keep your dick hard for a month. Now you git settled, she can join ya later on. Just be glad you're outa this jam. Don't worry 'bout your ol' ma, either. CC'll take care a' things. So look alive. Mex 'n the boys'll drive ya down to

Smolan. Got an old airstrip on back a' the hog barns there. Got a plane waitin'. Yessir, fly ya on down tonight."

Valentine saw no way out, breathing fast, heart racing, caught in a spin of events about to suck him down a drain and spew him out into some back alley of old Mexico. He wished he could slow things down and gain some footing. He worked his lips in attempt to phrase an argument, find an exit.

"Naw, naw, don't thank me," CC dismissed him with a wave of his cigar. "Just thank your lucky stars. And remember, Spanish is the loving tongue. *Hah! Hah!* No sir, don't you worry 'bout a thing. The boys'll see ya on that plane"—still laughing as he reached to pour some brandy.

"That's right, Val, ol' buddy," Mex smiled, gripping him by the neck, leading him from the room. "Then it's adios amigos and *hola Mejico!*"

They walked into the still night. Not a word spoken as they crossed to the truck. Mex opened the door and in the flood of light he stepped to the chrome running board. He nodded to his boot and said, "What do ya think?" The boots were red lizard skin, blood red to match his truck and the western shirt worn under his tan leather jacket.

"And check this," he raised his Levis to reveal the uppers tooled in swirls of blue, yellow, black, and green—all but poisonous to the eye. "Pretty wild, eh? The chicks dig it. They say it makes their skin crawl." Mex bared his teeth in a smile, stepped back and said, "Hop on in, sweetheart. You can ride in the middle next to me. Red, he's too leggy. And Straydog, I don't like his smell. Go on now, they won't bite."

Red and Straydog already sat shotgun and looked on in wait. Valentine climbed in and edged over as Mex got in and closed the door. The pickup spun around, spitting up gravel as they sped down the drive.

"You gonna have to spread your legs there, honey, so I can shift," Mex laughed. "Don't worry, Val my boy, I won't mess with ya. It's Straydog ya gotta watch for. He's kinda sweet on fellas. Right Red?" Mex laughed again as he reached in his pocket and said, "Here, Val, have a couple ludes."

"Thanks, man..." the other mumbled, barely audible, numb, hesitant.

"Sure thing. Hey, Straydog, fetch Val a cold beer."

Straydog reached in the cooler at his feet and popped open a can with a loud *ZLISSP!* Valentine grabbed the foaming can and tipped it up, took a greedy gulp and shook his head like a bird downing a worm as he swallowed the pills. Then he took another few gulps to wash it down, exposing the full length of his throat pierced by a sharp Adam's apple.

"Shit man, that was great," he gasped as if he were only now taking a breath after leaving the house and hearing CC pronounce his fate. "Man, I've been wound up tight these past few days."

"Sure you have. Being busted and all. You gotta relax, Val. Can't have you getting sick and puking on the plane. Got a long flight ahead and I'm your pilot, baby."

"No shit. Where you taking me? I mean, where at in Mexico?"

"A little place below Juarez called Cajonitos. A great place to rest your cajones," Mex grinned. "You'll see, you'll like it. Relax. *Rela-a-ax...*"

Valentine nodded and sipped his beer, gazing to the road, the darkness.

"What'll I be doing down there? Like...what's the game?"

"You'll play the coyote. It's kinda like a priest"—Mex nudged him and laughed. "You'll help lost sheep cross into the Promised Land."

Hearing this, Valentine laughed as well, could see himself in the role, beginning to sense some potential, a real possibility. Sure, he could play a coyote, no problem.

"Shit yes," he said, relaxing. "I can even yip like one—*Yippy-yip-yip-YOWL!*"

"There ya go, my man, a border coyote," Mex declared. "Just learn some Spanish, you got it dicked. Hey Red, roll us up a joint. Make it a big fat one. We gotta smoke to Val's new life. And don't slobber all over it like you did the last time. Damn..."

They continued down the highway, smoking the joint, talking and laughing in the crowded cab while white lines zipped into view as if borne out of the darkness, pointing to an unknown where they all peered in blind haste. Even Red and Straydog joined in the fun and chanced to speak now and then. Passing through Cibola, Straydog perked up.

"I could eat the ass end out of a skunk," he said, vouching his hunger. "Roadkill, any damn thing. Got the munchies bad. Gosh, there's the cafe. Smell that food? Liable to chew my tongue off. Sure would like a—"

"Okay, okay. Gotcha the first time," Mex said. "But we can't just stop by the Burger Bar and let the whole town know we're slipping Val here outa the country."

They drove on over the river bridge and in another few blocks they pulled into a dark alley next to Marley's Market, a little combination grocery/liquor store on the south edge of town. Mex handed Red a twenty-dollar bill. He hopped out and soon returned with a giant bag of barbeque chips, some beef jerky, and a 12 pack of Schlitz. He'd no more than snapped the door shut when Straydog tore into the bag of chips. Mex eased down the alley and circled the block, then headed south out of town.

They followed Highway 14 as it stretched into Lincoln County, then Saline, passing over a series of hills formed like rounded loaves left scattered through millennia on the broad tableland. The prairie lay dormant under the dark blanket of night, while a brisk wind promised the first hard frost. Red and Straydog gazed to the road, oblivious of the passing terrain, happily munching handfuls of chips and tearing at jerky like two hounds crunching chicken bones. Red finally let out a gaseous belch.

"That's a'nuff fer me," he said, handing the sack back to Straydog. "One thing I would like though, that's some chicken wings."

"Yah, yah..." Straydog nodded, shoving in another handful. "Usta eat 'em over in Gookland. Gooks had all kinds a' chicken wings. Any friggin' bird but a chicken they made inta chicken wings."

"That's no lie. Like them Gooney birds. 'Member? Big ol' birds we seen 'em there in port. Clumsy fuckers. Helluva time gitting airborne. But once up they's purdy much ta home. Dip 'n soar with nar a flutter. Dangest thing, a Gooney."

"That's an albatross, you fool," Mex said, winking to Valentine. "They have 'em down in Mexico too. All along the beaches. Them 'n seagulls shittin' everywhere."

"So?" Red answered back. *Al-bee-tross...Goo-ney* bird, them Gooks still made chicken wings of 'em. Same with any other dang thing with feathers. Bought me a chicken wing once there in Subric Bay. Sucker was as long as my arm. Sure as shit warn't no chicken. Had to be a Gooney bird."

"Talk a' chickens!" Straydog laughed. "Ever eat *Baluk*?"

"Oh shit no..."

"What's *ba-luk*?" Valentine asked.

Red leaned around and looked his way. "That's a chicken egg," he explained. "Gooks let it ink-u-bate then take n' bury it in the ground so it won't hatch out. In a week or so they dig 'er up 'n eat it."

"Man, that's...that's just a rotten egg."

"Purdy much, only it's already growed into a little chick."

"And I tell ya what, that shit stunk," Straydog added, facing Valentine, his own breath rank with barbecue, marijuana, and rotten teeth. "Walk inta some bar 'n see a Gook whore crack open one a' them eggs, sprinkle on a little salt 'n snarf it down. Nuff ta make ya lose yer appetite fer eggs or women."

"Ever try any?" Valentine asked.

"Baluk? Hell no! Nasty ol' stuff!" Straydog barked in a spew of chips.

"Ever kisst a bitch that had?" Red asked, his eyes keen with wonder.

"Gosh, I 'spose. Maybe a time or two. But only after I swabbed her mouth out with my dick!"

Red and Straydog both stomped their boots and laughed as Straydog chanted, *"Milk, milk 'n lemonade, 'round the corner choc-lat's made. Milk, milk 'n lemonade..."*—and Red joined in, spicing up their act like a Vaudeville team, both eying Valentine like two old salts tempting a young sailor, offering to show him what lay around the corner. They were soon trading more quips and anecdotes from their experiences in Asia and the South China Sea.

Time lapsed and the journey shortened, within an hour the pickup reached Smolan and they soon pulled into the Colonel's hog farm. They eased past the front office and the dozen trailers that housed the foreman and most of the crew, on down the long line of farrowing houses full of sows and piglets, the latter soon to be weaned and fattened for slaughter. Several Mexican workers nearly invisible in their dark coveralls and swarthy skin gave a slight nod and hurried on while others ducked back in the shadows—they all recognized the truck and none wished to be detained or harassed by the Colonel's son, *El Bastardo!* as they called him.

At the far end of the complex stood the pens with sows waiting to be bred by boars housed in barred closures across the way. Beyond that lay nothing but the catch pond, a foul lagoon full of drainage, and a charnel pit where they burned the accumulated corpses of dead swine. No one came near that sector at night, and few but the breeding crew during the day. The air hung heavy with stench like in a deep pit of hell where the black smoke never rises or dissipates.

The pickup rolled to a stop. Mex cut the lights and they got out.

"What are we doing here?" Valentine asked, uneased by the stench and the sound of the large boars crashing against their cages.

"We gotta walk from here," Mex said as he shut the door, leaving the night pitch black. The sky overcast and sullen. Nothing visible but the dim lights of distant sheds and the breath of man and swine in the chill damp air.

"Walk where...? Where's the plane?"

"A little further on south, about a hundred yards. But we gotta cross a dike and it's too narrow for the truck. Come on now, don't be a sissy. It'll smell better at the plane. Red 'n Straydog, you two head on down and set the flares to mark the runway."

They did as they were told, turned and started marching south. Valentine slowly followed. At each step he sensed the squish of mud around his boots and a sick feeling flood his flesh as the thick stench burned his eyes and nostrils. Nearing the end of the pens, he noticed Mex stop and kneel. He turned in question.

"No problem," Mex smiled, showing a glint of teeth. "Gotta pull up my sock."

Valentine nodded vaguely and turned back to see where the other pair had gone. In that moment Mex unsheathed a knife from his boot and in one rapid movement, like a spider to a fly, he seized Valentine by the neck and drove the blade through his back just below his heart.

"Kinda takes your breath, eh?" he said in a hard whisper as his victim went rigid.

The blade pierced his lung and Valentine could but faintly gasp, "*Uh god...*" And that only once as pain checked his breath and Mex twisted the blade deeper in the wound, using the hilt and handle to turn his victim towards the pens.

"Hey, don't fight it, Val," he urged in an oddly soothing voice. "It's like a woman, once you've got it in, she's already fucked. Except you can't scream. No, you can barely breath. There now, don't stumble," he softly coaxed. "Just a few more steps..."

Red and Straydog appeared like shadows, each grabbing an arm while Mex yanked out the knife. Valentine felt the world upend as he collapsed—his equilibrium lost in a rush of blood and pain spreading from his wound, every sense keenly alive like a leaf taking flame before it crumples into a frail white ash and dies. Red and Straydog held him splayed. He blinked his eyes in a climax of terror, thinking *What is this?* in the final moment as Mex's boot heel pressed his face aside and the knife sliced into his throat and his blood and thoughts spilled forth and emptied out. The last thing he saw before death sucked him down were four large sows grouped not a yard away, their gross flat noses shoved under the bottom rail, emitting loud snorts as the blood pooled near.

"Let's get busy," Mex said, wasting no time ripping the shirt from the body. Red and Straydog stood by, not certain what to do. "Go on. Pull off his boots 'n jeans. Get to it!" he snapped. "You've had lots of practice pulling down each other's pants."

"Naw we never," Straydog vowed even as he knelt to unfasten the belt buckle.

"Aw you *never*, my ass!" Mex jeered. "I'm on to you two bitches and your bunkhouse romance."

Red looked up after they'd pulled off the jeans, still reluctant to proceed.

"The Colonel just said to burn 'im."

"I know what the fuck he said." Mex leaned down and quickly worked the knife from gut to sternum as bowels steamed the air. Then he stood and answered, "But first I wanna feed the hogs. Got a problem with that?"

Red took one look at Mex holding that knife and shook his head "*Nope.*" His only problem was the thought of beating back the sows and digging scraps of meaty bone out of the mud to burn. But like it or not that would be his task, so he simply grabbed the ankles while Straydog took the wrists and with a hearty "*One, two, three...*" they heaved the body over into the pen where it plopped to the mud like a plucked chicken.

The sows wheeled about and plunged in as more humped apparitions emerged from the darkness, cloven hooves charging through the muck in rabid lunge. All rutted at the feast, squealing jowl to jaw, chomping down entrails yanked from the pale limp corpse that twitched alive amidst their feeding while the blank eyes stared in mute wonder to the misted sky.

XX. MOTHER'S GRAVE

Saturday morning the night shades quickly faded as the trees reached to catch the first rays of sunlight cast over Arcadia. Maple leaves along with ash and oak all bore a trace of red and yellow, presaging the golden hues of autumn. In the street below, Sheriff Hoss Wayne stood scraping frost off his windshield before heading to the Downtowner. The thermometer on Mrs. Wylett's back porch had read 29 degrees and the heater in the Bronco had no more than kicked in by the time he arrived at the cafe and parked.

Hoss got out and raised the collar of his windbreaker against the cool air, though he knew it would be plenty warm inside. News of the big bust in the neighboring county northeast had been the hot topic all week.

"Looks like Patch Hyland got the big catch this year!" one old boy shouted to Hoss.

"Hell's bells!" another one countered. "That was the state boys as done that. Patch Hyland couldn't catch a cold if ya sneezed in his face!"

"Why, he couldn't catch his tail if he was a dog!" another piped up.

Talk ballooned from there.

"I hear tell LaReese had a dozen gals living with 'im up there. Now it's a fact ya only need but one woman to cook 'n clean. What you s'pose they was doin'?"

"They's workin' for 'im. That's what I heard..."

"Yeah, but was they workin' standin' up or *layin' down?!*"

No need to answer that question as they slapped their tables, poked and laughed all around, envisioning a scene right out of the old west with LaReese the lone gunman entertained by a dozen saloon girls. Overnight the six women arrested had grown to twelve and the three men had shrunk to one. Hoss ignored their talk and took his ribbing in stride. He sat down at the far end of the counter and ordered his usual biscuits and gravy and coffee. Events in Hill County might as well have been a world away, like a typhoon in India or an earthquake in Guatemala—or the handful of refugees given quarter in the local convent for all he cared. If it didn't pertain to the murder of Joey Connors and Cathy Torres it was of little concern. He'd hardly reacted when Sheriff Craig called to say it looked like they'd found the rustlers and likely solved the mystery of the mutilated bulls.

—Some folks over there might be relieved to know. Ol' Homer for one.

Hoss supposed so and thanked him for passing word, but Guy might as well have said that the UFOs were friendly aliens from Mars come to check the price of corn. Hoss's sole question to him before hanging up had been: "Got any more on Mex?"

—No. Just LaReese and his gang...

This conversation had taken place Wednesday morning, two days following the bust. Thursday Hoss drove to Junction City, decided to try another tact while awaiting word from Captain Crohn regarding Father Michael. He didn't know why it hadn't occurred to him earlier, but that's the way his mind worked, one thing at a time, and still following the same routine each morning, dogging Father Michael at the church. Eyes caged, looking neither left nor right, focused—even now as he sipped his coffee at the counter. But he did acknowledge Meg's smile as he stood to leave, finding her smile more winsome every day, caught himself smiling back. Coughed up a "Thank you" for the refill and left another two-dollar tip.

Hoss had driven to Junction City to search for background on Mex's mother. He knew Mex's story in part, that following his mother's death he'd been adopted by the Colonel. All happened the same summer Hoss had joined the Corps. Even though the Colonel made his home on a ranch in Hill County, he cast a mighty shadow through the region and folks were always mindful of him and his doings. In fact he held greater sway through the immediate counties than if he were governor—for the governor changed name and shape every few years, a mere official, remote and diminutive compared to the vivid voice and presence of CC Holtz.

Hoss had no precise notion what to look for or what he might find, simply following his nose and playing a hunch as he reached Junction City. He didn't even know her first name and only presumed that her last name had been Orvano. But he knew the year.

"Summer of '64," he stated to the slouched clerk at the hall of records after giving a brief explanation, citing the woman's name as a possible clue to a murder in Sky County. Then he declared bluntly, "I'm Sheriff Hoss Wayne," and repeated, "That's *Or-van-o*. She died in '64." And that voice, that face, that 6'4" frame sparked an alacrity seldom witnessed in bureaucratic drones. The clerk snapped-to like a young recruit and shortly provided the requested information, that being her full name written neatly in longhand on legal paper: *Andrea Corina Marquez Orvano.*

Hoss elicited the same crisp response at the police station and the Junction City Herald. From the police he learned that Andrea Orvano had indeed been a known prostitute, though strangely enough she had never been arrested, at least not in their jurisdiction. As the old desk sergeant intimated, "She only serviced the brass at Fort Riley and other muck-a-mucks." At the newspaper he obtained a copy of her obituary, including her photo. In the photo Hoss found what he'd been looking for— saw Father Michael reflected in her delicate features, favoring her even more than Mex whose face was broader and bolder, though they shared the same darkly sensual expression through the eyes and lips.

Before leaving town Hoss drove to the cemetery and located her grave. It was marked by a large black marble stone, standing five-feet tall, softly arched at the top. Below her name the inscription read: "OUR BELOVED DOVE Born 1925 - Mexico Died May 15, 1964 - USA." No doubt CC had made the purchase and played a hand in choosing the words. But all Hoss saw mirrored in the polished black surface were the fluid features of the mother and two sons emerging to dissolve and interweave with the underlying veins. A cardinal lit in a nearby cedar and basked brilliant red in the sunlight. The wind hummed through the trees and bristly grasses mowed smooth about the graves. Hoss stood listening briefly then returned to his Bronco and drove away.

Friday afternoon Hoss sat in his office, typing up various scraps of information to add to the charges of rustling against Valentine LaReese; he'd typed the same form three times and still hadn't got it right, simply could not focus. Once again he caught himself gazing out the window and reflecting on the gravestone and the interplay of images. The phone rang. It was Father Thomas Crohn.

"Captain," Hoss perked up at the sound of his voice. "Good to hear from you."

—*Not so good, Sergeant. Afraid I don't have much. Mostly hit a brick wall.*

"Fire away, Captain. Sometimes a little is a lot."

—*Okay. Here goes… Father Michael Kairn grew up at Saint Mark's, a Catholic home for boys in San Antonio. He took his name from the headmaster, Father Charles O'Kairn. Although it appears his given name had been Miguel. They say a young Mexican girl left the child at the orphanage in the winter of 1941. No date of birth given, though the child was thought to be a year old at the time.*

"Did you get her name? The girl?"

—*No. My informant said that such arrangements were kept confidential by Father Charles. However, it seems he did correspond with the young woman over the years, relaying news of her son. But her name was taken with him to his grave. As for the boy, Michael, he was always highly thought of, though never out-going, quiet and reserved. He attended seminary at Saint Mary's there in Kansas. Which is something of a mystery, because Saint Mark's is Franciscan while Saint Mary's is Dominican. So there may have been a spirit of rebellion in the boy after all. And perhaps you are aware that he, Father Michael, has on occasion expressed sympathies with the Liberation Theology popular in Latin America. In fact he served his early ministry among the poor in Guatemala where his work was often noted in the radical press, and once praised by the high Bishop in El Savador. Which may not recommend him in some circles, but is hardly a black mark. So all in all he appears a highly exemplar young priest. Truly devoted. And I found nothing concerning a brother. No scandals or innuendoes, no negatives of any kind...*

"No sweat, Captain. You got me all I need. Thanks." Hoss sat tapping his pen to his notepad where he'd scrawled, "Saint Mark's, San Antonio, 1941," and directly under that the name, "Miguel," boldly underlined.

—Well, I hardly see how...?

"Believe me, Captain. This is like fresh ammo in a firefight."

—Then let me know how things turn out.

"Will do, Captain..." Hoss was already hanging up the phone as he said the words, anxious to get back to work, reacting as if he'd spotted the enemy and was drawing bead, warming to the scent, suspicion turning to cold certainty.

And Saturday morning after smiling to Meg and leaving the cafe, he drove to the church, got out and stood staring across the way, his arms folded on his chest. By his very stance making his accusation more public. His certainty shone through like the frost glinting on the intervening grass, a sharp silvery evanescence painful to the eye. Father Michael stood at the church door as parishioners filed in, squinting from the glare as he glanced to Hoss—and it wasn't simply the sunlight, it was the harsh eyes rifled straight at him, that cold certainty that made Hoss seem twenty-foot tall, then suddenly loom near as if standing at the base of the steps, on the very threshold, towering above the priest, bearing down.

And by late afternoon Hoss *was* there, standing at the front door of the parish, staring hard through the screen.

"You may come in," Father Michael said wearily, opening the door. Hoss stepped in but didn't remove his hat or avert his eyes. Father Michael likewise dispensed with further courtesy, returned his gaze and asked, "What is your interest today, Sheriff?"

"Just a couple of questions and I'll be off."

"Good. I must say that I prefer meeting face to face," Father Michael declared, unusually firm in tone and manner. "You sitting across the street day after day I find highly disconcerting. People are beginning to wonder, they're beginning to talk. They know you've moved out on your wife. Now they think you may harbor some sort of infatuation. For me."

The insinuation caught Hoss off-guard, but his scrutiny only hardened in answer.

"What people say behind my back I can't help. If they wanna say it to my face, let 'em. What troubles me is the murder of Joey Connors and Cathy Torres. It troubles me all to hell. Now I got a bit of information to pass to you…" Hoss edged closer, so close the priest could taste his hot breath, the scent of coffee and aftershave, the antiperspirant dampening his shirt as he stated, "Saint Mark's in San Antonio, does that ring a bell?"

The priest didn't flinch.

"How about Miguel?" Hoss continued. "Or how about this? A sixteen-year-old girl named *Andrea Orvano* who abandoned her son there in the winter of 1941!"

"She never—" Father Michael blinked his eyes and steadied. "Yes, I grew up at Saint Mark's. But believe me, neither I nor anyone knows who my mother was."

Hoss took out the newspaper photo and handed it to him.

"Take a good look and tell me that's not your mother."

Father Michael glanced briefly and handed it back.

"That's Javier's mother," he said simply, disavowing his mother as coolly as Christ disavowed his. "It's true, I knew the woman. But only in passing. I always remember the dying, their final words. I gave her last rites. You cannot know her sorrow."

"No, I don't know and don't care. But I do know this much. That son of hers is a murderer. He shoved a pistol up Joey Connor's ass and pulled the trigger. Gave him a horrible death. Think on that a minute. And he pressed the barrel to Cathy Torres's temple and the impact of the bullet popped her pretty eyes half out of her head. You talk about the dying and their sorrow, but I remember the dead and suggest you do the same. Or maybe you can go wave your hand and raise that boy and girl from the dead. Stand at their graves and call them up. While you're at it go to your momma's grave and wake *Our Beloved Dove!* and ask—"

"Stop it! Stop—"

"Ask her what she thinks of her darling boy, Mex!"

"Stop it! Please! You cannot say such things, cannot..." Father Michael pleaded, his lips trembling under the strain. "I insist that you leave. Please go."

Hoss slowly nodded and backed away.

"Sure, I'll be going. But I'll tell you straight out, my infatuation for you is gonna grow. I'm gonna stay on you like a fly on shit. I might start coming to church each morning. Sit right down in a front pew and listen to the good word. Wait for you to bear witness on that murdering bastard you refuse to call your brother. Can't say as I blame you. But I couldn't sleep at night, I couldn't face another day, if I knew what you know. You can pray all you like but you can't change what he's done. The only good you can do now is help me put 'im away. So you think on that and here"—Hoss handed him the clipping. "You might study on that some. You'll find it bears a striking resemblance."

Father Michael took the clipping in his limp hand and cast his eyes to the floor.

Hoss gave his hat a firm tug and walked out. This time stepping down off the porch into the warm sunlight he felt refreshed, buoyant, like a sinner having bared his soul to a priest. He marched straight to his Bronco and thought he might go check on little Rob and see if he wanted to take in a movie that evening. Go see Paul Newman in *Hombre.* They weren't making many Westerns these days and it was a crying shame.

Father Michael turned from the door and walked to the far room to seek its dark refuge. He stood before the image of the Virgin, the Holy Mother, and sank to his knees. How he'd longed for her, his real mother, had sought her in that image and in as much made himself a eunuch to enter into the Kingdom and seek her there. How much of his life and faith were formed to that end. But he knew his mother had been a whore—now a corpse embracing the earth. And his brother was a murderer like Cain whose victims' blood crieth from the earth. Now he found himself peering at the very brink of Hell with no hope of salvation. For her voice crieth out above all else in her final plea as she gazed to the young priest, her firstborn, her pride and hope, and said, "Look after him for me. Look after your brother. Will you…? Miguel…?"

Word of Valentine's various threats and doings had traveled to more ears than CC's. Bruce, for one, related his perilous adventures to his wife Julie who in this instance was positively enthralled as they discussed the probabilities and ramifications in hushed tones while seated on the sofa in his parent's house— for they were staying there through the summer and fall until they could decide where to move. And Bruce's mother, a quiet unassuming woman, stood in the kitchen doing dishes, folding laundry, pressing clothes, humming in a tuneless singsong manner, occasionally passing through wearing a bland "never mind me" smile as if she were no more sentient than the wallpaper. But she took in every word and the following afternoon while selling Avon door to door, which she did several days a week, she was not so quiet. Though her sly demurrals won nearly everyone's confidence, making her a prime purveyor of local gossip—what she didn't know, she could well presume.

Added to that Ry divulged a few salient details to his brother Rowdy who of course didn't "give a shit," not until he met up with his buddies at The Smoker and eagerly filled them in. And Will, who had the horse sense not to tell his wife JoAnn who would have spilled the beans to her sister Marcie, had to tell Tyke who'd proven his loyalty time and again down the years and who in turn shared his concern with at least a half-dozen good-old-boys he knew dead-dog-certain he could trust. And how could Rus, upon returning from Frankie's farm, hide his dark dread from Lori when even Dig sensed something wrong and started whimpering the moment he walked in. Lori took one look and had the full story in five minutes. She wanted to call *The FBI!* He said they couldn't do that.

"Well, for Pete's sake! Someone should lock him up!" she cried.

"They already tried that, peaches."

"Well what's he doing out?" she wanted to know.

"That's the way things work, honey buns. I don't like it any better'n you…"

Lori sat down, pressed her hands to her face and cried wet tears right through to the floor. Rus kept sweet-talking as he stroked her hair and finally calmed her down. But he couldn't follow her to work. Lori worked nights as a telephone operator in Hays City and once there she put her fists to her hips and told all the girls that some madman named LaReese had threatened to shoot her fellow. Before her shift ended the news had pretty much blanketed north-central Kansas.

So Guy had a fair notion of "happenings" by Saturday afternoon—he knew the boys had been run out of the patch by Valentine's gunplay, and he kept his ears tuned to subsequent threats. No telling about a snake like LaReese, once cornered he might coil and strike. The thought set Guy's stomach churning like he was riding a roller coaster that wouldn't stop, events spiraling out of control. Sunday afternoon he got a call from Web Dolson, a farmer north of town, reporting a car abandoned off Emory Road.

—Just south a' where Plum Creek forks to the Buff'ler…

This placed it in Guy's jurisdiction, the northwest corner of Range County.

—Been there two days n' I got to thinking that's too damn long…

Guy agreed and drove up to check it out. He searched through the glove box and found the registration. The car belonged to Naomi LaReese. Valentine's mother. Back at the office, Guy placed a call. She hadn't seen her son since bailing him out Tuesday.

—Why? Has he done something else? Has he wrecked my car?

"No ma'am, the car's fine. Just a routine check," Guy answered, not wanting to worry her. But when he called Valentine's wife, Janice, she was already upset. Her voice quavered as she said she hadn't seen Valentine since Friday noon.

—He should've been back by now. He knows I'm stranded without that car…

"Well, we'll get the car back to you. Don't worry, he'll likely show," Guy said to reassure her. But hanging up he had to wonder if the one of the boys hadn't gotten to Valentine first.

And Monday morning when Valentine failed to appear for his arraignment in Salina it was all but certain he'd either skipped the country or met with foul play. Yet if he had decided to run for it, a back road in Range County seemed an odd place to start—that is unless he planned to paddle a canoe all the way from Plum Creek to the Gulf of Mexico, as some joked. Before the day was out speculation spun in a whole other direction.

Three old farmers stood at the side of Emory Road, kicking at the dirt. One knit his hoary brows and pointed to the radius of burnt grass beyond where the car had been abandoned and swore it was sure sign LaReese had been abducted by aliens.

"Lots a' strange lights in the sky this past summer," he declared.

"They's stranger things at's happened in this ol' world," another vowed.

"Yuh-huh. No doubt a' that… *Patooie!*"—the third added his two-bits, spitting a long string of tobacco juice to puddle in the dust, as the three wise men stood beating plowshares into flying saucers, taking their logic to the very heavens where men have always looked for answers.

Guy received a call Tuesday morning from Special Agent Tillis regarding Valentine's disappearance.

—*We're drawing a blank here, Sheriff. As you may know, his wife and the others were arraigned yesterday. We questioned them at length, and I think they sincerely have no idea of LaReese and his whereabouts. In fact, I think they're scared. Have you heard any further rumors?*

Guy had filed a missing-person report on Valentine Sunday evening.

"Oh, there's rumors alright," he smiled, thinking of the radius of burnt grass and a dozen other wild conjectures. "But none that bear repeating," he added, not ready to share rumors of the boys.

—*Very well, Sheriff, I thank you for your time. Please keep me advised of any developments…*

Guy's smile faded as he hung up the phone; his stomach burned like a festered boil. He decided to drive over to Marley's Market. Preferred to buy his buttermilk there, due to the low inventory and rapid turnover he could count on it being fresh, not two months old like at Co-op or IGA. A brass cowbell jangled above the door as he stepped inside and said "Good morning" to the proprietor. Milton Marley stood behind the counter and gave a nod. He was even quieter than Guy. A plump little man and so pale he was nearly transparent, his features nondescript as doe patted with flour and left to rise. A wisp of white hair feathered past his ears. Guy reached in the cooler and grabbed a half-quart of "Sunrise" buttermilk, then set it on the counter along with a couple of crumpled bills. Milton rang open the cash register to make change and glanced to Guy already taking a good swig.

"Hitting that stuff a little early, aren't you?" he said with the dry wit of a man who sold both buttermilk and liquor.

"Maybe so," Guy said, wiping his mouth on his sleeve. "But LaReese never showed in Salina yesterday. And Sunday we found the car he'd been driving abandoned up there along Emory Road. I talked to his wife. She hadn't seen 'im since noon Friday. My stomach's telling me something's wrong."

Milton scratched his head where the hair once grew.

"That is a mite peculiar," he allowed, then thought a moment and added, "Here's something else peculiar. Ever know of that Mex fellow not to make a big show?"

"What are you driving at, Milton?"

"I mean he makes a big entrance wherever he goes. Biggest show-off around. But Friday night, around ten o'clock, I seen 'im come up the street in that new red pickup of his and pull off into the side alley here like kids do when they're looking to sneak in and buy liquor. He sent one of his boys in, that tall lanky fellow. He bought some chips and beer and ran back out. I saw them bunched up in the cab. Only got a glimpse, but I swear I saw LaReese in there. You know he delivered bread here till about a month ago. An awful foul mouth, but I'll say this for 'im, he was punctual. Anyhow, I watched for them to back out, but they headed on down the alley. A minute or so later I saw the pickup creep back out on the road and head on south pretty as you please..."

Milton had stood behind the counter gazing out that window for over thirty years. Opened at six each morning and closed at midnight. Quiet and observant, he knew who came and went, their habits and routines, as well as he knew his inventory. He always wore a grocer's apron and kept a notepad and fountain pen in the breast pocket to jot down items needed, rarely overstocked or under-ordered. The pen had been a gift from his father upon graduation from high school in 1927. He'd worked in the store alongside his father through the Depression and War years, taking over upon his father's death in 1951. He added air-conditioning in 1960, then upgraded the coolers and stood a coin-operated pop machine by the door in lieu of the old Coca-Cola ice chest that had always leaked and eventually rusted through. Otherwise everything remained fairly much the same—from the ceiling fans and cash register to the wooden floor that sagged under the tread of four generations. Milton had never married and was something of a local joke. Kids would drive by late at night and see his pale image beyond the window, point and laugh, "There's ol' Marley's ghost!"

One thing Guy knew, Milton was no gossip, if he said he'd seen LaReese, then he had likely seen him. A thought that settled Guy's stomach more than any ten gallons of buttermilk. But he took the buttermilk along in any case, returning to the office where he leaned back in his swivel chair and propped his boots on his desk. He sipped slowly in question as he saw events shift and adjust like a puzzle and mentally erased the boys' names from various blanks over and across. But what was Mex's involvement? Why was Valentine with him? There was certainly no law against giving someone a ride, and nothing suspicious about buying chips and beer. And if Mex had helped him skip the country, it was a clever ruse to abandon the car like that and leave people to wonder.

Guy continued to sip the buttermilk, puzzling over the situation, sorting out the whys and wherefores, when the phone rang. He sat the carton down and reached for the receiver. And he didn't actually believe in *coincidence* or *serendipity*, but both words sprang to mind upon hearing Mrs. Torres introduce herself as "*Catalina's mother*," her sweet gracious voice softly accenting each word. Guy swung his boots to the floor and leaned to the desk, fully alert.

—*I call you, Sheriff Craig, because of my husband, Carlo. I read to him in paper of the man, Valenteen LaReese. He is missing, no? My husband has news for you, perhaps. You see, Carlo works late many nights. And Friday night it was, Señor Orvano... the Colonel's son, who the men politely call El Segundo, but he has other name not so polite for he can be a hateful man. Carlo saw him and three men drive down to the pits, what Carlo calls la hoya de los muertos, the pit of death, for it is where they burn los puercos, the pigs. It is a bad place as you can imagine. No one goes down there unless they are told. Only men just up from Mexico do that job. But Friday night Señor Orvano and his three men went down there and burned the pigs...*

Silence followed as if she were letting him visualize the scene.

"Like you say, that is kind of unusual," Guy offered. "But that's his right."

—*Yes, that is so, Sheriff Craig. But four men went down and only three came back.*

Guy caught his breath and gripped the phone tighter.

"Mrs. Torres. Is your husband sure of this?"

—*Yes. He is certain what he saw. Others saw too.*

"That's good, real good. Can he identify the missing man?"

—*No, only that it was Señor Orvano and three others. It was too dark, too distant, you see. But also, Carlo says you will not find the missing man. For there is nothing in the pit but ashes and more dead pigs. And Carlo, his heart breaks, for he fears he is to blame...*

"To blame for what?"

—*For Catalina's murder. You see, something happened, and he did not think it so important at the time. Now he thinks he should have thrown Señor Orvano in the pit that day.*

"When was this? What happened?"

—*It was early in the summer during the festival of Fourth of July. Catalina wanted the car to go to parade, she was to march with the band, you see. So she drove Carlo to work and picked him up that evening. When Carlo come out of the work trailer after changing clothes, he saw Señor Orvano lean to the car in talking with Catalina. So it seemed. But when he come closer, he saw she had rolled up the window and looked the other way. And Señor Orvano, he was very angry. When he saw Carlo coming, he tried to laugh it off and said, "Your daughter is pretty but too proud to speak to me. You should teach her some manners, Torres. Or someone will." Carlo ignored the insult, thinking of his job, and walked away. In the car he asked Catalina what happened, and she said only that she did not like Señor Orvano for the way he looked at her, so she would not speak to him. Now Carlo fears that Señor Orvano maybe killed Catalina and Joey out of spite. And Carlo says that if the law cannot catch him, he will. One night he will take Señor Orvano to the pits and make him disappear.*

"No, Mrs. Torres. He must not do that. Do not let him."

—Yes. I tell him…

Her voice sounded faint and less than convinced. And waiting, silent, Guy had to admit it only seemed right to let a father lay hands on his daughter's murderer.

"I appreciate how he feels," Guy slowly answered. "I truly do. And I feel for you both. But these things must be proved in court. We do have a suspect. I'm sorry I can't say more. But I assure you we'll keep an eye on Mex Orvano, and at the proper time…" Guy could hardly stomach his own words, like all his efforts up to that point they seemed weak and dithering. "Just let us deal with it, okay?"

—Of course, Sheriff Craig. Thank you for to listen to me…

"And I thank you for calling, Mrs. Torres. What you've told me is real helpful. Believe me. Tell your husband that I appreciate it, I really do. But please be patient…" Guy tried his best to convince her that her husband must not act rashly. Right then his voice conveyed more warmth than it had since May's death. In his loneliness he felt a keen affection for Mrs. Torres and a deep sympathy for her husband. As for himself, he was out of patience.

Guy left the office in a quiet anger that overwhelmed his prior concern, his parsing of fact, rumor, and suspicion—determined this very day to take some kind of action and seek some clarity.

While driving to CC's ranch, a part of him, that which reasoned, said it was pointless, that there was nothing he could prove, while the greater part, that which had loved a woman and raised a family, begged to take hold of Mex Orvano and beat the living daylights out of him, then start asking questions. Guy clinched his fists to the wheel and drove a good deal faster than was prudent, speeding up back roads and topping hills with no thought of oncoming traffic, spinning out a cloud of dust that rose and settled in his wake, paling the roadside grasses as all acts pale in time.

Nearing sundown the dust-caked Chevy tore up the paved drive towards the grand stone mansion. CC paused in his stroll from the barn to the house. Chomped his cigar and watched Guy pull sharply to the gravel and get out.

"What's that piece a' shit Chevy doing in my drive?" he spat.

"Where's Mex?" Guy asked, bluntly ignoring the other's question, his fists doubled, standing toe to toe, a half head shorter and a hundred pounds lighter.

CC tipped back his hat and grinned, could see he was in for a session.

"Now that's a mighty big question for a runt, ain't it?"

"No, the big question is what's he done with Valentine LaReese?"

"What the fuck you mean?" CC scowled, taking the cigar from his mouth.

"I mean someone saw Valentine with Mex Friday night. And someone else saw 'em enter that Smolan hog farm of yours. Trouble is...they never saw Valentine leave."

"Now lissen here you scrawny little prick. 'Less you got a body..." CC growled, crushing his cigar like he intended to crush his opponent as their shadows cast to the far corral in the setting sun, their angry gestures playing back and forth till words fell away and their forms merged, both grappling as CC reached for his gun and Guy caught it like a steel trap and tripped him to the gravel.

CC hit face down, thinking—*Damn he's quick!*

But what made Guy so quick was he never thought at such moments, he acted.

"You little prick," CC repeated, raising to one elbow, spitting dust. "I oughta git up and kick your ass."

"Go ahead 'n try," Guy said, emptying the cylinder of bullets. "But you'll see boot leather in a blink. Sure hate to scuff my boots on your sorry head."

CC looked at Guy's boots wearing through at the toe and fallen down at the heel and laughed in spite of being thrown.

"Why shit, you ain't got boot leather to walk a mile let alone scuff my head."

"I can walk a mile and I can damn sure bust your head."

"Yeah, 'spect so…" CC wiped his mouth and caught his breath. "But you ever show your face up here agin, you better have more'n hot air and hearsay. You better have a gun, warrant, and backup. 'Cause I'll blow your ass to kingdom come 'n let my lawyers clean up the mess. Now git the fuck off my land!"

"All the same, you stay put and think on this. One more person gets hurt or disappears from around here, proof or no proof, you're gonna deal with me."

Guy hurled the pistol to the fence line, walked to his car, got in and drove away. In the rearview mirror he saw CC slowly climb to his feet and dust himself off, taking all the time in the world like an old bull, still potent, deliberate, sure of his ground. Meanwhile, Guy wasn't sure of a damn thing. Not even sure he'd made the right move. But he'd served notice and that made him feel a slight bit better.

XXI. BAD COMPANY

Sunlight glinted off clusters of frost in the east window like brilliant star patterns magnified to the eye. Diana observed the play of light while washing down the window casings in the kitchen. She wished they'd left the woodwork natural like through the rest of the house instead of painted, though she supposed it made it easier to clean. As Lee's mother had said, "Those old ranges put out an awful lot of smoke and grease. And hot, Lord, they were hot in the summer." Yet Diana wished she had one of those too, an old wood-burning range. Loved the thought of lighting a fire each time she baked. Clean as it was, she didn't care for her electric range and would have much preferred a gas one. But she wasn't complaining. Lee had gone to work for his brother Garret on Monday. Now Wednesday, their third whole day of normal life. Diana wrung out her cleaning rag and smiled, yes, she could be happy here if he could be.

She had raised the blinds on a number of windows, intending to clean the panes once the day warmed. Jesse peered over a lower sill and huffed his breath on the frosted pane. As the starry crystals warmed and faded, he watched in wonder like a little god turning night into day. He reached up and marked it with his finger then huffed again, creating yet another breath hole in the pattern.

Jesse pointed and said, "Lookit!" as his mommy knelt beside him.

"Yes, I know," she smiled. "Now watch this..." Diana fogged the pane above the frost and drew the letter 'J.' "See that, honey? That's a 'jay.' 'Jay' for Jessie."

He raised his eyes to the etched letter in dubious question, then smiled to his mommy and went back to huffing on the frosted edge. Clearly more fascinated by the melting magical stars than by the letter of any name.

Lee drove an old red farm truck following along behind the field cutter manned by Garret who kept checking back over his shoulder, holding steady at three to four miles an hour while the auger arched overhead shooting a stream of chopped silage into the truck bed where it swirled in a green fury. Random leaves were carried off in the wind as flecks and hulls floated to the windshield. From time to time Lee hit the wipers to clear the debris, otherwise he merely gripped the wheel and enjoyed the slow hum and pace as warm air blew up from the vents mixing with odors of engine oil and fresh cut sorghum, both as sweet in their own way as the coffee he occasionally sipped from his thermos.

They'd been in the field since daybreak, the same each morning, and planned to work twelve-hour days straight on through till they finished. Which to Garret's mind should have been yesterday—glancing to the sky in fret of the weather, had to wait for the first hard frost to start cutting and no telling when the snow might hit. An early blizzard would not only cut the nutritional value of the feed, it would knock down the stalks and complicate things considerably.

"Two weeks of clear weather, that's all I ask," Garret would vow each day. "Two good weeks and no breakdowns"—kept up a running monologue of all the factors, time being the most urgent. Out by four o'clock each morning, he already had the trucks and tractors gassed up and idling, having checked the belts and greased a score of points on the field cutter by the time Lee and other hired hands arrived. Lee drove an old Willy's Jeep that Garret insisted he use so Diana wouldn't be stranded without a vehicle, worried about her and Jesse like he worried about everything else. He'd round each truck, kick the tires, then point in at the heat gauge and say, "Keep an eye on that needle. If it starts edging to red, drive to the station and have 'em blow out the radiator. Might lose a little time but that's better than burning up an engine. Got that?"—reminding each man of his task and what was expected. "And don't forget to double clutch!" he'd shout, mounting the tractor, preparing to lead them out, "Saves wear on the transmission." Practical and hardheaded as a top sergeant, and would have made a good one, ready to fight to the last breath. Like his senior year in football against Arcadia—Garret the fullback, a soggy field, Cibola getting stomped and Garret still driving through the mud and blood till he finally scored.

Once again it was Garret's game and Lee gladly let him lead the way, ready to sit back and merge with the flow. The money wasn't great, $2.65 an hour, but a welcome break from dodging bullets and ducking the law. Definitely felt at ease up in the cab, one hand to the wheel, the other nursing his coffee, the cup only half-full or it would spill in his lap and give him a hot jolt. Other than an occasional bump or two, smooth sailing.

He kept the radio tuned to 91-Country out of Kansas City, ingesting the current Nashville hits. Not many he cared for, but a few weren't half bad. He liked Jessie Colter's, "Don't It Make My Brown Eyes Blue"—nice voice and piano, laid back and melodic, more like sweet blues than country. But Arlo Guthrie's new hit, "The City of New Orleans," really made him sit up and take notice. It spoke of old men drinking whiskey and playing cards, of passing landscapes and a rolling train— written by an unknown named Steve Goodman. Lee hoped to be another unknown that would write such a song. Still facing the quandary over Diana and the house and whether to move to Nashville. If the hemp didn't sell, they couldn't buy the place, not without a loan and a long commitment, and he wasn't about to sign on as a farm laborer for the rest of his life. Two weeks looked about right. But he'd see how Frankie fared, then decide.

Frankie and Gabe were headed east that very morning, cruising through St. Louis around noon, the old green van loaded with a ton of market-ready hemp destined for a rendezvous in central Pennsylvania at a little place called Johnstown, famous for the flood, where the boys hoped to make a deal. But in truth they were on a desperate run, clutching at straws in high water, anxious to unload the stuff and tidy up loose ends, for they still had a thousand pounds stashed in California—like farmers paying storage on grain during a down market.

Gabe had made a number of phone calls, checked with contacts in Kansas City, Atlanta, Dallas, and came up empty. Then he bumped into a quasi-vagrant who lived upstairs with a waitress in the third-floor apartment. His name was Junes. A tall skinny slum-cowboy who wore greasy blue jeans and boots, a part-time welder and small-time dope dealer with half his teeth missing and the remainder capped in gold—he spent most of his time chain-smoking and tinkering with a baby-blue '57 Ford Fairlane. Gabe knew him in passing and in a last-ditch effort he chanced to ask where he might unload a ton of hemp. Junes ran a hand through his greased-back hair and said, "Naw, nowhere near that much"—which won Gabe's confidence, unusual for a petty dealer not to make extravagant claims—"But I might know someone that does." He jotted down a name and phone number on a matchbook cover and handed it to Gabe.

Sunday evening Gabe placed a call and set up the deal. A new source was always "iffy" and Gabe and Frankie each had their doubts, but doubt never made a dime and money being their prime object if a junior high teacher in Johnstown, Pennsylvania said he could sell a ton of hemp, *Then by God he was their man!*

Frankie presently leaned over the wheel, eager as a kid on the way to a carnival, all but certain to make a dollar on a dime at the rat roulette, tapping out rhythmic prospects on the dash with his free hand as they crossed over the Mississippi into Illinois.

"Who'd of thought? A god-damned junior high teacher," Frankie laughed in mock scandal. "Hell fire, what's the world coming to? Think he's dealing to the kids?"

"Who knows?" Gabe yawned, not nearly so amused, hadn't slept a wink the previous night in worry of what was in store. "All he said was that he could put us in touch with the right people and that they had the cash. Lots of it."

"Then bring it on! *Bring it on!*"—Frankie slapped the dash with a shout as the lowering sky began spitting rain.

Garret drove himself hard and expected his crew to keep pace, but he wasn't relentless, they broke a full hour for lunch. And he didn't skimp on the meal. Being a cattleman, he counted it a patriotic duty to eat beef and ordered beefsteak all around.

They ate at a restaurant off Highway 24 named "The 24"—flashed in red neon above the front entrance twenty-four hours a day, owned and operated by a Chinese couple, Joe and Dotty Wang Chi, emigrants from Taiwan. Quick-witted and tough, they took numerous ribbings for their background and broken English. Even suffered for their name, Wang Chi. Hardly a day went by when one local or another didn't ask for some "chi" on a sandwich or hamburger. Dotty would shake her tiny fist and yell, "I give you chi, buster!" then laugh, or maybe not, depending on their tone, her mood, any number of subtle factors that determine a slight from a jest. She and her husband spit in the eye of whatever prejudice they met and forged on, plucky strivers, serving good food at fair prices, Chinese being their specialty. They soon won people over and had them lining up at the door, making a small fortune feeding the descendants of prior emigrants: Germans, English, Scotch-Irish, French, Swedes, among others.

While Joe ran the kitchen, Dotty took charge of the service. And Garret always cheered up seeing Dotty. They shared the same work ethic and blunt sense of humor, liked to give each other a hard time. Garret opened his napkin, preparing to cut into his steak, and found only a knife and spoon.

"Hey Dotty, you shorted me here. I can't eat meat with a spoon."

"Oh Gaw'it, so saw'ry," she said, reaching to the tray of utensils. "You need *fok*?"

"No Dotty, not today, I'm too busy," he answered with a quick grin. "And you better not let Joe hear you talking like that."

"Oh Gaw'it, you—" She blushed and whacked him with the fork then tossed it to the table before hurrying on to the next order, the next booth, the next customer waiting by the register to pay their bill.

So Garret had his lighter moments. And he loved good food;

it kept him stout for his labor and helped ease his mind. Going bald at age thirty trying to make a go of the farm and placate his in-laws. But such moments were always brief. The banter ended with lunch. Back to the field and back to form with a grim set to his jaw by one o'clock, ready to grind on through for another six or seven hours.

By mid-afternoon the wind whipped up, leaves and chaff taking flight in the constant shift and swirl. Black birds descended by the hundreds in wake of man and machines, settling over the field like a long black veil in search of scattered grain. And when the field cutter roared back their way they'd rise up like a great spiral of smoke, then loop and wheel out over the field as if tracing the very wind before settling once more to feed, gathering to fly south for the winter. Beckoning to all their brethren, *Fly south…fly south.* Lee watched the birds take wing like a thousand notes played on a wild fiddle and couldn't help wanting to fly with them.

But Diana's thoughts remained grounded, centered on her child, her husband and her home. When she observed a bird, she savored its song, its color and flight. Yet when it flew away, she did not wish to follow. After cleaning the kitchen, she had taken Jessie outside to play. They saw an Oriole land on the naked branch of a dead elm. It fluttered in the bright sunlight like a splash of yellow then tucked its head beneath its wing in act of preening.

"Lookit, mommy," Jessie pointed. "Ka-bird, he hide."

"No, honey. See…he's using his bill to smooth his feathers. It's called *preening,*" she explained, smoothing his fine hair with her fingers.

Later, while he napped on the sofa, she stood upstairs in front of the mirror, her hair in a cascade of curls following her bath; she turned as she smoothed her dress about her hips, glimpsing in back to check the fit. Lee's favorite, the one with all the buttons down the front that he loved to unfasten. A ritual she loved as well, feeling her breasts fall free to his hands as the dress slipped from her shoulders to her waist, her thighs tingling in anxious want to spread like wings in flight. Poised before the mirror, she arched to her toes and spun in pirouette, chin up, arms gracefully extended, then caught herself and blushed at her rapt flight and fancy, feeling warm and sensual.

Suddenly she frowned and hurried downstairs, fearing she'd burnt the pie in her absence. But checking the oven everything was fine, the apple and cinnamon juices only now seeping up through the widened slits in the dainty brown crust. She soon took it out and sat it on the table and draped it with a towel to slowly cool. She planned a special evening for Lee, a surprise evening. She wanted to show him how fine life could be even following a long day of labor. That normal needn't prove boring, but poignant, lasting, and good. That life and the flesh were indeed the finest art.

Diana heard a vehicle drive in. Glancing through the window, she saw a nice-looking man step out of a red pickup. Rue and Keeps nudged his hand in greeting and wagged their tails. Diana didn't recognize him but assumed he was one of Lee's circle of friends, perhaps an old team-mate from football, for he moved with the ease and grace of an athlete, taking strong supple strides up the stairs to the porch.

Diana opened the door and nodded in greeting.

"Hi there," he said with a frank smile, his dark handsome features accented by his smile and white shirt tucked neatly in faded blue jeans fit snug to his thighs. "I'm Jay, Jay Orvano," he added, extending his hand to hers with a brief appreciative grasp, noting her delicate touch, her long slender fingers.

"Is Lee around?" he asked, his voice soft and languid like his smile, for Mex could use his charm and exotic looks to good effect when he wished.

"No, he's...I'm sorry. I'm Diana, his wife," she answered, a bit flustered and flattered by his gaze. "Lee's at work. Do you know Lee?"

"The finest guitar player in these parts? You bet I know Lee," he laughed. "We go way back. But hey, I didn't know he had such a pretty wife." His smile broadened. "He keeps you hid away, huh?"

"No. I like it out here," she answered pleasantly. Though his manner was fairly direct, she did not find him overly forward so much as relaxed and playful. He stepped back and examined the doorframe and windows and cast his eyes down the length of the porch.

"You know, I've heard about this place for years. The old Tannis place," he said, marveling at the structure. Then he turned back to Diana. "Sorry I missed Lee. But do you think…I could maybe take a look inside? Curious, you know. Only be a minute."

"Well, I suppose…*you may*…"

His question caught her off guard, but more so his manner as he breezily walked past and entered. He stopped at the threshold to the dining room, laid his palms to either jamb and leaned in, gazing at the woodwork, the high ceilings, and the grand staircase in the foyer beyond. That's when Diana noticed "MEX" tooled on the back of his leather belt. She'd heard references to the name and none of them good. She raised a hand to her throat, feeling her breath constrict.

"What is it you want with Lee?" she asked, attempting to stay calm while her heart hummed like a tuning fork struck with fear—wishing she hadn't put away the gun, that she hadn't opened the door.

"Aw, just business…" he answered absently, still taking in the house. "This is fine…really fine," he said, gradually turning his voice and eyes to her as he walked her way. "Yeah, just a little business," he repeated, adding a certain swagger missing till now, lowering his eyes to her dress, her form. "You see, the Colonel…that's Colonel Holtz, he wants to talk business with Frankie Sage. And we've had a devil of a time reaching him. Thought Lee might help us out."

"You don't really know my husband, do you?" Diana said, keeping her hand to her throat, unnerved by his approach.

"No, not really," Mex laughed. "But hey, that doesn't mean we can't talk business. Like you 'n me," he smiled, backing her to the table. "We could talk business…get to know each other. Say, what's this?" he asked, reaching aside to raise the towel. "*Yum-yum*…apple pie. Smells good. Might want a piece."

"That's for my husband," she answered coolly.

"Uh-huh. Keeping it warm, aren't you? Keeping it under wraps just for him. Like you keep yourself."

"I think you better go..." Diana stiffened at his touch; felt the table at her back.

"No-no-no. Not so fast," he said, leaning his face to hers, noting her lush hair and green eyes, her soft ivory skin and the pale blue veins of the *sangre azul* as he fingered her throat, her tender throat, his hot breath whispering, "I wanna taste you like that sweet pie, pretty one..."

Diana tried to break free of his grip, but his grip tightened as he roughly penned both her arms in back with one hand, pulling her to him, letting her feel the bulging heat of his loins and the pain of his grip while he began unfastening the buttons of her dress, smoothly working his free hand under her bra to her breasts, her nipples, kneading them like doe till her breath rose, quickening, as he tasted her lips. "Open for me my pretty, open..." he urged, pinching till her nipple burned and she at last relented, opening her lips to him as his hand moved lower, button by button, to the breach of her thighs and the moistening heat that she could not quiet or tame answering to that which she resisted with all her will yet was about to happen like death as she sensed the killer in him and she his frightened prey. Mex lifted her to the table, wedging his knee between her thighs while she whimpered in raw ache and fear, stifling her cries in greater fear she'd awaken Jessie and bring him harm.

But Jessie, hearing her faint cries, had already awakened. He stood at the door to the kitchen and watched her struggling with the strange man. Saw something that did not belong—like a ghost in the night. He screamed. Clutched his pillow and screamed hard and long. A scream of instinct and rage.

And as suddenly Mex eased his grip and glanced around. For a moment he saw himself hidden in the shadows while his mother serviced a john—the heavy musk, the scent of tobacco and booze, the man's sweaty bulk and rude thrust, and a ray of light coming through the drawn shade to his watching eyes like the shared breath of a greater witness. Again, he saw himself staring on in bitter rage, and he remembered well and understood the boy's scream.

"Hey there, little man," he said. "I didn't know there was a man around."

Diana wrenched free and ran to Jessie, clasping him to her as she grabbed a bread knife from the pie-cabinet and crouched, trembling, prepared to defend self and child.

"Don't come near us," she warned, her eyes teared with hate and shame.

Mex tossed back his head and laughed.

"No problem, pretty one. I won't mess with your little man." Then he grabbed his crotch and groaned, "Ohhh, but you had me going there. You really did. And I think I had you going too." He raised his hand and slowly licked his finger, the one he'd had in her, and smiled. "Like I said, I only wanted a taste..."—with that he snapped his finger and said, "Don't forget. The Colonel wants to talk with Frankie Sage. Got it? And you 'n me, maybe another time, huh?" he winked. "When your little man's not around."

Mex waved *Bye-bye* to Jessie and swung his braid with the jerk of his head and walked casually to the door where he gave her one last smile. Diana dared not answer, dared not provoke him. She simply held tight to Jessie and the knife and watched him go. She heard the truck start up and drive to the road. At that she laid the knife aside and hugged Jessie tight, embracing him in both arms, shedding warm tears of gratitude and relief. Jessie gripped a fold of her hair and listened quietly while she sobbed; he had no idea what was happening, only that he felt safe with his mommy now that the man was gone. Diana soon caught her breath and wiped her tears; her hair had matted to her face, she brushed it back and smiled.

"You sweety," she said, gazing to his eyes. "You saved mommy, you know that? You scared the ghost away."

"Man is ghost?"

"Yes, honey. A very bad ghost. But you scared him away, like mommy scared the old woman away. But we must never tell daddy about the bad ghost, okay? It must be our secret. If we tell anyone, even daddy, the ghost may return. And we don't want that, do we..."

Jessie shook his head in slow earnest—he understood little, but for certain he didn't want the old woman or the bad man to return. Diana patted his cheek, then stood and buttoned her dress. She fixed him his favorite sandwich, peanut butter and jelly sliced four ways, and poured him a glass of milk. "Mommy has to go upstairs for a minute," she told him. "But I'll be right back down, okay?"

He nodded, grape jelly dripping down his chin.

In the bathroom Diana took off her dress and threw it in the hamper, doubted if she could ever wear it again. She stood at the sink and washed, scrubbing wherever he had touched her, erasing the scent, every trace of him. All except the memory. Determined to erase that too as best she could, assuming a fierce expression as she pulled back her hair and tied it in a ponytail. She checked her neck for any sign of a bruise; she found none. The only bruises were to her wrists which she covered by putting on a long-sleeved sweatshirt. Then she slipped into her work jeans and tennis shoes. From the bedroom closet she fetched the shotgun and made sure it was loaded before returning downstairs where she stood it by the door in the kitchen, reminding Jessie *not to touch*. Through the remainder of the day Diana cleaned the windows in the south and east rooms of the main floor, working at a feverish pace, as if cleaning were the cure for the foulness she felt, all the while keeping an eye to the road, making certain the ghost was gone.

Lee came home about an hour past sundown. Jessie was already asleep. Diana tried to appear buoyant, happy to see him, though she didn't exactly leap into his arms as she had earlier planned. She simply stood at the door and smiled, had his place set at the table and hot food waiting—pork chops with diced potatoes smothered in gravy, a fresh salad, and hot rolls. Not to mention the apple pie. Lee washed his hands and eagerly set to, hadn't eaten since noon. He seemed relatively cheerful after three days of work.

She asked him how it was going.

"Not so bad," he said, taking a bite of a roll. "The day just gets kinda long 'n boring." He chewed fast and swallowed. "But I heard some good songs. Got some lyrics jotted down," he added hopefully, looking to her. And she knew that look and could read his thoughts like they were mapped out on the table. Dreaming of Nashville, dreaming of playing guitar and writing songs. Well she wasn't going to play along. Not this time. That's why she hadn't told him about the ghost upstairs, nor mentioned one negative thing about the house—she wanted it to be their home. Her smile faded as she turned away, her hopes fading too under the weight of the day's event settling in like a dark sludge. In lieu of words she leaned to the sink and scrubbed a pan.

Lee sat silent, knew he'd touched a nerve with his talk of songs. And that look she gave him, like she could read his thoughts and in as much as said *No!* How in hell could she know what he was thinking? And why feel guilty? What was the harm in *thoughts* or *songs* or *plans* for that matter? But Lee said nothing. Too soon to make a decision anyway.

After finishing a piece of pie, he carried his dishes to the sink and let them slip under the suds. He stood back of Diana and watched her work, trying to fathom the workings of her mind. He knew she was hiding in her work, like if she stood real quiet and said nothing she couldn't be seen. She was like that sometimes; the quieter she got the prettier she looked. Her ass shimmied and her breasts swayed as she scrubbed his plate. A loose curl had fallen to her cheek. He lifted her ponytail and gave her a peck on the neck. She shot a sharp elbow to his ribs.

"Damn!" he said, rubbing his side. "What was that for?"

"I don't want to be touched," she said, knitting her brow. "I've had a long day. I washed all the windows and I'm tired. Okay?"

"Sure, I understand," he nodded, trying to make small talk. "Glad to see you got the gun back out. Good to keep it handy."

"No, it's *not* good! *Not* one bit! I *hate* that thing in my kitchen."

"Well then! Let's put it away..."

"No! I *want* it right there, thank you."

"All right. There it is. As you like it."

"No, I don't like it," she answered flatly, staring into the soapsuds, watching them blink and vanish one by one and wishing she could do the same. "But I thought of that dog again today and I think I should have it there."

"So you should. He might come back. It's—" He thought better of saying anything more, realized she was having one of

those moments, maybe her time of the month; he'd been around
so little lately, everything out of sync. Lee turned to the fridge
and got a beer, sat down and popped it open. He took a double
swig; it tasted good. He took another and her silence deepened,
hard and impenetrable, like a stone wall—all he could hear was
the clink of dishes and himself swallowing. Still he watched her
at the sink even as she tried to disappear behind her wall, but
she couldn't hide from his eyes, not with that body, no matter
what she wore. Lee watched her ponytail bobbing above the
nap of her neck and thought he might finish his beer, edge right
up to her and get her laughing, then carry her upstairs and love
her like she needed.

"I nearly forgot," she said.

Ah, a voice, he smiled, leaning forth, encouraged.

"What's that?" he asked.

"A man came by today," she answered, still facing the sink.
"Jay Orvano."

Lee rolled the name through his mind then set his beer on
the table.

"You mean Mex…?" he said, losing his smile. "Mex Orvano?"

She gave a slight shrug and turned her face in profile.

"So, do you know him?"

"No. But I've seen 'im around. What the hell was he doing
here?"

Which struck her as an accusation.

"Looking for *you*," she answered sharply. "About *business*. He
said that some Colonel wants to talk to Frankie about *business!*"

By now Lee was on his feet walking towards her.

"Why the hell didn't he call?"

"How should I know? I didn't invite him here?"

"You mean he was here? In this house?" Lee demanded,
pointing to the very space they stood.

"Well, yes…he—"

"You let him in?"

"No! He let himself in," she answered, looking Lee full in
the face. "Just walked right in. What am I supposed to do? Lock
the door anytime someone shows up?"

"No, but you seem awfully upset."

"Well he was...rude."

"How do you mean, Diana? Did he touch you?"

"No! I said *rude!* Just...rude. He lifted the towel and looked at the pie."

Lee smiled at the thought, imagining Diana shooing him out, defending her pie.

"That was a good pie," he said.

But Diana wasn't smiling, her face twisted in a grimace, fighting back her tears. Lee touched her shoulder. She jerked away and turned back to the sink.

"I'm sick of it, Lee," she gasped, straining with each word. "Sick of the guns...the threats...you being gone...the whole business. And every week one more thing...and now the songs...I'm sick of them too...and you talking about other places...I don't—"

"I know, I know..." he soothed, gently grasping her shoulders, rubbing her back. And she longed for his touch, but she knew he would soon reach for her hands as was his wont and see the bruises on her wrists and she had felt Mex's brutal strength and feared Lee was no match, for he was neither brutal nor so strong. And she wanted it to stop, everything to stop.

"It's just that I..."—she struggled against her fear, his warm caresses.

"What is it, Dita? Tell me—"

"I'm not *Dita*, Lee! I'm *Diana!* And I just...just feel like I'm falling in love with someone else..."

At those words he dropped his hands—felt he had no right to touch her if she no longer loved him. A thought so unexpected it took his breath like a blow to the gut. Like when you hear a loved one has died and you shake your head, *No, no, this cannot be.* He slowly backed away, numb, his thoughts in spin like the sink water gurgling down the drain. All he could manage to say was "Yeah, well, that happens I guess..." as he turned to the dark sanctum of the living room, leaving her to slowly dry her hands. He entered the darkness like a ghost haunted by the question of who she'd fallen in love with.

But for Diana it was no one specific, yet anyone not her husband. Anyone who could protect her and Jessie. Though she'd said it to distract him, she meant it well enough. Weary of Lee's rife ambitions, his chaotic transience, seemingly doomed to drift. She longed for one place, one certainty. So she'd fallen in love with Will's staid good humor, with Ry's gentlemanly manner and good looks, with Frankie's dash and shameless greed that placed a high premium on ready cash and plenty of it. And all possessed one quality that Lee lacked, a sense that they belonged and would stay anchored to that region. Lee's wanderlust churned inside and out and threatened to tear him apart. She dreaded seeing him in his moments of determined urge, when he was most kinetic and attractive, in turmoil like a whirlwind that drew her in and bore her off. For three or four months he seemed tranquil, solid, steady as a captain at the helm, then *Boom!*—another storm. And instead of safe harbor he steered into the wind. So her fears ran far deeper than Mex.

Lee listened to her climb the stairs and enter their room. He wanted to follow but felt shut out and distanced, like he were the dead and she the living. Her love was his constant, his compass pointing north. Whatever happened he could look to her and know one thing that was good and true. Aware of her hopes and resentments, he weighed them against his dreams, juggling till he hardly knew which spun where. But he could not simply fold his hands and cease to dream. There was more to life than cooking, cleaning, and caring for a child. Something more than getting up each day to shuffle off to some mindless task, some job that left you empty no matter how much love waited at home. His father's death had taught him that. And he had not run a gauntlet of risks simply to sit at the edge of life and wait till time made him dust. So she hated his songs. *Well to hell with her!* There was more to a song than to any damn job— something intrinsic that held a key to the meaning of things, like a dialogue with the wind. And when he held his guitar as now, it seemed perfect in form and intent, meant for his hands. He plucked a few chords in listless search, but every note rang hollow, somehow dead, like fallen leaves compared to budded stems. He laid his guitar aside and leaned his face to his hands, wondering *What the hell? What the hell anyway?*

A sentiment echoed half a continent away in a motel room outside Johnstown, Pennsylvania—"Motel 6" as indicted by the neon flashing red against the curtain. Gabe, usually calm, a tome of reason, at that moment was seeing nothing but red. "You what? No money? You fucking what?" he cursed, pumping his fist like a pistol at the pockmarked dweeb of a teacher named Wilson, backing him into the corner. "What the fuck you mean, the money's in fucking Florida?"

"I-it's there. It is. Th-the money...is...there," he stuttered like a startled parrot, pawing at his face as if his acme flared anew. His blondish hair cut in neat long bangs above his gold wire-rimmed glasses, he no doubt thought himself the spitting image of John Lennon, humming "Bridge Over Troubled Waters" each time he stepped into the shower to jerk off.

"Then what the fuck are we doing in Pennsylvania?" Gabe asked, tempering his tone, attempting to reason. "Why didn't you just meet us in Florida?"

"The thing...thing is. I need to call...s-see if...they will—"

"If? If? What the fuck If? You mean they don't know about this?"

"No. N-not yet. I need to call...s-see if they might. Then I get my cut. But it's cool. I-it's my cousin, so I'm p-pretty sure..."

"Pretty sure? You mean we drove twelve hundred miles to see *If* your cousin *Might*?" Gabe raised his fist in sheer frustration, needed something to grip, thought of the fool's neck but instead pulled out his pistol and waved it for emphasis. "Well I'm pretty sure you're a fucking moron. Got that? You fucking, fucking moron!"

"Whoa-whoa-whoa!" Frankie declared, stepping between them. "Put that thing away, Gabe. Come on now. Simmer down here, that's right..."

Then the teacher started to speak, and Frankie shoved his finger in his face and said, "One word from you and I'll smash your fucking face, understand?" And that finger and those fierce eyes seemed more menacing than Gabe's gun. The teacher swallowed hard and said nothing.

"Do you even know who *Pythagoras* was?" Frankie asked. The teacher stood flummoxed, unable to answer. "You haven't a clue, do ya?" Frankie continued. "I hate teachers, always have. Know why? Because they're stupid. So listen up, stupid. You better stick with teaching school. The next bunch you deal this way are liable to rip your guts out 'n dump ya in the river." Frankie fixed him with another hard look for good measure then turned in disgust.

"Come on, Gabe," he said, "let's get going"—hurrying himself and his friend out before they both turned violent and there'd be one less teacher to plague young minds.

Outside, Gabe gave the guardrail a hard kick with his tennis shoe and didn't flinch from the pain, so angry he could hardly breathe, wheezing as he reached for a cigarette, his thin hair and the lighter flame blowing wild in the cold dark wind. The night brooded dense and dark through the parking lot and beyond, while in the distance big trucks raced spewing oily fumes to thicken the air warmed by the fresh-lit tobacco. Gabe snapped the lighter shut and slowly exhaled, shaking his head as they walked to the van, feeling the brunt of Frankie's hard eyes, knew he'd nearly lost it back there.

They got in and drove out, Gabe at the wheel. They followed a clover leaf onto the interstate then headed back the way they'd come. The engine hadn't even cooled, the heater still blowing warm air. The wipers soon flapped an intermittent scrape as the foul mizzle turned to sleet. They joined the flow of traffic, mostly trucks with tandem trailers weaving through the alien landscape. The dark hills loomed like heaps of mining sludge remnant from generations of incessant toil and industry relieved only by seasonal deer hunts and an occasional war. Neither Gabe nor Frankie said a thing. They rode on in silence as the old van groaned over the rising hills and sunken valleys like a plodding mule, too burdened for speed, but tireless, stubborn, determined to plow its way home.

Passing below Pittsburgh, the "Elrama Exit" caught Frankie's eye.

"*El Rama*, my ass!" he blurted. "Look at this place! What a shithole! And what a crock!"—switching to a high whiny voice—"*My cousin in Florida might want it…*"

"Okay, you're right. It's bullshit," Gabe tried to explain. "But

I swear he sounded solid on the phone. Said the money would be there."

But Frankie wasn't hearing a word, on a roll, in full rant. "How in hell did you come up with that guy? Sure as shit not out of central casting! And Johnstown, Pennsylvania, no goddamn less. We're talking off-off-off Broadway, bubba. Way the fuck off! This whole fucking state is nothing but a junk heap! Just take a look. I swear it's been nuked 'n seeded with a zillion retards and one squirrelly fucking teacher!"—hitting every harsh note through a four-octave range.

"All right, already. I fucked up. So lay off, will ya?" Gabe attempting a mea culpa, trying to diffuse Frankie before he hit critical mass. "Think I like this any better than you?" he asked. "Just lay off..."

Neither of them wanted to take the blame nor were they eager to face the boys. Especially Will's stern jaw set in firm expectation of *His* share, *His* money. Every hundred miles or so Gabe snorted another line of coke to stay alert, driving straight through, it kept his thoughts dancing, his hands quick and steady. Entering Ohio, the road smoothed out and the sleet turned to rain. He relaxed his grip on the wheel and welcomed the coming daylight even amidst the drab scenery and back-spray hitting the windshield as big trucks roared past like freight cars loosed from the rails, mighty and majestic in their tandem sweep. Frankie ignored all, sat in a deep funk except when he roused to declaim whatever *Godforsaken!* city or state they were passing through. Otherwise he remained sober and sullen, didn't snort any coke all the way back. Didn't want to feel one bit better. Preferred his dark mood.

He dropped Gabe off in Kansas City the following evening and drove on to the farm, kept the hemp stowed in the van, didn't want any fool but himself setting up the next deal. But he was glad to be back in any case, back on familiar terrain. He rolled down the window and breathed in the night air rich with scents of autumn grasses, cattle grazing, the milo harvest, and the broad blankets of turned-up soil where dormant seeds lay in pregnant want of another spring, another harvest.

When Frankie finally arrived at the old house and stepped

through the door, the Kid perked up from the couch, hopeful of a party like always following a big sale. But one look told him there'd be no party. He puffed his cheeks in disappointment and told Frankie that Lee had called.

"He says Colonel Holster...or whoever, wants to talk business."

Frankie didn't bat an eye, shuffled on past like he hadn't seen or heard.

"Hey? Am I invisible here or what?" Kid called out, baffled at the zombie that just passed through. "I say-yed *Ker-Nail Hol-Ster wants—*"

"Sure, Kid," Frankie mumbled. "I'll sleep on it..."

He hadn't any more than dozed in the last seventy-two hours. Ridden in the van, except for pit stops, the whole time. His body ragged, his head ached, he kicked the tick mattress against the wall and collapsed like a sack of grain.

Kansas grown, thank God...

XXII. THE DEAL

CC's stomach had been bothering him for quite some time, more each passing day, all kinds of rumblings and pain down there, so stove-up that morning he couldn't pass gas let alone take a shit. He would have skipped a good fuck for a good shit. Felt a shift in his lower bowels like a rock loosened by a pry bar. Milk-a-Magnesia might be kicking in. He drank a half cup with a shot of whiskey first thing each morning. So far so good, still maintaining, still avoiding the scalpel. Chalk it up to all those years of whiskey and whoring, he supposed. Added to which all the worry of running half the business in the county. You didn't become King of the County by ingesting moderate portions. You bit off more than you could chew and kept right at it.

CC presently sat gripping one of Greta's "Big Man" hamburgers, two-fisted jobs with a half-pound of ground beef, a quarter inch slice of onion, longhorn cheese, lettuce, tomato, ketchup, mustard, and pickles, the whole works, including a basket of home fries dripping grease. CC loved Greta's fries—he figured grease was the best gut lubricant going. He sat at the far back table in Carl's Bad Tavern, a little roadhouse bar and grill off Highway 36, a couple miles into Hill County. Friday morning, 11 a.m., the place was mostly empty except for two roustabouts playing pool, and Carl and Greta busy behind the bar in wait of the noon crowd comprised mostly of farmers and road crews. The jukebox enlivened the empty space with Johnny Horton singing "Honky-Tonk Man," one of CC's all-time favorites and a good song any time of the day. He took a shot from his silver flask and chased it with a beer, starting to feel like his old self. He lit a cigar, waved out the match and tossed it spiraling to the floor.

Through the savory drift CC gazed idly at the pine-paneled walls darkened by nearly thirty years of tavern smoke, scarred by pool cues, fistfights, and various initials and dates whittled in the grain, some etched black by time, others carved as recent as yesterday. Calendars nailed about head-high along the walls marked every year since 1946 when Carl returned from the war and opened the place; and each calendar depicted a winter scene in January, except for the current one showing a covey of quail in flight above a milo field—October 1975, Carl and Greta's thirtieth year. Carl had served as a cook in the 3rd Army; his hot chow kept Patton's boys on the march from the Battle of the Bulge on through to victory. Greta was his war bride, a smitten fraulein who liked his easy humor and saw her chance to escape the rubble and grief and never looked back. A lively little blonde, cute as a kitten in her day, and still lively on occasion but the cute had gone to fat, like her accent, once coy Dietrich, now pure Kansan, broad and flat as the rolling plains. CC reflected briefly on years gone by, what they'd taken and given, but he was a businessman and little given to reflection. He checked his gold pocket watch, 11:10, thinking *The boy's running a little late* as he snapped it shut. A minute later Frankie walked in. CC smiled, liked to see a man prompt for business.

Frankie stepped to the counter and ordered a beer. Greta filled a frosty mug from the tap and set it before him. "That'll be four-bits," she said, sober as a potato. Frankie tossed a half dollar to the counter where it hit and spun in a dribble of beer. He took a couple of swallows and glanced around, noted CC sitting like an old king in wait at the back table. Frankie took another deep draft and wiped his lips, in no great hurry, still taking in the place, letting his eyes adjust to the dark interior. And CC liked that too, Frankie's style, watching him turn and slowly walk his way, didn't come running like a damn lap dog.

Frankie edged back a chair and sat down.

"How's Colonel Holtz today?" he asked briskly, brushing back his mane of hair.

"Fair to middling, Frankie...fair to middling." CC licked his cigar and took a casual puff, eased the basket of fries towards his guest and said, "Here, have some…"

"No thanks. I already ate," Frankie said, staring through the haze of smoke, studying the dim gray eyes. "Just what business do you have in mind, Colonel?"

CC chuckled and shook his head. Yessir, he liked the boy's style. Direct like his mamma, not to be trifled with. "You young bucks always running late 'n raring to go. Well then, I'll tell ya." He laid his cigar to the edge of the table and folded his hands like a poker player showing his cards.

"Hemp," he said. "I hear you got hemp for sale."

"Where did you hear that?" Frankie answered, a hint of challenge in his smile.

"Never you mind where. The fact is I'm ready to do business."

"Since when have you been interested in hemp?"

"Since there's been a healthy profit to be made, that's when. Farm economy like it is. Hog 'n cattle prices down. A man can always use a healthy profit."

Of course that wasn't the whole story. CC said nothing about being in hock to heavy hitters in Kansas City. Serious people, bigger players in a bigger game. He'd let himself get sucked in for a hundred grand, confidant of an inside straight and lost to a full house, thought he could bluff it home but got called. He had to sign an IOU on his house and ranch to cover the debt. That was in mid-July and it had been a hard scramble, he now had close to seventy grand, but they wanted no less than the lump sum by November or else. Serious people. He would have sold a sale barn, but no one was buying. Same with the ready-mix and hog operation—everything tied up and leveraged. Besides, you never pulled ahead by pulling back. At the first sign of trouble most people ducked for cover. That's when the smart money sniffed opportunity. CC was smart and not about to duck for cover. And he'd rather lose his life than lose his ranch, to him it was one in the same—self, house, and ranch—like the Trinity. His religion, his very soul.

"So how much you want?" Frankie asked.

"How much you got?"

"I've got a ton."

"Then I want a ton."

"How much they paying?"

"The going rate...forty a pound."

"That's eighty thousand dollars. What's your cut?"

CC chomped his cigar a moment.

"Like any landowner, I want a third a' the crop. Thirty grand."

"That's too much. Do the math. A third of eighty is twenty-seven, rounded up. And that's still too much"—Frankie driving hard, eyes intent, jaw flexing. "We'll give you twenty and take sixty, cash on the barrel head. Otherwise we hold out. We've got all winter and no one's starving."

"Frankie Sage, you drive a harder bargain'n your ol' man, Justin."

"My old man pawned the farm for the next bottle and you know it."

"S'pose he did. I wouldn't be so hard on 'im. There's parts to Justin you don't know." CC laced his fingers and popped his knuckles. "What say we do this," he offered. "Split the difference. I take twenty-five and you git fifty-five...once it's sold."

"No deal," Frankie countered, not the least sentimental. "I said cash on the barrel head. You pay up front, I'll take fifty-five."

"Look son, you grew up on a farm. I sold stock for your daddy, your grandaddy. You know how it works. I'm an auctioneer. Folks bring me cattle, hogs, what have you, all on consignment. Once I make the sale, they git paid. That's the way it is and always has been. Take it or leave it."

Frankie scooted back his chair, ready to *leave it.*

"Hold on there—" CC reached out to delay him. "Lemme level with ya, son. Fact is I'm cash poor right now. Couldn't slap down sixty grand to save my soul from the devil. Couldn't buy a used truck. My only guarantee is my word 'n I ain't goin' nowhere. I got a reputation 'n I git things done. I don't run out on nobody. Never have. I'm good to my word no matter what the business."

"This isn't normal business."

"Sooner or later it's all normal business. A dollar don't smell no different whether you sell wheat, barley, milo, or hemp. Ain't no banker gonna turn his nose up at a buck whether fished from a skunk or a snake's ass. No sir…'n damn few women either."

A pool cue struck the balls at a distant table echoing the clash of thoughts in Frankie's mind as he considered the offer and whether to trust the old devil. Wondering whether he had any real choice. Already had a thousand pounds starting to dry rot in California. And only just returned from a dry run back east. Selling hemp was always a gamble. Might as well gamble on the devil he knew.

"How soon do we see the money?"

"How soon can you git the hemp to my ranch?"

"In about twenty minutes"—deciding then and there not to run it past the boys, least of all, Will. "It's out in the van."

"By God, boy," CC grunted, tapping his cigar. "Late or not, you got the goods."

"So when do we get the money?"

"We head up to the ranch. Git Mex loaded 'n on his way. Should be no problem gittin' your money by Monday night. How's that sound?"

"Mex is working the deal?"

"He's Mexican, ain't he? They're the ones as deal the bulk of it."

"I heard he was dealing with LaReese."

"Yeah, was…or hoped to. But that little rat-fuck never delivered. Got his ass caught then run off. Left his ol' momma holding the bag on his bail."

"Some think he did more than run. Some think he was done in…" Frankie left the statement pending like a question, studying the puffed, red-veined features for any sign of interest. CC betrayed nothing other than his usual cagey indifference.

"Look. Maybe he lit out for Timbuctoo, maybe he got hisself ground into sausage. Who knows? What's more, 'side from his ol' momma, who cares? And just 'tween you 'n me, are you really so sorry the little bastard's gone?"

"No."

"Well then, let's do some business and make us both some money." CC set his elbows to the table and extended his big hand, adding, "What say you, Frankie Sage? Have we got a deal?"

"Fifty-five grand by Monday evening," Frankie asserted, holding him to his word.

"Yessir, that's the sum agreed to."

Frankie gave a firm handshake and they both stood to go.

The pool players never took their eyes off their game. Carl stood at the grill, scraping off the grease, while Greta walked back to clear the table—the cigar left to smolder amidst the uneaten fries and the sweaty half-drank beer.

Father Michael neatly laid his vestments out on the bed. He fit his shirt and collar, donned his cassock and biretta, held the crucifix and rosary in his gloved hand, assuming the role of a priest as he had each dawn since being ordained, imbued by the spirit in the very act of touching the cloth, the accouterments of his calling, and now prepared to meet his Father. But who was his father? Some wretch or rogue or wandering Jew, forever nameless, unknown like God, yet present from the beginning and with him in witness of each moment, each breath? And his mother a distant icon, a grainy image in a photo, her dying voice whispering, *Look after your brother...will you, Miguel?* Then the light faded from her eyes, and they no longer saw or answered to his. The one he'd longed for his whole life and to whom he'd been near but a few days, lost to him forever, mute and cold, remote as statuary. Now as before he had nothing but a graven image where his mother and the Virgin merged. And whether as a whore or the Virgin, she was beautiful and dear to him. Yet he was cursed by his love for her and damned by his promise, a guilt he could never confess, for he could never betray his brother or his promise. A vow deeper than faith.

"*Mother...*" he answered softly, placing her photo by the crucifix on his bed.

Then he loosened the silk cord girding his waist and stepped to the chair. He tied one end of the cord to the brass light chain pendant from the ceiling and with the other fashioned a crude noose which he looped to his neck and secured just above his collar. He stood a quiet moment gazing to the Virgin across the way then whispered his last breath, "*De nihilo nihilum*"—from nothing to nothing. He kicked the chair away and swung: the weight of his body pulled the cord taut and the heat of his pulse surged in his ears like a deafening echo as the noose tightened, choking off his breath while his eyes burned in wonder of the raging panic then the quiet faint that soon fell like succor to his soul. His legs jerked and stilled. Warm urine dripped from his shoe to the carpeted floor as sunlight through the window cast his shadow to the wall. His hanged body slowly turned to the left then the right, like a slowed pendulum that marked no time.

When Hoss pulled up across the street that morning, the church doors remained closed and the elderly parishioners milled about the front steps somewhat perplexed in wait of early Mass. Hoss stepped out of his Bronco, curious of the priest's absence as were a couple of ladies who presently circled around to the parish to see what was keeping him. They weren't inside a minute before they rushed back out and hurried down the steps, heading straight towards Hoss. Their breath frosted about their gray hair as they hunched their autumn coats tight to their shoulders, mostly focused to the ground, careful of their footing. Hoss sensed their alarm and walked across to meet them. They were visibly upset, tears streaming their powdered cheeks.

"He's…he's hanged himself," one managed to say, wringing her hands in want of reason while the other poor woman simply shook her head and gasped for air. "He did. He…hanged himself," the first repeated more adamantly, looking to Hoss like he should undo the horror she had witnessed. "You plagued that poor man," she said, breaking into tears. "Why…why did you…plague him so…?"

Hoss nodded matter-of-factly and answered, "That I did. I had to."

But he said nothing more by way of explanation or self-defense, he simply laid a hand to the old woman's shoulder. And no, this was something he hadn't expected or wished. He wanted a witness, not a dead man.

"Would you two ladies help me here?" he asked calmly. "Would you let the others know what's happened? There now, that would be a big help," he added, directing them back to the fold. "I'll take care of…Father Michael"—employing the term of respect in the tragic moment. His demeanor and tone worked to reassure them as they nodded and walked back towards the others waiting by the church.

Hoss walked grimly to the parish, marched up the steps and through the front door left open by the women in their hasty exit. Inside he noted the deathly silence and the ticking clock. The time, 7:10. Further on he met the sweetly sick odor of loosed bowels and followed the odor to the corpse. He found the priest hanging in the bedroom; his eyes rolled upward, his mouth gaped in silent plea as if to cry: *Stop it! Stop it!* Hoss glared back in accusation and wanted to shout: *You damned fool! You had more guts than good sense!*

Yet words could not speak to this. He knelt and picked up the biretta, tossed it to the bed. He reached and touched the gloved hand—it was as slender and fine-boned as a woman's. And still warm. He stood the chair upright and stepped to the seat. Lifted the body in the brace of his arm, paying no mind to the foul stain soaking through his shirt as he removed the noose. Then cradling the body, he stepped down and laid it on the bed. He gently closed the eyes and mouth and arranged the arms and legs. He stood gazing down at the priest, his eyes set hard with hate. Not for the priest, but for Mex. Nor was Hoss prone to pity. But right then he pitied the priest more than he had pitied Joey and Cathy and could not say why.

But he would not dwell on it. The news clipping lay on the bed beside the rosary and crucifix. He picked it up and examined the photo, comparing it to the death mask before him: the priest resembled his mother even more now that his features had stilled, both equally remote in death. Hoss folded the clipping and slipped it in his shirt pocket. He turned away and glanced to the bureau. On the edge rested an old brown shoe box, stained and crumpled, the lid partly caved in and secured with a string under which lay a crisp white envelope addressed simply: *Sheriff Wayne.* Hoss opened the envelope and removed the letter—his hands trembled uncertain of what he might find, like holding the last words penned by a dead soldier, often too intimate and poignant to bear reading.

"*Dear Sheriff Wayne,*" it began, written in a graceful cursive.

"By the time you read this you will have witnessed my fate. Please know that the guilt is mine alone. I bear you no animosity, and I am sorry to trouble you in such a manner. I'm sorry as well that I cannot help in your investigation. You were right, knowing what I know, I cannot face another day. Yet what I know cannot be divulged. I have obligations as a priest, as a son, and as a brother. And against my brother I cannot bear witness. I can only bear witness before God. As you see, I have already done so. Though I fear I failed to fulfill my obligations. Most importantly, I failed my brother, and thereby failed my mother and God. For I never reached out to my brother to embrace and acknowledge him. Of our deep bond, I alone was aware. I confess I envied him with our mother; all the years they shared in which I had no part. Out of envy and pride I remained aloof in my sanctuary, in hope to preserve my priestly virtue against his virile nature. I should have told him who I was, at least announced myself. By remaining silent, I renounced him.

"In the box you will find various letters sent to me over the years by our mother. They are written mostly in Spanish and in broken English, and they contain nothing that will help you. They simply concern Javier and myself, and our mother's hopes and dreams for us. What a tragic price we pay to hope and dream. To purchase virtue, we barter sin until we have only sin. Though I think it is time Javier knew he had a brother. It is my hope and wish that you give him these letters. They need no explanation, he will recognize her handwriting and her words, and through them learn of me. Then who knows? Where I could not reach him, perhaps God will. That is my final hope. May God have mercy on my soul..."

Signed, *Miguel Orvano*—

Hoss folded the letter back in the envelope, then untied the string and lifted the lid from the box. He sifted through the cluttered pages, gave several a cursory glance and recognized not a word. Further down he found a creased black-and-white photo of a toddler in diapers attempting to walk—on the back was written: *Javier, su hermano, de diez meses.* Beneath it lay another of the boy posed with his mother as she knelt smiling, and again on the back was written: *Javier, de tres años.* At the bottom were even more photos of various holidays and class pictures, mostly marking the boy's growth through the years. Hoss looked no further, replaced the lid and retied the string. Sensed meanings too private, too personal—a space in which he did not belong. Like the bedroom. Still, he intended to use them, the photos and letters, and tucked the box under his arm as he walked to the kitchen to phone the coroner and have him come verify the cause of death.

With that Hoss ended his duties there. The Church and parishioners could arrange the funeral in whatever manner they saw fit. It being a suicide there was bound to be a scandal with a hot debate over where to bury the body. Whether in holy ground or amongst the heathen. *Let 'em bicker,* thought Hoss. He had no more sympathy for the Catholic Church and the proprieties of faith than did Mrs. Wylett. His sole concern as he stepped down off the porch and crossed to his Bronco was how to make use of the box. He would make damn certain Mex received it along with a photocopy of his brother's last letter. Send them like a fuse to a powder keg. No predicting how or when, but there would be an explosion, of that Hoss had no doubt. Sooner or later Mex was going down if it took his full weight to do it.

Hoss drove directly to his office and wrapped the box in brown paper, folded the corners and taped it neat as a present. He addressed the top in bold black print with a magic marker— *Mex Orvano RR#4 Mankato, KS*—knew the address from prior legal dealings. He carried the package across the street to the post office and set it on the counter by 9:15. Paid the postage and directed the clerk to make certain it went out that afternoon so it would arrive at the Colonel's ranch with the next day's delivery, right about the time news of the priest's death appeared in all the papers. Bound to make headlines. Hoss had left a note regarding that too, placed a wry message inside the priest's letter that stated bluntly: *"I grant him this much, he was his brother's keeper. But now that your brother's dead, Mex, what's going to keep you from me?"*—the last underlined with a stabbing pen.

So the hunt had shifted. And by-and-by, as with the priest, Hoss aimed to make his presence felt. For the time being he'd let Mex sweat the question of how much he knew and how far he'd go.

But Mex wasn't sweating a thing except the prospect of snow further west as he headed for Denver later that day, his pickup loaded with a ton of hemp underneath his new red camper shell. He had the goods, and he had the contact, and the Mexican bruja, Sanita Teresa, had the money. She always flashed her smile as collateral, every tooth capped in gold, saying, "If I do not pay, you may pull them one by one, no?" and not a one was missing. Though with her five burly sons standing by, who would take issue? Mex liked her moxie, and The Old Bitch, as he called her, liked his. No sentiment, no remorse. All instinct and savvy.

Meanwhile Frankie headed back to the farm, the van empty, his mind filled with doubts of who he dealt with—if not for the Colonel, he wouldn't have trusted Mex to stand by his own shadow. And now the cold leaden sky that had followed from all the way back east settled in a lowering mist like a great dark shroud dousing every shred of optimism he could muster.

Garret, too, watched the sky, pushing on through the afternoon and evening, determined to keep cutting till the trucks and tractor bogged down. The field grew steadily more sodden and gummy, the tractor tires spinning out clumps of mud that stuck to the wheel wells like fresh manure, while amidst the roar of machinery Garret carried on a raging soliloquy against *Whoever* was in charge up there, telling Him what kind of a such-n-such He was for bringing on such weather. Lee could read his lips and read his thoughts: *Two Goddamned weeks is all I asked. Is that so Goddamn much to ask?*—cursing at the ceaseless mist and continually checking back to make certain the cutter heads cleared the ground and were free of mud—*Enough to give a man a good Goddamned pain in the neck!*

Lee followed along in the truck, glum and silent, nothing but cold coffee to sip and down to dregs at that, tormented by the loss of Diana's love and the thought of her in love with someone else. He didn't like the sky any better than Garret, hadn't seen one bird all day or listened to a single song. Left the radio turned off and listened to the groan and grind of the truck. Didn't want to hear or think of any kind of song, good or bad, and certainly none bright and cheery. Hit the wipers on occasion to clear away drops of moisture edging one to the other in jagged descent down the windshield.

"Drizzling rain," he mumbled absently. Then the thought took hold and grew: *"Drizzlin' rain...runnin' down the alley, runnin' on down...chasin' after me, runnin' on down to the bottom of the river...runnin' on down...to the bottom of the sea..."*

A rather somber lyric, definitely not cheery, but it cheered him nonetheless. He reached over and snatched a gas receipt from the glove box and jotted down the words. And soon had more, a ballad starting to form:

"Where have you been to, my lady?
Where have you been to till now?
"I've been waitin' the whole night thru,
me, the moon, and the owl.
"I'll take my heartache down to the bar
and order a whiskey 'n beer.
"Hold the memory of you in my arms
and laugh away all the tears..."

It wasn't really about Diana; he knew she wasn't stepping out. It simply spoke to his mood, the rain, and his fear of losing her—a variation on an old, old theme. He began humming up a tune to fit with the lyrics, letting the wipers mark the time. He couldn't help but express the feeling flooding him that warmed and filled his emptiness and made him smile. He couldn't deny the song any more than he could deny Diana. And she'd smiled to him that morning, a brief fleeting smile, though she still shrank from his touch. So he didn't push it. He'd wait, take his time, and in time he hoped to woo her back. Maybe not with song, but he would prove to her that he could write songs and still hold steady, and together they could *laugh away the tears*. He already had the chorus, singing in a low tone, *"Drizzlin' rain runnin' down the alley..."*

XXIII. THE HAUNTING

Diana had watched the sky mist over and thicken through the day, forming droplets on the windows in echo of those witnessed by Lee as she gazed out from time to time, hoping he might come home early due to the rain. The only man she wanted to see drive in was Lee. Feeling lonely and cold from the weather, she longed to be held, simply held, not seized, groped, or touched. Still wary. In part it was her violation, but that was merely the catalyst. The greater part was the uncertainty. Never knowing Lee's next mood or move. Not to mention his drinking. Sometimes he'd be off with a friend and not return till the next day. Though lately he'd stayed sober. Maybe he'd settle down and maybe not. Maybe she'd stay with him and maybe not. But such thinking filled her with disgust, reminding her of the school-girl game, "Love me, love me not…" and she didn't want to play any games with Lee and force him to be something he wasn't.

Over the past two days to suppress such questions she'd cleaned every room in the house, waxed the floors, polished the woodwork, including the entire grand staircase—rails, stiles, newel posts and all. At times she stood and straightened her back in wonder whether the house wasn't too big, too much for her, then instantly shunned the notion and bent to work, in fever to clean and caress its every surface, for she loved the house and was determined to stay. To possess and be possessed. There belong.

Diana even removed three old dresses she'd left hanging in Jessie's closet, having thought someone might return to claim them. Which was doubtful, for they were simply old summer dresses of flowery pattern with capped sleeves: two dark and one light, like those in style during the 20s that she'd seen her grandmother wear in old photos or like the one worn by the sweet old lady who'd asked to see the house. And there were photos as well dating from the same era, a dozen or so scattered in a dusty corner of the upper shelf—one of a young woman coyly posed in front of a Ford coup; another of a young man standing proudly before the same, his arms cocked to his hips; while the remainder were mostly group portraits from family gatherings and picnics.

To make a clean sweep of things Diana decided to burn the dresses and photos. This marked the day's big event for Jessie as he tagged along curious, watching her pour kerosene from the lamp into a tin can and grab the box of kitchen matches. He followed her outside to a low depression far back of the house where she burned all their trash. A good day for burning, damp and misty. Rue and Keeps slunk off towards the red shed east of the cedars, for they knew the routine and were wary of fire. Diana plopped the dresses down on the blackened bed of prior burnings and scattered the photos on top like fallen leaves. She doused all with the kerosene and warned Jessie to stay back.

"Careful, honey, it's hot," she said, striking a match and tossing it to the heap.

Blue and yellow flames leapt into the air to warm their faces. Jessie stood enrapt, watching the fire eat into the fabric as it burned bright-orange then a ghostly black and white— the pattern and weave bleeding through an instant before disintegrating. The photos caught like dried leaves, the images briefly given life in the hiss of flames while the edges curled and flaked away. Within a minute the last ember had blinked and died, leaving nothing but a thin breath of smoke, and soon that too withered in the ashes.

Staring there Diana felt a pang of remorse at the burning, like a window closed forever on another life and time. Then she raked it over and left it, anxious to fill the house with her life and time. Jessie simply wished the fire had lasted longer as he grasped his mommy's hand and returned to the house.

Like the fire the day ended too soon, without its customary

slant of shadow and soft evening light. The sun having not once shown its face, it was like they inhabited a lone, isolate world, she and Jessie, closed in by a deep mist and fog while beyond the big house and lawn laid nothing but trackless wastes and indefinite forms. Every tree and limb etched black against the enveloping night; what leaves remained hung shriveled, their colors damp and muted, browned in decay, awaiting the earth, lifeless, unburied. She felt utterly abandoned, forlorn. More than loneliness it was a haunting she sensed, like she and Jessie were the last of the living and all else lay dead in wait.

She turned from the window, the darkening scene, and shuddered at the thought of night. Jessie had grown fussy after his supper, and she'd put him to bed with a story that seemed to quiet him. But nothing could quiet her own unease; she wished Lee were there. The darkness grew so dense that light bulbs barely lit the immediate space. The same when she stepped into the living room and gazed through to the grand staircase ascending to the shadows—witnessed a heavy encroaching darkness, indistinct, without shape or form, yet incipient and strangely hostile, like she'd felt while cleaning out the third floor earlier in the day. A broad empty space where she'd dreamed of dancing, but working there she felt watched at every turn, a looming resentment of her very presence that seemed to intimate, *No dancing, no cleaning...* wishing to be left undisturbed. Floors bare and unfinished, like the walls simply plastered over and left unpainted through the years, etched by ugly brown stains from the leaking roof. Diana had touched her broom handle to a damp spot on the ceiling and the plaster fell away, exposing the lath like an open wound. She quickly swept up the debris and soon finished cleaning, glad to return down the short flight of stairs and latch the door. She glanced to the diamond-shaped window and wondered for the hundredth time at its odd placement there at the end of the hall above the grand stair and before the entrance to the attic—like a stern red eye set glazed in warning. But she would not be intimidated. That's when she went to Jessie's room and cleaned out his closet. Though now, gazing through to the grand staircase and the shadowy glum, she again sensed the threat. She switched off the light and returned to the kitchen, clutching her shoulders against the rising chill and the darkness seeping in through every window and door.

Then she heard something. *A voice? No...*several voices. Upstairs. Seemingly from her bedroom. Her first thought was that the clock radio had abruptly turned on. But the voices quickly spread through every upper room and down the grand stair. And no horrendous howls or screams or grave whisperings as one might imagine, just peculiarly common voices of people engaged in conversation, exchanging pleasantries and mild laughter like at a party—she even discerned the clink of a glass, the swish of a dress, the light rhythmic footsteps of couples dancing, as if all her cleaning had somehow awakened the house and every memory was being replayed. She stood vaguely amused, curious at what was happening, then transfixed in terror as the voices drew closer, louder, nearly deafening, passing all around and through her like shadows, only willful shadows, voices too numerous to decipher or name. And suddenly one did name her.

Jessie cried from his room, calling for his mommy.

Diana broke and ran up the back stair, following the rise of her shadow, frantic to reach him. She turned at the mid-landing and saw a further shadow leaning into Jessie's room. Diana, angered at the violation of her child, continued up the stairs, determined to walk through ghost or wall of fire if need be. At her approach the shadow whipped like a dark wind and vanished, leaving nothing but a chill space before the door.

From the room Jessie stood crying: "Old woman! Old woman!"

Diana rushed in and held him in her arms, clasping his warm life to her.

"It's okay, honey. We're leaving now," she said and gathered him up.

She carried him down the stairs through the spawn of voices clinging like broken webs, no longer the least familiar but emphatically dark and menacing. She snatched her purse hanging from a chair and rushed out the door. She didn't stop till they reached the pickup, nor once look back. She could still hear the voices spilling onto the porch. She strapped Jessie in his car-seat and started the truck, both of them in tears as she revved the engine and sped down the drive then swerved onto the road, all the while blinking her eyes to see, trying to calm herself and Jessie. And she didn't slow down till she'd passed the Shafer place and turned east on the pavement—at last breaking free of the haunting, ready to follow the road anywhere but back to the house.

Lee might have met her on the road had he not left from a field further north; he turned off the pavement only minutes after she'd headed south for town. He drove the old Willy's Jeep that Garret had insisted he use. "Can't leave her without a vehicle," he'd said. "She might need groceries. And you never know what might happen. Jessie might step on a nail like I did that time..."—as a five-year-old he'd ran across a barnyard plank and drove a nail clean through his foot. "If Dad hadn't saddled ol' Pat and swum me 'cross that flooded creek to reach a doctor, I might've died of lock-jaw..."

Though at times Garret wondered if that wouldn't have been best, to lay gripped by a hot fever, a weak fledgling having not yet escaped the nest, watched over by his mother and father as he passed into a cool slumber never to learn more of life and its many trials and disappointments. A thought he best not dwell on, like the weather, nothing he could change—but he could give the equipment another thorough going-over to make certain nothing broke down once the weather cleared. His plan for next morning as he leaned to the Jeep and told Lee to go ahead and sleep in.

"Too damn wet already," he said. "But you might call around noon. I might could use some help moving cattle."

Lee nodded "Okay" and goosed the Jeep, cutting down through the ditch and back up on the road. It was a temperamental old beast built in '49, mud-splattered on the front and side which blended with the rust and undercoat showing through the chipped yellow paint. Caterpillar yellow like a dozer. And sometimes they used it for one, put a blade on front to plow through snow or to muck out cattle pens. No doors, just a metal topper bolted on like a tin helmet rattling at every rut. Noisy as a combine and every bit as dirty, especially rolling down country roads, churning up dust. Tires knocked out of balance from bounding over fields and rough pastures. Lots of play in the steering due to the shot rocker arms which Garret vowed to replace once harvest ended. "Just don't drive over forty," he advised. Being so low-geared, 45 mph was about top speed in any case. Every few miles the headlights cut off and you had to pound the dash in hope they blinked back on. No falling asleep after a long day while driving that thing.

Lee steered up the drive, glad to be home. Saw Rue and Keeps, their yellow eyes reflecting in the headlights, cowered before the shed instead of up by the porch where they usually lay. Scared of the Jeep, he supposed as he turned off the engine and cut the lights. Hadn't noticed till then that the pickup was gone. Lights on in the kitchen and in Jessie's room upstairs. Guessed Diana had made a late run to town in need of milk or eggs or some such item. He grabbed his thermos and headed inside, pausing at the door in wonder of why it was left open. Diana seldom did something without a reason, so he left it open and stepped on in, setting his thermos to the counter. It wasn't exactly warm out, but seemed even cooler inside, so why would she air the kitchen?

He fetched a beer from the fridge, kept cold in back of the milk, popped it open and sat down at the table. Licked the foam off the top and took a sip, savoring its crisp bite fizzing down his throat, clearing his head of the numbness brought on by hours of driving the old truck behind the howling cutter. Good to simply sit and drink a beer and relish the silence. She'd probably be home most any minute. Then he might get her to smile. Maybe show her the lyrics he'd penned.

With that thought Lee heard the faint sound of the radio upstairs—hadn't noticed it till now, but reception was often poor, sound fading in and out, depending on the weather and the station. And it sounded like a weather forecast, a lone voice droning in the static monotone that Lee dreaded waking to each morning at 4 a.m. But then another voice answered, and several more somewhat brighter up and down the hall. One giddy with laughter. Lee stood and walked to the back stair, wondering *What the hell?* Then to his immediate left, in the living room, still more voices, like from a 1920s' soiree, only there wasn't a soul in there, nothing but a shadowed room and soft disembodied voices. Lee stepped back into the kitchen and took a deep breath, still too numb and tired to register more than puzzlement. Perhaps the house did need airing. He opened a south window and leaned to the sill to clear his head.

Not a breath stirred beyond the screen, though he plainly heard two voices approaching across the lawn, men's voices, one older, one younger, exchanging views in the frank, droll tones of farmers accustomed to hedging their efforts against vagaries of the weather and markets. A conversation that Lee had heard a thousand times and all the more frightening for its familiarity as the voices drew steadily closer and more distinct, like those in the rooms above and at his back, initially thin and distant, indifferent to his presence as if on another wavelength, now coming into focus, tuning in, closing around, visceral as the cold touch of a corpse.

Lee left his beer on the sill and shot out the door, leapt stumbling to the ground and ran for the Jeep. He saw Rue and Keeps running for the barn and had no thought of why or what was happening. No thought but utter fear, worse than any he'd known. Worse than being shot at because at least there was a reference, something tangible in the threat of a bullet. He jumped in the Jeep and hit the starter—it cranked and groaned while he pumped the gas, playing the choke for fear he'd flood the engine.

"*Dammit!*" he cursed and tried again. Nothing. Felt like a fool in "Night of the Living Dead" trying to escape the risen. On the third attempt the engine sputtered and shook, then threatened to die as he eased in the choke and gave it full throttle. In a roar of blue smoke he shifted to first, wheeled around, stomped the clutch and skipped to third, anxious for speed.

Approaching the road, the lights bumped off and he had to guess the turn, edging into the ditch as the passenger side tipped weightless, the front fender clipping stalks and limbs with a sharp *thack-thack-thack!* Then the tires sought purchase and in a hail of gravel the Jeep swerved back up on the road. Lee didn't slow down, driving blind and desperate, following the ruts till he hit a washed-out depression in front of the low bridge that bumped the lights back on. In passing the long-abandoned place south of the road, he didn't give it a single thought, nothing that lurked there could surpass what he'd just witnessed. Nor did he see the yellow-eyed hound suddenly shrink from the oncoming lights as the Jeep veered past the Shafer place and turned north. Lee didn't once brake or downshift, his lone thought was to distance himself from the dread voices—whether real or imagined, they were clearly imminent.

Near the railroad crossing he glanced back at the huge house, dimly lit, ill-defined, framed by the mist like a dark mausoleum, massive, cold, sealed by the night. Looking back to the road, Lee caught the flash of a light beaming at his left periphery. He hit the brakes and skidded sidelong towards the siren blast of the belated whistle, large, oceanic, plowing out the night, sounded less in warning than in vow to crush any in its path.

The Jeep stopped a breath shy of the great black train engine and lone car roaring past with the thrust of an angry sea, tons of iron and churning steel spewing hot cinders and a spray of diesel fumes in through the passenger side, rocking the Jeep like a tiny boat in its brute passage and wake. It appeared out of nowhere and vanished like a ghost train highballing through the night. And for an instant Lee swore he did see a ghost as a jagged white shape rose up and caught on the fence. But it was merely a plastic feed sack buffeted in passing. Lee took a slow deep breath and shifted to reverse. Chanced a smile and counted himself lucky. He backed out onto the road and proceeded into town with greater caution—lest he'd become a ghost himself in haste to flee the same.

Lee found the pickup parked in the alley beside his mother's house. He figured Diana and Jessie might be there. He parked the Jeep and switched off the engine; it gave a mulish shutter, firing on its own fumes till he popped the clutch to kill it. Inside, Diana and Jessie sat at the kitchen table; both looked up bright-eyed and smiling as Lee stepped through the door. Jessie was still dressed in his PJs and had his right fist wrapped around the handle of a tablespoon. He liked the "Big Spoon" as he called it for eating Cheerios, which he presently slurped, milk running down his chin.

"Why, there's a stranger!" Lee's mother announced, turning from the stove with a big smile. "Looks like we've got your whole family in tonight."

"Guess so," Lee nodded, glancing from one to the other.

He was a little surprised at how cheerful everyone looked. Because Diana and his mother hadn't gotten along all that well in recent months, no real estrangement, mostly Diana's resentment at having to stay there through half the summer. But Vera, in her late 50s, her hair nearly white, could be quite obstinate and opinionated. A widow of twenty years, her sole passion was her children. And Diana didn't want any advice regarding her own child and husband. Like it or not she usually got some.

"Got home and no one there," Lee added with a faint smile. "Thought I'd check in here."

"I had to come to town for milk," Diana explained as if it were no matter, though her smile grew as tentative as his. "So we…stopped by to see your mother."

"Well I'm glad you did," Vera said. "You guys have been awfully scarce lately."

"Things have been pretty hectic, Mom," Lee answered. "And what with Garret and the silage, it looks to stay that way for a while."

"Yes, I know," she said, rubbing her arthritic hand, flexing it absently. "Garret's anxious to be done, worried about being caught by the weather and such. But that's farming for you." She pursed her lips, knew the risks better than most, having lost her husband to the gamble. "Anyway, now that you're here," she brightened, "no sense in you running off. Might as well stay and have supper. I can fry you up a hamburger and some sliced potatoes. And there's left-over corn…?"

Lee glanced to Diana; she seemed in no hurry.

"Sure, Mom," he said. "Sounds good to me."

Sitting down at the table, he asked, "Where's Tory?"—Lee's little sister, now a year out of high school.

"Oh, she's on a date," Vera answered. "On a date seven nights a week it seems."

"Still the same fella?"

"Yes…" she answered slowly, betraying some concern. "I hate to see her get so serious so young. But I can't say much, I was the same age myself when I married your father. And Danny seems like a fine young man."

Lee asked no further and made no comment, knew he caused enough worry on his own. They mostly spoke around things, avoiding deeper issues, keeping it lighthearted while he ate. Their attention centered mostly on Jessie showing off for his grandmother, jabbering about all of his adventures with Rue and Keeps.

"They gots ka-bird in grass," he told them, arching his brow, raising his spoon. "But ka-bird fly to the sun and gots night come. Rue 'n Keeps not find ka-bird…"

The story only grew from there, the bird assuming other shapes, an old box, a rag that Rue and Keeps tug and fight over while Jessie trails along in witness and narrative, watching it escape time and again…till they find the cicada shell, the "Wee-oh bug"—a thing so finely made and mystifying that he fell silent at the thought of it making all that noise as his mommy assured him it did when it was awake inside its shell. Mother and Grandmother both proud of his clever and inquisitive nature, of how many words he knew. One thing they could truly agree on: What a fine boy he was.

About a half hour later Lee stood up from the table, finished with his meal.

"Hate to eat 'n run, Mom, but it's been a long day," he said. "And we need to get Jessie to bed. Need to get to bed myself."

"No, no. I understand. I'm just glad you made it in." She traded smiles with Jessie as she walked them to the door and said, "Don't take so long coming back, okay?"

But standing there, watching them go, she knit her brows over the recent rumors she'd heard concerning Lee and Frankie and others. Dangerous rumors that caused her some sleepless nights. She wished he would find another way to make his money, hated to think where that path might lead. Yet in spite of all she had faith in him, a mother's stubborn contrary faith. And apparently things had smoothed over, for the rumors had died down. Still, she sensed something edgy between Diana and Lee, the way they kept looking across the table at one another in search and question. Something she couldn't put her finger on.

No one could, not by way of answer. Certainly not Diana or Lee, the question of those voices at the fore of their minds as they turned up the drive, the Jeep leading the way. The house stood stately and quiet, the kitchen light on, the door open in welcome, the picture of innocence and tranquility.

Rue and Keeps lay by the front porch steps, which Diana counted as a good sign; they hadn't come near the house since the burning, and she had to wonder if burning the dresses and photos hadn't triggered something. But she didn't pursue the thought. Shut it from her mind and said nothing, fearing any word or thought would conjure all again. Lee operated under a similar assumption, walked up the steps and stopped by the door.

"Guess I left it open," he offered faintly.

Diana merely shrugged and walked on in carrying Jessie. Lee shut the door and the south window. He retrieved his beer and stood taking a sip, attempting nonchalance, glancing from the side room to the corners. Diana likewise braved a flicker of a smile and said, "Looks like we're home." Lee gave a nod. Both looking, listening past one another, expectant of the voices. But they heard nothing but Jessie's yawn as he rubbed his eyes, having fallen asleep on the way home. And he was getting heavy. Diana gave him a heft and shifted his weight.

"Think he could sleep with us tonight?" she asked. "He was a little upset earlier in his room."

"Sure, if you think so," Lee answered vaguely, letting his thoughts drift to the faded wallpaper, images emergent from the old walls like voices as he wondered how many shadows had passed that way, in what state of hope or worry, and were they listening like him to the shift and rustle of the vast house, to their own breath and heartbeat? Lee laid his beer aside, switched off the light and followed upstairs, thinking it best they stick together. Tonight he'd have let the dogs in if they were willing—but strange thing, you couldn't coax them through that door with a chicken bone, never could. Which made him wonder what their uncanny senses told them. Same with his own sense and instinct, beginning to doubt his own mind and what had happened, given nothing to reference to. And Diana wasn't about to say a thing, dared not say a word.

Preparing for bed, she asked Lee to leave the bathroom light on.

"For Jessie," she said. "In case he has to go in the night."

"Sure thing," Lee answered, didn't mind leaving it on for himself either.

After using the bathroom, he flushed the stool, noted the low gurgle and swirl and listened to the pipes rattle and groan all the way to the basement. Definitely a series of ugly sounds, but nothing at all unusual or frightening. And nothing voiced in answer. Though he did avoid looking in the mirror while brushing his teeth for fear he'd see an image back of his own. A ridiculous fear, the stuff of movies. For there was nothing in the old house except Diana, Jessie, and himself. So he reasoned returning to bed.

Diana and Jessie were already under the covers; he switched off the light and joined them. Jessie, snug in the middle, felt wholly safe between his mommy and daddy, secure in his reason, knew the old woman wouldn't dare come in there with his daddy around. A certainty that lulled him like a lullaby. Lee shared no such confidence, stared at the ceiling and slaked his breath in wait, watchful of the shadows, of the lighted hall, listening for the slightest stir, and heard nothing but ringing in his ears and the steady *thump-thump* of his heart. Finally he closed his eyes and slept like a zombie, without thought or dream. But Diana lay awake for hours, listening to Jessie's peaceful slumber and Lee's low deep breath, listening for the voices and hearing none but the inner voice telling her that she would not stay in that house another night.

An interminable night, grains of time mixed with grains

of fear like countless seconds falling away inside an hourglass and every breath a mere pause that started all again. A few minutes till four she reached to the clock radio and switched off the alarm, at last falling into a fitful sleep until daybreak. A chill gray dawn, dreary and drizzling. Lee and Jessie still slept. She crept out of bed and dressed in the bathroom. Then she went downstairs and fixed herself a hardboiled egg and a slice of toast.

Diana decided to call her mother in Oklahoma; she needed someplace to go that very day and wouldn't stay with Lee's mother, not again, not so soon and so close. She needed distance and time to think. A chance to sleep. Away from all the guns, ghosts, and threats, and Lee's next enthusiasm or quest, each so immediate and intoxicating that she felt swept up in the moment and helpless to resist. And she wouldn't have called her own mother if her father were still alive, for he was Lee's opposite, rigid in life and faith, easily offended, quick to anger, alternately meek and stern like any bully. Her mother had learned to walk a minefield and adapted by wearing a complacent facade, creating a neutral zone in which she and her children could survive his rages and tantrums. Diana needed that neutrality just then. A place to stand quiet and reach a sober decision. And she didn't wish to discuss it with Lee or with anyone.

"Is something the matter?" her mother asked, quietly puzzled, surprised, for Diana had sounded so excited in recent letters, relating details of the house and how happy she would be if they could buy it.

"No, it's just…things have gotten kind of awkward here. A little unsettled. We need to make a change. So if you don't mind, I'd like to bring Jessie and stay for a while…"

Her mother asked no further questions, pleased for any excuse to see her daughter and grandson, and said she didn't mind in the least and would be happy to come and get them. Diana's hand trembled hanging up the phone, a cold irrevocable moment giving up her dream of the house. And perhaps leaving her husband.

When Lee came down a while later, she told him she was going to her mother's.

"You were right," she said. "I need to go and let things blow over"—coloring her decision in his terms. Though to Lee's mind things had pretty much already blown over. All that waited was the rest of their money. He studied her warily.

"Does this have to do with you and someone else?" He braved the question that had gnawed at him the past two days.

She smiled wanly and shook her head.

"No, Lee, there's no one. That was...something I said. I was upset."

His blood warmed and the constriction eased like a gripped hand releasing his heart. Still, they kept their distance, too many uncertainties unresolved.

"So, you no longer want to stay and buy the place? Even if I get the money?"

"No...there's..." she paused, hesitant, again looking to the walls and corners.

"What is it, Diana? What happened last night? I know you didn't go to town for milk. There was milk in the fridge when I got home."

She raised a hand to her throat and looked to him in wistful plea and answer.

"I haven't told you and don't know quite how," she began. "I didn't want to believe the rumors about the house because I wanted to live here. Wanted to so badly. But ever since we moved in Jessie has awakened in the night, crying. Not every night. But once or twice a week. And for several weeks not at all. Then it would happen again. At first I thought it was only a bad dream. But it was always the same. He'd point to the hall and say, 'Make the old woman go away!' And I would answer, 'What old woman?' But he would insist and keep on pointing. He claimed that she cried and told him the old man was hurt and needed help. Eventually I would calm him and rock him to sleep, telling him there was nothing, that it was only a dream. But there is always a cold spot there, Lee. At the top of the stair where he would point."

Lee had noticed it in passing and remembered Will commenting on the same. Will had also mentioned hearing from Ned Furburgh that the farmer who built the place, a McLeon or McLoid, had been injured in a fall and died sometime after. And over time folks swore it was haunted. This was long before John Tannis bought the place and it had sat empty for years, tied up in estate. And when John's wife failed to take to the place, claiming it was too far from town, there'd been a succession of renters, none staying for long. Lee was beginning to understand why.

"Last night, after putting him to bed," she continued, "I heard something upstairs. *Voices*," she said more emphatically. "Too many to be mistaken for the wind or creaking woodwork. Then I heard Jesse cry and I ran up and I saw something, Lee. It looked like a shadow standing at Jesse's door, and he cried, 'Old woman!' like he saw her. Then I passed on through and nothing happened, thank God..." She watched him start to smile and was on the verge of anger, thinking he meant to patronize or ridicule her.

"You heard voices...?" he asked, still smiling.

"Yes!" she insisted, her lips pressed firm, ready to cut him short.

"So did I!" he laughed. "A whole house full!"—anxious to escape his doubt and share the experience like the morning he'd pulled her out of bed to observe the strange light in the east. "Christ, they were coming from everywhere, Diana. Every last room. Like I was trapped inside a radio with someone turning up the volume. I threw open the window and heard more coming from the yard. I ran out the door, cleared the steps 'n hit the ground running. Never been so scared. Diana, I don't know how or why, but I think this place is haunted!" Declared like a blind man given sight.

Both of them relieved they weren't the only one to witness such a thing.

"So, you ready to move out of here?" he asked, taking her hand.

She smiled and nodded.

"Want to move to Nashville?" he urged.

"I don't know about that, Lee," she answered, losing her smile. "I don't know about lots of things..."

He let go of her hand and stepped back. He didn't want to

press it, just happy to make contact and bridge the moment. He searched her green eyes studying him and wondered of her thoughts and what she would decide. There was no doubt in his mind that he could make her happy, one way or another. And no doubt in hers that whatever Lee did would entail a whole lot of uncertainty. She feared he may never settle.

Diana went upstairs to wake Jesse and give him a bath, then pack their clothes and make ready to leave. Lee called Garret and said he wouldn't make it in that day. Said he needed to help Diana with some things. Didn't explain. Didn't want to tell anyone that she was leaving. Not ready to admit it himself. He sat in the kitchen sipping coffee till she was packed, then went up and carried down the suitcases and helped her gather a box of toys for Jesse. They didn't say much more, and the morning passed in mere seconds like time does when you feel something precious slipping away.

Diana's mother Norma arrived shortly after one. Diana and Lee started carrying bags and suitcases out the minute she drove in. She couldn't fathom their hurry, wanted to see the house, pause a moment after her long drive and satisfy her curiosity. The biggest house she'd ever laid eyes on—it had loomed even from the distance, big as the forty-stall milk barn on the farm where she'd grown up. And now walking in through the dining room and foyer, she gazed at the grand staircase, marveling at the fine woodwork and all the space.

"Why would you possibly want to leave all this?" she asked, at once flummoxed and overwhelmed.

What could Diana say—that a hellhound had nearly snatched Jesse, that she'd nearly been raped and nearly shot Lee. That she'd seen a ghost and heard a hundred haunting voices but the night before?

"Mom," she answered wearily, "the house is simply too big. Too much for me." And having cleaned it thoroughly the past two days served proof to the fact. It was too big, and too weighted with the past.

Norma followed her out, still shaking her head as she stepped down off the porch and gazed to the corniced fascia and upper windows, taking in the width and breadth of the structure, giving it all one more look before heaving a deep sigh of exasperation and returning to the car. Hard to figure her daughter sometimes. Lee, she had always been a tad skeptical of, but *Good Gracious!*—what woman would leave such a house? Lee picked Jesse up and carried him to the car, told him to be a good boy, that he'd see him soon. Then he looked to Diana. "Gotta help Garret finish up," he said. "Shouldn't take more than a couple weeks. Then I'll come down and we'll talk, okay? See how you feel...?"

"Okay, Lee. You take care"—her answer noncommittal, reluctant to say more.

She leaned close and shared a light embrace, feeling oddly constrained by her mother's presence and the implication that she was leaving Lee, and she didn't know if she was or not. Seated in the car, riding away, she glimpsed to the side mirror and saw him standing alone in front of the big house, the two dogs at his feet. She wanted to stop the car and run back, fill his arms and claim him and the house come what may. But looking to the road she also wanted to escape, keep on going and never look back.

Jesse simply wondered why his daddy was standing back there and why Rue and Keeps couldn't come along.

XXIV. SACRIFICE

By mid-Sunday morning the mist lifted and the sky cleared. The sun shone bright and welcome in the crisp autumn air. A dry wind stirred through the stalks and tassels and long-bladed leaves. Garret and his crew, including Lee, returned to the field right after lunch and harvested on till nightfall. The sun set so suddenly they hardly noticed. The stars appeared in sheer instantaneous glory, spreading their icy glitter like specks of frost against the night's black pane.

Further north, at the Colonel's ranch in Hill County, Mex stepped from his warm truck, his breath fogging the very air as he scanned the dark hump of surrounding hills. Quite a shock returning to those lonely vistas after a wild night in Denver. La Bruja liked to cap business with a good time and kept a stable of fine dark-eyed fillies eager to buck and romp at a slap of the ass. Mex had sold the hemp for $90,000 and carried the money in a small black duffel minus the ten grand he'd stuffed in his boot, no need to mention or share the bonus—five dollars a pound for timely delivery.

In the house he set the bag on the table alongside the newspaper and miscellaneous mail. There was a package addressed to him. He picked it up and gave it a shake, not very heavy. He grinned, thinking some sweet thing might have sent him her underwear as a come-on. But the grin didn't last. Hoss's package lit a fuse the instant Mex opened it and read the words: *Now that your brother's dead...what's going to keep you* from me?

Fire ate into his brain as if following twisted strands of memory dusted with gunpowder, burning a thousand paths to the deadened center of his fissured soul, awakening raw nerves as he stood reading the letters. He recognized his mother's writing, her fond words, and could hear her voice echo in his mind, could sense her ache and longing, her scented presence in the hint of perfume that lingered on the pages like a whiff of lilac, reminding him of her favorite color, purple. Transfixed by the letters, the photos, and the revelations of a brother—his thoughts tore at him, at his certainty. For Mex had always been alone, the son of a whore...*son of a bitch,* and for certain alone ever since her death, and that certainty let him act without regret to avenge every slight. But learning of his brother Miguel and realizing that he, Mex, had actually seized and threatened him, bore down like a curse, burned his heart and left him hollow. For yes, he felt remorse for his brother, saw that he too had been alone, alone forever and now gone. But he sneered at his brother's final hope of God reaching him, and with that sneer his rage returned, filling him with a new certainty. Certain that the Colonel had known all along.

Sunday evenings were CC's night out. He customarily ate a 16-ounce sirloin at the Buffalo Inn in Mankato then retired to the private club in back to sip bourbon and play pinochle, or preferably poker if there was a game. If there wasn't, he usually tied one on. Needed a game or a good drunk to clear his system. Red and Straydog always tagged along to keep him company and drive him home.

Mex took the box of letters and the bag of money, tossed them in the seat of his truck and drove to the barn. He took a lasso and a can of oats from the tack room then opened the gate and drove into the pasture. Mex knew how to hurt, and he planned to hurt the Colonel in a way the old bastard would feel it. He honked the horn and shined the spotlight, hunting for Brutus. The old bull always came to the sound of a horn, looking for the Colonel to give him a treat of oats or alfalfa. Soon his dark hump and spike horns emerged from a draw, the paired eyes reflecting the lights as the old monarch lumbered forth. Tame as a pony he stepped right up and put his head in the noose, lowering his nose to sniff the oats spilled in the grass, lapping up the grain with his black tongue while Mex wrapped the loose end of the rope twice around the bumper hitch and secured it with a slipknot. Brutus continued munching on the oats, wholly unaware as Mex shoved the truck in gear and peeled out, tires digging into the sod. The rope drew taut and jerked the old bull's head in rude surprise, pitching him forward as he lunged and fell, his spike horns twisting and plowing through the rock-studded grass behind the tires burning all the way up through the pasture.

At the berm of the hill stood a lone broad oak. Mex pulled under the lower bough and backed up a few feet to give slack. By now the old bull had nearly strangled, his haunches quivered, slimed with shit, his eyes bulged while his tongue begged in want of air. Mex aimed his pistol at an upturned eye and fired—the shot quickly muffled in the night wind as the old beast tensed its legs and quietly went limp. Mex knelt by to loosen the noose then yanked it from under the head. He coiled the length and arched it over the near bough then lashed it to the hind hooves. This time he eased the truck forth, pulling the rope taut, dragging the body up in a slow pivot till the dead bull hung fully extended, its black tongue dripping blood to the grass.

Mex set the brake and cut the lights and engine. He unsheathed his K-bar knife, walked back and slit the belly from the pizzle to the throat, opening the carcass as the stomach and bowels fell in ripe folds steaming to the ground. Then he reached up and deftly sliced the foreskin and seized the length of the pizzle—cut it free and whipped it through the air with a sharp wet hiss. He tossed the pizzle to the mound of guts then reached in the chest cavity and ripped out the heart. He gripped it in his bloody hands like it was the Colonel's, touched it to his brow then dropped it by the pizzle.

Deadfall from past storms lay about the tree. He dragged out several large limbs and stomped and busted them till he had a ready pile. From the truck he fetched the bag of money and the box of letters—several of which he wadded up for kindling. He knelt down and snapped open his lighter and cupped a blue flame that soon spawned red and yellow snakes licking up through the limbs, hissing in hunger to blaze. Mex stood back from the heat, ripped off his shirt and laid it over the flames as if he was blanketing a horse, preparing to ride. The shirt caught fire, fluttered up and fell aside while one fiery piece carried off in the wind like a severed wing.

Mex took his knife and hacked off a green branch, sharpened one end to spit the heart, then propped it to roast at the edge of the fire where the hot coals glowered black and red. He wiped his bloody hands on his chest and stood baring his flesh to the night, the wind, and the fire as if he were the question and they the answer. Then he knelt once more and reached in the shoe box and one by one crumpled and tossed the letters to the flames, indifferent to the words, their sentiment and meaning, severing all ties, making certain he remained alone in the world, savagely alone, unloved and unloving. Only once did he glance down, saw a picture of his mother with himself as a child fallen by his boot; he picked it up and gazed a moment then pitched it to the fire like a lame card. The rest of the letters he delivered to the flames box and all, looking only to the flames and the night beyond—to fire and darkness, making them his sole companions, would not risk another glimpse to the past. Leave his mother buried, his brother unknown.

He reached for the spitted heart, raised it to his teeth and tore off a chunk and chewed, returning to his vengeance, clearing his mind of all else like a knife finding its edge. Squatting by, he bit off yet another chunk then laid the whole to the flames and watched the heart blacken and sizzle in the coals. And the heart within felt as black and blistered as the one he burned. The fire danced and flared, shooting sparks to the night, lighting his cheekbones and brow, his large dark eyes, the muscles of his broad shoulders and chest. Gazing there, riveted, as if divining his own essence, he palmed a silver snuff box and repeatedly dipped a wetted finger to the white powder and sniffed, inhaling the drug like fire and air, increasing his strength and potency, his clarity of mind, enhancing all his senses till in an urgent sweat he stood and screamed a primal howl that carried through the night, tapering in the distance where coyotes cried in answer. Given release his howl turned to laughter and again he knelt, his laughter cunning, calm, clairvoyant, approaching the act that would pain the Colonel more than death itself.

Mex grinned like a voodoo priest preparing to drive pins through his victim as he pitched a bundle of money to the flames, then another and another—20s, 50s, and 100s, pitching all $80,000 to the flames, using a stick to snag any straying to the wind and drive them deeper into the coals, making certain they burned and in their burning he saw the Colonel twitch in agony.

Long past midnight, about halfway through the ritual, CC returned lounged in the backseat of his "Caddie" chauffeured by Red and Straydog. Both hired hands noted the fire on the north hill but said nothing as they pulled to a stop. CC roused and got out. Held the door open to steady himself as he yanked his dick out and dribbled a puddle. He glimpsed the fire and growled, "Wha' in tarnashun's 'at?"—too drunk and his eyes too poor to detect anything but a distant fire. He shook his dick and stowed it in his pants, didn't bother to zip up.

"Wull, wha' is't?" he asked, more demanding.

"Looks like Mex built hisself a fire. Maybe campin' out," Red answered and said nothing more. But even at a quarter of a mile he and Straydog could clearly discern Mex squatted by the fire, the bull hanging in the backdrop, the truck posed like an accomplice in the darkness beyond. CC grunted, took a step and staggered back; Red and Straydog each grabbed an elbow to escort him to the house.

"'At damn Mex turned Injun on uz," he slurred. "Hell'uf ah care. He kin roz mars'mellows 'n freeze 'iz balls fur'z ah care…"

They herded him on in and helped him out of his jacket, set him on his bed and pulled off his boots. CC did the rest—fell back spread-eagled and started to snore. They lifted his legs to the bed, covered him with a blanket, and switched off the light. Standard procedure. And they stuck to their routine. Walked straight to the bunkhouse without once looking to the hill or raising a question. Neither of the pair was overly bright, nor were they overly curious. They weren't about to walk up on Mex in the middle of the night and question him or his doings.

CC groaned at first light, his mouth a wad of dry crud he'd

rather not taste. Like he'd sooner not think. He could've died and woke feeling better. Enough alcohol in his veins to keep him well preserved. He stumbled into the kitchen, broke three eggs in a glass and swallowed them raw. An egg was the only part of a chicken he cared for and only when he had a hangover. He uncapped a bottle of aspirin and tapped a half dozen tablets in his palm then popped them in his mouth and washed them down with a glass of water. Followed directly by a shot of Jack Daniel's home remedy which helped clear his head and settle things a mite.

The *Hill County Weekly* lay open on the table. CC had perused the paper along with the rest of the mail Sunday morning. The priest's death hadn't made headlines, but it did make the front page, lower left hand corner. No details regarding the death of the 35-year-old priest other than the fact that it had been an unexpected shock and had saddened both the parish and the community at large. Though CC didn't gloat, the priest dead suited him fine, one less headache to worry about. But the package to Mex had him a trifle concerned, postmarked from Arcadia the day of the priest's death. No, he didn't like the timing. Didn't like coincidence and didn't like mystery. The contents of the box nagged at him. And seeing the empty wrapping reminded him that Mex was back, which further called to mind the fire on the hill.

Then his head did clear with a sudden profound sense that something was wrong. He stormed into the bathroom, leaned over the black marble basin and splashed cold water on his face. Ran his damp hands through his thin gray hair and blinked his red eyes at the rude sight of himself grown haggard and old. He turned away and tucked his shirt in his pants, pulled on his boots and jacket, and headed outdoors, his eyes watering in the chill dawn air. He walked back through the shelter belt and squinted to the hilltop. A large dark form hung from the tree. CC winced, knew it was Brutus from the sheer size of the carcass, like seeing an old friend butchered. He'd bottle-fed Brutus as a yellow calf, named him for his size and strength, the only animal he'd doted on since he was a kid. Saw the old bull as his natural counterpart, monarch of the pasture.

CC's eyes blistered with rage. In crossing the fence, he ripped his pants on a barb and gashed his leg. He didn't feel a thing, strode on up the long slope, his barrel chest and great belly carried on his long spindly legs, his wisp of hair blown awry in the wind, and he didn't slow his pace, in a huff and fury, aimed to get there if it took his last breath and with his last breath demand an answer—*By God!*

He marched straight to the truck and opened the door, expected to find the *low-down sonuvawhore* passed out in the seat. But the cab was empty. He wrenched the door back against the fender and left it hanging like Brutus. Then he kicked the empty duffel and kicked the ashes. And in the drift of ashes he noticed the black evidence of hundreds of burnt bills, many still retaining their bundled shape like pages of a burnt book curled and flaking to the wind, disintegrating at the slightest touch. He felt his gut drop out.

In desperation CC dug his tooled boots deep in the still-hot coals and uncovered monies only half burned, tantalizingly green and tempting. He knelt to save what few remained, burning his hands on live embers as he clutched the ruined bills and stuffed them in the duffel. Finally he stopped, aware of the futility, raised a sooted hand to his teared cheek, leaving a black smear. The same with his pant legs as he placed his hands to his thighs and slowly stood. He looked to the fire, the gutted bull, the empty truck. Nothing made any sense. CC liked things reasonable and business-like—even violence he considered a reasonable option if it gained a reasonable end. Namely money. To steal, strong-arm, even kill for money, yes, within certain limits and given a reasonable chance of success. But to squat by a fire and actually burn a pile of money entailed a violence too subtle and hellish, wholly beyond his understanding.

CC snatched up the duffel and started down towards the barn, too nauseous and drained after his climb up and too bewildered for haste, his only thought was to find Red and Straydog, then find Mex and ask him, *Why, why in God's name did you do this?*

Red and Straydog were busy mucking out stalls and pitching

hay to the quarter horses CC kept for working stock. The barn doors at either end were left open to catch the breeze and a broad shaft of sunlight slanted in from the east, defining every line and shadow of the stalls to about mid-aisle. Red and Straydog worked in and out of the light, raising a glitter of dust to the upper reaches of the haymow. Both paused upon seeing the Colonel enter; they stood clasping their fork handles more or less like soldiers at parade rest as he approached carrying the duffel, his dark silhouette framed in the west opening. Closer up they saw his face and clothes blackened with soot, his mouth strangely twisted minus his clinched cigar as he voiced his stern consternation.

"Either of you two seen Mex?" Both stood mute till he barked, "*Well*?!"

"No sir, Colonel," Red answered. "Not as yet we ain't."

CC peered to the shadowed rafters and crossbeams and with the last of his rage leaned back and bellered, "*MAY-Y-Y-EX!*" Figured he was up there somewhere waiting. And so summoned, Mex appeared above them like a shadow gazing down. The next moment he leapt from the haymow to the aisle in a swirl of straw and dust like a winged devil landing crouched. He tossed off the blanket that draped his shoulders and stood flexing his muscled plumage—intent, poised, silent as a statue, his hair unbraided and matted, his flesh blood-caked from the sacrifice and naked from the waist up except for his gold medallion.

"Why did you do *this*?" CC demanded, raising the duffel to Mex. "And why old Brutus?" he asked, more baffled than angry. "Why butcher the poor ol' beast?"

Mex's eyes burned from the drugs and hate and from all he'd learned upon opening the package.

"Because he was a prick like you," he grinned, tapping his thigh with the dried pizzle. "Nothing but a big prick"—slapping harder as he advanced. "And *why?* Like you have a right to ask? Why is my mother dead and buried, huh? Because of pricks like you. Because of all you fucks. Fucking her till she rotted inside and *died!*"

"Now wait a minute. I loved that woman. It wasn't like—"

"It *was* like that. Ex-*act*-ly like that. I was *there! I watched!* And my brother, Miguel? Why didn't you tell me about my brother?"

"Hold on here. What the hell you talkin' 'bout, Mex?"

"The priest, you bastard. You sicced me on him like a dog on meat!"

"Now wait...just wait...hold on, Mex...?"—CC steadily giving ground, trying to reason, suddenly fearful, yet even more, perplexed. "I don't know a damn thing 'bout any a' this, boy. Ya gotta believe—"

"I believe you're a lying *fuck!*" Mex struck him with the crude whip, knocking him back against a stall. CC grabbed for his pistol but didn't have it on him as Mex reached down and slipped the K-bar from his boot. "I'm gonna gut you, old man. Then cut out your dick like I did your *dumb fucking bull!*"

Mex raised his knife to lunge—then froze in grave surprise at his sudden arrest. He cocked his head in wonder at the second thrust as Straydog speared him through the back with a pitchfork, the sharp tines emerging in a stream of blood either side of the nipples, the third driven through the sternum. Mex touched a finger to the bloody point that had pierced his heart, dropped to his knees and raised his palms in languid pose as if hoping to rise, then slowly collapsed and lay. He rolled his eyes, gasping for air as CC knelt and cradled his head in both hands.

"Damn you Mex, damn you boy," he cried. "Why? Why this? I knew you as a baby...crying in your crib. I picked you up 'n hoped you was mine. Don't you know? Don't you...? Damn you...damn..."

But the other heard nothing beyond *Why? Why this?*—his eyes blank, his head limp as CC raged on in grief, recounting his love for the mother, his plans and dreams, slowly choking back his tears. For a few silent moments he simply gazed to those dead eyes then gently laid the head aside. Wiped his nose and staggered to his feet. Ran a bloodied hand through his hair and stood grimed in grief.

Red and Straydog shrank before his visage, not knowing whether they'd done right or wrong in saving the Colonel, both paired in the act as their shadows rippled across the body. Anxious to turn tail and run but each stayed out of long habit, if not loyalty. Not certain where they belonged or where they stood.

"Ah'm...ah'm sorry, Colonel," Straydog stammered, chewing on his bearded lip in wait of what might come. Red griped his pitchfork in wonder of the same.

CC looked from one to the other then back to Mex.

"Yeah...I know," he said with a pained sigh. "We're all sorry sonsabitches."

"What we do with 'im, Colonel?" Red asked.

"Born of a whore, bury 'im in a beast," he declared, still gazing there. Then he fixed his cold gray eyes on them and said, "Stuff 'im inside ol' Brutus. Stitch 'em up with bailing wire 'n cake it with manure. Load 'em on the dump truck along with that heifer that died a' scours the other day. Haul 'em to the rendering plant. *Born of a whore, bury 'im in a beast!*" he repeated bitterly. Then lowered his eyes one last time and with all the tenderness he could muster, added, "Mex, ya crazy bastard...it coulda been yours. All yours."

"So what we do with his truck?"

"Take it to that shop in Omaha. You know the place. Then take what money ya git 'n skedaddle. Make yourselves scarce, ya hear? Don't dare show up here agin..."

XXV. BURNT OFFERINGS

After watching Diana and Jessie leave, Lee returned to the house and packed a bag of clothes along with his toothbrush, razor, a bar of soap and a towel, grabbed his guitar, shotgun, the Coleman lantern, and a sleeping bag. He moved into the red shed along with Rue and Keeps. The dogs were glad of his company and Lee likewise, feeling abandoned and fearful of the house.

A stack of straw bales lined the north wall—Lee had busted one open for his bedding and had slept there the past two nights. Returning late each day from the fields, he'd wash off in the hydrant outside the shed then crawl into his sleeping bag and stare at the darkness till he dozed off, waking again to the ding and rattle of his wind-up alarm at 4 a.m. Same routine Monday evening as he kicked off his boots and lay back on the straw, the clock ticking a quarter past eight, the lantern pumped up, hissing a steady warm glow. He gazed to the shadows in wait of another lonely night. Hadn't told anyone that Diana and Jessie were gone, not Garret or his mother. Nor had he seen any of his friends or once returned to the house now haunted by his own memories as well. He wanted to see Diana waiting at the door and Jessie playing by the steps, but the house stared back dark and empty as a hollow skull in accusation of his dreams and failures. And if he lacked the courage to face whatever haunted its interior, what of his own?

The wind whistled past the shed door left open to give the dogs exit and entry. The yard light slanted through on Rue and Keeps where they lay in the nearby corner, curled muzzle to tail, occasionally blinking an eye or raising a brow to Lee's shifts and turns, all and all content with their situation. Lee was anything but, he'd never felt so emptied out and drained, like a cold void ate at his center, sapping his will. To shake his funk he'd played guitar a while but laid it aside, his fingers too stiff and uninspired from gripping the wheel all day. He had no lyrics, no gems of thought for his notebook. He simply stared at the weathered planks of the old shed and watched his breath fog the air.

Overhead, the lamplight glittered on a drop of pine sap set like a jewel in the heart of a burled plank where seepage from a thousand rains had etched the image of a plowed field. On other boards around the door and window more exposed to the sun and the constant rasp of elements, the etchings deepened and grew more sculptural, revealing swirled ridges and valleys, knots, voids, and splintered ends, gnawed on and warped by span of time till he could almost read a history written in the hieroglyph of wood like veins and bones jutting through weathered skin. Faces were like that and so were hands. Hands that had fought, labored, and aged. And lying in his makeshift cave, entranced by the crude images, Lee recalled his father's hands, every finger bent and broken, yet they could cup a harmonica and play a tune palmed in soft vibrato, grasp a tender note and make it sing. But now those hands were simply bones that neither fought, labored, nor played. He dared not imagine their grip and embrace, dared not conjure or reach to them, but let them rest folded on the heart rib beneath the skull that had been his father. Yet vivid as the night he sensed him near and dreaded his coming, whether in the rising wind or his mind's eye, did not wish to hear that voice added to recent hauntings.

The dogs suddenly pricked their ears and bristled in a low growl at a shadow cast through the door. A man shadow. Lee tensed and reached for his shotgun.

"Anyone at home...?" Frankie looked in, surprised to see Lee with the dogs. Even more surprised to see the shotgun aimed his way.

"Hey! Hold your fire!"

"Damn!" Lee gasped, taking a breath. "I didn't hear you drive in."

"Guess not. The wind's kind of whipping up. Sorry to give you a start. But Jesus, Lee, what you doing out here? Trying to catch a possum?"

"Naw," Lee grinned, laying the shotgun aside. "Nothing so exciting."

"I tried up at the house"—Frankie gestured to the door. "No one there. Then I saw a light out here. Where's everyone at? Where's Diana and Jessie?"

Lee just gazed to the lantern and said, "They're gone."

"Gone? You mean up and left? Gone for good?"

"Well, I hope not. But…yeah, they're gone from here for good."

"How's come? Something wrong?" Frankie squatted by in quiet concern.

"Oh, this 'n that," Lee answered, forcing a smile. "It's been a pretty crazy harvest, ya know. Then the house…" His smile faded. "Just too much I guess."

"I thought you were gonna buy it? Thought she loved the place?"

"She did…" Lee thought a moment, not certain what to say. "You've heard tell of the house being haunted?"

"Shit yes, all my life," Frankie laughed. "Grandad Reggis always said that Clyde McLellon, the ol' boy that built the place, was crazy as a loon. And a fool to boot. Lost a section of ground building that house. Then died there rather than go to the hospital to have his leg tended. Too stubborn to leave the place."

"Yeah, well, I think he's still in there. His ghost…or something is. 'Cause Friday night we heard something real strange."

"Strange?" Frankie's curiosity deepened, as did his doubt. "Hell, that's an awful big house, Lee. Probably settles extra loud at times. Just timbers creaking."

"No, it was voices," Lee answered simply, certain of his experience if little else. "Diana and I heard voices. Only she heard 'em first and left for town before I got home. I found the door wide open, lights on, the place empty. Wondered what had happened. Then I heard voices…"

"Come on, Lee? What're you feeding me?" Frankie narrowed

his eyes, thinking he was about to be suckered by one of Lee's tales.

But Lee didn't blink or smile; he stared straight ahead and waited.

"Okay," Frankie said. "What kind of voices?"

"Just natural voices. Like you 'n me talking. Only there were lots of voices...all through the house. Like the house had trapped bits and pieces of conversation, events from another time and played them back all at once. Ghost voices, Frankie. As plain as day. And Diana did see a ghost. She told me next morning. Neither of us said anything that night. You see something your mind can't explain, it's pretty damned spooky. But next day she said she'd seen a shape...or shadow at Jessie's door. And that ever since we'd moved in Jessie had woke in the night crying about an old woman. And here's the thing, the old woman kept saying that the old man had hurt his leg."

Hearing this put Frankie's doubt in suspension.

"No shit? Said he'd hurt his leg...?"

"That's right," Lee answered without a trace of guile. "And I'm not going back in there except in broad daylight. Only to get our things once I finish helping Garret."

Frankie nodded in odd wonder of the old house, of the stories he'd heard, the blend of fact and circumstance as related by Lee. There was no doubt something had happened. Something strange enough to drive a woman from her home and make a man sleep out in an old shed. Something so strange he couldn't phrase a question let alone an answer. Besides, there were more pressing and tangible concerns.

"Wanna help me finish up a deal and get our money?" he asked.

"What deal's that...?" Lee said as he roused at the prospect.

"I worked a deal with the Colonel. Haven't told anyone and didn't want to till it was over and done with. I fronted the stuff. He said he'd have the money by tonight. Not that I expect any trouble, we'll just drive up 'n get our cash. But I don't trust Mex. So you might ride along and watch my back. Might bring that shotgun too."

"Sure thing," Lee grinned, getting up. "Gotta guard the

payroll"—willing to do most anything rather than be alone right
then. And the chance of another six or seven grand was enough
to lift his desperate mood. He pulled on his boots, grabbed his
hat and jacket, and checked his shotgun. Thought to douse the
lantern but gave it a good dozen pumps instead. Wanted a light
on when he returned.

As the green van sped north over a maze of Range County roads,
CC sat at his desk in wait. He hadn't forgotten his appointment
with Frankie Sage, his last note of business to conclude the day.
He'd expected him by sundown or shortly after—and here it
was past nine, not business-like, but he knew the lad would
show soon enough. Two things called a young man nearly
every time: the promise of money and the promise of pussy.
Though each lost their allure in time, especially when time runs
out. Then what? What does a man want in his final breath? One
more chance at having all again? CC held up his empty hands
and chuckled at the thought of all the money and pussy they'd
grasped. He lit a fresh cigar and poured a glass of bourbon,
sipping slow, by now relaxed, at ease. *Yessir, and meaning,* he
supposed...*a man wants meaning.*

Earlier he'd taken a bath and shaved, donned his best suit,
knotted his tie, then slicked back his silver hair and slapped
his face with English Leather. For a moment he gazed to the
mirror and fingered the welt Mex left on his cheek then turned
away and gave it no further thought. Let bygones be. Retiring
to his den, he arranged his papers and scribbled instructions to
his accountant and lawyers—he'd spread his interests over the
years between three different firms, knew that his best chance
to ensure a legacy lay in keeping the greedy bastards in a legal
stand-off. By such precaution the structure of Holtz Enterprises
looked to be secure.

And upon his death the house and ranch were never meant
to go to Mex, instead they were to be placed in public trust to
create a county park and museum: the central pond fenced off
for camping and fishing; the exotic herd maintained to provide
a scenic vista and fresh meat for various holiday barbecues and
celebrations; and lastly, the house would serve to display the

Colonel's extensive collection of antique saddles, pistols, and rifles along with numerous Indian artifacts unearthed through adjacent counties. An oil portrait of the benefactor already hung above the fireplace. As for his gambling debt, if the Kansas City boys tried to press their claim they'd be laughed out of court. With Mex gone, their sole threat and leverage was his own life and he planned to play a hand that no gambler dared call. He palmed his pearl-handled snub-nosed .22, checked the cylinder, then fit it neatly in his vest pocket. A precise little weapon sufficient to the task.

CC tapped his cigar at the edge of the marble tray and watched the ash tumble to the center. The gold horse-clock read 9:15. A minute later headlights laced in through the curtain, dappling the wall as the van pulled to a stop. Then the lights shut off—followed shortly by an insistent knock at the door.

"Late 'n impatient," CC muttered, then growled out, "C'MON IN! It's open…"

Darkness pervaded the house as usual, only the green-shaded lamp left on in the den. Frankie entered and wove a path through to the light. CC eyed his approach.

"Why looky here, if it ain't Frankie Sage," he noted dryly. "King of the hemp pickers come to collect. You a mite late ain't cha?"

"You said Monday evening, Colonel."

"So I did…" CC leaned back in his chair, hands folded on his belly. "You alone?"

"Lee Clayton's waiting outside," Frankie answered, searching those cagey gray eyes all but hidden in shadow. "How about you, Colonel. You alone?"

"Oh, absolutely, Frankie," CC grinned, leaning forth. "Alone as the Lord a'fore he made Adam. Go ahead 'n have a seat, son."

"Thanks. Think I'll stand."

"Suit yourself. Take a shot a' bourbon…?" he offered, setting by another glass.

Again Frankie declined. "No thanks, Colonel."

"Why hell, can't hardly believe this? A son of Justin Sage turning up his nose at good bourbon?"

"Look, Colonel, I've had a long day. Just want the money."

"Well there it is..." CC pointed to the duffel at the edge of the desk. "Least ways what's left of it," he added as Frankie reached in and pulled out a handful of crumbling bills. "Mex burnt the lot," he stated bluntly in answer to Frankie's puzzled look. "Sat up there atop the hill last night and burnt eighty thousand dollars in cash. Ask me why? Spite, I reckon. But I don't really know."

The words hit like a hard slap. Frankie's mind blurred in anger and confusion. Then his eyes set like flint in thought of the Colonel playing him for a fool.

"Don't you piss down my back, old man."

"No, Frankie. I'd sooner piss up a rope."

"You expect me to believe this?"

"It's the damned truth."

Frankie's eyes twisted even harder as he asked, "Where's Mex?"

"Like to git your hands on 'im, would ya? Well the devil got 'im first. He's gone to hell like raw meat plucked to stew..." CC tried to play it hard, thought he could say such words and not feel his heart twinge, his voice choke, his eyes well up. But he blinked away and took a deep breath and softened his tone. "I ain't lying here, son. Now I can lie, you know that. We both can lie so's to make an angel listen. We're two of a kind, Frankie Sage. But I'm an older meaner kind that you don't wanna be. Mex is dead, that's a fact. How 'n why is my business. You lost a whole lot a' money today. Believe you me, I understand. But I lost a son. Be he mine or not, that's how I saw 'im. You may think I'm a black-hearted devil and maybe I am. But lemme tell ya..."—he raised his hands in futile gesture—"My house 'n land is all I got a' life. You may think it's a whole lot, but it ain't spit in the wind compared to a son. Now you think on that, Frankie Sage. And think on your daddy, Justin. Miserable as he was on his dyin' day, whatever his regrets, he was a far happier man than me for leaving a son."

"Bullshit. My dad's only regret was leaving a bottle half drank."

"You're wrong there, Frankie. Dead wrong," CC countered in a weary voice. "His one regret might a' been not killing me.

Maybe you'd like to do it for 'im? Maybe take that brass horse 'n bash in my head? A' course I'd prefer not," he said, pulling the pistol from his vest pocket as Frankie drew back wary.

"Here, use this, it's not so messy..." CC laid the pistol by the proffered glass. "Go ahead, you got reason and I'll give ya more. God knows your daddy had reason. All the reason in the world. And had his chance. Caught me with your momma one night way back when. Parked off in that pasture east a' your home place. Caught me pullin' up my pants 'n pressed the gun to my head. But didn't pull the trigger, just run me off. No sir, didn't have the guts. And I think it ate at his gut ev'ry time he seen me in town, and ev'ry week at the sale barn, the thought of me with your momma ate at 'im till he tried to kill it with whiskey and kilt himself instead. What you think a' that, Frankie Sage?" His eyes squinted like shards in question. "Did you know I had your momma?"

Frankie wasn't particularly surprised, though the details had their impact and for a moment he felt his center churn, sorely tempted to shove the pistol in the grinning mouth and pull the trigger till it clicked on empty.

"It's no big secret, Colonel," he answered, leaving the pistol lay. "Mom always you said weren't worth a fuck. Called you 'One-shot' Holtz. Said your cannon lasted about a minute. It worked for a dip stick and that's about all."

CC leaned back and chuckled.

"Yeah, that sounds like your momma," he said. "Bless her heart. She sure had a way with words. That sharp Irish wit. 'Member one time, we's at a dance. Marv Griffith sat at our table. Your mom'ud just come back from the ladies room. Harv asked, 'Did ever'thing come out all right?' Your mom didn't bat an eye, looked at him 'n said, 'Funny thing, Harv, all I did was mention your name and got a seat right away.' Hearing that Harv 'bout shit too. Shut 'im up good. Yessir, she had a clever tongue. And what a beauty. Had 'bout any man she wanted. Even as a man, I gotta say I almost envied her. Yeah, I 'spect we're all sonsabitches..."

"That may be, Colonel. But I don't want to hear about my mom and dad. Much less your confession."

"Now lissen here, Frankie Sage"—CC snatched up the pistol and waved it part in emphasis and part in warning. "Don't argue with a man fixin' to die. And don't piss 'im off! Like I said, we're all sonsabitches 'n that ain't meant to mock you or your momma. 'Cause we're all sons a' God and the devil too. And that's the devil of it. Cast 'tween the two like rolled dice 'n chance is good we'll turn to bad. Roll snake eyes as offen as the righteous seven. And I ain't confessing shit! Chance brought me up in the world and chance brings me down. Sure, I want mercy. We all do. Like we want pussy 'n cold cash. Any gut-shot fool kicking in the dirt at high noon wants mercy. But the sun blazes on and the wind howls black as night 'n I doubt there's any—"

"Colonel," Frankie cut-in sharply, "I know the whole smear"—not keen on a lecture from someone who owed him $55,000. "I ain't no fool and I'm not looking for mercy. Right now all I want is my money. So what's your point?"

"You're one hard nut," CC allowed. "Yessir, one hard nut..." Then he knit his brow and said, "Look son, I'm trying to square things. That's all. Now maybe I can't square things with you. Damn sure can't git ya your money. But see this black book here," he said, tapping the Bible on his desk. "I thumbed through it agin today. Do so now 'n then. Take a good look at the Bible sometime, Frankie. Take a good long look. Find you one note a' humor. There ain't none. Can't trust a man that's got no humor. Can't trust a book neither. Seems there's something wrong with this book, something dead wrong. Still we cling to it like to our momma's memory. Maybe 'cause it's stern black words remind us of our fathers. Yeah, I looked there agin and you can bet I'll git no mercy, none at all. There's that place in Job it says...*He frustrates the devices of the crafty, so they find no success...and they meet with darkness in the day 'n grope at noon as in the night...* This day has been my night, Frankie. Thought I was wise, but it was far from me. Yessir...*and that what is...is far off 'n deep, exceedingly deep...* But I wanna laugh at death, grin back at the bastard 'n spit in his eye. 'Cause this land right here is my Bible, Frankie. That's how I square things. I go back to the dirt and let the wind sift the good 'n the bad..."

Lee stood out by the van—the shotgun held ready as he listened to the wind blowing down off the pasture from the northwest, a cold wind hinting of winter, old and calloused, void of sympathy. Nothing moved in the sky, not a falling star or a passing plane. Nothing moved. Lee watched the shadows in wait and sensed his wait lengthen. Frankie had said he'd be right back out, but that had been a quarter an hour ago. Lee scanned the night, wondering of Mex and where he might be, growing edgy, fingering the trigger. The house stood quiet and dark except for a lone lit window. He kept staring to the window, growing more anxious by the minute, thinking Mex might be in there and Frankie in trouble. Sensed a dark certainty, like a cold gust of wind.

Lee hurried across the drive, urged on by every threat experienced that autumn, fearing he was already too late. He paused at the door and eased on in, the carpet lush and thick as the darkness that yielded like a satin veil as he crept towards the light and the low voice that seemed to drawl from the depths of a cave. He rounded the corner and saw their shadows cast on the wall. Beyond the doorway he spied the Colonel holding a pistol on Frankie. Lee braced the shotgun and clicked back both hammers.

"Lay it down, dammit! Do it now! NOW!"—he cried, advancing into the room as if entering a misty tunnel, himself disembodied and obscure, mixing with the dim light and shadow as he leveled both barrels on the Colonel whose voice and person seemed made of mist as well, silent and slowed like forms underwater, and Frankie the same as he turned in a sidling movement, raising his hand to Lee, his mouth gaped in soundless appeal, while Lee heeded nothing but his own far voice demanding:

"Drop it...! DROP IT...!"

Everything focused and stilled in the fatal moment of whether to pull the trigger? Whether to kill? A question formed not of words, but from his very breath like a fierce pulse connecting heart, mind, and hand.

Through his pending aim a voice edged in—*"Easy now... easy..."*—it coaxed, quiet and steady. "That's it, easy now..."

Frankie repeated as he gripped the gun barrel and firmly raised
it to the ceiling.

"Frankie? What the…"—Lee jerked the gun away in question.

"It's okay, Lee. The Colonel…we were just talking. That's
all."

Lee glanced from one to other, kept the barrel raised, but
the hammers clicked back and ready.

"You got the money?" he asked.

"No. That's part of what the Colonel was explaining."

CC quietly laid the pistol on the desk. Reached down and
relit his cigar.

"There for a minute, boy," he said, tossing the match to the
tray, "thought you was gonna make a mess a' me and my wall."

Lee eyed him warily. "Then you don't have the money?"

"No, the money…went up in smoke," CC declared, puffing
his cigar with a slow sardonic smile. "Mex burnt it. Sat up under
that tree on the hill and fed it to the flames. Now him 'n the
money is both beyond reach. Nuthin' up there 'cept a pile a'
ashes and a million stars blinking in the sky…each one bright as
a diamond in a billy goat's ass. And you can't touch them either.
Only money left is in that bag and there ain't a bill worth shit-
wipe. But to be right honest, boys…and at this point 'bout all I
got's the honest truth. Earlier in the day I did have money. Not
this money…other money. Near seventy grand locked in that
safe on the wall yonder…"

Frankie and Lee looked to where the Colonel indicated. Felt
like they were being led through a maddening maze where
every turn met another dead end. If there was a lesson, they'd
learned it—numbed and sickened at ruined prospects. Frankie
foremost, frustrated by the old con's shell game, yet tantalized
and curious nonetheless.

"So where's the money, Colonel?" he asked.

"Like to git your hands on that too, I bet?" CC grinned.
"Can't say as I blame ya. But I sent it off for safe keeping. Ain't
nuthin' in there now but my will and deeds 'n such. 'Spect
you boys could blow it open if you had dynamite. There's only
three feet a' concrete poured round it. Or you could try 'n break
my arm and get me to fess up the combination. Still wouldn't

do you no good, wouldn't find nuthin' but a batch a' papers. Here's the thing…and a good part why the money's gone. The combination is known only by me 'n three others. And they each only know one number. That's my accountant here in Mankato, my lawyer down in Salina, 'nuthern back in KC. Yessir, I got to thinkin' as how them three buzzards might come to a quick agreement at seeing all that cash in there. Use it in ways I had not intended. No sir. So to keep it out a' their grubby paws I sent it by registered mail to the Sister's Convent in Arcadia. Thought 'bout giving a share to you boys as seed money, to help even the score. But it's best used to redeem the blood that earned it. Ain't nuthin' but bad come of that money. It's a crying shame what's happened. An all-round crying shame. And today's been nuthin' but payment. Believe you me, once burnt, twice shy. Take it from an old boy 'bout to settle accounts with this world…" CC looked to both and gave an earnest nod.

"So you think on what I had to say tonight, Frankie Sage. Think on it a spell. And you keep playin' that guitar, Lee. Keep raising that son a' yours. Now you two git on out a' here. Go live your lives. Go on now," he urged, lifting the receiver. "I aim to call Sheriff Craig 'n settle up. Don't think you wanna be part a' this conversation…"

Wry, convincing, still King of the County—his voice tinted in deepening blue with traces of a sunset fading to night. Lee eased down each hammer, cradled the shotgun and backed away, his heart beating fast in question of all he witnessed. Frankie grabbed the duffel as grim consolation, evidence of so much effort laid waste. Gave one last look and left the Colonel to his reckoning.

CC watched them go. He listened for the door to latch then dialed and waited for the sheriff to answer.

"Craig, this is Holtz," he announced in his gruff baritone.

—*Okay. What do you need?*

"Never mind need. What I got to say won't take long. Then you do what you like."

—*I'm listening…*

"I called you 'cause I figured you could handle it. You guessed most the story already and the rest don't matter. Plus

I don't want Patch Hyland sniffin' over me like a damn bird dog. Call Al Harris there in Cibola, me 'n him go way back, he'll arrange the funeral. You'll find several names and a phone number here on my desk. Might give 'em a call. Now if ya don't mind, I'm gonna finish up..."

CC laid the phone down on the Bible, took a sip of bourbon, licked his lips and smiled. Left the cigar to smolder in the marble bowl. Everything set to his liking. He pressed the pistol back of his ear and pulled the trigger.

At the sound of the shot, Guy jerked his feet off his desk and sat up—held the receiver gripped to his ear, listening to the ethereal void of line static. Fairly certain of what he'd heard, sensed nothing solved, merely a shrewd brisk finality characteristic of the caller. Guy hung up the phone, pulled on his boots, and slowly stood. Looked like another long night ahead.

Frankie and Lee heard the shot as they reached the van. A single sharp note muffled by the thick walls and the wind. Both gazed back at the house. It appeared even darker and quieter than before.

"Think we should go check?" Lee asked, not really wanting to.

"No, it's finished, Lee. Nothing in there but a dead man."

Both thought on that death, that fate and their own in driving away. Neither spoke for a mile or so. Lee reached in the duffel and held up a handful of ashen bills, remnants of a booty that had recently totaled thousands of dollars.

"Jeez..." he sighed in disgust. "Burned it. Damn our damn luck." Then he looked to Frankie and asked, "Did he say why? Why Mex burned it?"

"No, not really. I don't think he really knew."

"Guess we better show Will, huh?"

"Yeah, might as well get it over with. Wolfer's gonna really howl."

"Afraid so. But he'll simmer down. Ry'll take it better. Same with the rest."

"How about you? You okay with this?"

"No, not even close," Lee answered with a shallow laugh like a fighter too beat to answer the bell. "But there's no blaming you, Frankie. Can't argue acts of God or madmen. And we each still cleared six to seven thousand. That ain't so bad..."

They rode on in silence until they reached the highway and headed south.

"You ought to come in with us, Lee," Frankie offered. "Gabe wants out. Doesn't like the farm. Chip in with me 'n Jack. We'll grow Colombian next year. Cultivate some sinsemilla. I've already got the seed. Won't deal with near the hassle or near the bulk. A couple hundred pounds of Colombian will make us a lot of money."

"Well, I don't know..." Lee actually considered the notion for a moment, tempted. Then he said, "No, I don't think so, Frankie. Think I'll go on to Nashville 'n try my luck with songs. Just hope I can get Diana back." He felt his stomach knot up at saying her name, wanted her and Jessie like his next breath and feared them lost.

"Where'd they go?"

"Down to her mother's."

"Aw hell, Lee," Frankie said, waving it off like a puff of smoke. "If she's half the woman I think she is, after a week with her mother all you have to do is just show up at the door. She won't think twice. She'll be ready to pack 'n go most anywhere."

"Think so?"

"Shit yes, I'd bet the farm."

Lee smiled at Frankie's bluff confidence, heartened by those words: *Aw hell...just show up at the door.* Same old Frankie, hadn't lost his faith. Shared it with one and all. Lee gazed out the side window at his reflected image passing over the broad nightscape like a ghost in another dream.

EPILOGUE

Guy found CC's body slumped to his desk, his head in a tiny pool of blood like a blot of spilled ink. As Hoss had hoped, the package wreaked its judgment, though the murders of Joey and Cathy were never solved, only guessed at. Like Mex had said, "*Los muertos no hablan.*" But it is also said, "As you sow, so shall you reap." Mex's body was never found, only the bloody pitchfork; foul play was suspected, but again, only guessed at. In stripping off Mex's boots, Red and Straydog found the $10,000 in cash. They split the money as due payment, delivered the dead for rendering, the truck to Omaha, then disappeared like two strays in the night never to be heard of again.

Hoss took no pleasure in the Colonel's demise, merely sensed a frayed conclusion and got on with his job, his life. He started dating Meg the waitress and married her later on. Drank less beer and went to bed a much happier man.

The following summer they found Guy slumped over his desk much like he'd found CC. Only there was no blood. His heart simply gave out. He lay as if resting, his face turned to the side, staring off—from his expression still puzzled by it all. They laid him beside May in the graveyard; his name chiseled on the red granite stone. The last three spaces filled in.

In time the Colonel's legacy grew, the misdeeds and rumors largely forgotten, his largess affirmed. Families drove past the Holtz Ranch on weekends to view the buffalo and longhorn. Ladies from the Hill County Historical Society managed the house and contents, and hosted teas and luncheons for various social groups and politicians, their benefactor always fondly referred to, his portrait hung above the fireplace like the image of a patron saint. And the monies sent to the Sisters of Mercy did reap some benefit as the Sanctuary movement blossomed in the 80s and refugees were given aid and asylum from the violence in Central America. Though once again motive and intent formed unlikely alliance with mixed results. Two of the sisters who traveled south on the funds disappeared in El Salvador. But they were neither raped nor murdered by death squads; both ran off with the guerrillas and ended up pregnant. And while they knelt by metates and learned to slap tortillas, a meager few they came to succor shuttled north.

Frankie's faith was right on target. When Lee showed up at Diana's door several weeks later, her cool greeting soon warmed and within an hour they were in bed making love so loud it made her mother blush and concede that her daughter was hopelessly in love with the rambling fool. They moved on another dozen times in the next few years and had another son before they finally settled. By then even Lee was ready to plant a garden and paint the house. They found a cozy little bungalow with no wasted space and no ghosts. Though he hadn't entirely given up his rambling ways—he still stayed out late many nights playing his guitar in taverns. Friends, especially the women, shook their heads in collective wonder why Diana let him.

Frankie kept to his venture and eventually bought out both Jack and Gabe. The first crop he lost to grasshoppers and drought; the second to torrents of rain, though his milo fared well enough to make the land payment. But third time was charm: he raised a bumper crop and did so with an occasional setback for any number of years till he finally paid off the farm and simply farmed and ran cattle, not one of which was rustled. And he took to sweet Alice, married her in fact—but never convinced her to live at the farm. *Not in that house.* So he spent considerable time on the road traveling between his and hers. Which suited him fine; he could only suffer domesticity in small doses. And she suffered him likewise. In spite of which they soon produced two sons who grew tall and handsome. Both good boys.

But not so good they didn't give Ry fits in eying his two daughters. He and Kara had also married and in tat for his youthful philandering the fates granted him daughters, each one pretty as a peach. Watching them and the drove of boys they attracted, Ry gritted his teeth and grinned, not so ironic as in the old days, more a gutsy concession to come-what-may. He'd learned long ago that remaining watchful never altered a single course or fate, whether of man or the stars. He sadly watched his father Cole take to the bottle in one last wild ride to the grave as if pulled by gravity to his fevered end.

Will and JoAnn also raised a pair of daughters who grew into fine young ladies under their parent's vigilant care. Will, cautious as ever, was always ready with a bit of wisdom— "Damn sure smart enough not to front a ton of hemp to the biggest crook in the county!" as he exclaimed to Frankie that very night. "What the fuck were you thinking...?"—carrying on in such manner while Frankie took his scolding and quietly ate crow. Will soon had his say and calmed down like Lee said he would. Then he brewed them some coffee and they sat up half the night in attempt to fathom why the Colonel had shot himself and why Mex had burned the money. Each trying to divine undercurrents that would never surface.

Rus was simply happy to have done with such business. The fun had ended with Valentine's threats. And once that faded, he wasn't all that concerned about the money. Though for arguments sake he still believed in an even share and kept one of the burnt bills as token against further foolishness. Lori soon made an honest man of him. And they eventually had a boy and a girl. Rus quit chewing and shaved off his beard, joined the church and coached little league. Still, he loved to play the fiddle and remained by turns colorful and cantankerous. He worked as a pumper in the oil fields and always had a dog riding along in his truck. But never another one quite like Dig.

Jack married a pretty redhead from Wichita. He brought her home and took over his father's farm. Like most of the boys in growing older he grew more conservative, fretful of their lone child, a daughter, also a redhead. Seeing her off to college, he stood at the door, his one eye cast in doubt of all the folly youth is prone to, while the other, the glass orb, urged her on, ever wayward, prescient, unaging.

For a time the Parks brothers remained seemingly ageless in their remote realm. Their mother Fay lived for another two years, dying at age 103. The boys survived her well into their eighties then passed on much as they'd lived, in their unique brotherly way. One day while returning from town, their car veered off the road and rolled down an embankment—threw one clear and left the other pinned beneath. Evin suffered a heart attack in vain attempt to free Ellwood. And still the tough old soldier made the steep climb to flag down help before collapsing at the side of the road. He died a week later strapped to a hospital gurney, dreaming he was back in the trenches fighting for breath against a piece of hot shrapnel lodged in his throat.

Lee's brother Garret continued farming and never ceased to fret and worry. And while haunted by their father's memory, he never made their father's choice. In time he raised two strong sons and a beautiful daughter who helped him mellow and see the worth of all his doings. He continued to plow, plant, and harvest as his face weathered and his hair grayed till his very voice and presence seemed a fixture of the land.

Nor can the Kid, the irrepressible, be denied a footnote herein. And no, he didn't remain a kid forever, though the boys referred to him as such even after he became a grandpa; for yes, even the Kid had kids. Along the way he served time down in Texas, which became something of a running joke—"So you're a graduate of State U," he'd say; "Well, I'm a graduate of the state pen!"—asserting his prison pedigree for a good laugh and any reference to Penn State, he slam-dunked. He'd been nabbed north of Dallas while running a load of Colombian for his ex-wife; he'd taken the gig in lieu of paying child support and took the rap for sake of the kids. Once out he was more plagued by child support than by parole, for she could be every bit as relentless as Fascisto in collecting her due. But he fared better in his second marriage. Wed a beautiful Latina, beautiful enough to make Frankie pop his eyes and rant against the injustice of it all. Which was justice enough for the Kid. Great to have the last laugh against "The Ol' Cow-Codger," as he tagged Frankie in later years.

"Dixie" Dave, who'd laughed as he watched the other boys gradually marry and become fathers by their mid-thirties, calling them all *late-urban-reproducers*, or *lurps* for short, turned 40 a confirmed bachelor still playing the field. Then on a jaunt to Saint Paul to see a friend, he fell for a wily blonde who matched his urgent energy and could drink him under the table. Impressed, he moved to Minnesota and married her. They kept each other warm through those long cold winters, and he turned 50 with a rambunctious two-year-old in tow and another boy on the way. Seeing which, Ry's grin reclaimed its old irony. Like with the VC tank and the UFO, things never ceased to amaze him.

No one was surprised when Bruce and Julie divorced a year or so later. About as compatible as a bird and a snake and best they parted. Bruce bummed around for a time in a nihilist funk then headed west for L.A. He met and married a Valley girl with a sharp mind and a more amenable heart. They ended up on "The Rock"—not Alcatraz, but the big island of Hawaii—where they raised a son and a daughter, each bright and precocious. They also raised orchids, breeding new varieties and sending their exotic bouquets to upscale markets around the world. A tad more lucrative and respectable business than selling "Ditchweed," although it retained a certain wry botanical link to prior endeavors. Living so proximate to fuming volcanoes and a vast surging ocean, Bruce grew more thoughtful and privy to the elemental, while in spare moments he continued to ponder various philosophical questions: the accelerating universe as opposed to the decelerating flesh, worm holes of orchids and time, black holes of mind and space, and just where in hell did his own singularity fit in the midst of the whole chaotic swirl? Attempting a philosophical Houdini in effort to escape the snare of thought and theory, yet ever more at play and enticed by the play, not so stymied by definition.

Oddly enough Pete also gravitated to a contemplative life. Busted at age 40 for dealing cocaine and given a stern five-year probation, he didn't chance worse. Went to detox, swore off drugs and drinking, and returned to school. Reined in his urges and sought stimulus in hard study and graduated Phi Beta Kappa in biology. He later took a doctorate in Environmental Studies, writing his thesis on the impact of road construction on various soils and substrata. By then his thinning hair had turned snow white and he spent most weekends out birdwatching, walking the woods and pastures in search of further sightings, learning their habits and songs, identifying a rare species with the palpable rush of a youth in love. He eventually taught at the University of Kansas and few of his colleagues or students suspected the large dragon and other tattoos on his back and chest, let alone the reckless youth who'd once flaunted them. Quite the opposite, he grew quiet and reflective, humbled by the interconnectedness of life and experience.

Of all the boys, only Gabe made good by ill-gotten gains. The Florida connection proved out after all, though not by way of the fool in Pennsylvania. Later that fall Gabe loaned Junes and the waitress upstairs a couple hundred dollars so they could move to Fort Lauderdale. Of course he never expected to see them or the money again. But that next spring Junes called, said he knew some people, the right people, and they were looking for a good man in the Midwest, someone they could trust. Gabe took him up on the offer, drove down and made contact. Over the next two years he cleared better than a half million dollars running cocaine to various points across the U.S.A. After that he more or less retired, indulged his habit now and then, dabbled in the stock market, read book after book, rode a Harley, drove a BMW, lived a life of casual ease—often alone, quiet, brooding, sought out old friends on occasion, always good-natured and generous, but troubled, in search, in thought, could not perceive a synthesis in self or society. He even entered therapy for a time and dated his analyst, flew her to Europe and vacationed together in the Caribbean, but never felt settled or attached. Maybe it was the angst of having money and seeing it dwindle, or love and its emotional void, or his precarious health and premonitions of death—for his father had died in his late-forties of a heart attack. Gabe made it to age 53, saw the turn of the century and little more. His brother found him alone in his apartment one day after he'd failed to answer the phone, seated in his big chair, eyes open to the curtained window, lips parted as if he meant to say something. Perhaps he had achieved a final synthesis and simply went there.

The new millennium saw the boys middle-aged with one of their number gone. Soon they were all old men and the ensuing years turned them under one by one like seeds planted in the ground, each surprised at the manner and moment of their passing, giving up the ghost with whatever dread, hope, or conceit they carried.

And when the snows recede in early spring revealing artifacts of a pasture junk pile, some flush-faced youth with his dog in hunt may kick through the rummage and happen on an old boot once worn in work or a broken crock jar once tipped in thirst. Then searching through the sagging interior of a nearby shed, he may find a corn knife, untouched in sixty years, hanging from a nail. Will he grasp its handle in wonder of its story as the wind whistles over weeds and grasses through the cracked siding, speaking of many things, of past harvests and buffalo hunts, of night fevers and muffled voices, of lives lived and those yet to form even as it moves the dust?

ABOUT THE AUTHOR

Melvin Litton's latest work, The Kansas Murder Trilogy, presents three novels of shared theme, but separate time and character: *King Harvest* (1); *Banks of the River* (2); and *Skin for Skin* (3) – all published by Crossroad Press. He has three previous novels (also from Crossroad): *Caspion & the White Buffalo*; *Geminga*; and *I Joaquin*. His stories and poems have appeared in *Chiron Review, Pif, Mobius, Foliate Oak, Floyd County Moonshine, Broadkill Review*, and *The Literary Hatchet* among others. He has two books of poetry: *From the Bone* (Spartan Press), and *Idylls of Being* (Stubborn Mule); and a collection of short stories, *Son of Eve* (Spartan). He is a retired carpenter and lives in Lawrence, KS, with his wife Debra and their shepherd Jack. Formerly captain of the Border Band, he now performs as The Gothic Cowboy with Mando Dan: www.borderband.comperforms songs as The Gothic Cowboy: www.borderband.com

Curious about other Crossroad Press books?
Stop by our site:
www.crossroadpress.com
We offer quality writing
in digital, audio, and print formats.

Made in the USA
Middletown, DE
24 September 2022

10887438R00250